JUST BEYOND ™

THE HORROR AT HAPPY LANDINGS

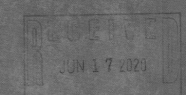
Publi

More Books in the

JUST BEYOND™

Graphic Novel Series

THE SCARE SCHOOL

THE HORROR AT HAPPY LANDINGS

WELCOME TO BEAST ISLAND

JUST BEYOND™

THE HORROR AT HAPPY LANDINGS

Written by
R.L. Stine

Illustrated by
Kelly & Nichole Matthews

Lettered by
Mike Fiorentino

Cover by
Julian Totino Tedesco

Just Beyond created by
R.L. Stine

Designer
Scott Newman

Assistant Editor
Michael Moccio

Associate Editor
Sophie Philips-Roberts

Editor
Bryce Carlson

JUST BEYOND: THE HORROR AT HAPPY LANDINGS, May 2020. Published by KaBOOM!, a division of Boom Entertainment, Inc. Just Beyond is ™ & © 2020 R.L. Stine. All rights reserved. KaBOOM!™ and the KaBOOM! logo are trademarks of Boom Entertainment, Inc., registered in various countries and categories. All characters, events, and institutions depicted herein are fictional. Any similarity between any of the names, characters, persons, events, and/or institutions in this publication to actual names, characters, and persons, whether living or dead, events, and/or institutions is unintended and purely coincidental. KaBOOM! does not read or accept unsolicited submissions of ideas, stories, or artwork.

For information regarding the CPSIA on this printed material, call: (203) 595-3636 and provide reference #RICH – 883297.

BOOM! Studios, 5670 Wilshire Boulevard, Suite 400, Los Angeles, CA 90036-5679. Printed in USA. First Printing.

ISBN: 978-1-68415-547-7, eISBN: 978-1-64144-713-3

3765873

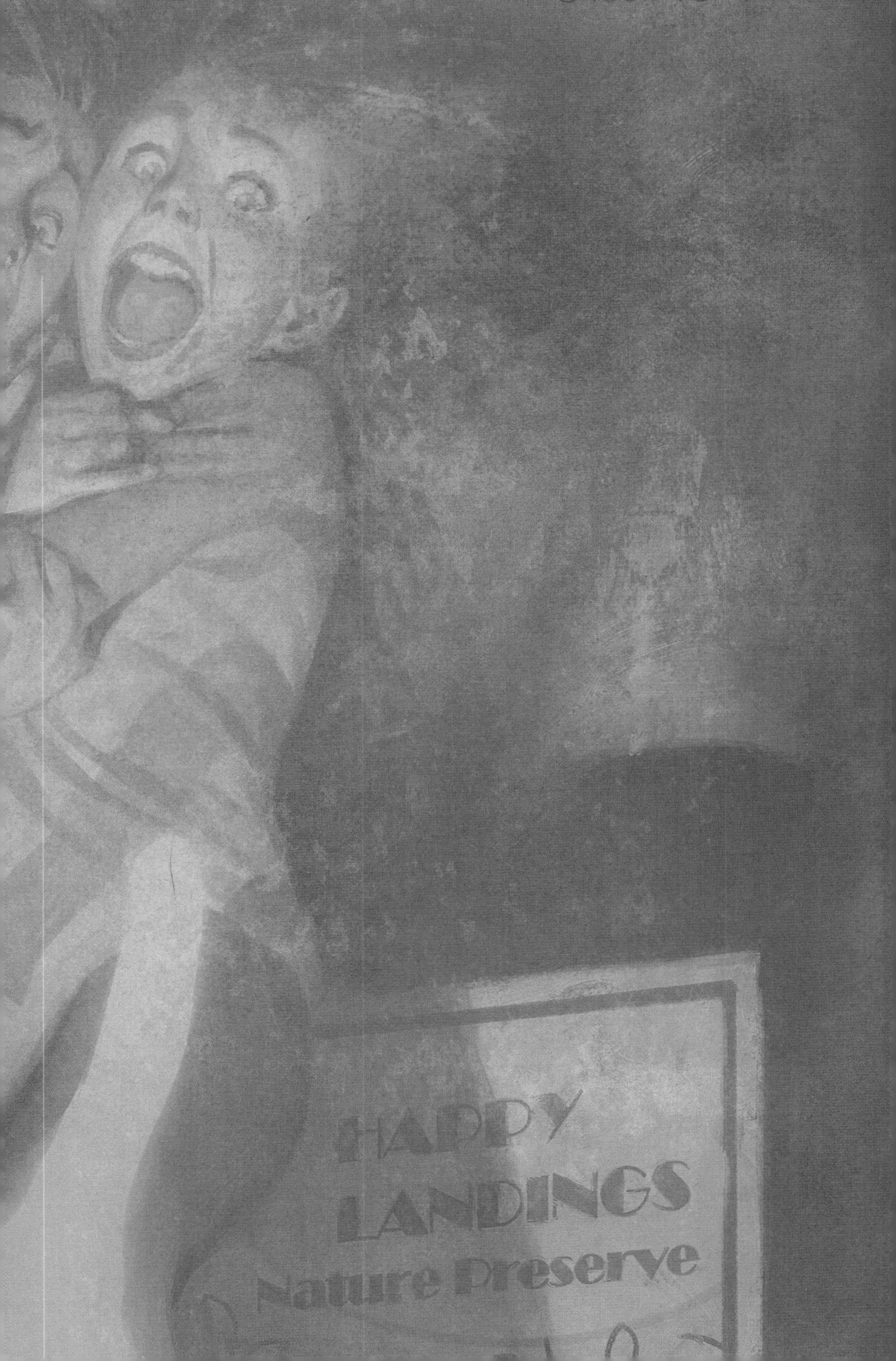
HAPPY
LANDINGS
Nature Preserve

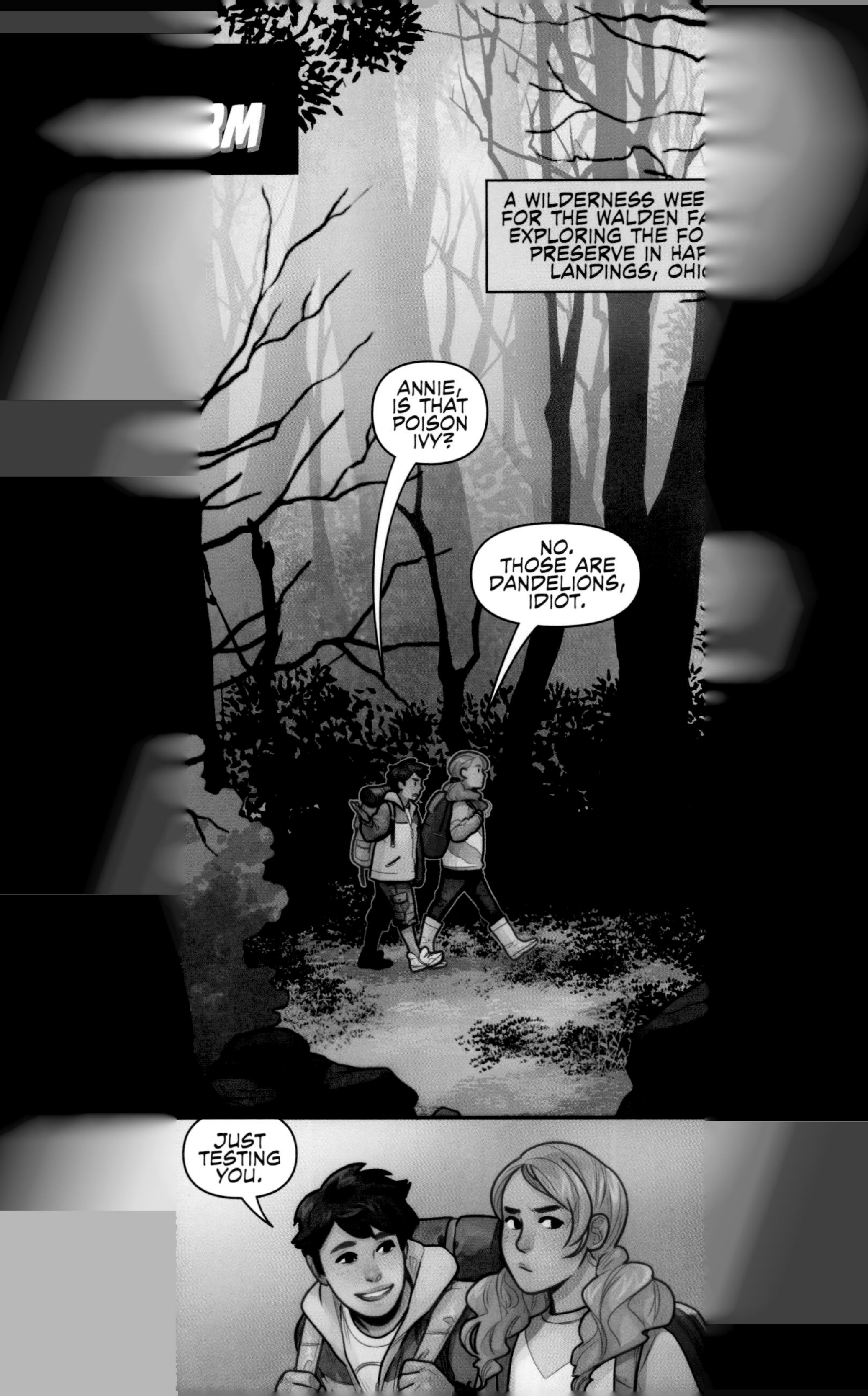
A WILDERNESS WEE
FOR THE WALDEN FA
EXPLORING THE FO
PRESERVE IN HAP
LANDINGS, OHIO
ANNIE, IS THAT POISON IVY?
NO. THOSE ARE DANDELIONS, IDIOT.
JUST TESTING YOU.

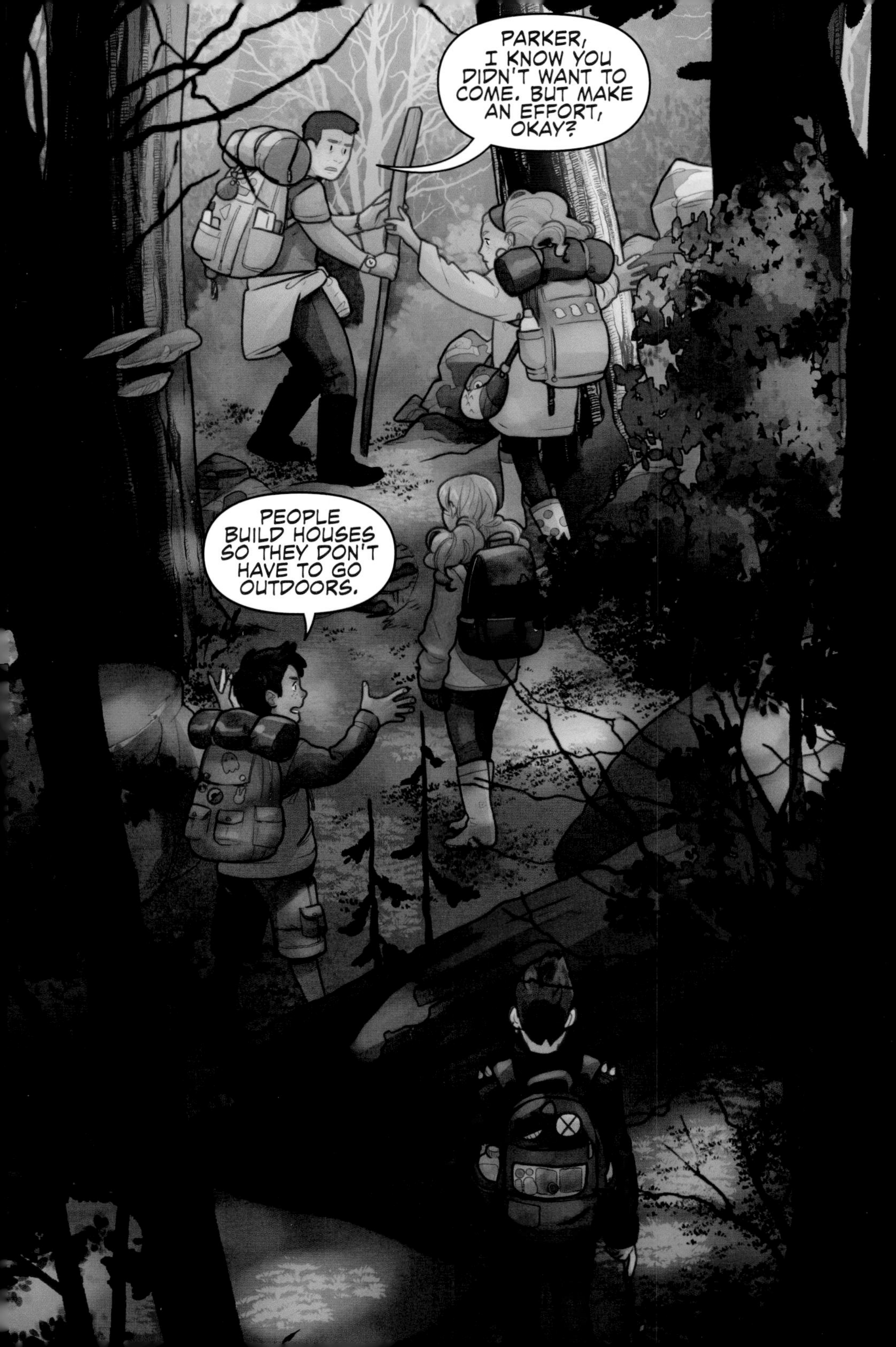
PARKER, I KNOW YOU DIDN'T WANT TO COME. BUT MAKE AN EFFORT, OKAY?
PEOPLE BUILD HOUSES SO THEY DON'T HAVE TO GO OUTDOORS.

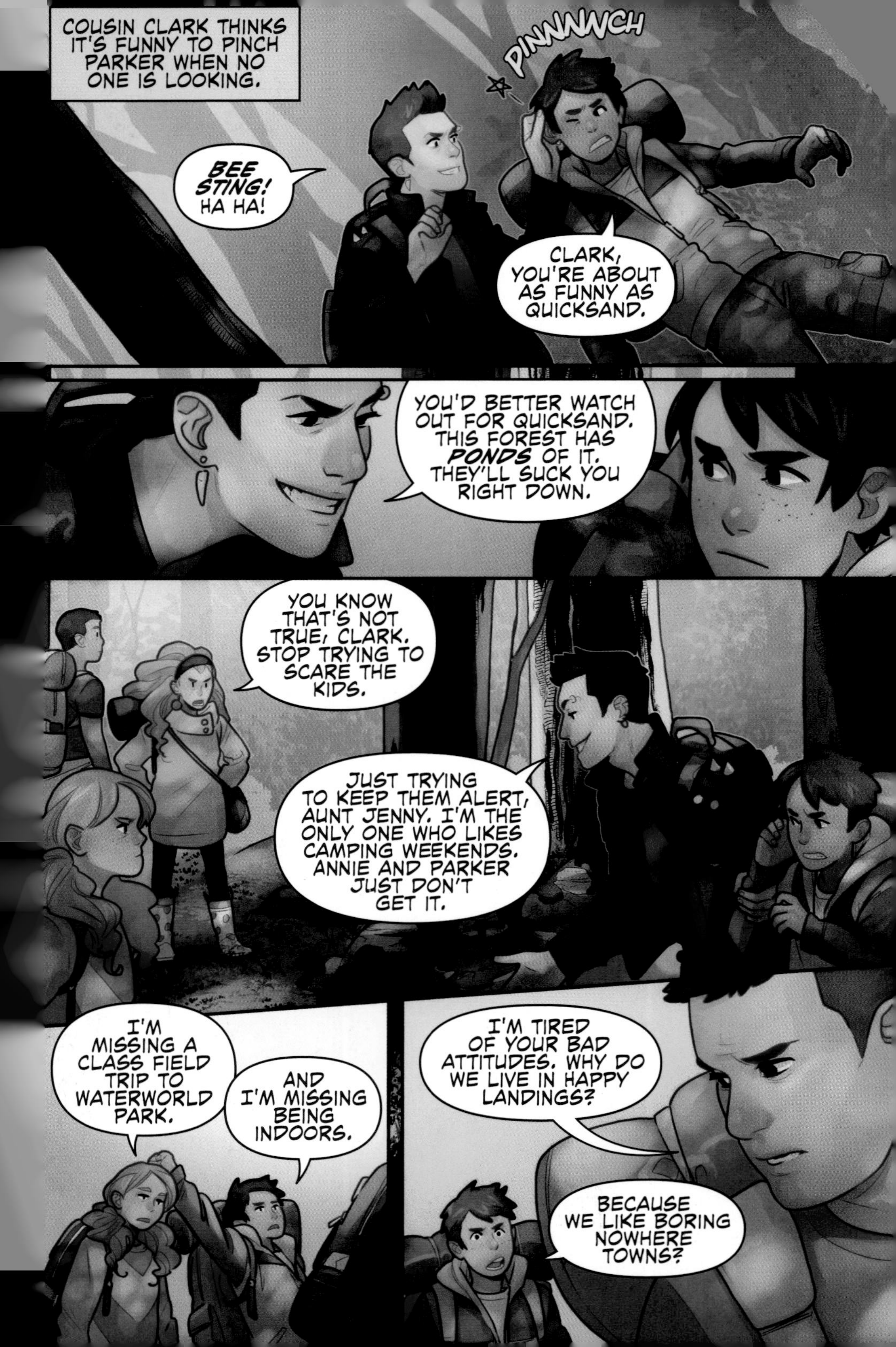
COUSIN CLARK THINKS IT'S FUNNY TO PINCH PARKER WHEN NO ONE IS LOOKING.
PINNNNCH
BEE STING! HA HA!
CLARK, YOU'RE ABOUT AS FUNNY AS QUICKSAND.
YOU'D BETTER WATCH OUT FOR QUICKSAND. THIS FOREST HAS PONDS OF IT. THEY'LL SUCK YOU RIGHT DOWN.
YOU KNOW THAT'S NOT TRUE, CLARK. STOP TRYING TO SCARE THE KIDS.
JUST TRYING TO KEEP THEM ALERT, AUNT JENNY. I'M THE ONLY ONE WHO LIKES CAMPING WEEKENDS. ANNIE AND PARKER JUST DON'T GET IT.
I'M MISSING A CLASS FIELD TRIP TO WATERWORLD PARK.
AND I'M MISSING BEING INDOORS.
I'M TIRED OF YOUR BAD ATTITUDES. WHY DO WE LIVE IN HAPPY LANDINGS?
BECAUSE WE LIKE BORING NOWHERE TOWNS?

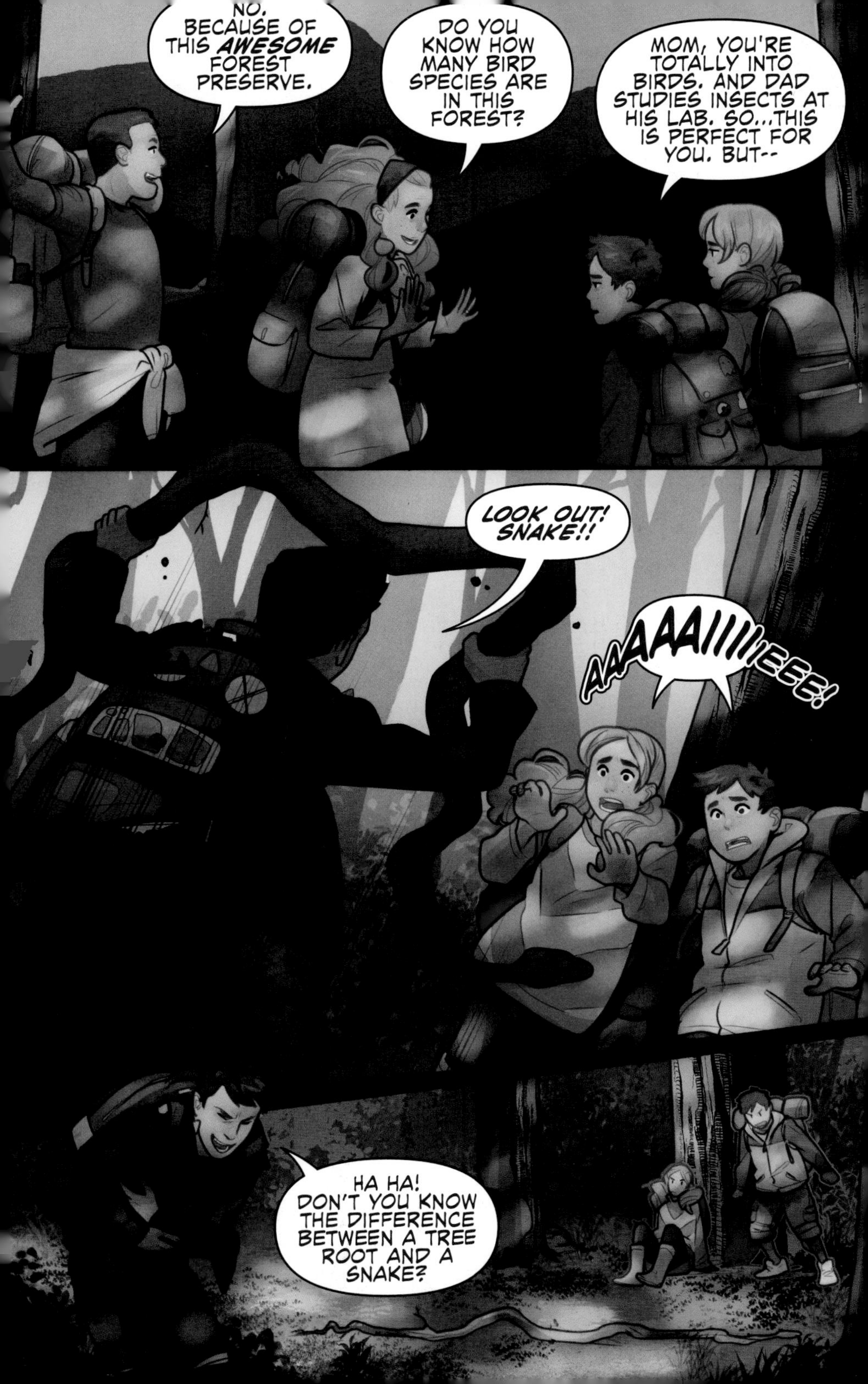
NO. BECAUSE OF THIS *AWESOME* FOREST PRESERVE.
DO YOU KNOW HOW MANY BIRD SPECIES ARE IN THIS FOREST?
MOM, YOU'RE TOTALLY INTO BIRDS. AND DAD STUDIES INSECTS AT HIS LAB. SO...THIS IS PERFECT FOR YOU. BUT--
LOOK OUT! SNAKE!!
AAAAAIIIIIEEE!
HA HA! DON'T YOU KNOW THE DIFFERENCE BETWEEN A TREE ROOT AND A SNAKE?

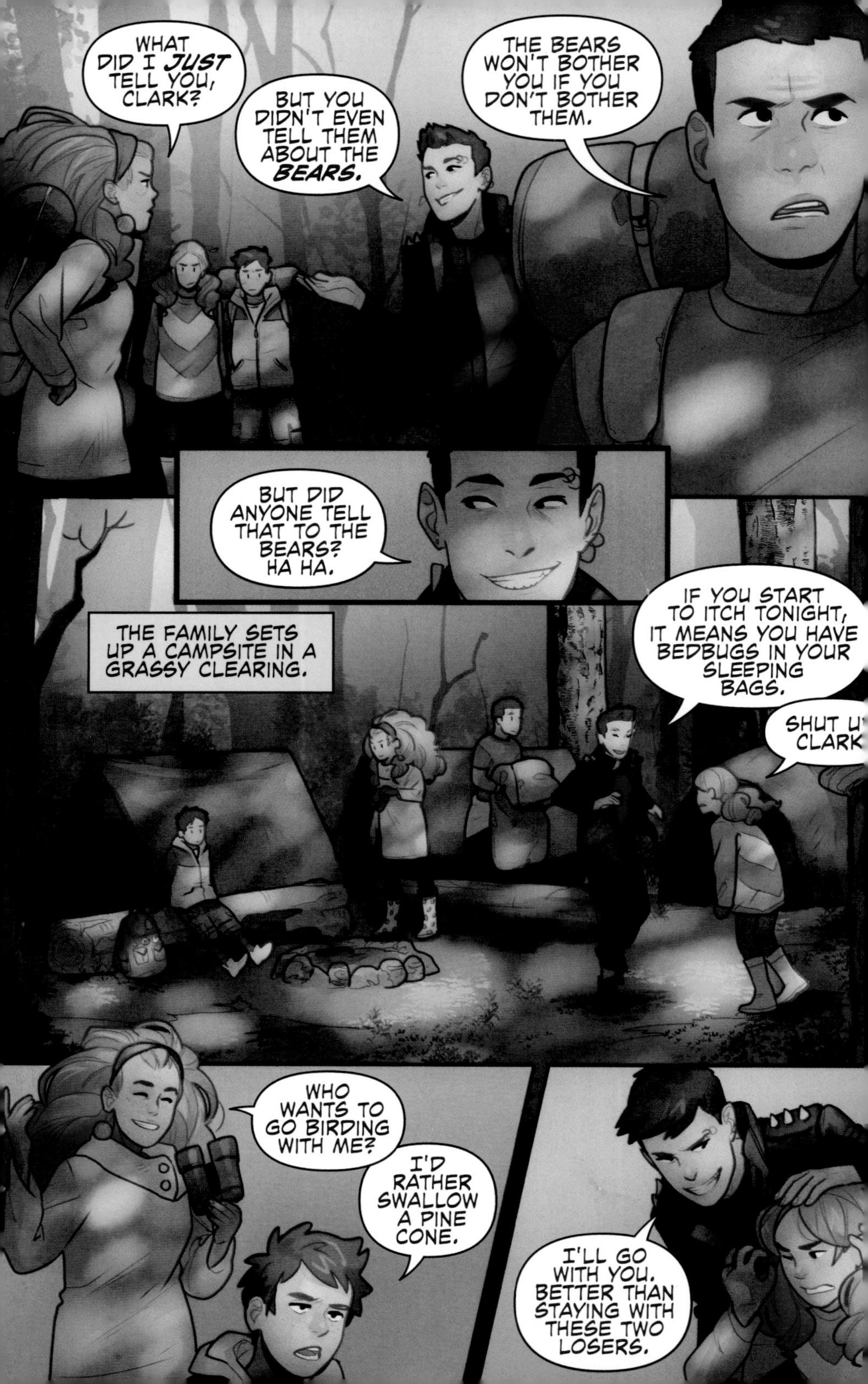
WHAT DID I *JUST* TELL YOU, CLARK?
BUT YOU DIDN'T EVEN TELL THEM ABOUT THE ***BEARS.***
THE BEARS WON'T BOTHER YOU IF YOU DON'T BOTHER THEM.
BUT DID ANYONE TELL THAT TO THE BEARS? HA HA.
THE FAMILY SETS UP A CAMPSITE IN A GRASSY CLEARING.
IF YOU START TO ITCH TONIGHT, IT MEANS YOU HAVE BEDBUGS IN YOUR SLEEPING BAGS.
SHUT U CLARK
WHO WANTS TO GO BIRDING WITH ME?
I'D RATHER SWALLOW A PINE CONE.
I'LL GO WITH YOU. BETTER THAN STAYING WITH THESE TWO LOSERS.

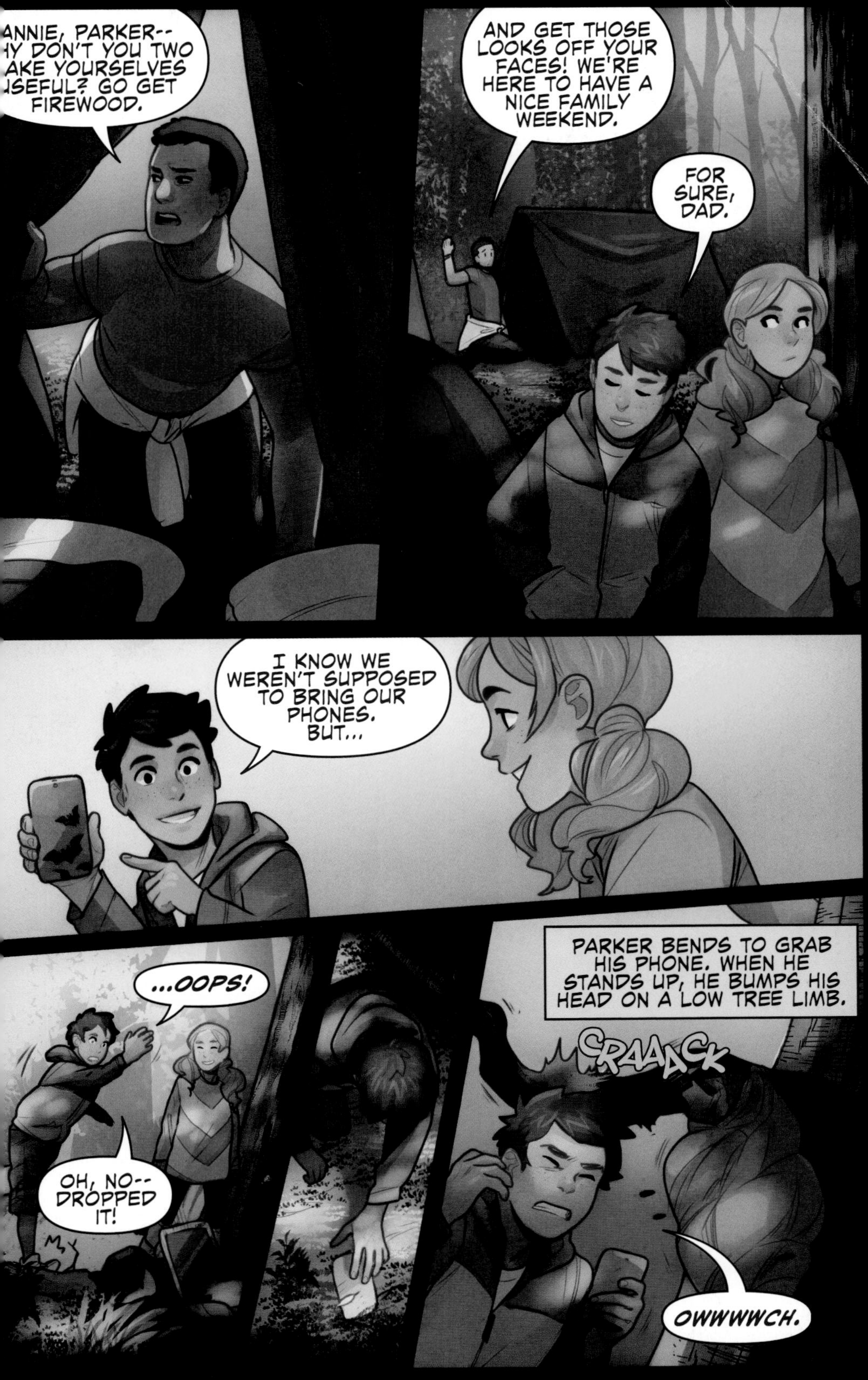
ANNIE, PARKER-- HY DON'T YOU TWO AKE YOURSELVES ISEFUL? GO GET FIREWOOD.
AND GET THOSE LOOKS OFF YOUR FACES! WE'RE HERE TO HAVE A NICE FAMILY WEEKEND.
FOR SURE, DAD.
I KNOW WE WEREN'T SUPPOSED TO BRING OUR PHONES. BUT...
...OOPS!
OH, NO-- DROPPED IT!
PARKER BENDS TO GRAB HIS PHONE. WHEN HE STANDS UP, HE BUMPS HIS HEAD ON A LOW TREE LIMB.
CRAAACK
OWWWWCH.

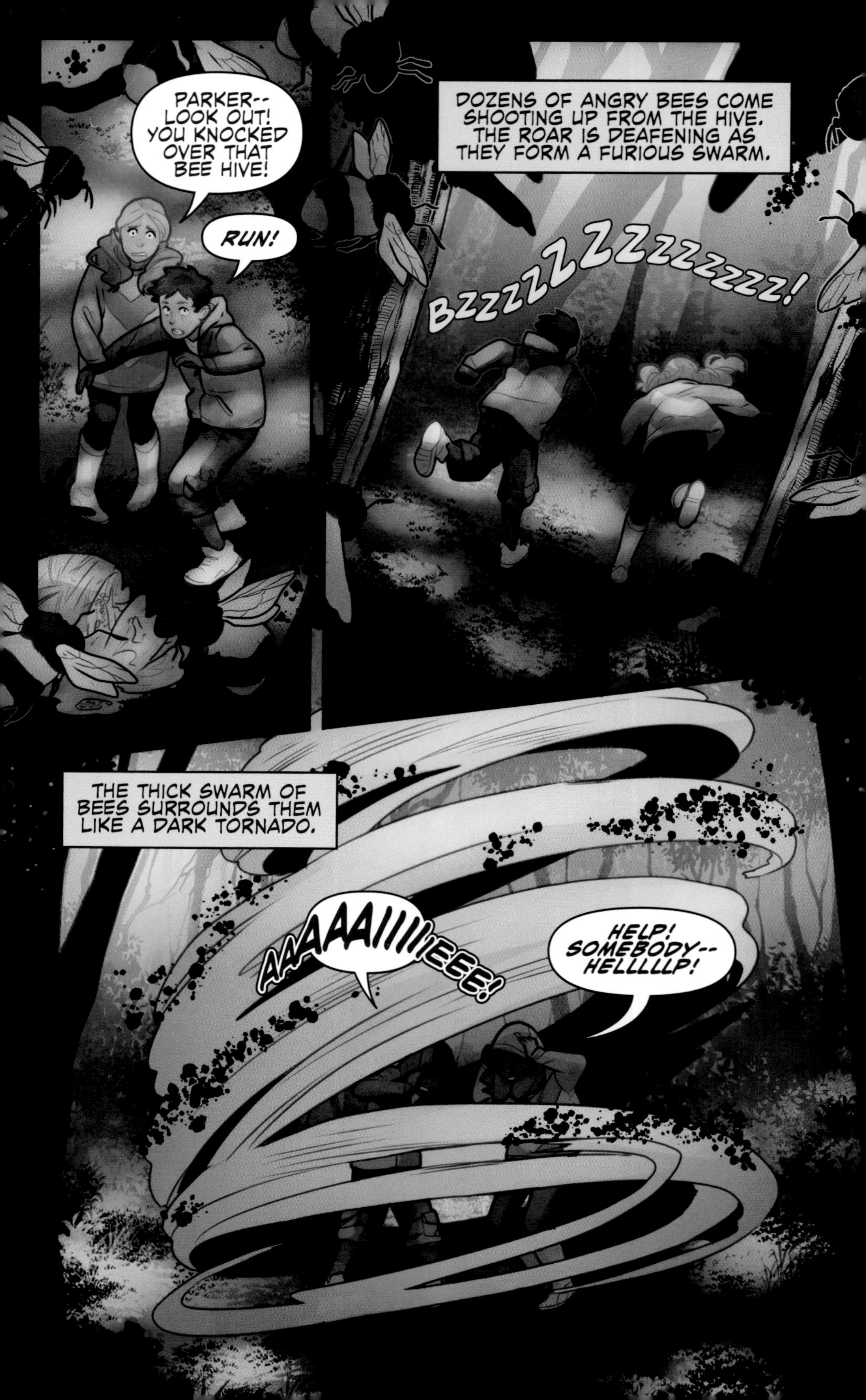
PARKER--
LOOK OUT!
YOU KNOCKED
OVER THAT
BEE HIVE!
RUN!
DOZENS OF ANGRY BEES COME SHOOTING UP FROM THE HIVE. THE ROAR IS DEAFENING AS THEY FORM A FURIOUS SWARM.
BZZZZZZZZZZZZZZZ!
THE THICK SWARM OF BEES SURROUNDS THEM LIKE A DARK TORNADO.
AAAAAIIIIIEEE!
HELP! SOMEBODY-- HELLLLLP!

CHAPTER TWO
MORONS FROM MARS

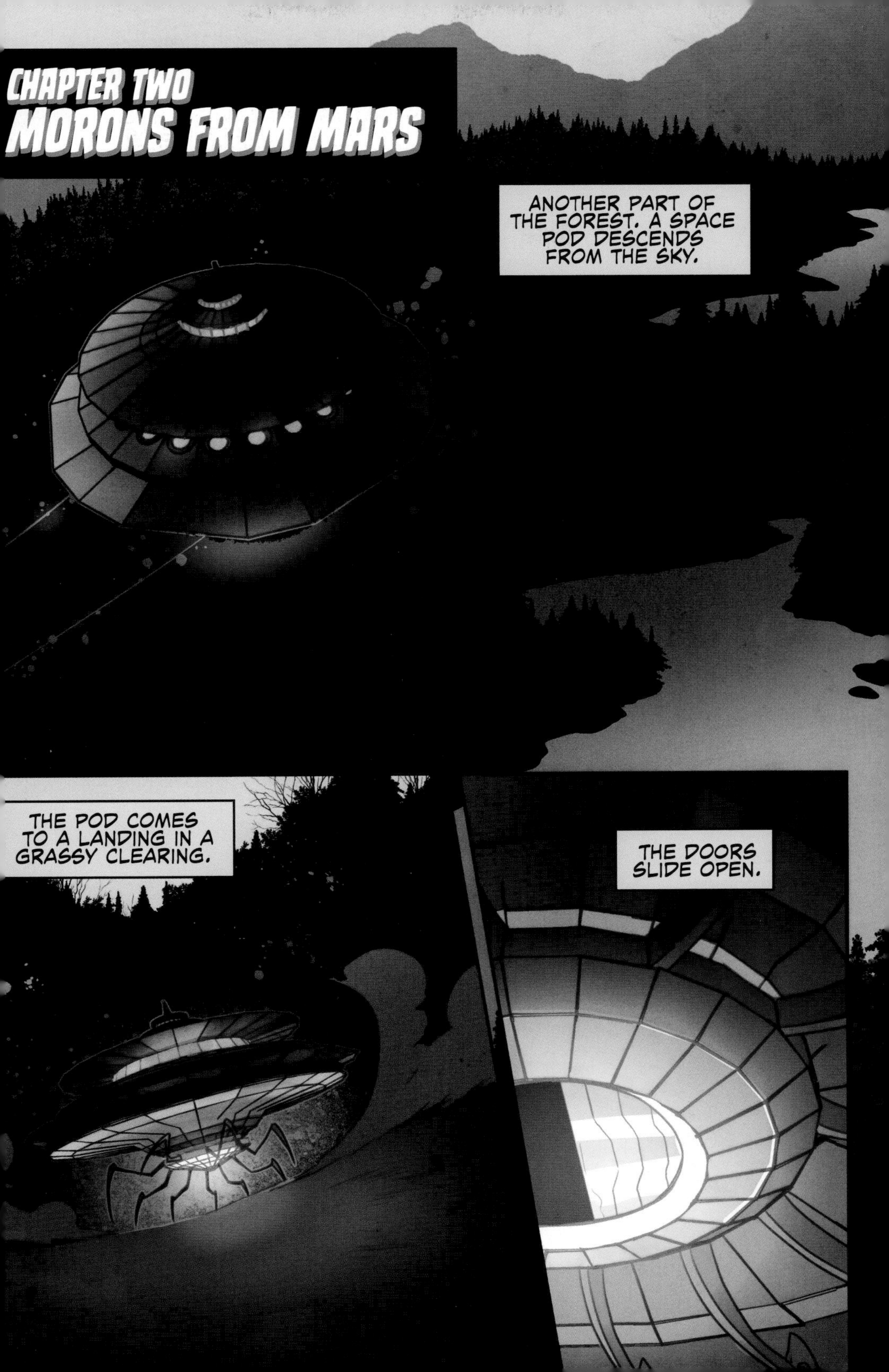
ANOTHER PART OF THE FOREST. A SPACE POD DESCENDS FROM THE SKY.
THE POD COMES TO A LANDING IN A GRASSY CLEARING.
THE DOORS SLIDE OPEN.

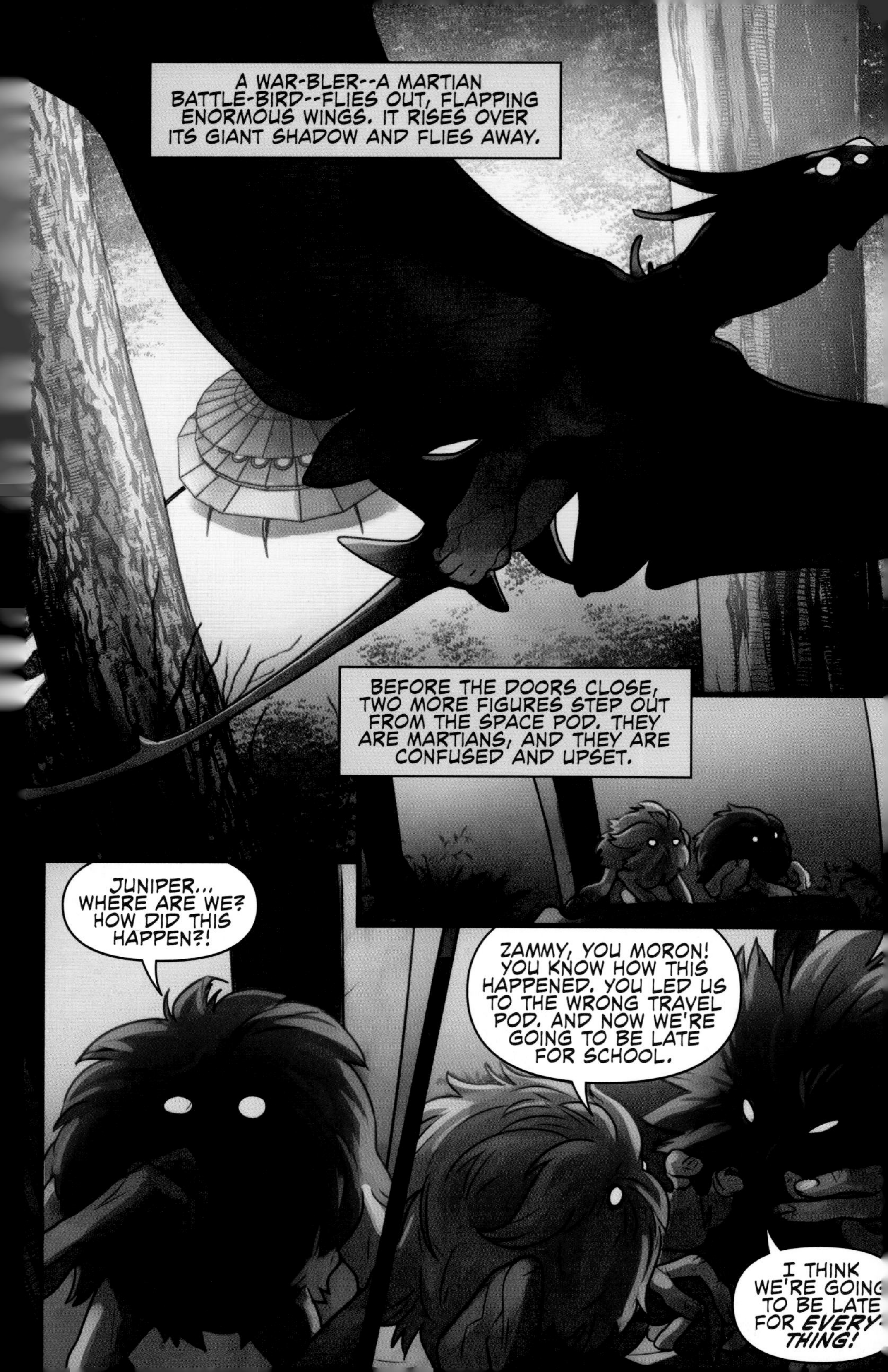
A WAR-BLER--A MARTIAN BATTLE-BIRD--FLIES OUT, FLAPPING ENORMOUS WINGS. IT RISES OVER ITS GIANT SHADOW AND FLIES AWAY.
BEFORE THE DOORS CLOSE, TWO MORE FIGURES STEP OUT FROM THE SPACE POD. THEY ARE MARTIANS, AND THEY ARE CONFUSED AND UPSET.
JUNIPER... WHERE ARE WE? HOW DID THIS HAPPEN?!
ZAMMY, YOU MORON! YOU KNOW HOW THIS HAPPENED. YOU LED US TO THE WRONG TRAVEL POD. AND NOW WE'RE GOING TO BE LATE FOR SCHOOL.
I THINK WE'RE GOING TO BE LATE FOR *EVERY-THING!*

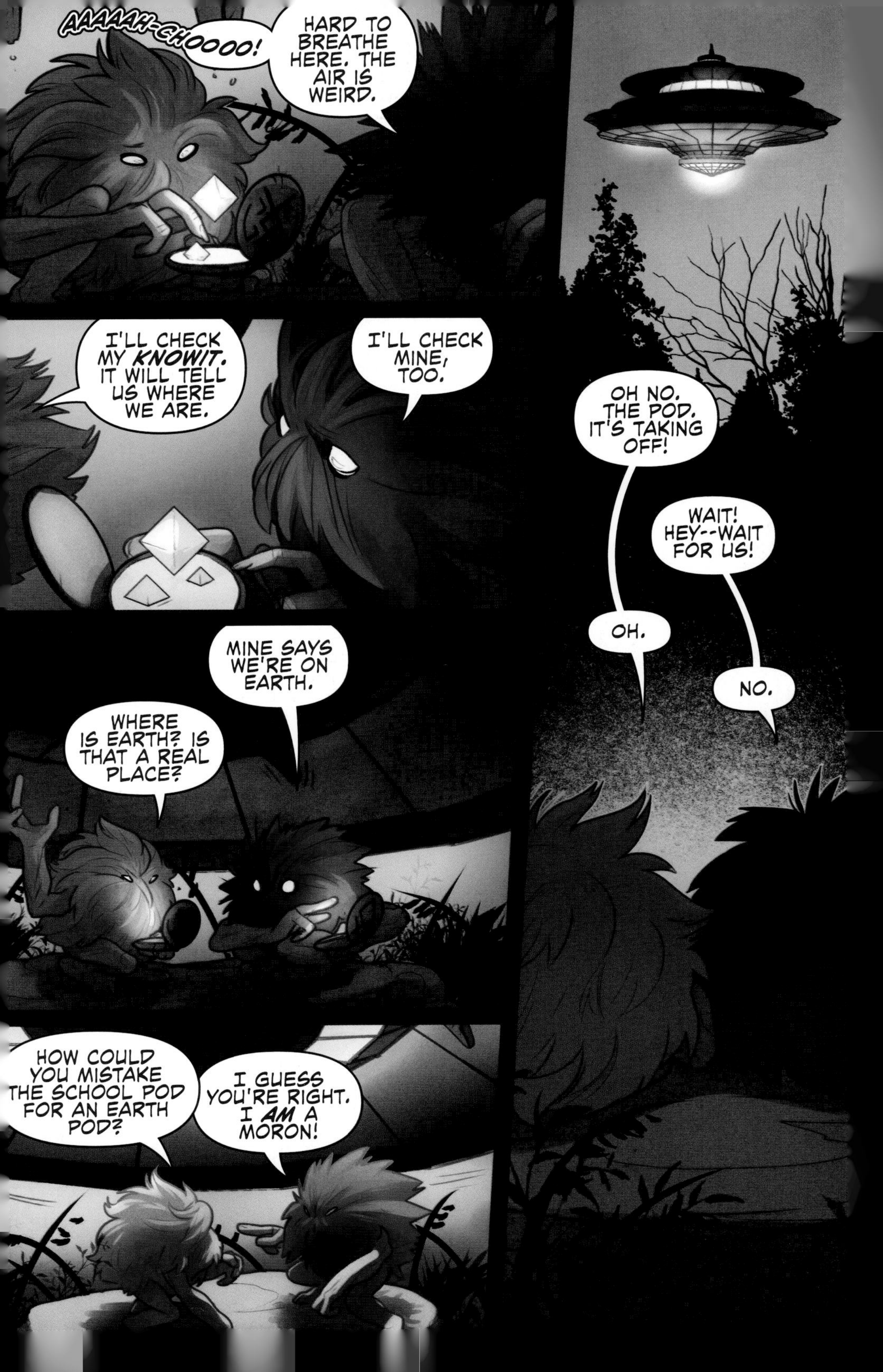
AAAAAH-CHOOOO!
HARD TO BREATHE HERE. THE AIR IS WEIRD.
I'LL CHECK MY ***KNOWIT.*** IT WILL TELL US WHERE WE ARE.
I'LL CHECK MINE, TOO.
MINE SAYS WE'RE ON EARTH.
WHERE IS EARTH? IS THAT A REAL PLACE?
HOW COULD YOU MISTAKE THE SCHOOL POD FOR AN EARTH POD?
I GUESS YOU'RE RIGHT. I ***AM*** A MORON!
OH NO. THE POD. IT'S TAKING OFF!
WAIT! HEY--WAIT FOR US!
OH.
NO.

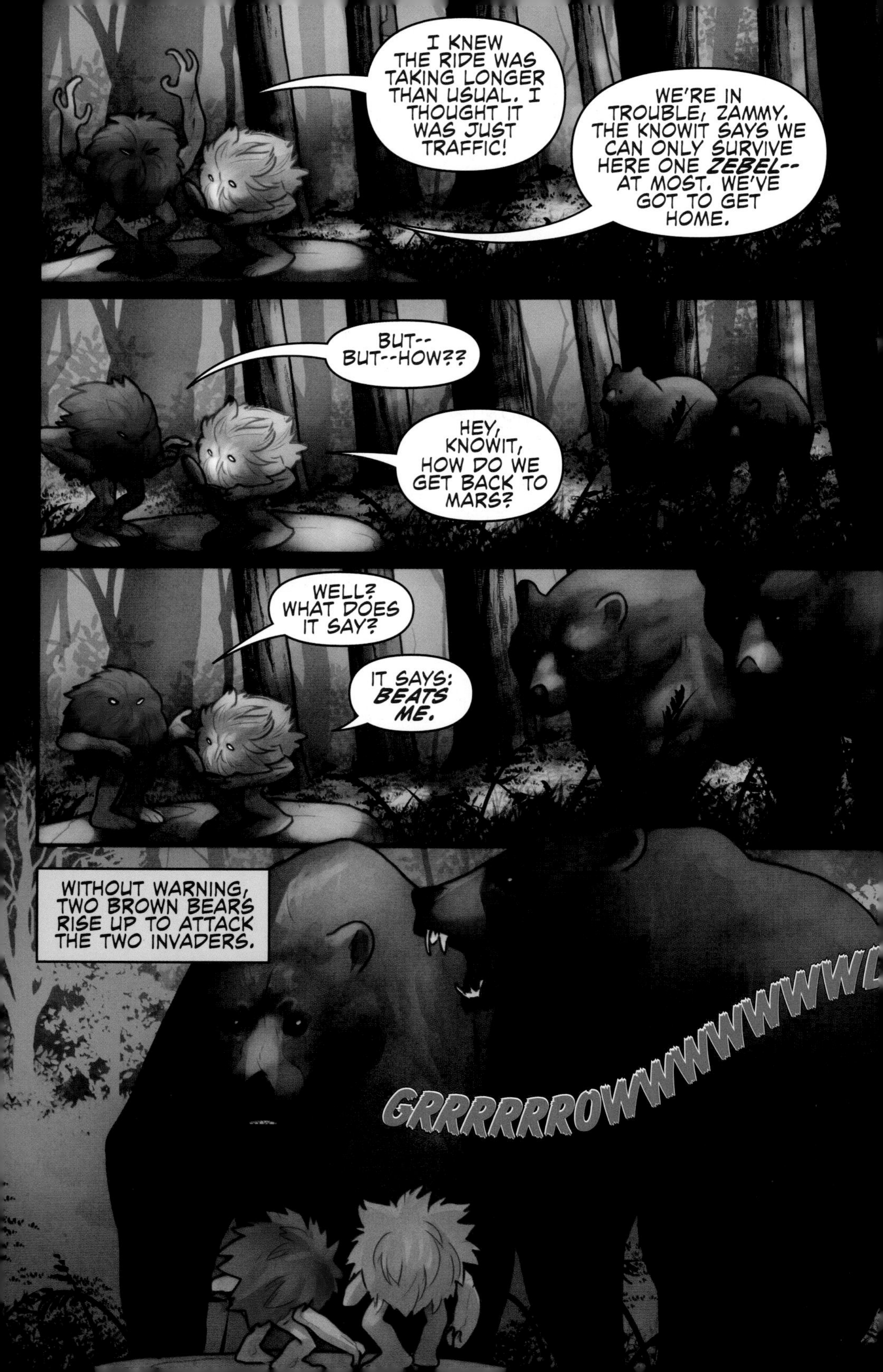
I KNEW THE RIDE WAS TAKING LONGER THAN USUAL. I THOUGHT IT WAS JUST TRAFFIC!
WE'RE IN TROUBLE, ZAMMY. THE KNOWIT SAYS WE CAN ONLY SURVIVE HERE ONE ZEBEL-- AT MOST. WE'VE GOT TO GET HOME.
BUT-- BUT--HOW??
HEY, KNOWIT, HOW DO WE GET BACK TO MARS?
WELL? WHAT DOES IT SAY?
IT SAYS: BEATS ME.
WITHOUT WARNING, TWO BROWN BEARS RISE UP TO ATTACK THE TWO INVADERS.
GRRRRRROWWWWWWWWWL

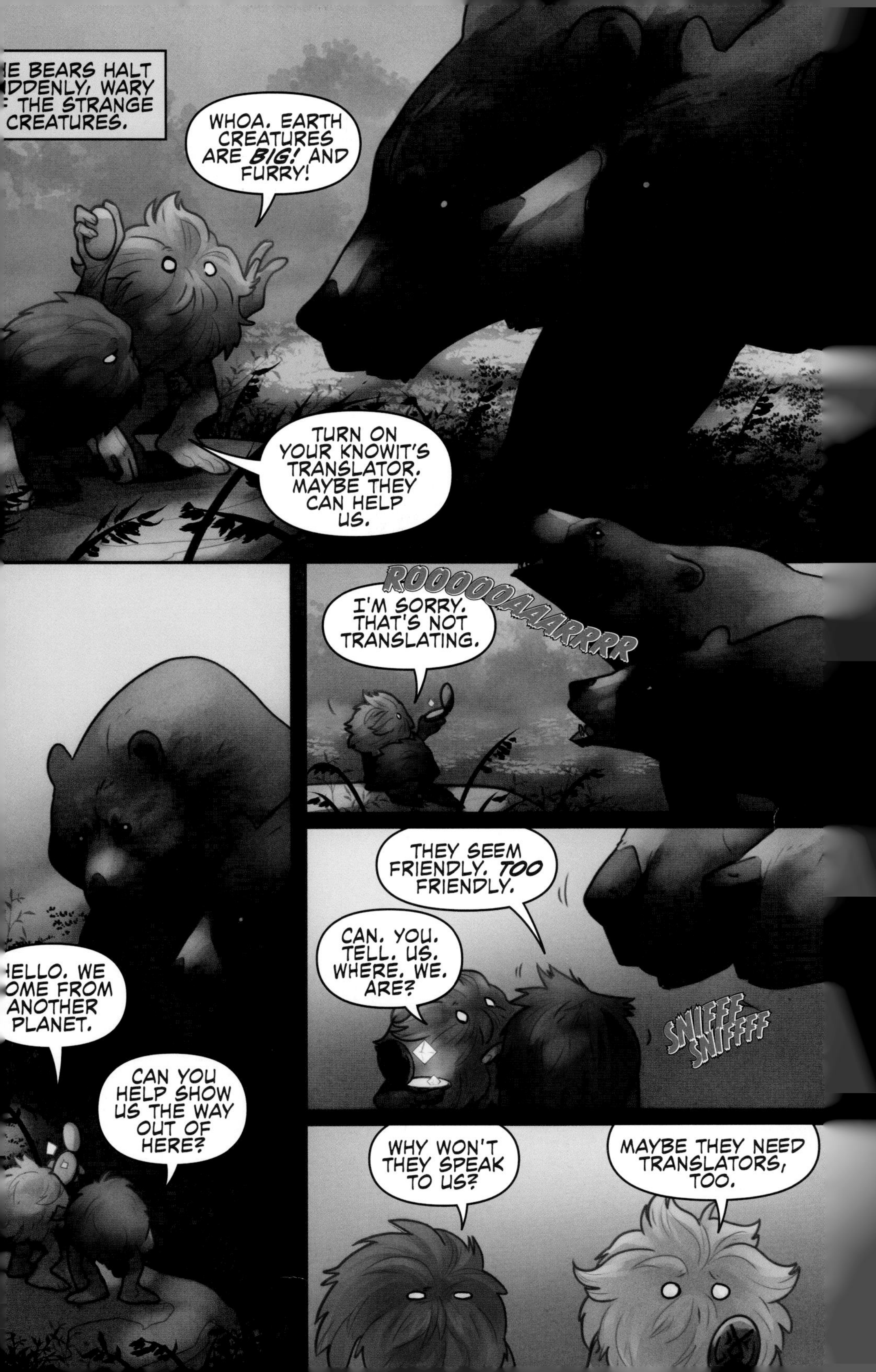

E BEARS HALT
DDENLY, WARY
F THE STRANGE
CREATURES.
WHOA. EARTH CREATURES ARE BIG! AND FURRY!
TURN ON YOUR KNOWIT'S TRANSLATOR. MAYBE THEY CAN HELP US.
ELLO. WE OME FROM ANOTHER PLANET.
CAN YOU HELP SHOW US THE WAY OUT OF HERE?
ROOOOOOAAAARRRRR
I'M SORRY. THAT'S NOT TRANSLATING.
THEY SEEM FRIENDLY. TOO FRIENDLY.
CAN. YOU. TELL. US. WHERE. WE. ARE?
SNIFFF SNIFFFFF
WHY WON'T THEY SPEAK TO US?
MAYBE THEY NEED TRANSLATORS, TOO.

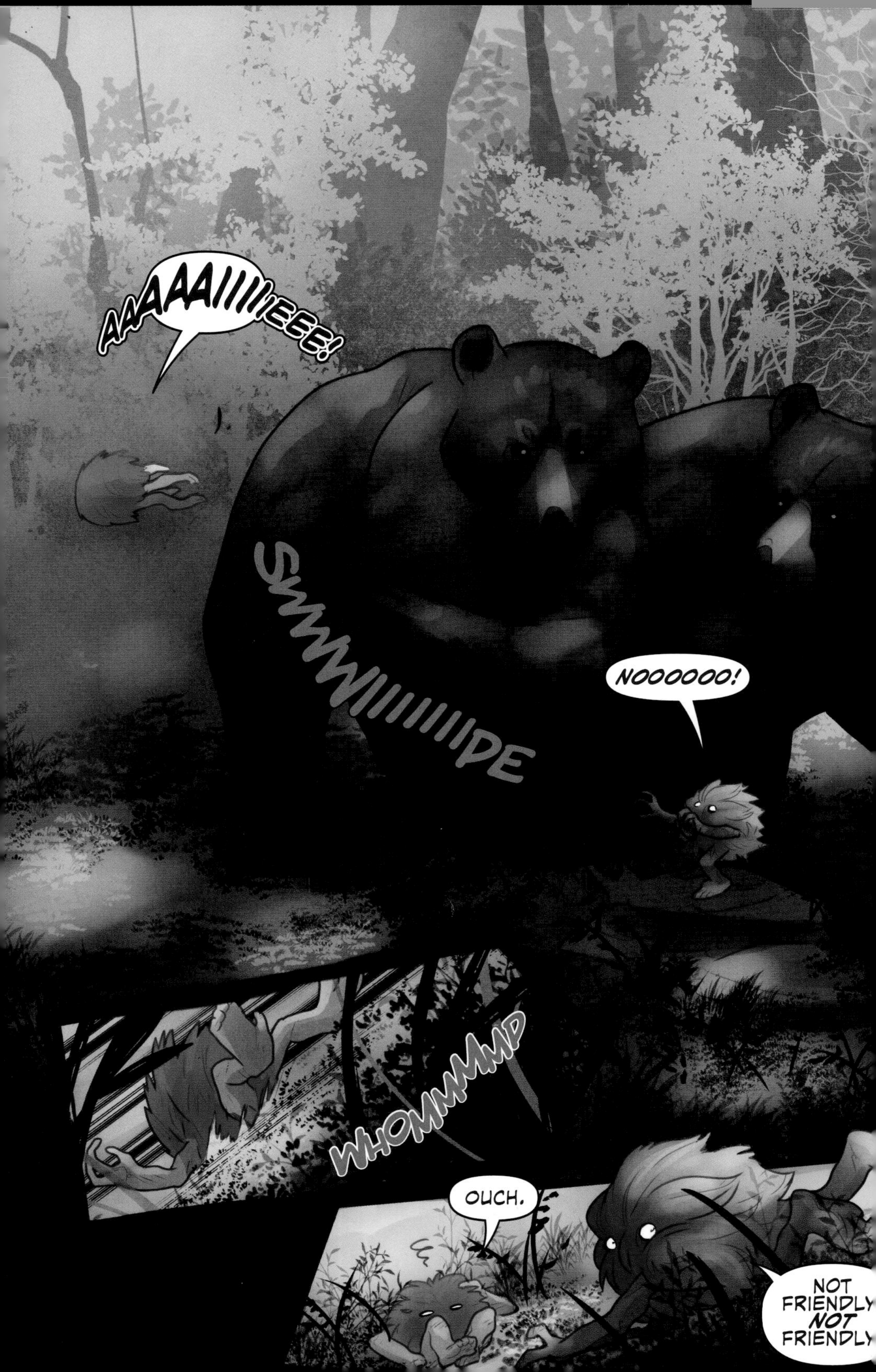
AAAAAIIIIIIEEEE!
SWWWIIIIIIIIPE
NOOOOOO!
WHOMMMMMP
OUCH.
NOT FRIENDLY NOT FRIENDLY

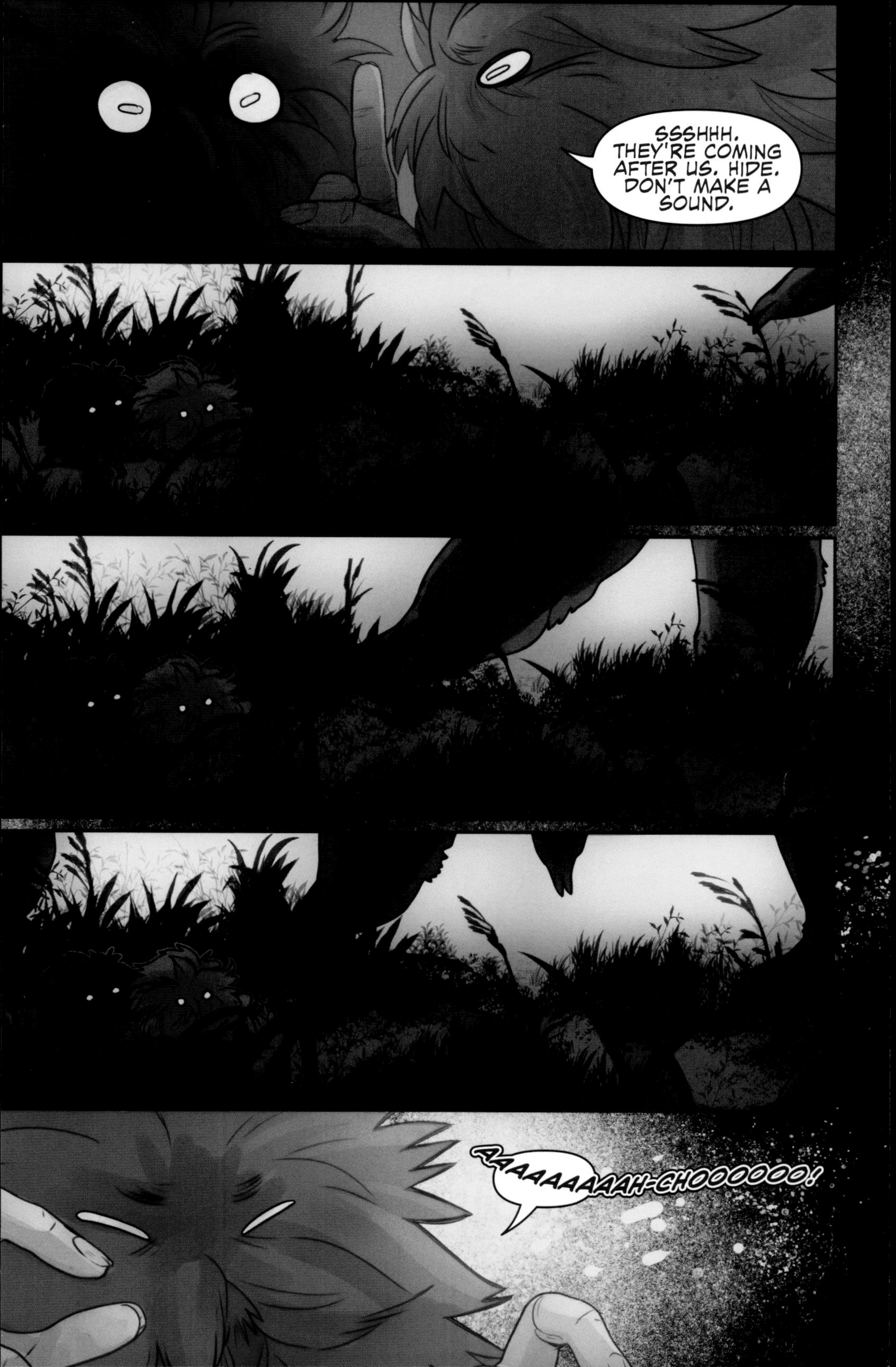
SSSHHH. THEY'RE COMING AFTER US. HIDE. DON'T MAKE A SOUND.
AAAAAAAAAAH-CHOOOOOOO!

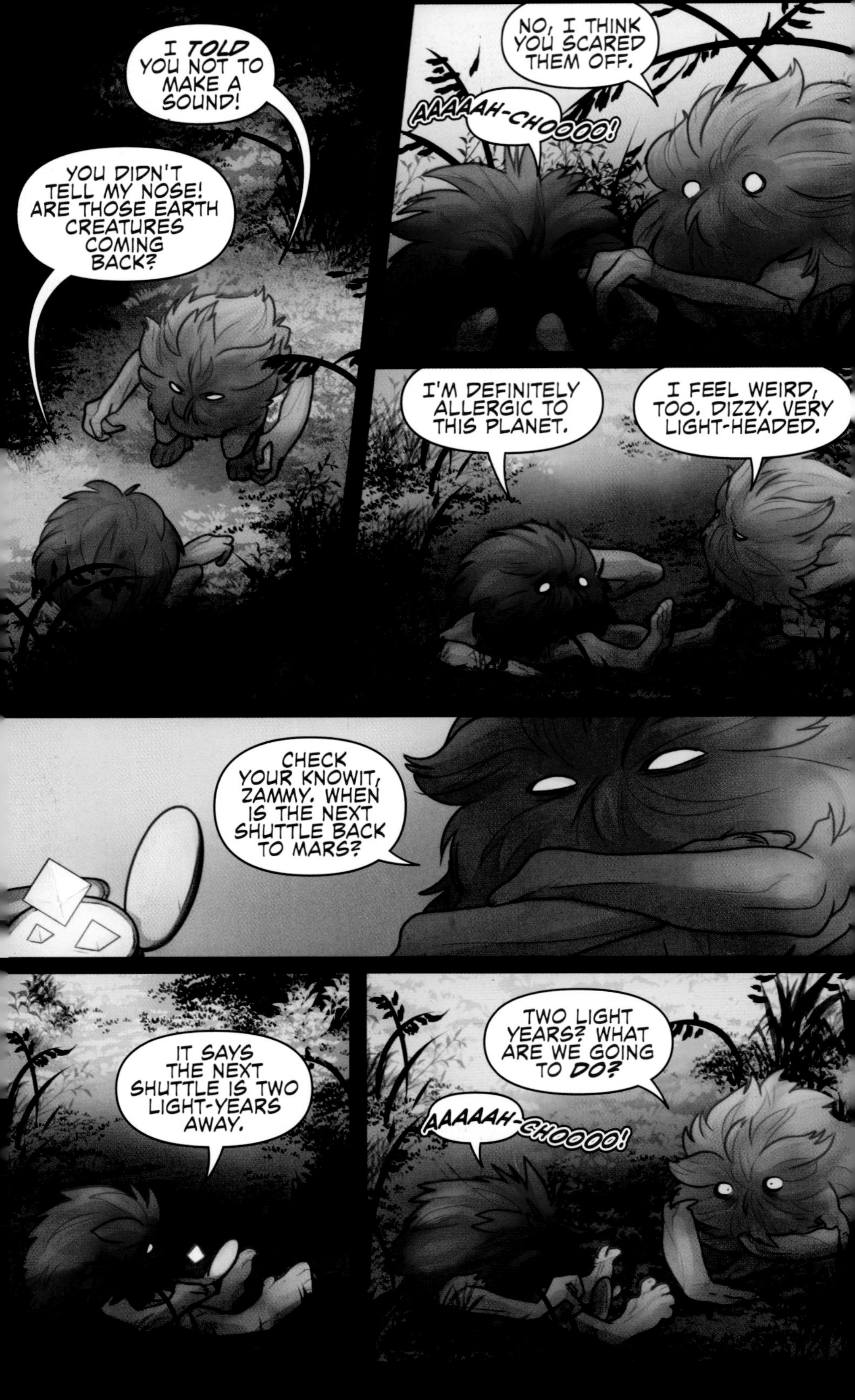
I *TOLD* YOU NOT TO MAKE A SOUND!
YOU DIDN'T TELL MY NOSE! ARE THOSE EARTH CREATURES COMING BACK?
NO, I THINK YOU SCARED THEM OFF.
AAAAAH-CHOOOOO!
I'M DEFINITELY ALLERGIC TO THIS PLANET.
I FEEL WEIRD, TOO. DIZZY. VERY LIGHT-HEADED.
CHECK YOUR KNOWIT, ZAMMY. WHEN IS THE NEXT SHUTTLE BACK TO MARS?
IT SAYS THE NEXT SHUTTLE IS TWO LIGHT-YEARS AWAY.
TWO LIGHT YEARS? WHAT ARE WE GOING TO *DO*?
AAAAAH-CHOOOOO!

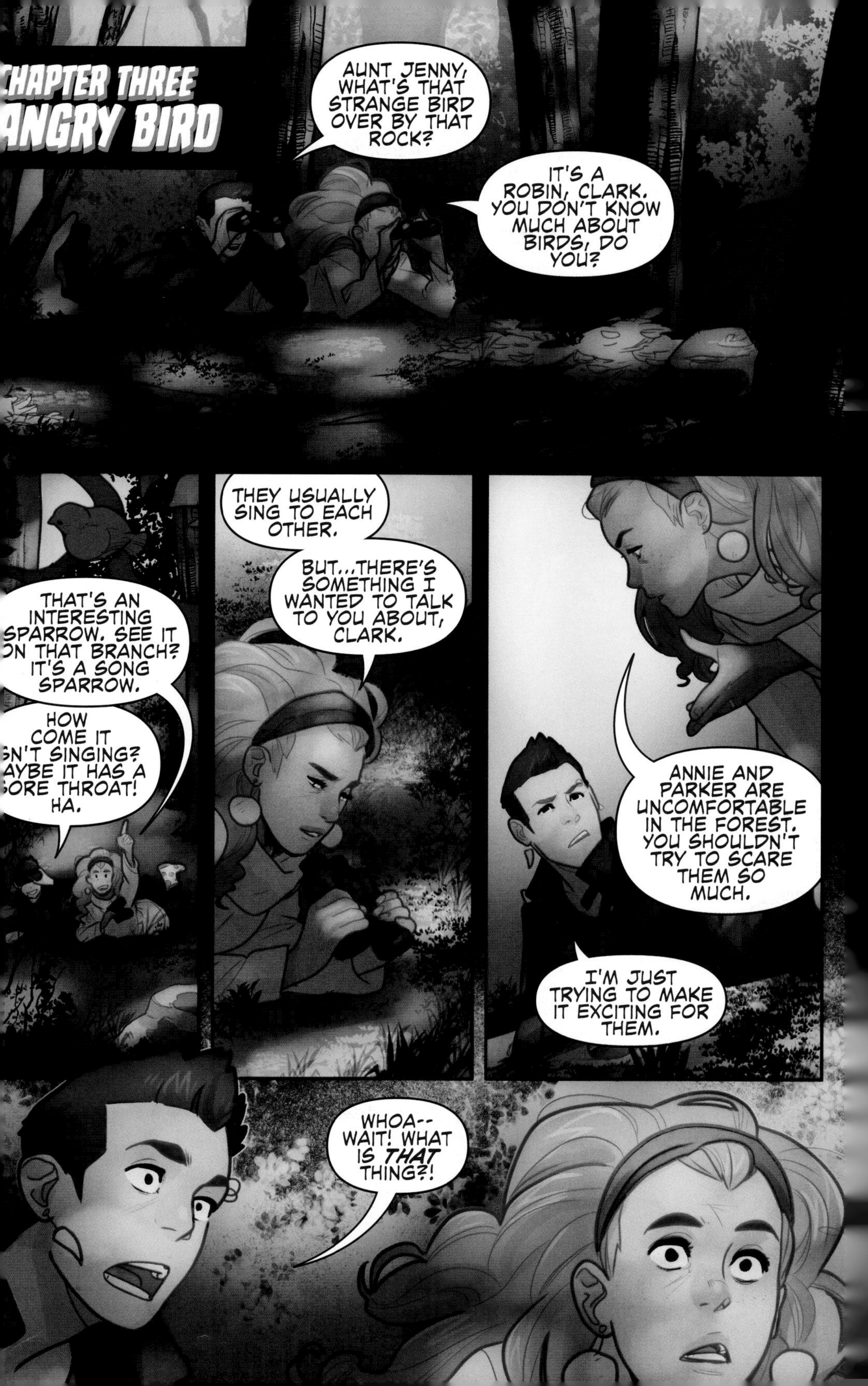
CHAPTER THREE
ANGRY BIRD
AUNT JENNY, WHAT'S THAT STRANGE BIRD OVER BY THAT ROCK?
IT'S A ROBIN, CLARK. YOU DON'T KNOW MUCH ABOUT BIRDS, DO YOU?
THAT'S AN INTERESTING SPARROW. SEE IT ON THAT BRANCH? IT'S A SONG SPARROW.
HOW COME IT ISN'T SINGING? MAYBE IT HAS A SORE THROAT! HA.
THEY USUALLY SING TO EACH OTHER.
BUT...THERE'S SOMETHING I WANTED TO TALK TO YOU ABOUT, CLARK.
ANNIE AND PARKER ARE UNCOMFORTABLE IN THE FOREST. YOU SHOULDN'T TRY TO SCARE THEM SO MUCH.
I'M JUST TRYING TO MAKE IT EXCITING FOR THEM.
WHOA--WAIT! WHAT IS *THAT* THING?!

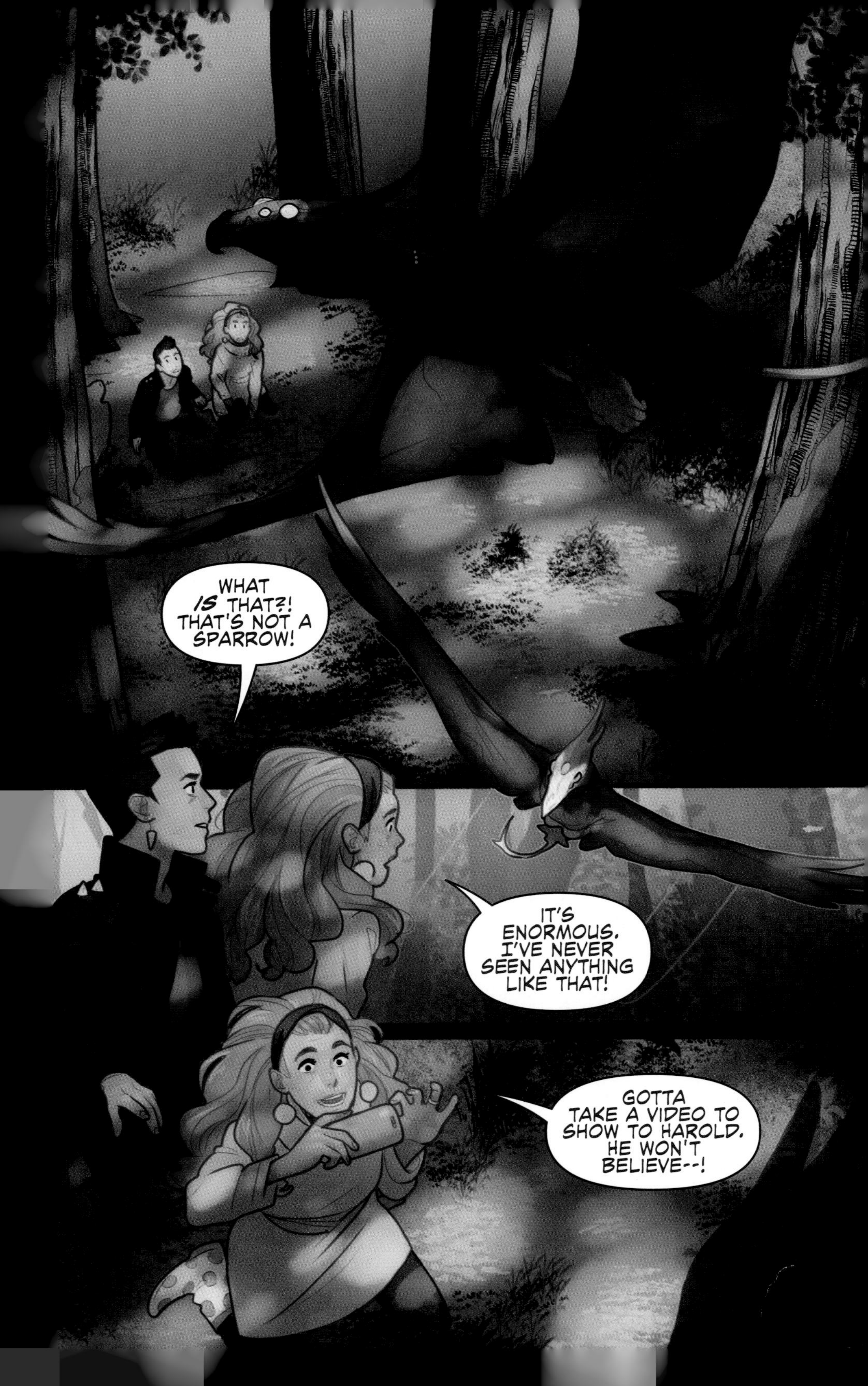
WHAT *IS* THAT?! THAT'S NOT A SPARROW!
IT'S ENORMOUS. I'VE NEVER SEEN ANYTHING LIKE THAT!
GOTTA TAKE A VIDEO TO SHOW TO HAROLD. HE WON'T BELIEVE--!

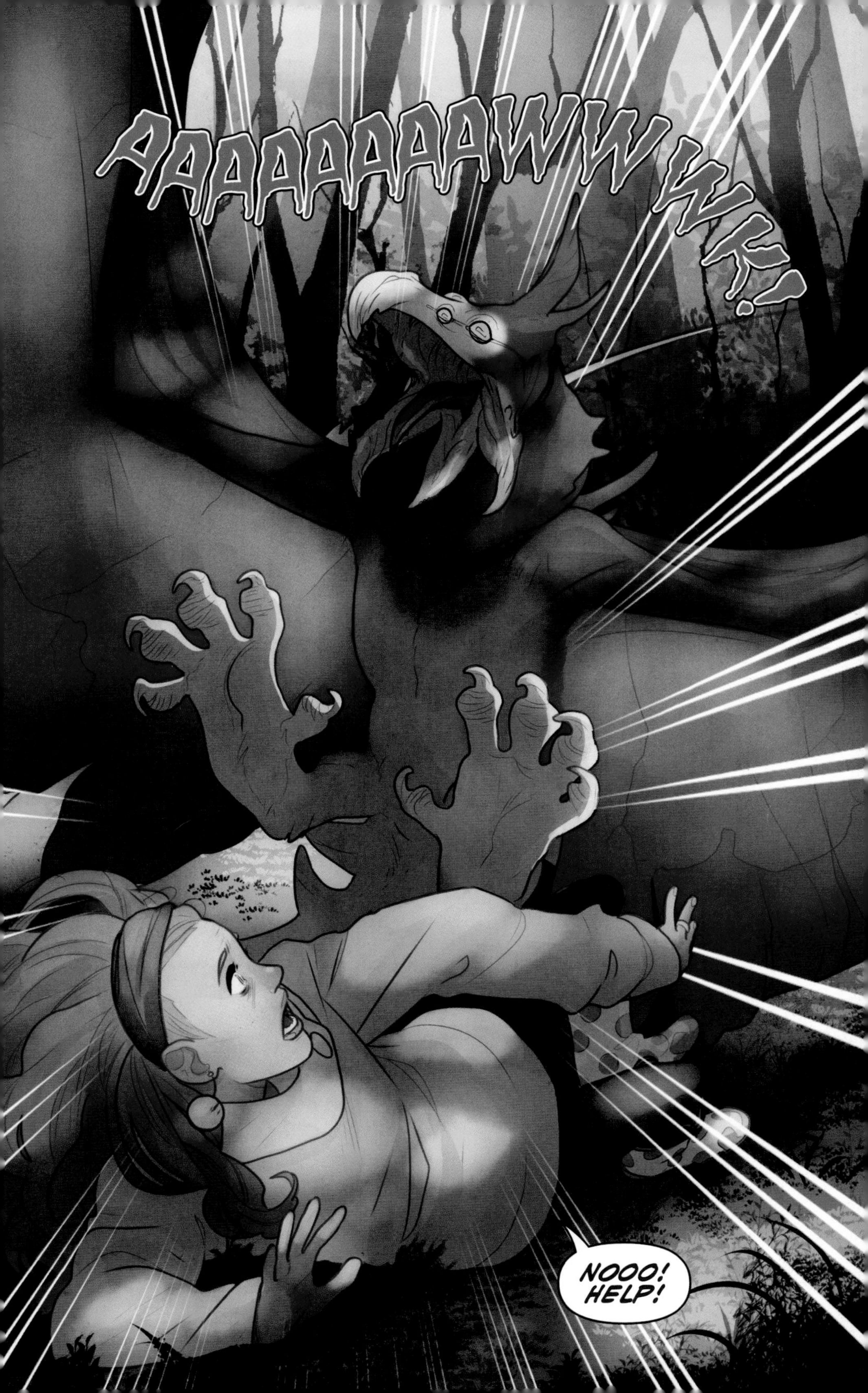
AAAAAAAAWWWK!
NOOO! HELP!

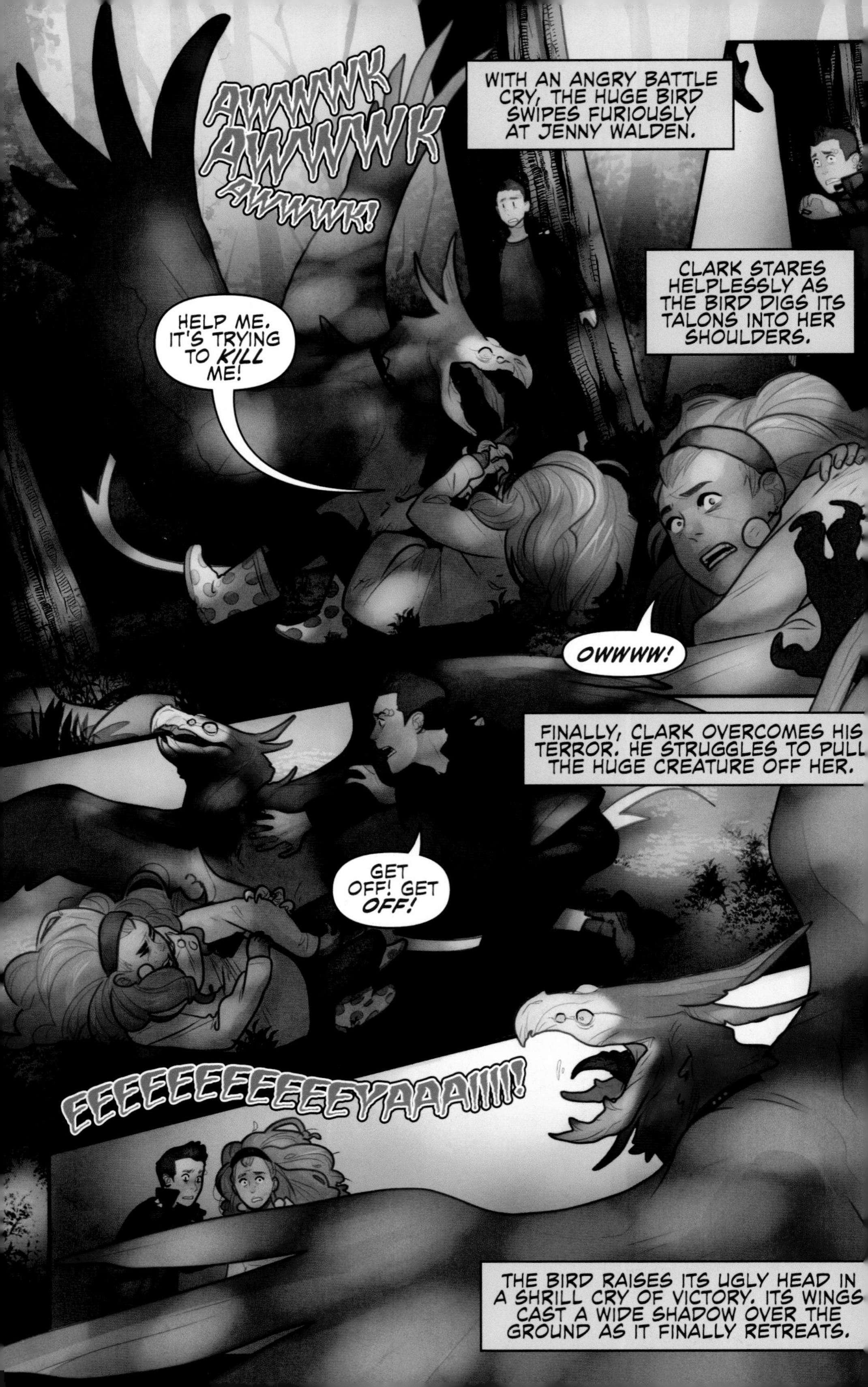
AWWWK AWWWK AWWWK!
WITH AN ANGRY BATTLE CRY, THE HUGE BIRD SWIPES FURIOUSLY AT JENNY WALDEN.
HELP ME. IT'S TRYING TO KILL ME!
CLARK STARES HELPLESSLY AS THE BIRD DIGS ITS TALONS INTO HER SHOULDERS.
OWWWW!
FINALLY, CLARK OVERCOMES HIS TERROR. HE STRUGGLES TO PULL THE HUGE CREATURE OFF HER.
GET OFF! GET OFF!
EEEEEEEEEEEEYAAAIIIII!
THE BIRD RAISES ITS UGLY HEAD IN A SHRILL CRY OF VICTORY. ITS WINGS CAST A WIDE SHADOW OVER THE GROUND AS IT FINALLY RETREATS.

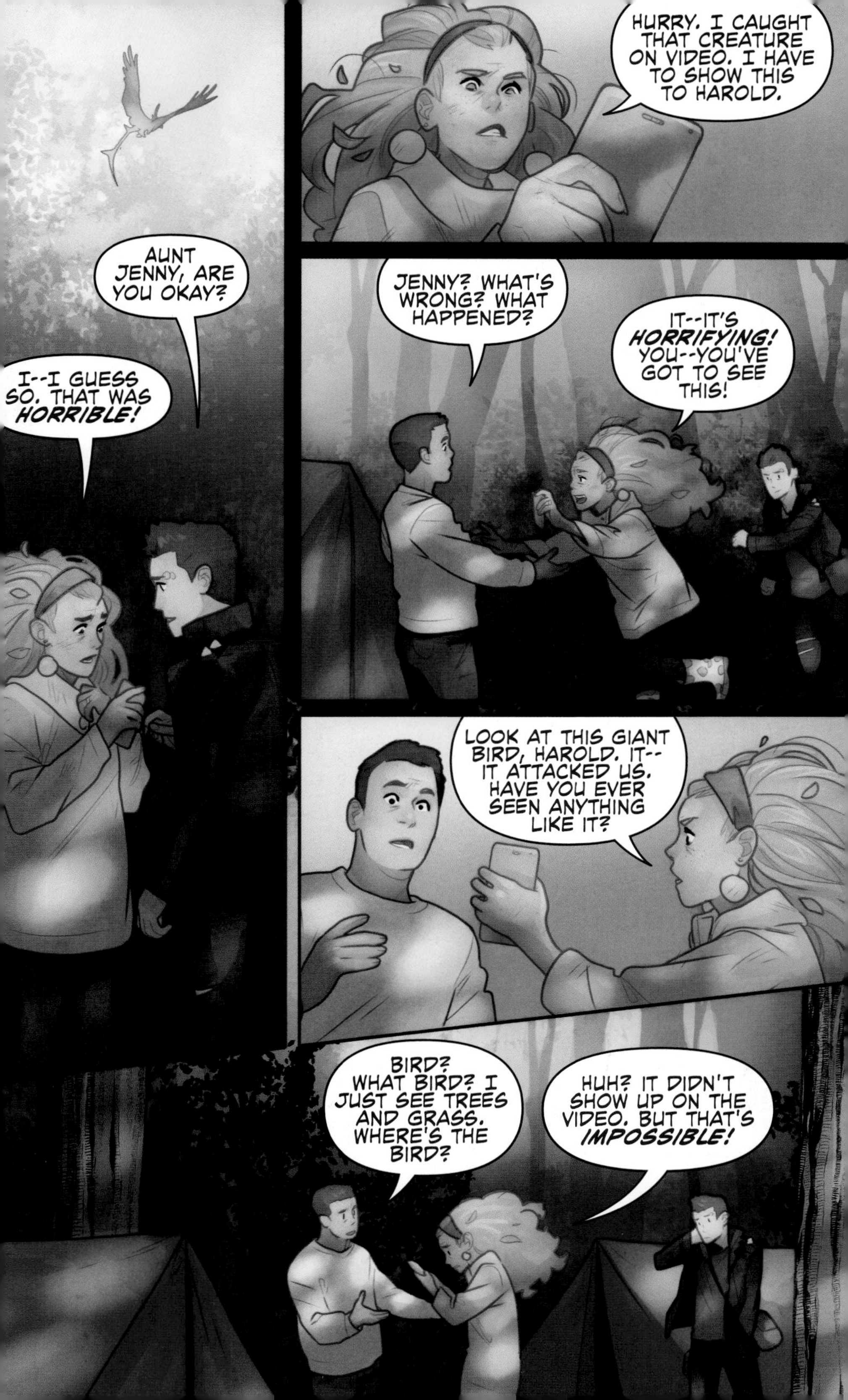
AUNT JENNY, ARE YOU OKAY?
I--I GUESS SO. THAT WAS *HORRIBLE!*
HURRY. I CAUGHT THAT CREATURE ON VIDEO. I HAVE TO SHOW THIS TO HAROLD.
JENNY? WHAT'S WRONG? WHAT HAPPENED?
IT--IT'S *HORRIFYING!* YOU--YOU'VE GOT TO SEE THIS!
LOOK AT THIS GIANT BIRD, HAROLD. IT--IT ATTACKED US. HAVE YOU EVER SEEN ANYTHING LIKE IT?
BIRD? WHAT BIRD? I JUST SEE TREES AND GRASS. WHERE'S THE BIRD?
HUH? IT DIDN'T SHOW UP ON THE VIDEO. BUT THAT'S *IMPOSSIBLE!*

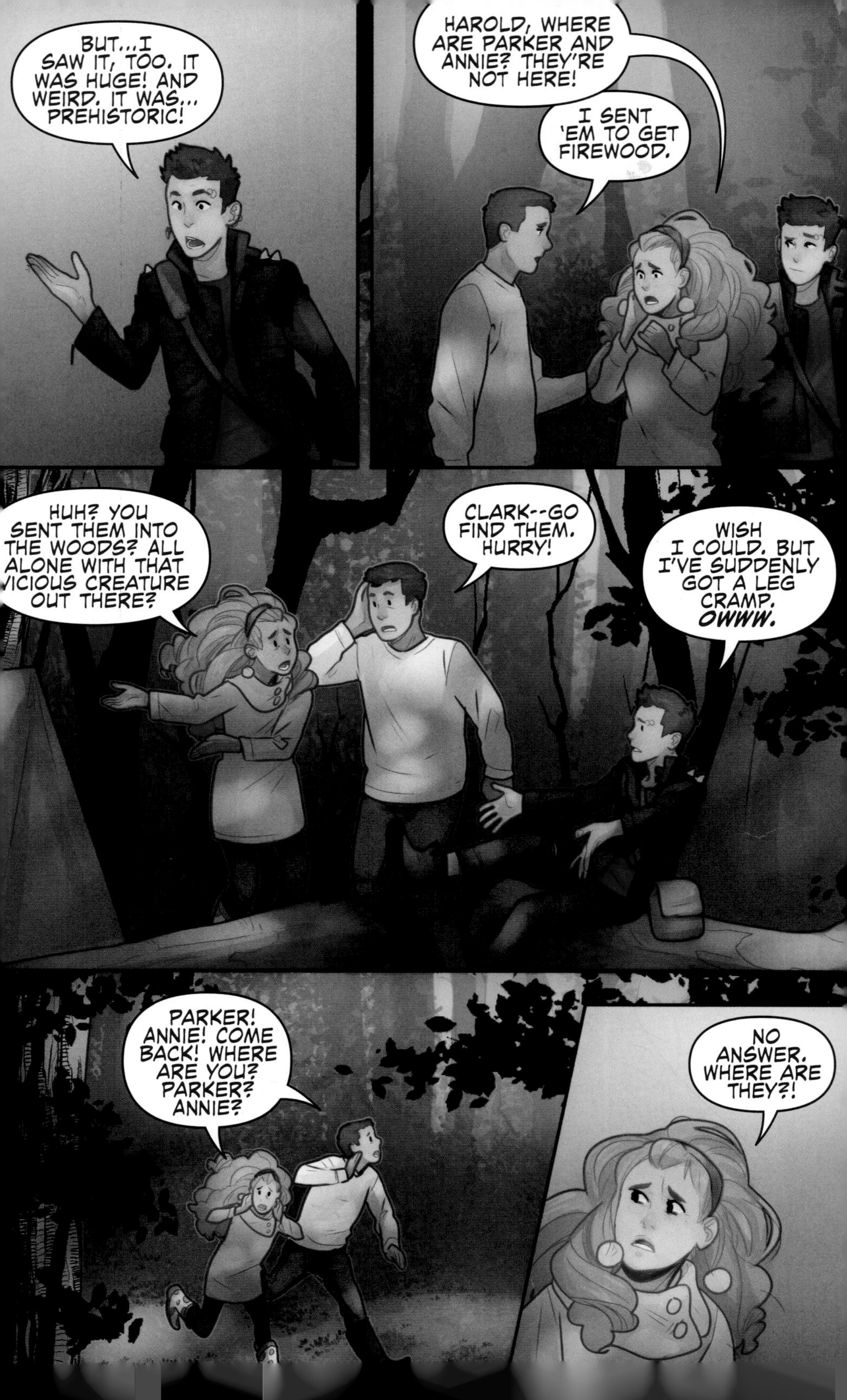
BUT...I SAW IT, TOO. IT WAS HUGE! AND WEIRD. IT WAS... PREHISTORIC!
HAROLD, WHERE ARE PARKER AND ANNIE? THEY'RE NOT HERE!
I SENT 'EM TO GET FIREWOOD.
HUH? YOU SENT THEM INTO THE WOODS? ALL ALONE WITH THAT VICIOUS CREATURE OUT THERE?
CLARK--GO FIND THEM. HURRY!
WISH I COULD. BUT I'VE SUDDENLY GOT A LEG CRAMP. OWWW.
PARKER! ANNIE! COME BACK! WHERE ARE YOU? PARKER? ANNIE?
NO ANSWER. WHERE ARE THEY?!

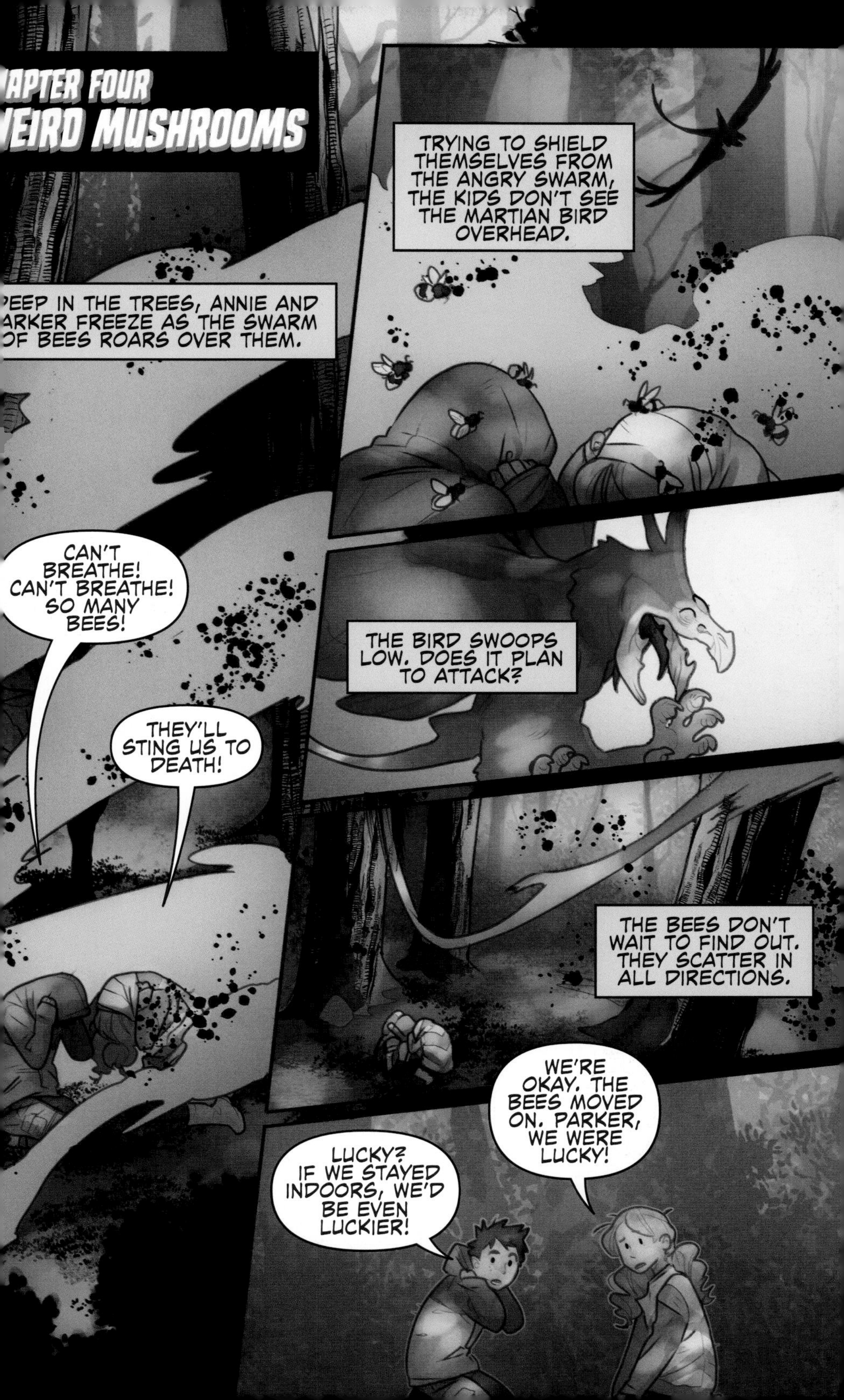
APTER FOUR
EIRD MUSHROOMS
EEP IN THE TREES, ANNIE AND ARKER FREEZE AS THE SWARM OF BEES ROARS OVER THEM.
TRYING TO SHIELD THEMSELVES FROM THE ANGRY SWARM, THE KIDS DON'T SEE THE MARTIAN BIRD OVERHEAD.
CAN'T BREATHE! CAN'T BREATHE! SO MANY BEES!
THEY'LL STING US TO DEATH!
THE BIRD SWOOPS LOW. DOES IT PLAN TO ATTACK?
THE BEES DON'T WAIT TO FIND OUT. THEY SCATTER IN ALL DIRECTIONS.
WE'RE OKAY. THE BEES MOVED ON. PARKER, WE WERE LUCKY!
LUCKY? IF WE STAYED INDOORS, WE'D BE EVEN LUCKIER!

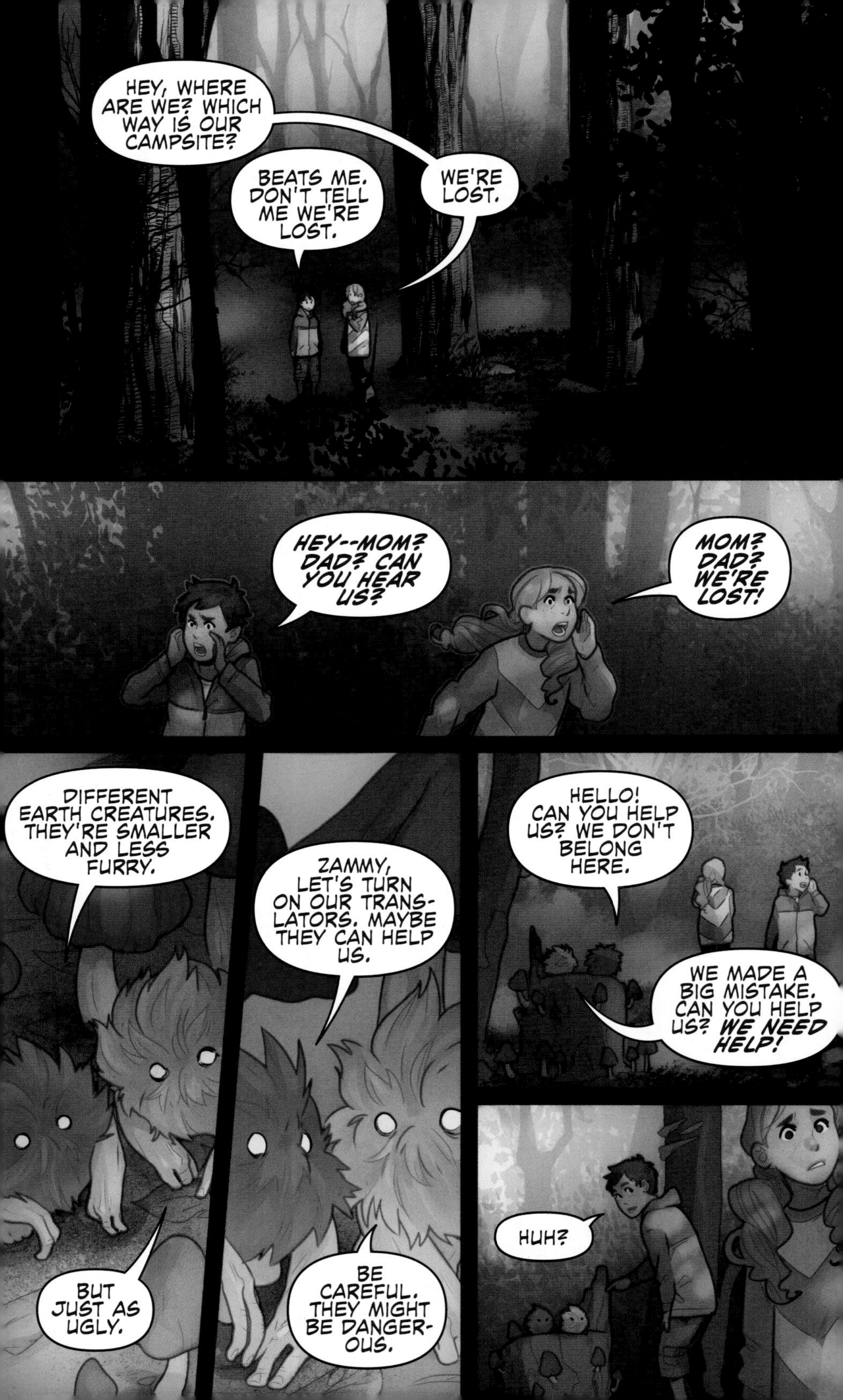
HEY, WHERE ARE WE? WHICH WAY IS OUR CAMPSITE?
BEATS ME. DON'T TELL ME WE'RE LOST.
WE'RE LOST.
HEY--MOM? DAD? CAN YOU HEAR US?
MOM? DAD? WE'RE LOST!
DIFFERENT EARTH CREATURES. THEY'RE SMALLER AND LESS FURRY.
BUT JUST AS UGLY.
ZAMMY, LET'S TURN ON OUR TRANS-LATORS. MAYBE THEY CAN HELP US.
BE CAREFUL. THEY MIGHT BE DANGER-OUS.
HELLO! CAN YOU HELP US? WE DON'T BELONG HERE.
WE MADE A BIG MISTAKE. CAN YOU HELP US? *WE NEED HELP!*
HUH?

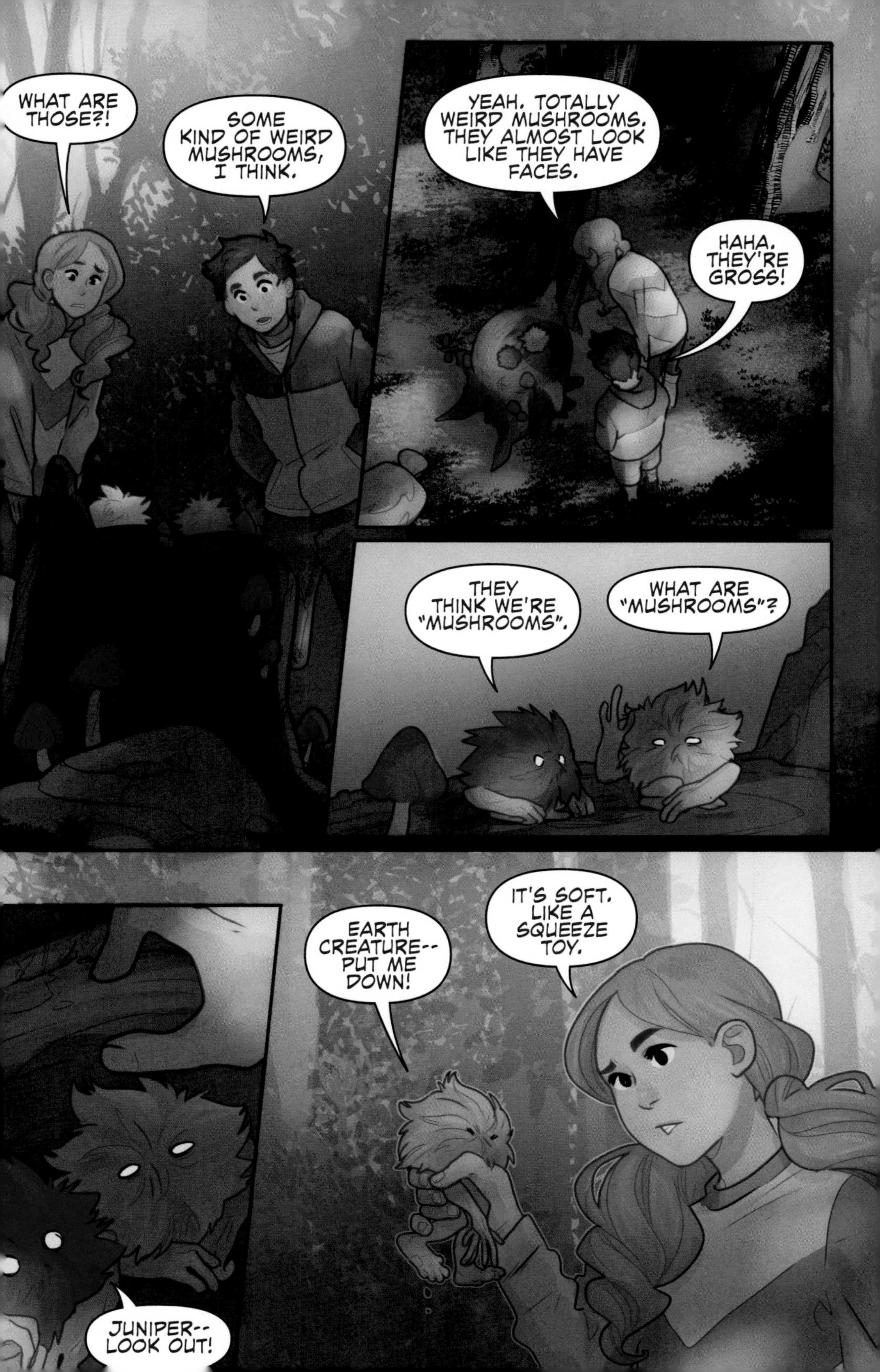
WHAT ARE THOSE?!
SOME KIND OF WEIRD MUSHROOMS, I THINK.
YEAH. TOTALLY WEIRD MUSHROOMS. THEY ALMOST LOOK LIKE THEY HAVE FACES.
HAHA. THEY'RE GROSS!
THEY THINK WE'RE "MUSHROOMS".
WHAT ARE "MUSHROOMS"?
IT'S SOFT. LIKE A SQUEEZE TOY.
EARTH CREATURE-- PUT ME DOWN!
JUNIPER-- LOOK OUT!

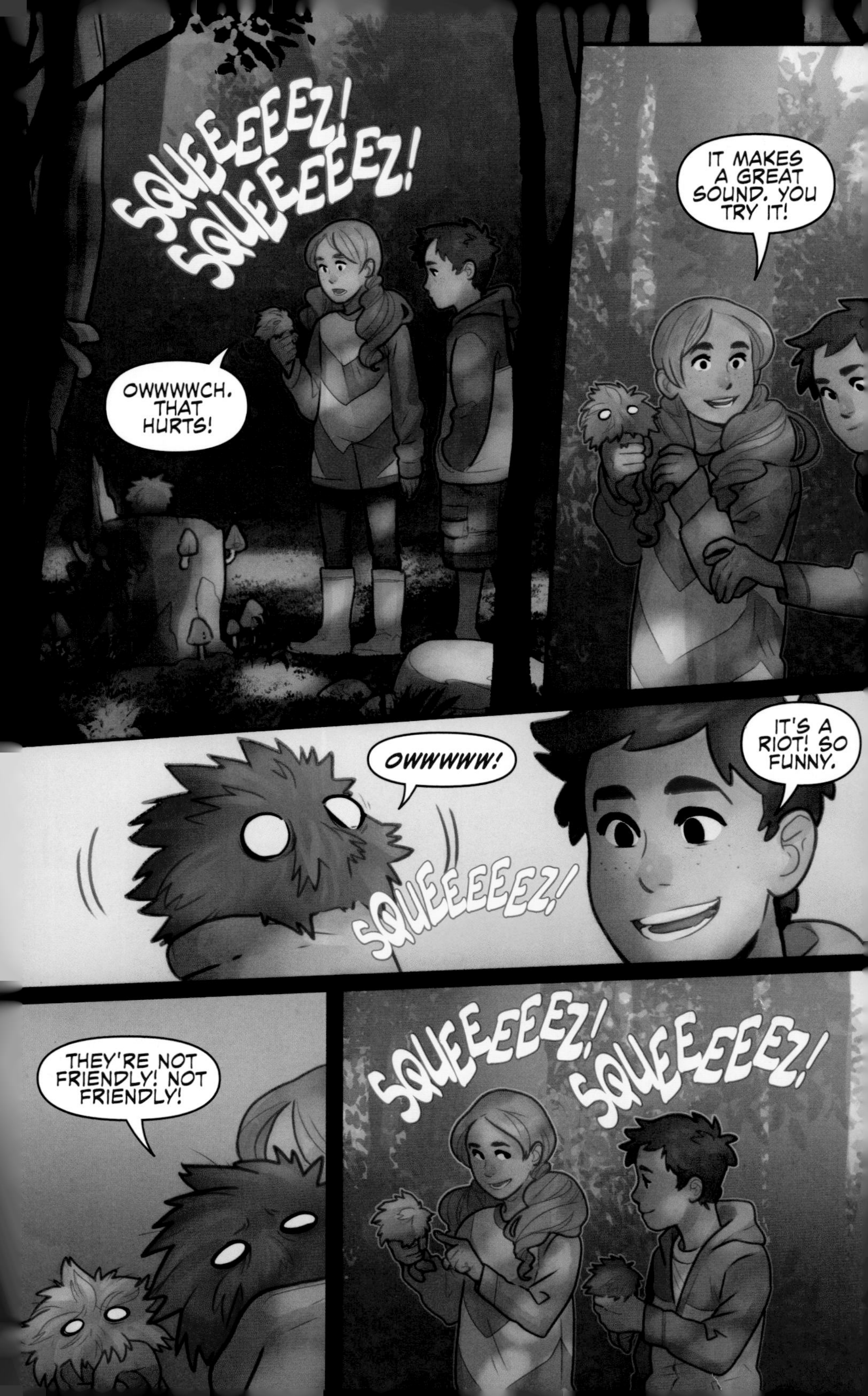
SQUEEEEEZ! SQUEEEEEZ!
OWWWWCH. THAT HURTS!
IT MAKES A GREAT SOUND. YOU TRY IT!
OWWWWW!
SQUEEEEEZ!
IT'S A RIOT! SO FUNNY.
THEY'RE NOT FRIENDLY! NOT FRIENDLY!
SQUEEEEEZ! SQUEEEEEZ!

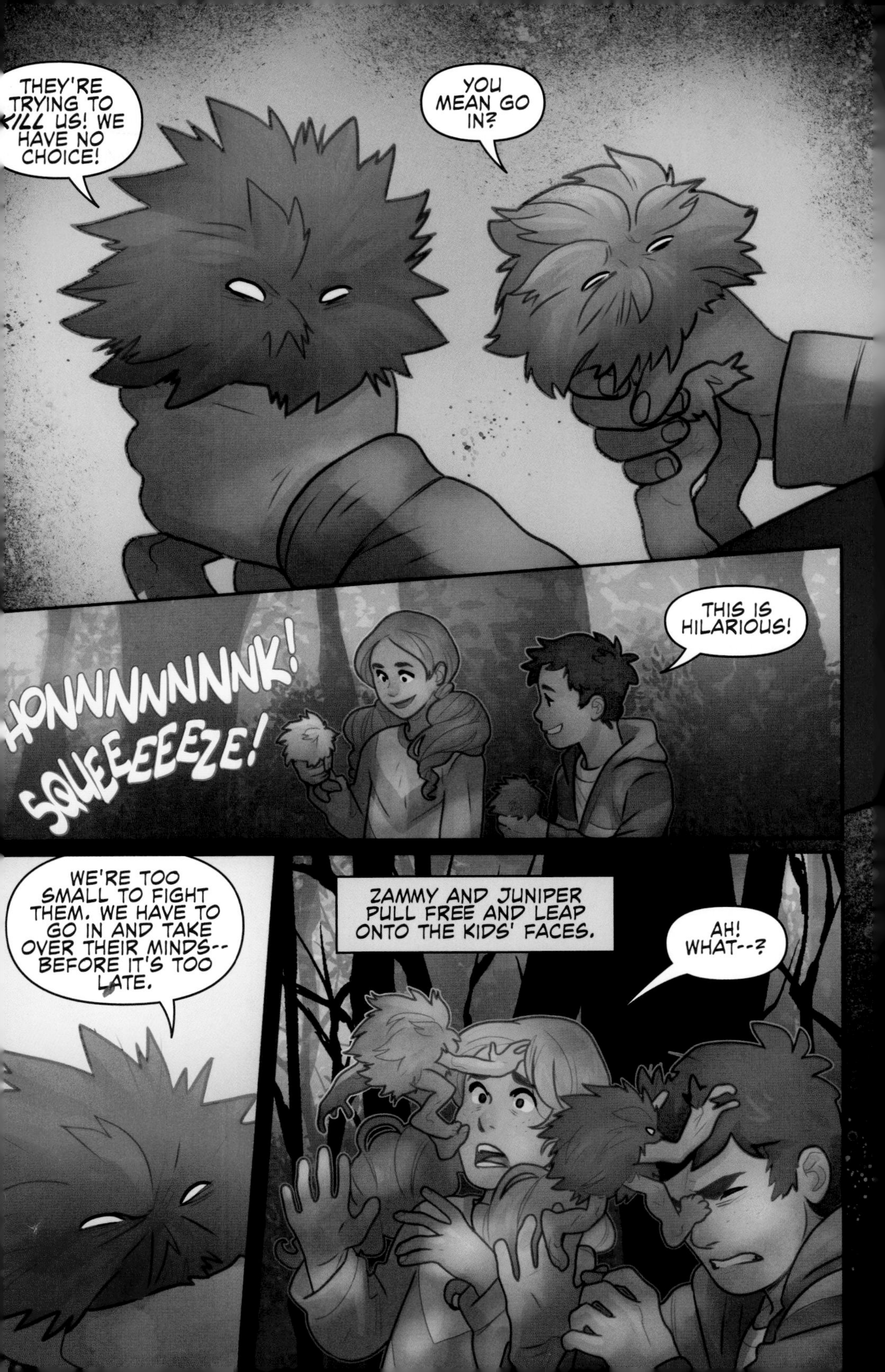
THEY'RE TRYING TO KILL US! WE HAVE NO CHOICE!
YOU MEAN GO IN?
THIS IS HILARIOUS!
HONNNNNNNK!
SQUEEEEEEZE!
WE'RE TOO SMALL TO FIGHT THEM. WE HAVE TO GO IN AND TAKE OVER THEIR MINDS--BEFORE IT'S TOO LATE.
ZAMMY AND JUNIPER PULL FREE AND LEAP ONTO THE KIDS' FACES.
AH! WHAT--?

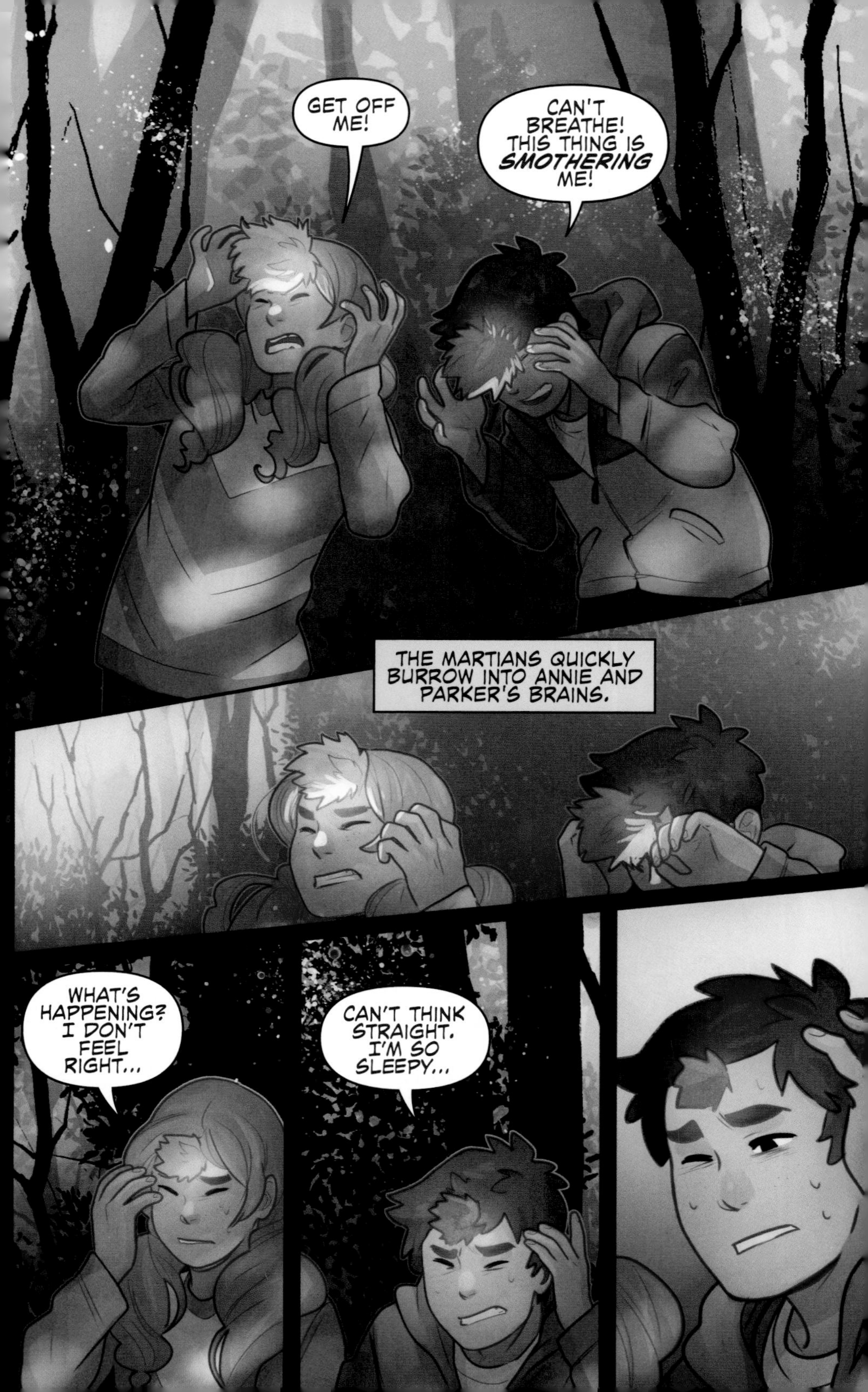
GET OFF ME!
CAN'T BREATHE! THIS THING IS SMOTHERING ME!
THE MARTIANS QUICKLY BURROW INTO ANNIE AND PARKER'S BRAINS.
WHAT'S HAPPENING? I DON'T FEEL RIGHT...
CAN'T THINK STRAIGHT. I'M SO SLEEPY...

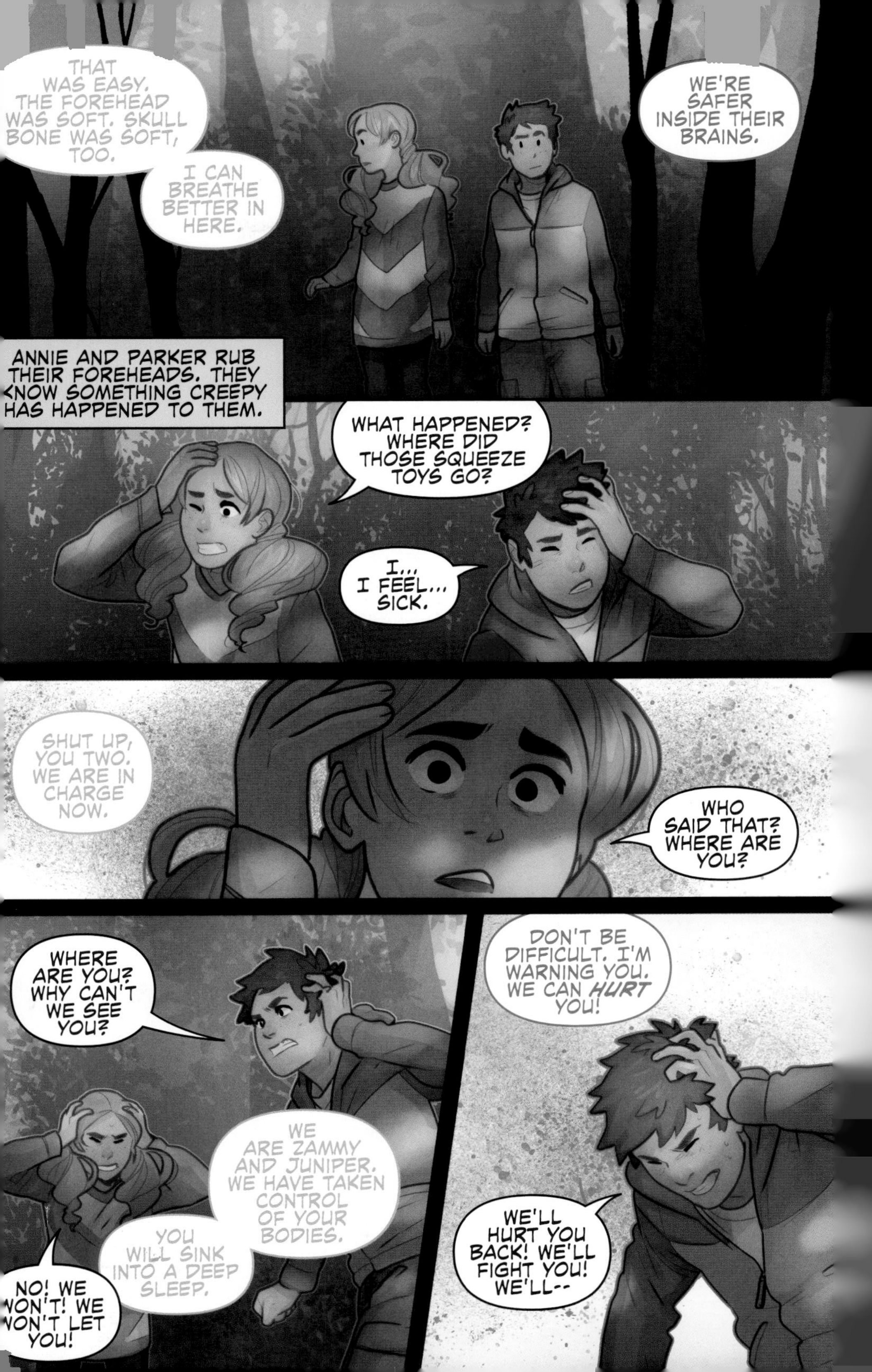
THAT WAS EASY. THE FOREHEAD WAS SOFT. SKULL BONE WAS SOFT, TOO.
I CAN BREATHE BETTER IN HERE.
WE'RE SAFER INSIDE THEIR BRAINS.
ANNIE AND PARKER RUB THEIR FOREHEADS. THEY KNOW SOMETHING CREEPY HAS HAPPENED TO THEM.
WHAT HAPPENED? WHERE DID THOSE SQUEEZE TOYS GO?
I... I FEEL... SICK.
SHUT UP, YOU TWO. WE ARE IN CHARGE NOW.
WHO SAID THAT? WHERE ARE YOU?
WHERE ARE YOU? WHY CAN'T WE SEE YOU?
WE ARE ZAMMY AND JUNIPER. WE HAVE TAKEN CONTROL OF YOUR BODIES.
YOU WILL SINK INTO A DEEP SLEEP.
NO! WE WON'T! WE WON'T LET YOU!
DON'T BE DIFFICULT. I'M WARNING YOU. WE CAN *HURT* YOU!
WE'LL HURT YOU BACK! WE'LL FIGHT YOU! WE'LL--

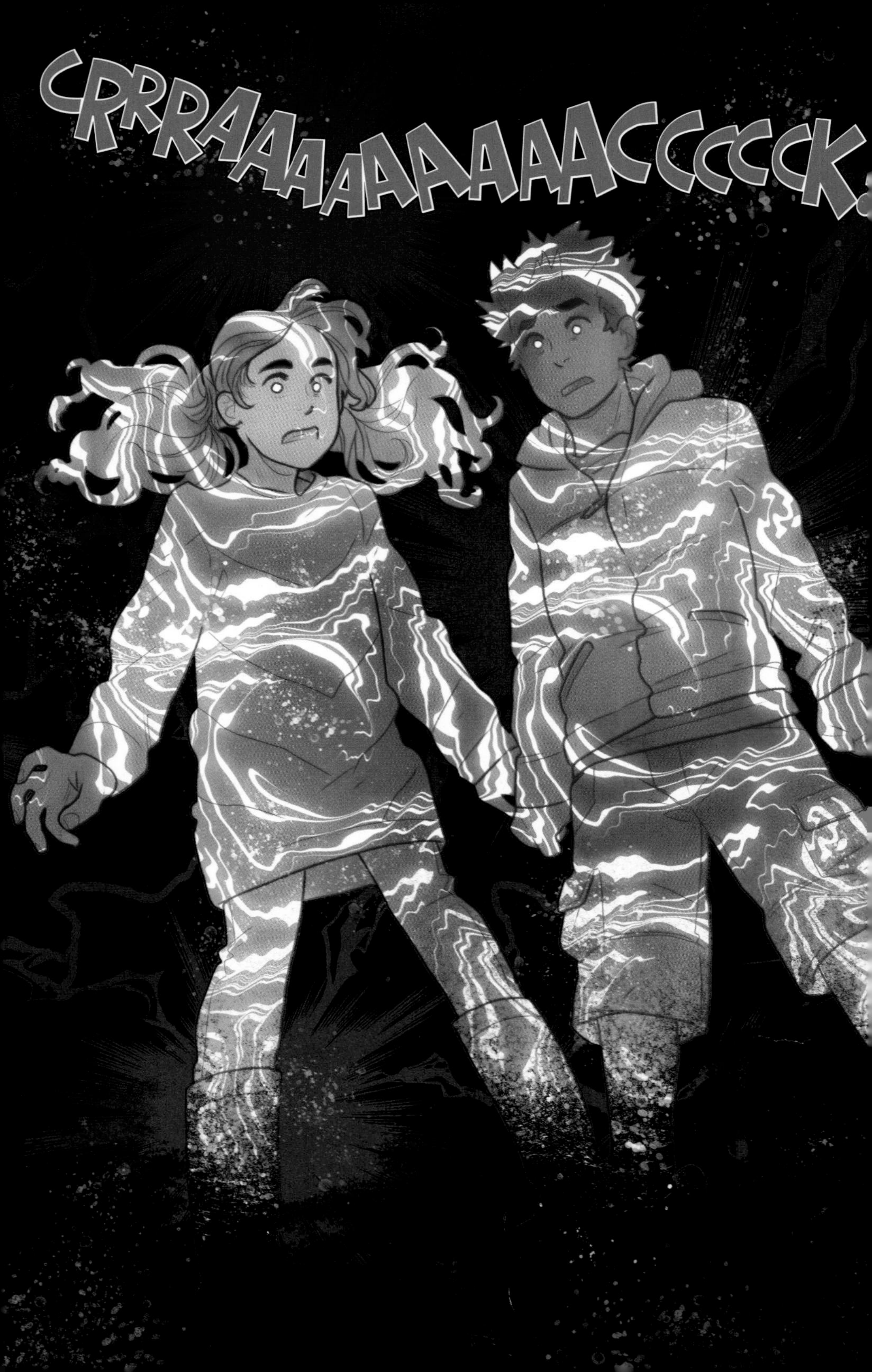
CRRRAAAAAAAAACCCCCK!

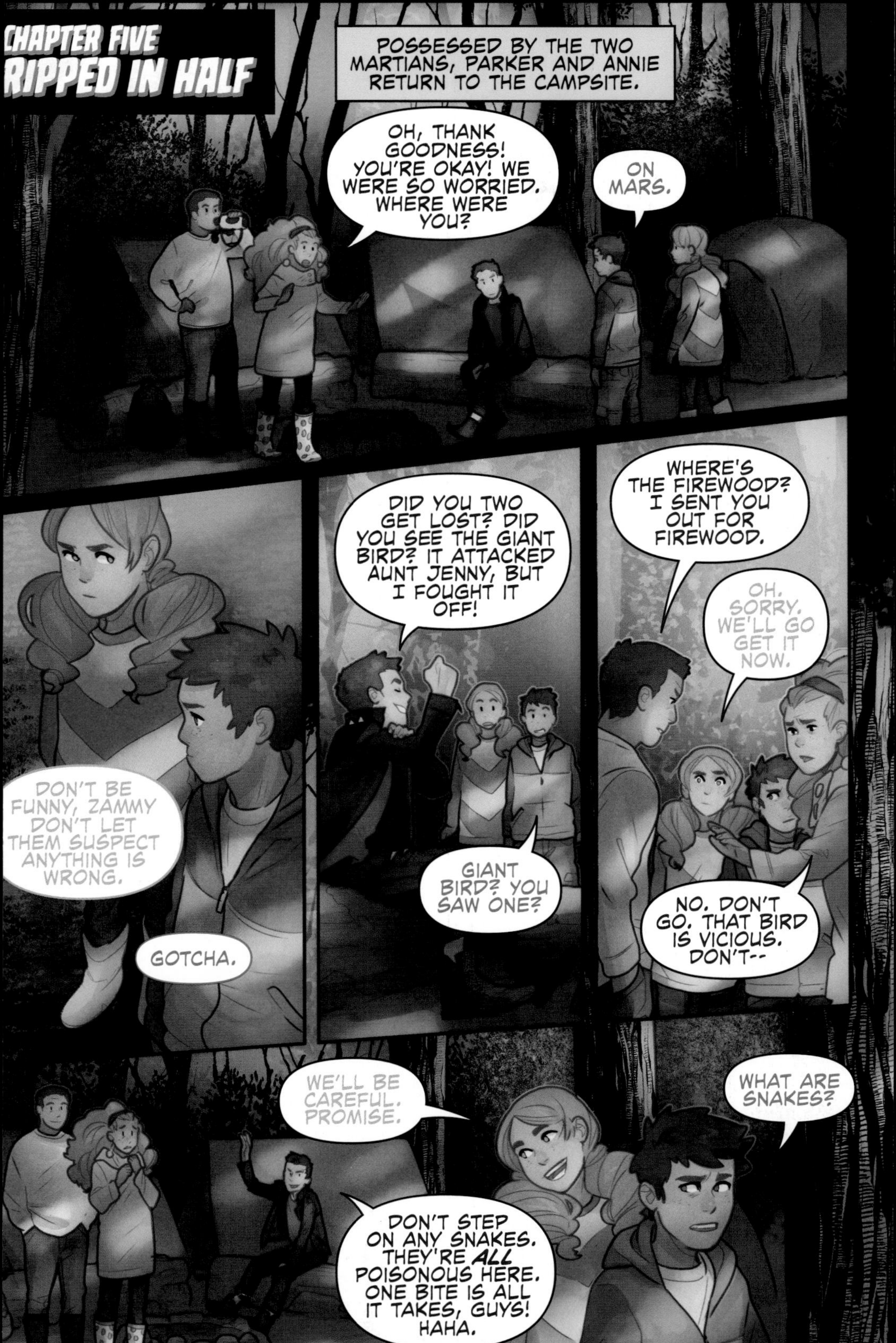

CHAPTER FIVE
RIPPED IN HALF
POSSESSED BY THE TWO MARTIANS, PARKER AND ANNIE RETURN TO THE CAMPSITE.
OH, THANK GOODNESS! YOU'RE OKAY! WE WERE SO WORRIED. WHERE WERE YOU?
ON MARS.
DON'T BE FUNNY, ZAMMY DON'T LET THEM SUSPECT ANYTHING IS WRONG.
GOTCHA.
DID YOU TWO GET LOST? DID YOU SEE THE GIANT BIRD? IT ATTACKED AUNT JENNY, BUT I FOUGHT IT OFF!
GIANT BIRD? YOU SAW ONE?
WHERE'S THE FIREWOOD? I SENT YOU OUT FOR FIREWOOD.
OH. SORRY. WE'LL GO GET IT NOW.
NO. DON'T GO. THAT BIRD IS VICIOUS. DON'T--
WE'LL BE CAREFUL. PROMISE.
DON'T STEP ON ANY SNAKES. THEY'RE ALL POISONOUS HERE. ONE BITE IS ALL IT TAKES, GUYS! HAHA.
WHAT ARE SNAKES?

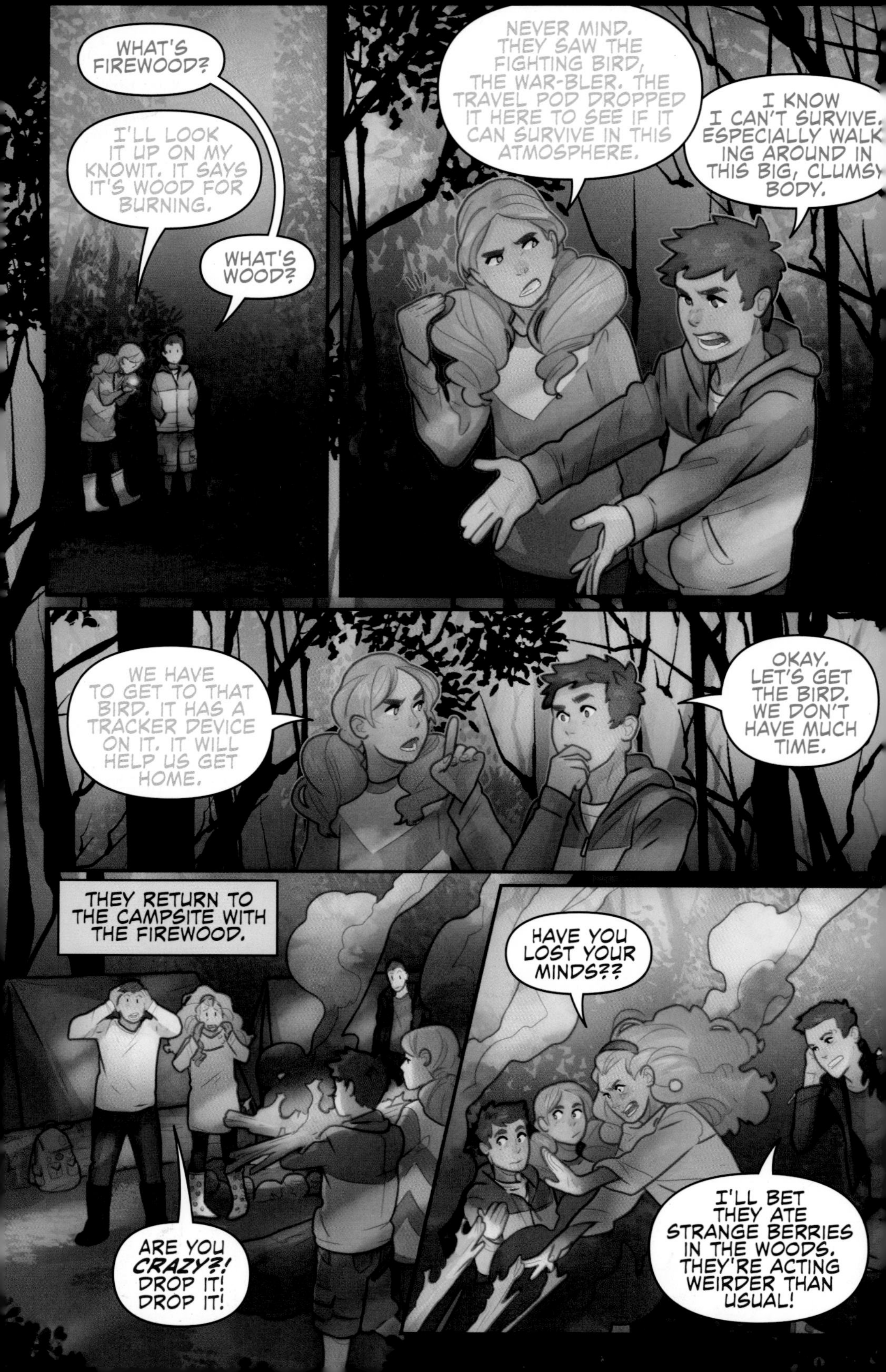
WHAT'S FIREWOOD?
I'LL LOOK IT UP ON MY KNOWIT. IT SAYS IT'S WOOD FOR BURNING.
WHAT'S WOOD?
NEVER MIND. THEY SAW THE FIGHTING BIRD, THE WAR-BLER. THE TRAVEL POD DROPPED IT HERE TO SEE IF IT CAN SURVIVE IN THIS ATMOSPHERE.
I KNOW I CAN'T SURVIVE. ESPECIALLY WALKING AROUND IN THIS BIG, CLUMSY BODY.
WE HAVE TO GET TO THAT BIRD. IT HAS A TRACKER DEVICE ON IT. IT WILL HELP US GET HOME.
OKAY. LET'S GET THE BIRD. WE DON'T HAVE MUCH TIME.
THEY RETURN TO THE CAMPSITE WITH THE FIREWOOD.
ARE YOU *CRAZY?!* DROP IT! DROP IT!
HAVE YOU LOST YOUR MINDS??
I'LL BET THEY ATE STRANGE BERRIES IN THE WOODS. THEY'RE ACTING WEIRDER THAN USUAL!

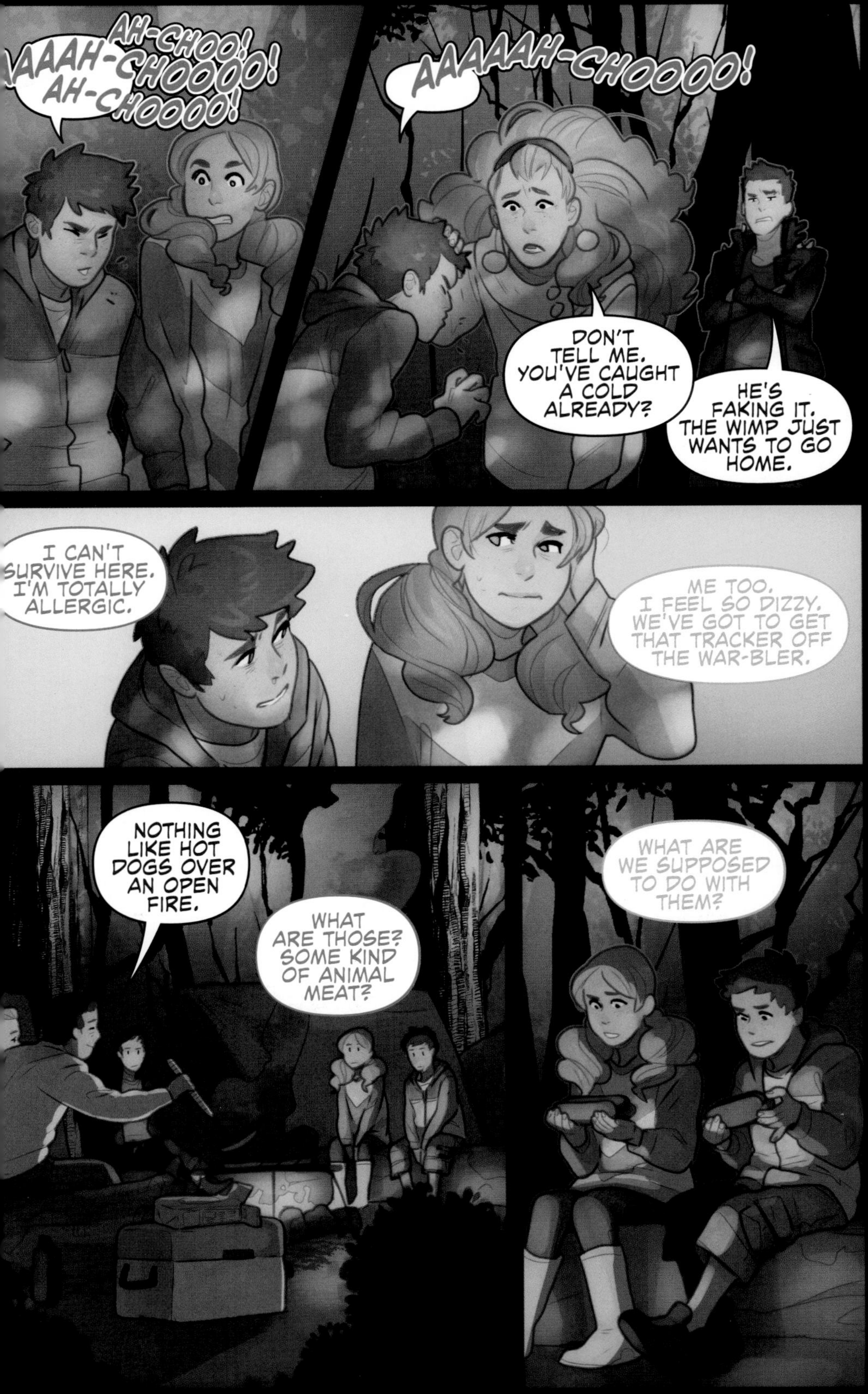
AH-CHOO! AAAAH-CHOOOO! AH-CHOOOO!
AAAAAH-CHOOOOO!
DON'T TELL ME. YOU'VE CAUGHT A COLD ALREADY?
HE'S FAKING IT. THE WIMP JUST WANTS TO GO HOME.
I CAN'T SURVIVE HERE. I'M TOTALLY ALLERGIC.
ME TOO. I FEEL SO DIZZY. WE'VE GOT TO GET THAT TRACKER OFF THE WAR-BLER.
NOTHING LIKE HOT DOGS OVER AN OPEN FIRE.
WHAT ARE THOSE? SOME KIND OF ANIMAL MEAT?
WHAT ARE WE SUPPOSED TO DO WITH THEM?

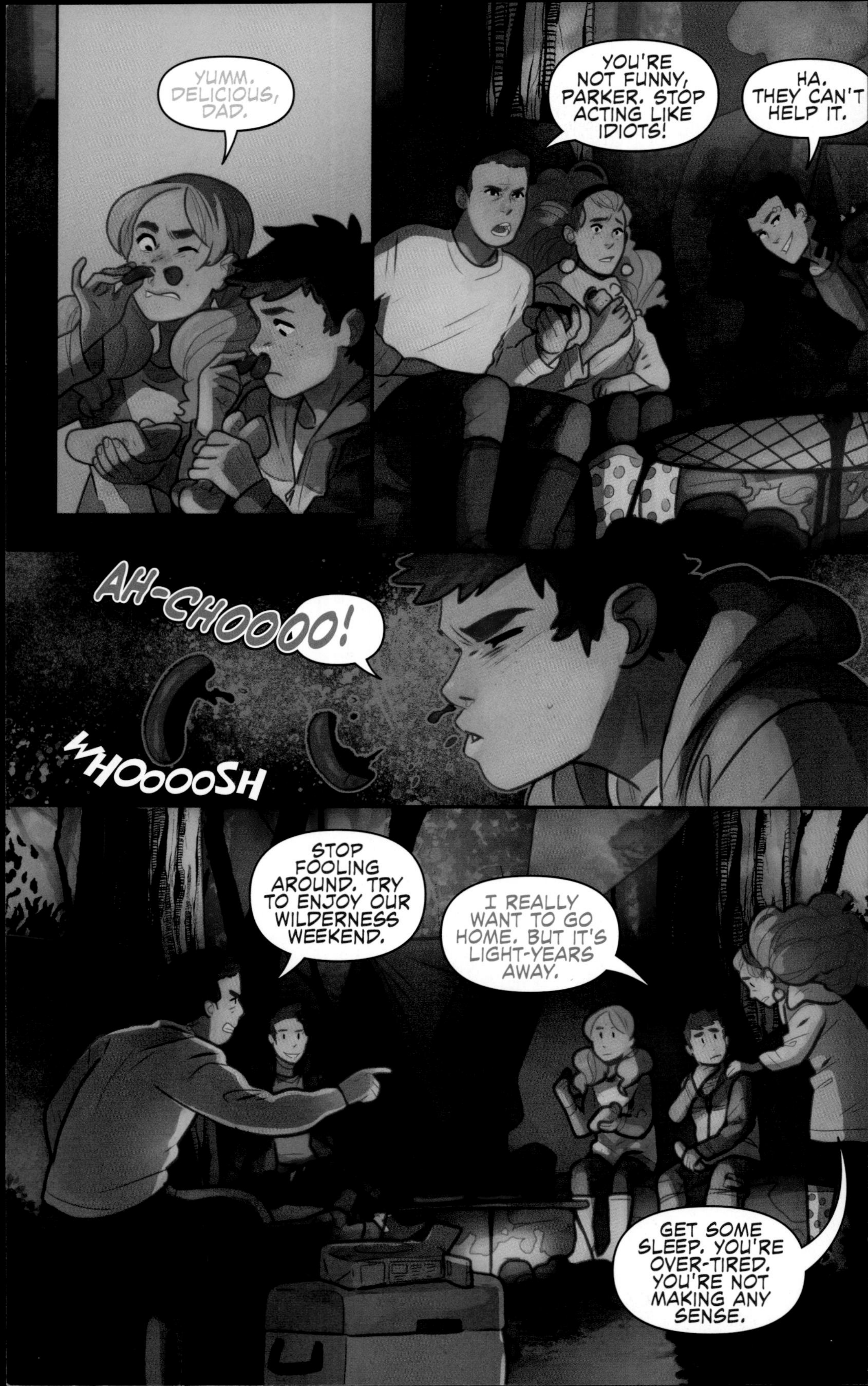
YUMM. DELICIOUS, DAD.
YOU'RE NOT FUNNY, PARKER. STOP ACTING LIKE IDIOTS!
HA. THEY CAN'T HELP IT.
AH-CHOOOOO!
WHOOOOSH
STOP FOOLING AROUND. TRY TO ENJOY OUR WILDERNESS WEEKEND.
I REALLY WANT TO GO HOME. BUT IT'S LIGHT-YEARS AWAY.
GET SOME SLEEP. YOU'RE OVER-TIRED. YOU'RE NOT MAKING ANY SENSE.

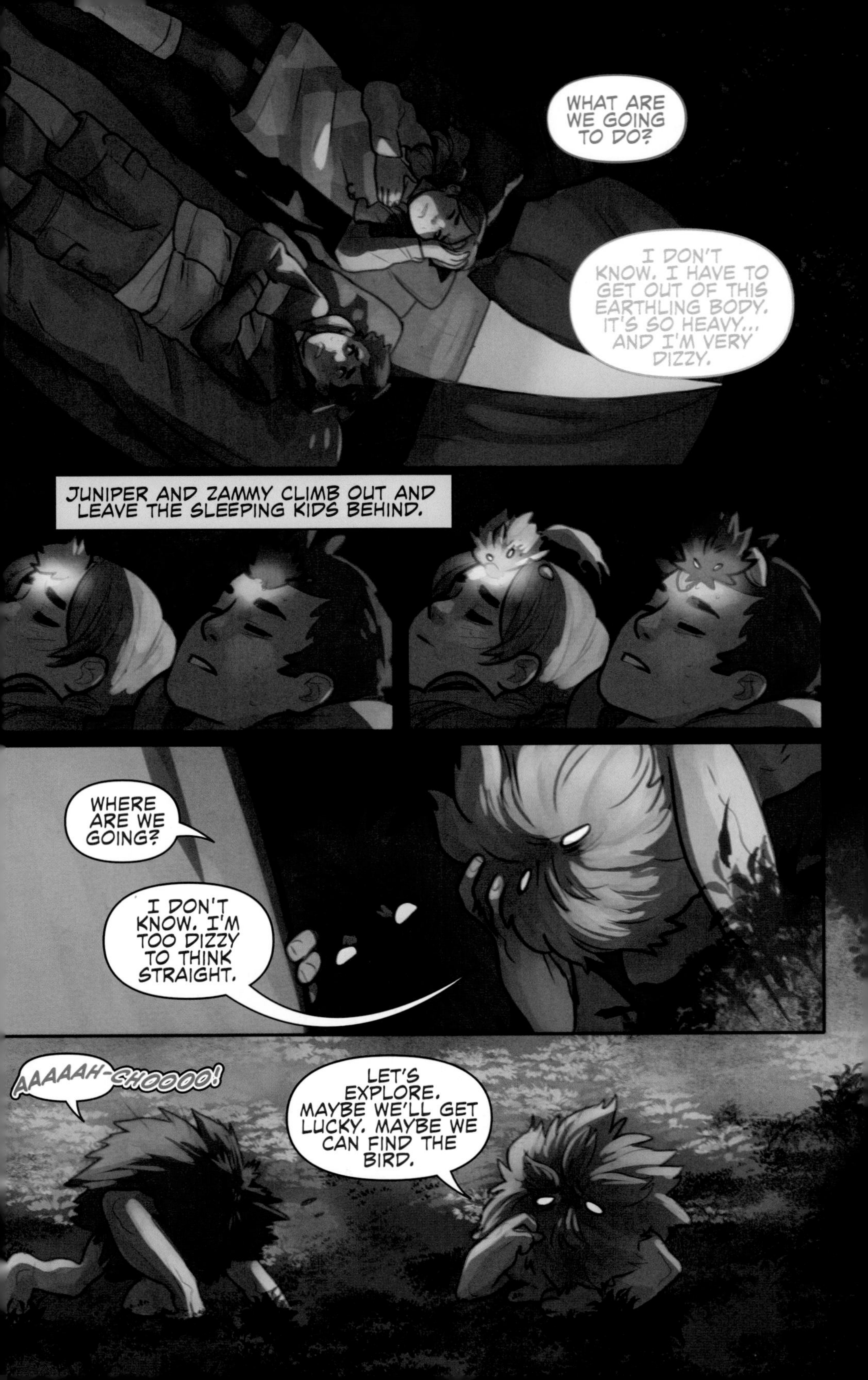
WHAT ARE WE GOING TO DO?
I DON'T KNOW. I HAVE TO GET OUT OF THIS EARTHLING BODY. IT'S SO HEAVY... AND I'M VERY DIZZY.
JUNIPER AND ZAMMY CLIMB OUT AND LEAVE THE SLEEPING KIDS BEHIND.
WHERE ARE WE GOING?
I DON'T KNOW. I'M TOO DIZZY TO THINK STRAIGHT.
AAAAAH-CHOOOOO!
LET'S EXPLORE. MAYBE WE'LL GET LUCKY. MAYBE WE CAN FIND THE BIRD.

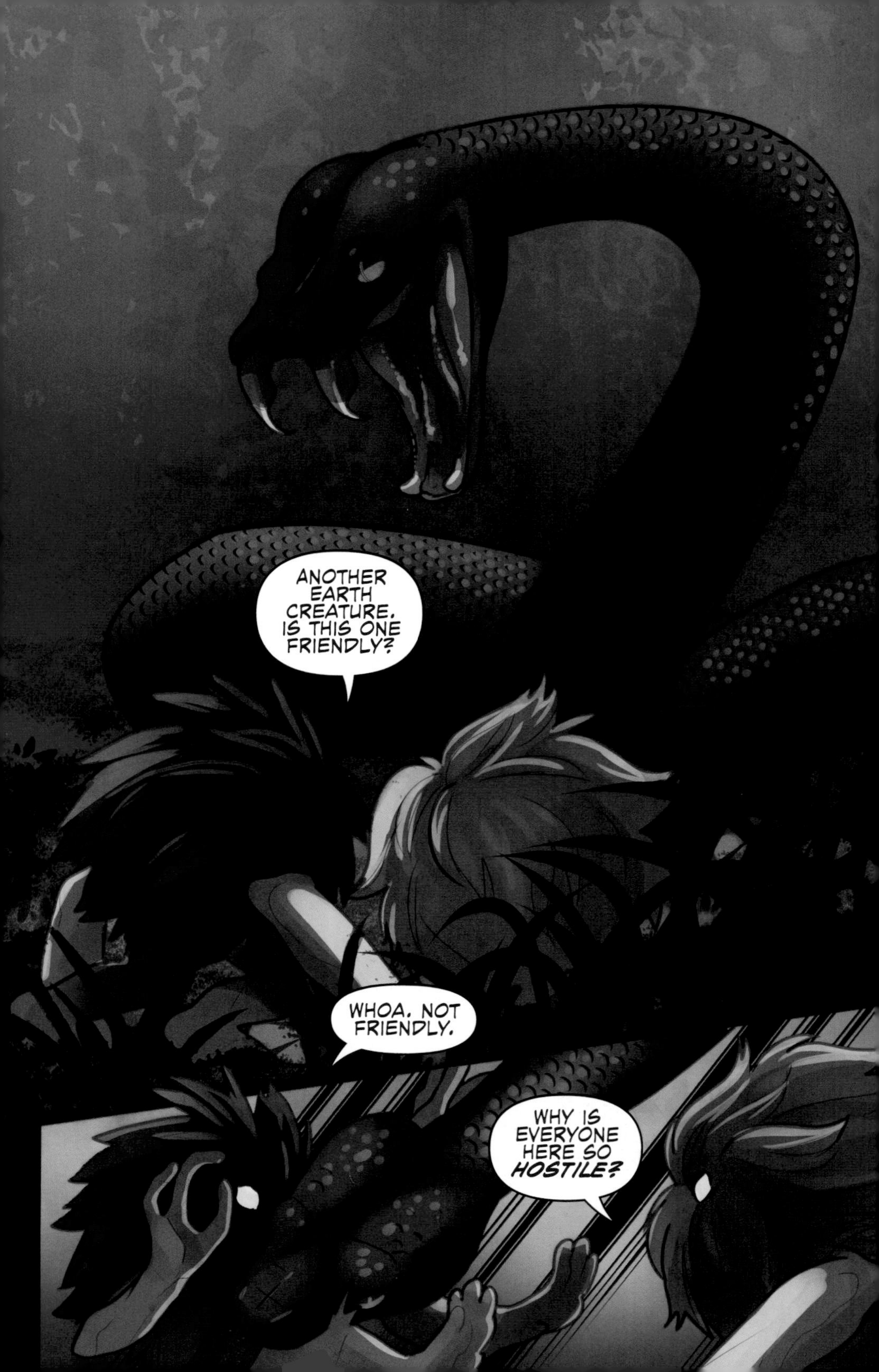
ANOTHER EARTH CREATURE. IS THIS ONE FRIENDLY?
WHOA. NOT FRIENDLY.
WHY IS EVERYONE HERE SO *HOSTILE?*

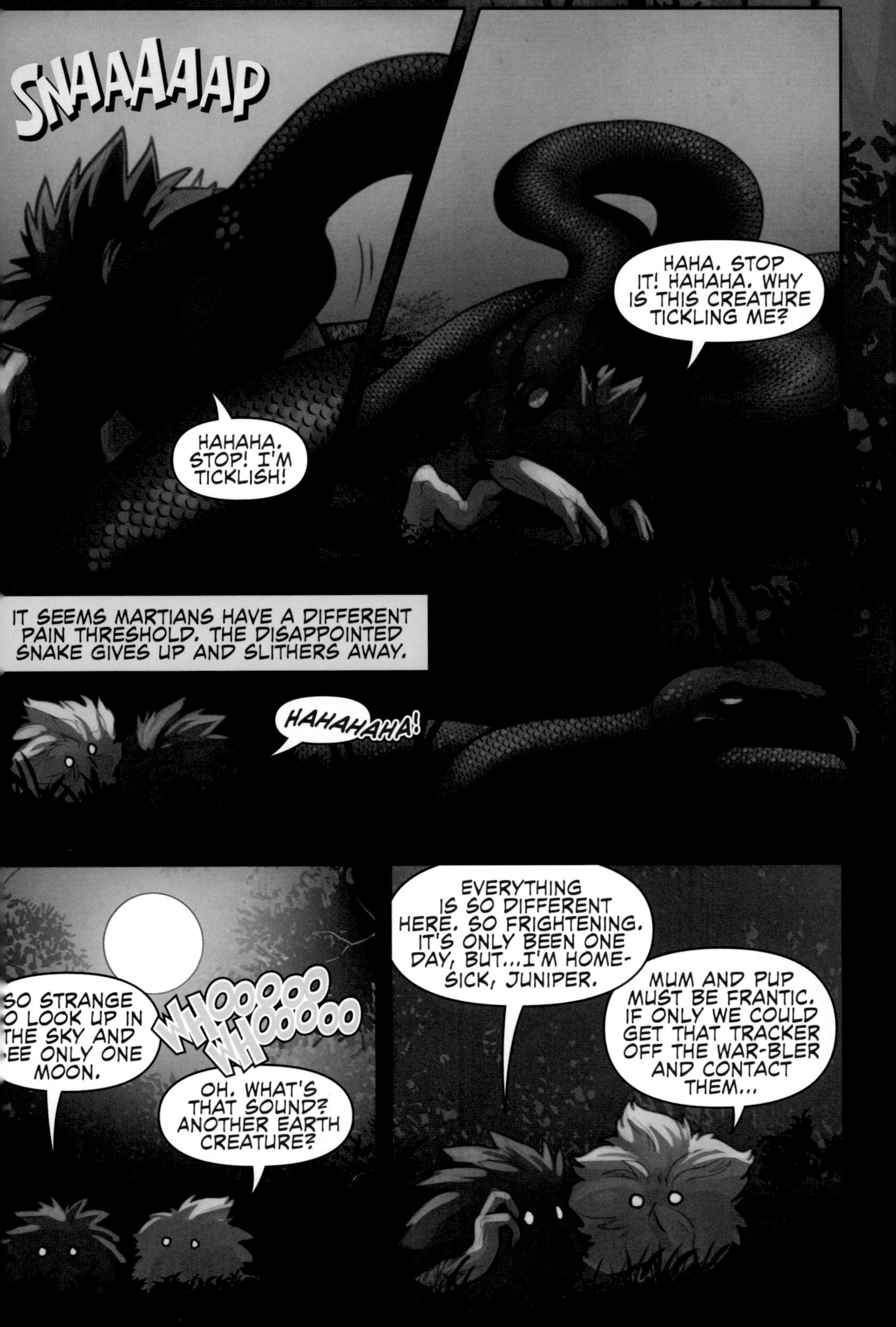
SNAAAAAP
HAHAHA. STOP! I'M TICKLISH!
HAHA. STOP IT! HAHAHA. WHY IS THIS CREATURE TICKLING ME?
IT SEEMS MARTIANS HAVE A DIFFERENT PAIN THRESHOLD. THE DISAPPOINTED SNAKE GIVES UP AND SLITHERS AWAY.
HAHAHAHA!
SO STRANGE O LOOK UP IN THE SKY AND EE ONLY ONE MOON.
WHOOOOO WHOOOOO
OH. WHAT'S THAT SOUND? ANOTHER EARTH CREATURE?
EVERYTHING IS SO DIFFERENT HERE. SO FRIGHTENING. IT'S ONLY BEEN ONE DAY, BUT...I'M HOME-SICK, JUNIPER.
MUM AND PUP MUST BE FRANTIC. IF ONLY WE COULD GET THAT TRACKER OFF THE WAR-BLER AND CONTACT THEM...

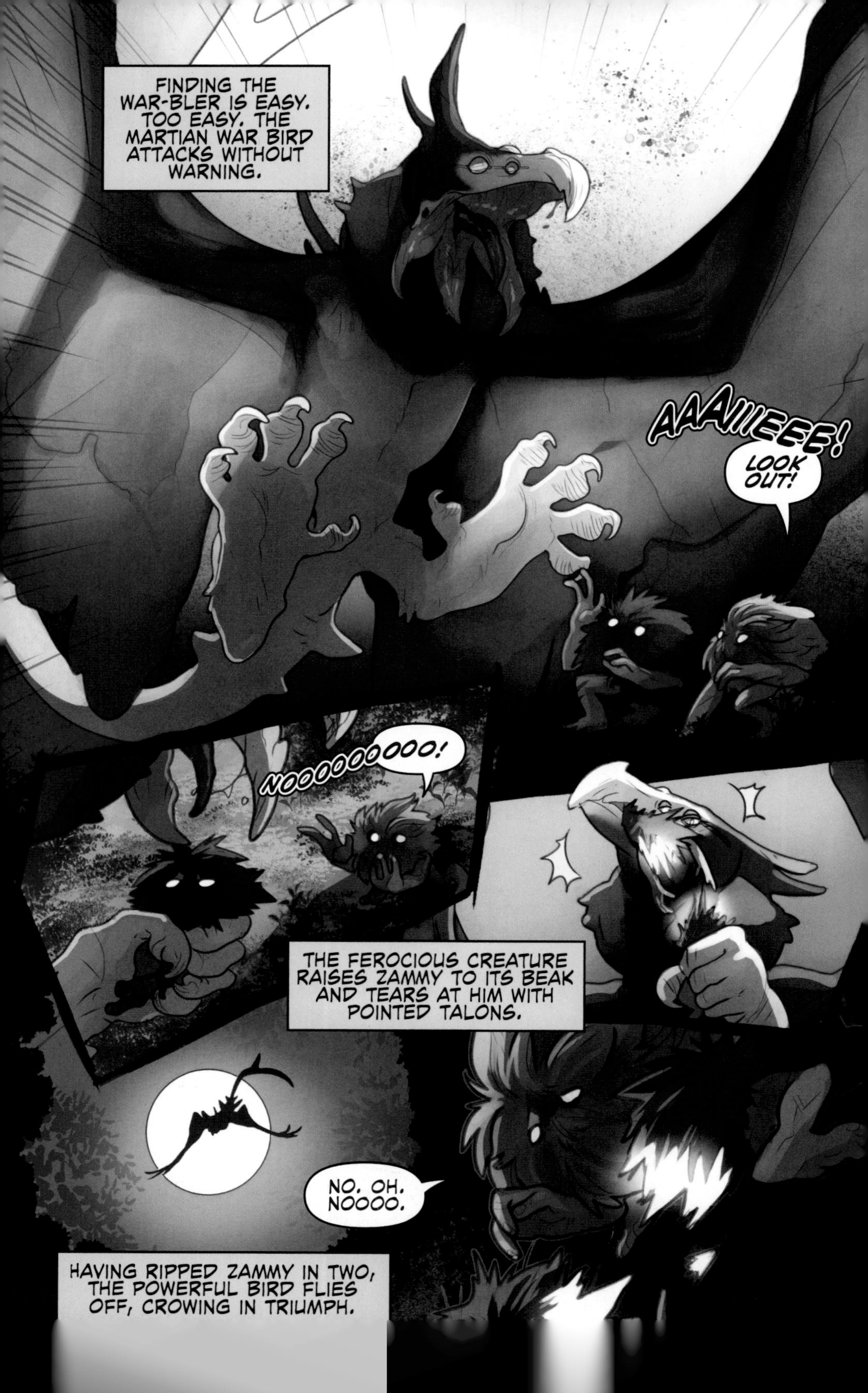
FINDING THE WAR-BLER IS EASY. TOO EASY. THE MARTIAN WAR BIRD ATTACKS WITHOUT WARNING.
AAAIIIEEEE!
LOOK OUT!
NOOOOOOOOOO!
THE FEROCIOUS CREATURE RAISES ZAMMY TO ITS BEAK AND TEARS AT HIM WITH POINTED TALONS.
NO. OH. NOOOO.
HAVING RIPPED ZAMMY IN TWO, THE POWERFUL BIRD FLIES OFF, CROWING IN TRIUMPH.

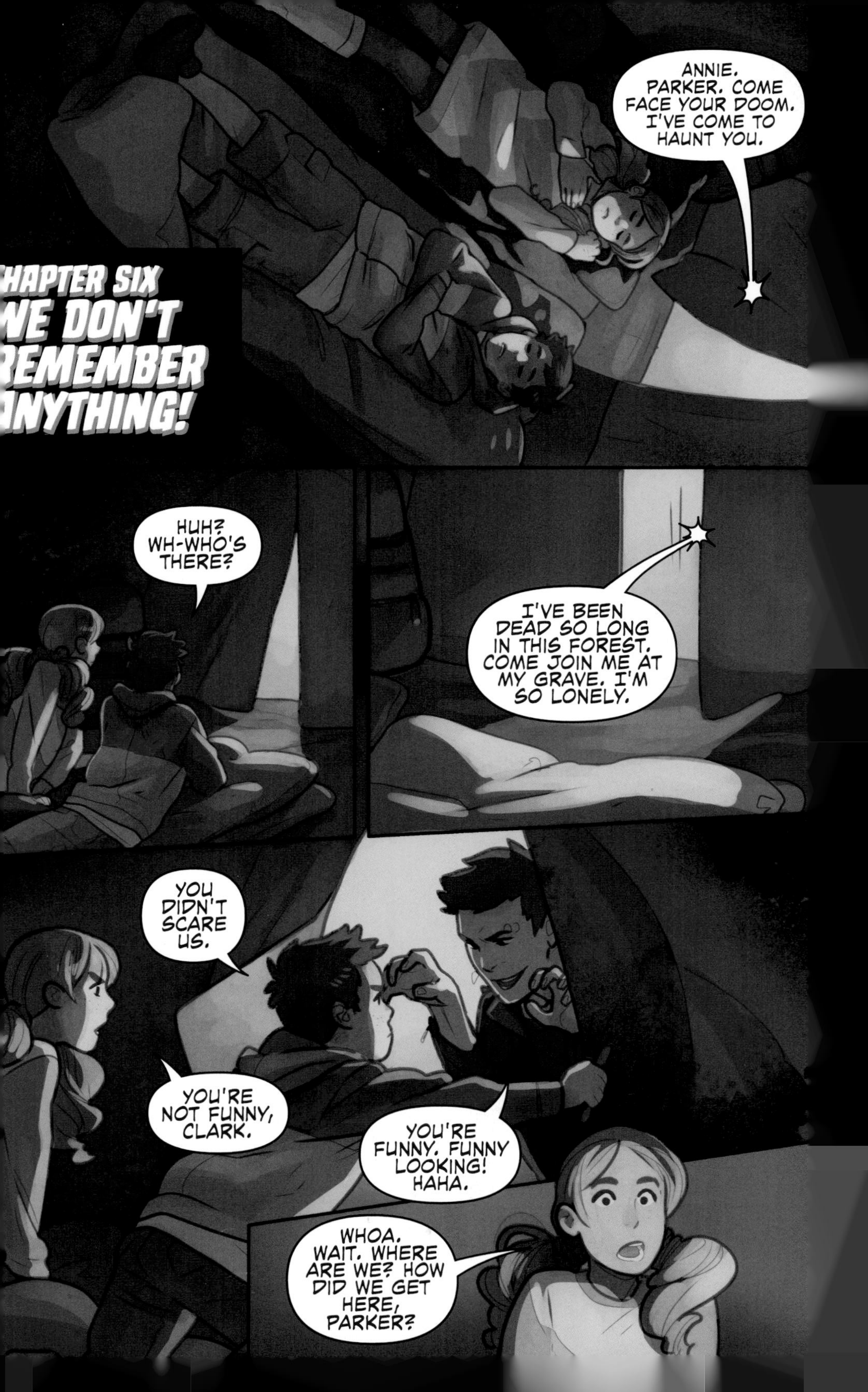
CHAPTER SIX
WE DON'T REMEMBER ANYTHING!
ANNIE. PARKER. COME FACE YOUR DOOM. I'VE COME TO HAUNT YOU.
HUH? WH-WHO'S THERE?
I'VE BEEN DEAD SO LONG IN THIS FOREST. COME JOIN ME AT MY GRAVE. I'M SO LONELY.
YOU DIDN'T SCARE US.
YOU'RE NOT FUNNY, CLARK.
YOU'RE FUNNY. FUNNY LOOKING! HAHA.
WHOA. WAIT. WHERE ARE WE? HOW DID WE GET HERE, PARKER?

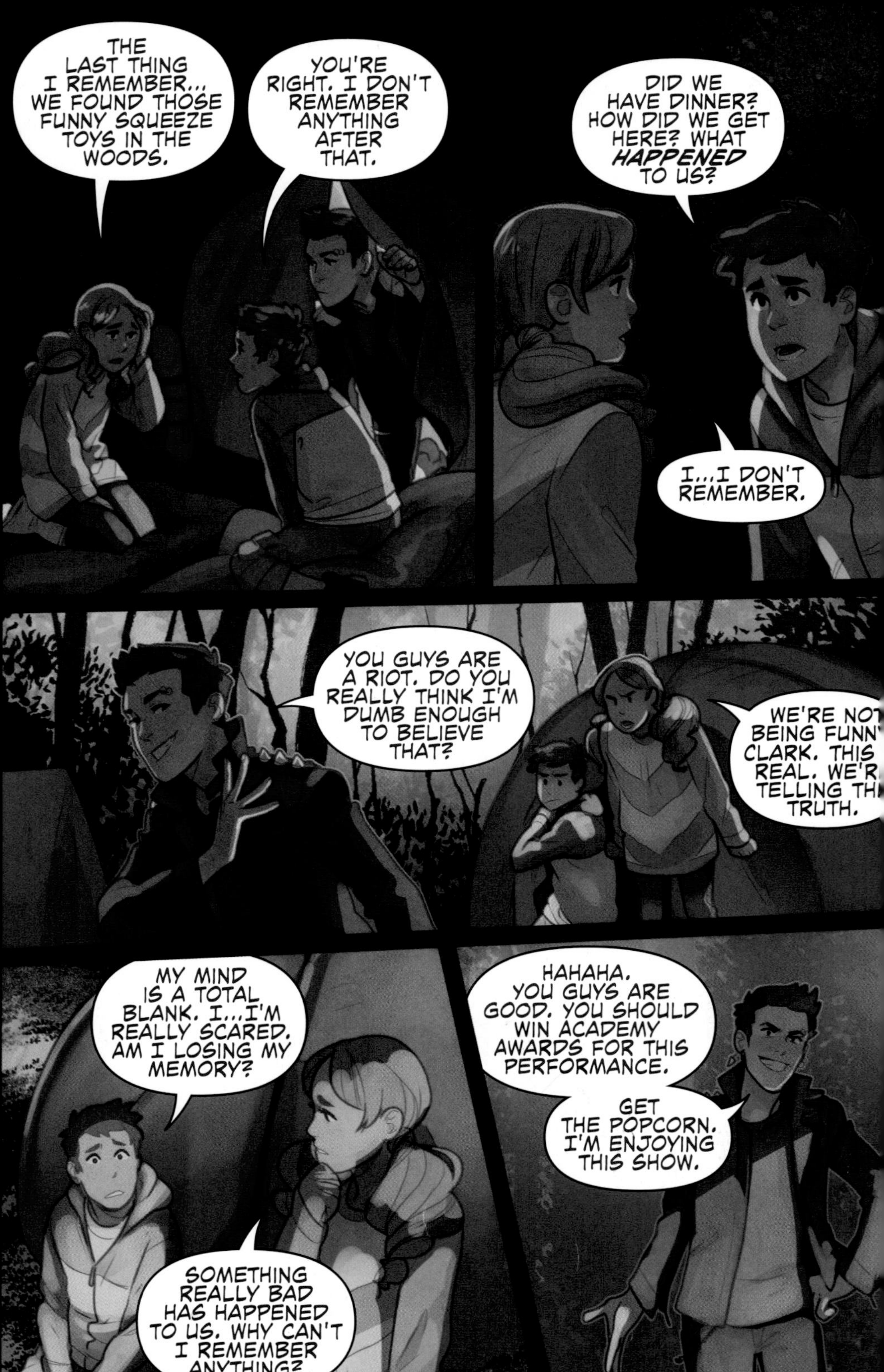
THE LAST THING I REMEMBER... WE FOUND THOSE FUNNY SQUEEZE TOYS IN THE WOODS.
YOU'RE RIGHT. I DON'T REMEMBER ANYTHING AFTER THAT.
DID WE HAVE DINNER? HOW DID WE GET HERE? WHAT *HAPPENED* TO US?
I...I DON'T REMEMBER.
YOU GUYS ARE A RIOT. DO YOU REALLY THINK I'M DUMB ENOUGH TO BELIEVE THAT?
WE'RE NOT BEING FUNN CLARK. THIS REAL. WE'R TELLING TH TRUTH.
MY MIND IS A TOTAL BLANK. I...I'M REALLY SCARED. AM I LOSING MY MEMORY?
SOMETHING REALLY BAD HAS HAPPENED TO US. WHY CAN'T I REMEMBER ANYTHING?
HAHAHA. YOU GUYS ARE GOOD. YOU SHOULD WIN ACADEMY AWARDS FOR THIS PERFORMANCE.
GET THE POPCORN. I'M ENJOYING THIS SHOW.

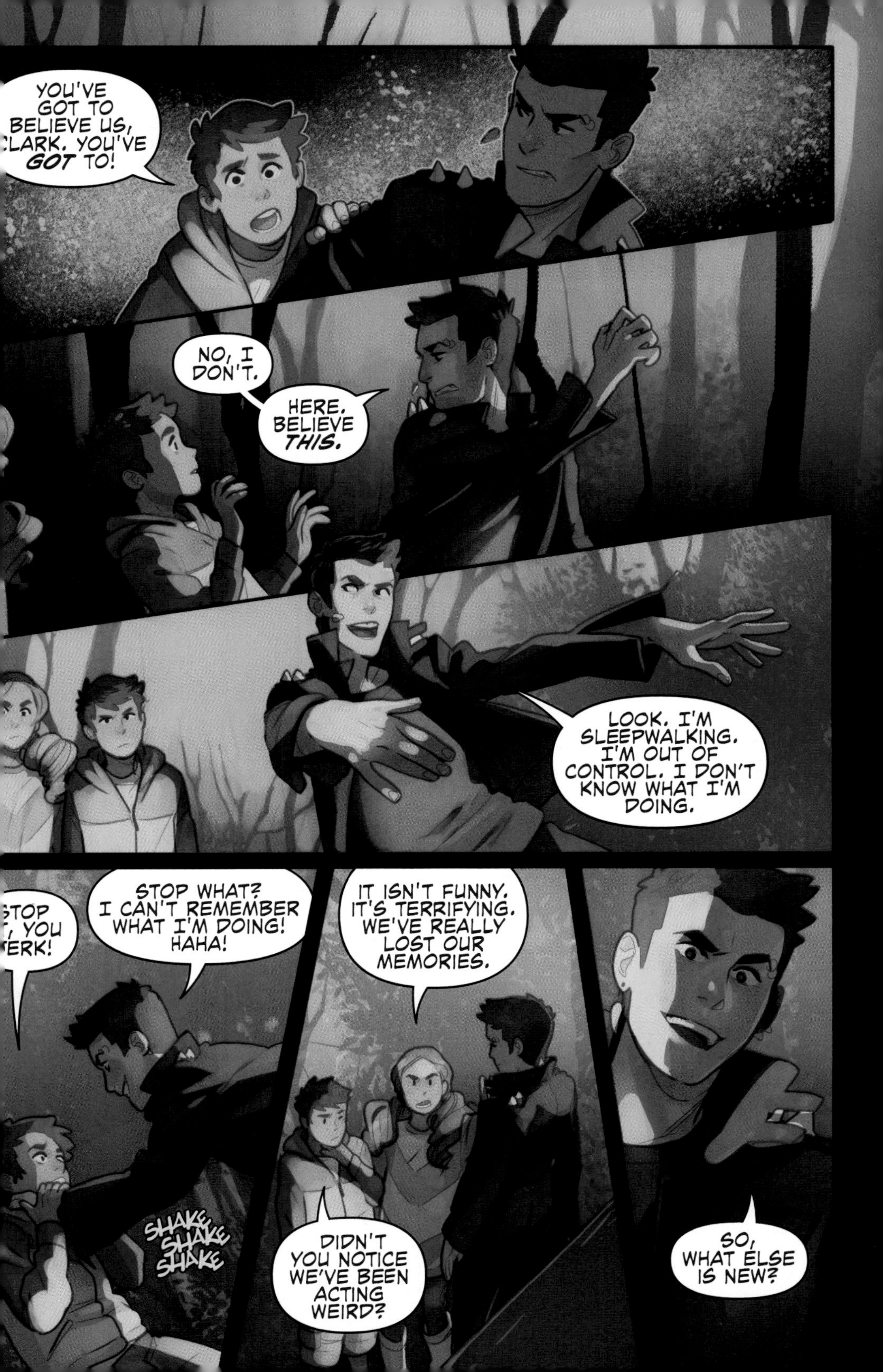

YOU'VE GOT TO BELIEVE US, CLARK. YOU'VE *GOT* TO!
NO, I DON'T.
HERE. BELIEVE *THIS.*
LOOK. I'M SLEEPWALKING. I'M OUT OF CONTROL. I DON'T KNOW WHAT I'M DOING.
STOP WHAT? I CAN'T REMEMBER WHAT I'M DOING! HAHA!
SHAKE SHAKE SHAKE
IT ISN'T FUNNY. IT'S TERRIFYING. WE'VE REALLY LOST OUR MEMORIES.
DIDN'T YOU NOTICE WE'VE BEEN ACTING WEIRD?
SO, WHAT ELSE IS NEW?

CHAPTER SEVEN
POSSESSED AGAIN

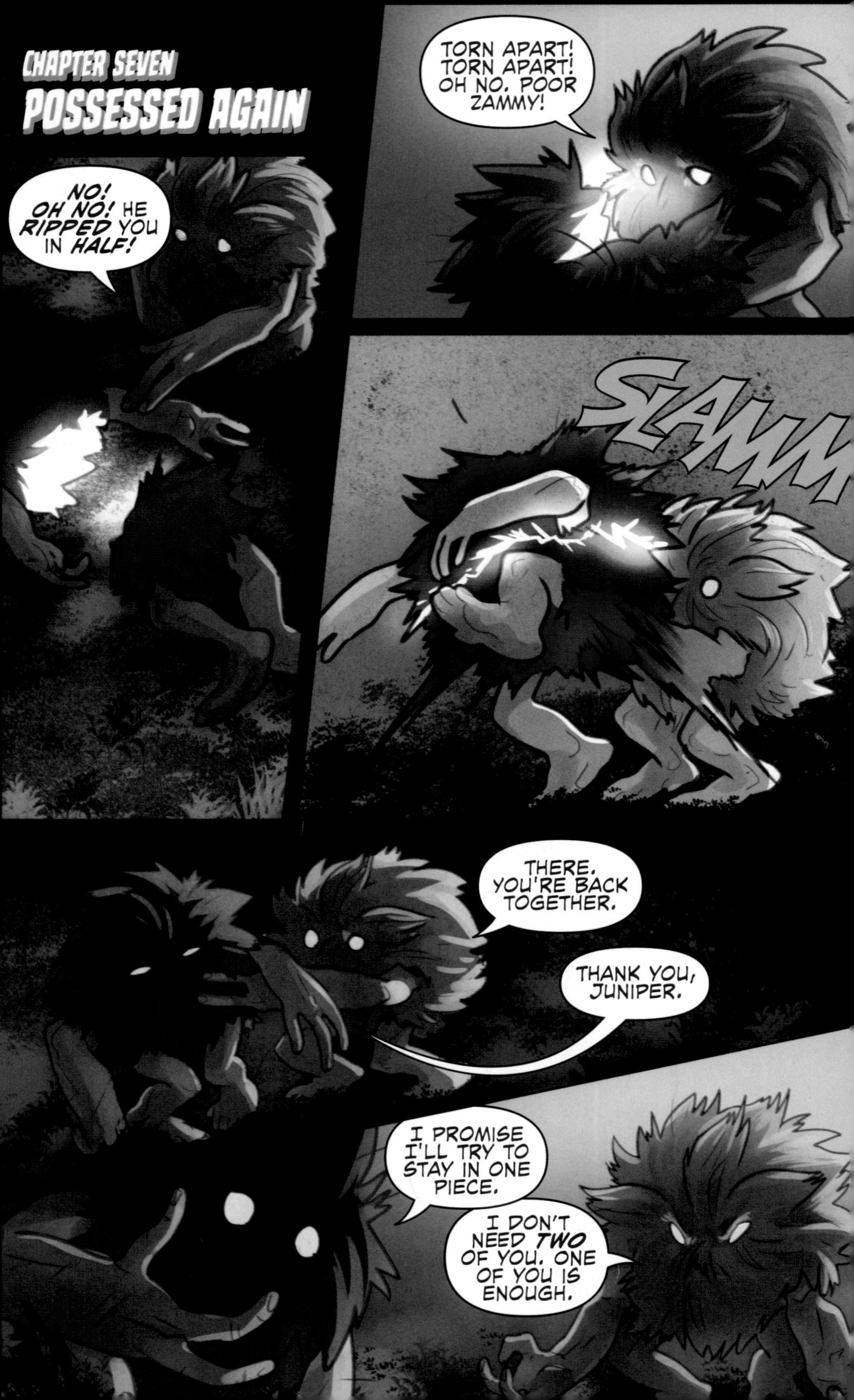
NO! OH NO! HE RIPPED YOU IN HALF!
TORN APART! TORN APART! OH NO. POOR ZAMMY!
SLAMM
THERE. YOU'RE BACK TOGETHER.
THANK YOU, JUNIPER.
I PROMISE I'LL TRY TO STAY IN ONE PIECE.
I DON'T NEED TWO OF YOU. ONE OF YOU IS ENOUGH.

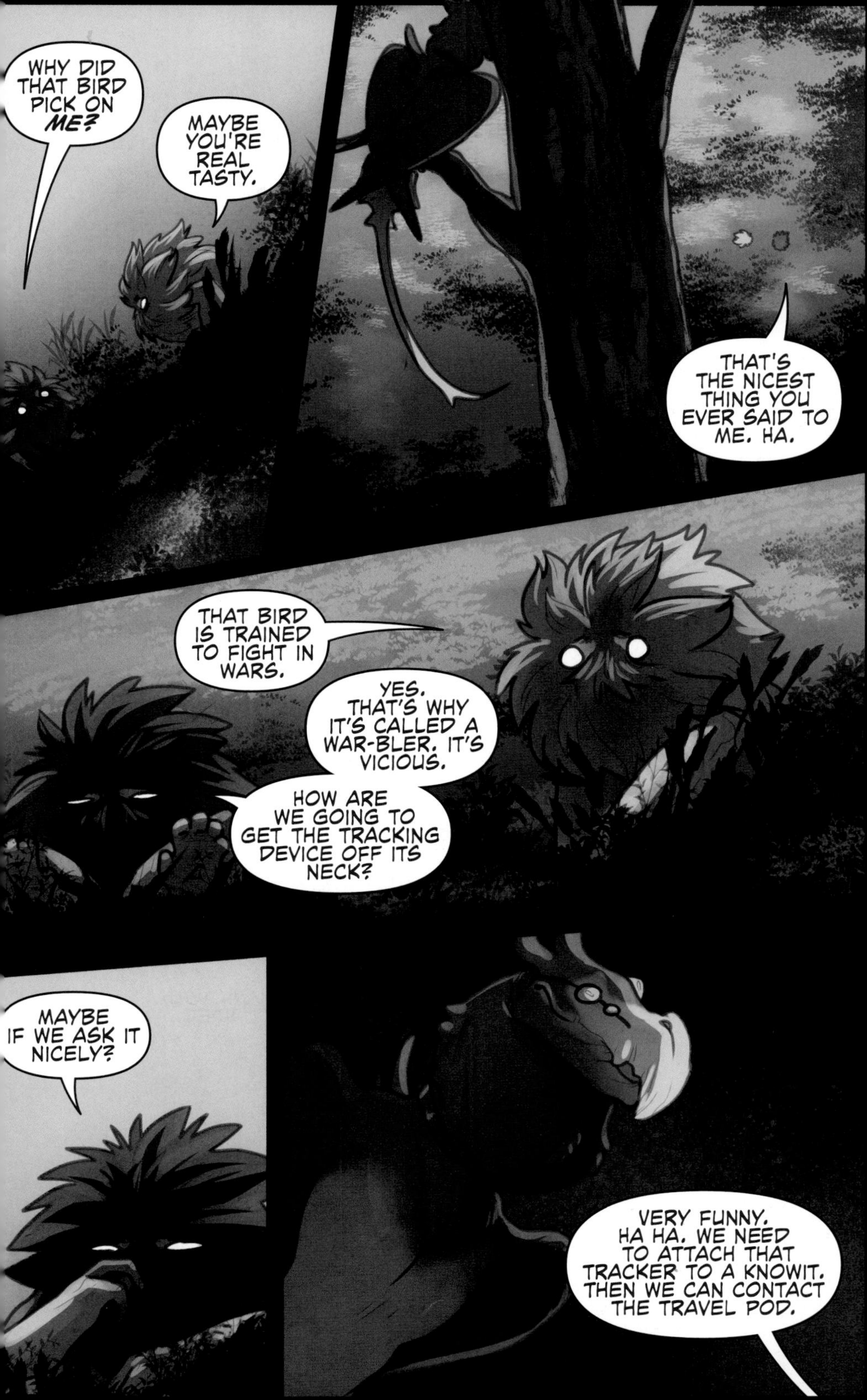
WHY DID THAT BIRD PICK ON *ME?*
MAYBE YOU'RE REAL TASTY.
THAT'S THE NICEST THING YOU EVER SAID TO ME. HA.
THAT BIRD IS TRAINED TO FIGHT IN WARS.
YES. THAT'S WHY IT'S CALLED A WAR-BLER. IT'S VICIOUS.
HOW ARE WE GOING TO GET THE TRACKING DEVICE OFF ITS NECK?
MAYBE IF WE ASK IT NICELY?
VERY FUNNY. HA HA. WE NEED TO ATTACH THAT TRACKER TO A KNOWIT. THEN WE CAN CONTACT THE TRAVEL POD.

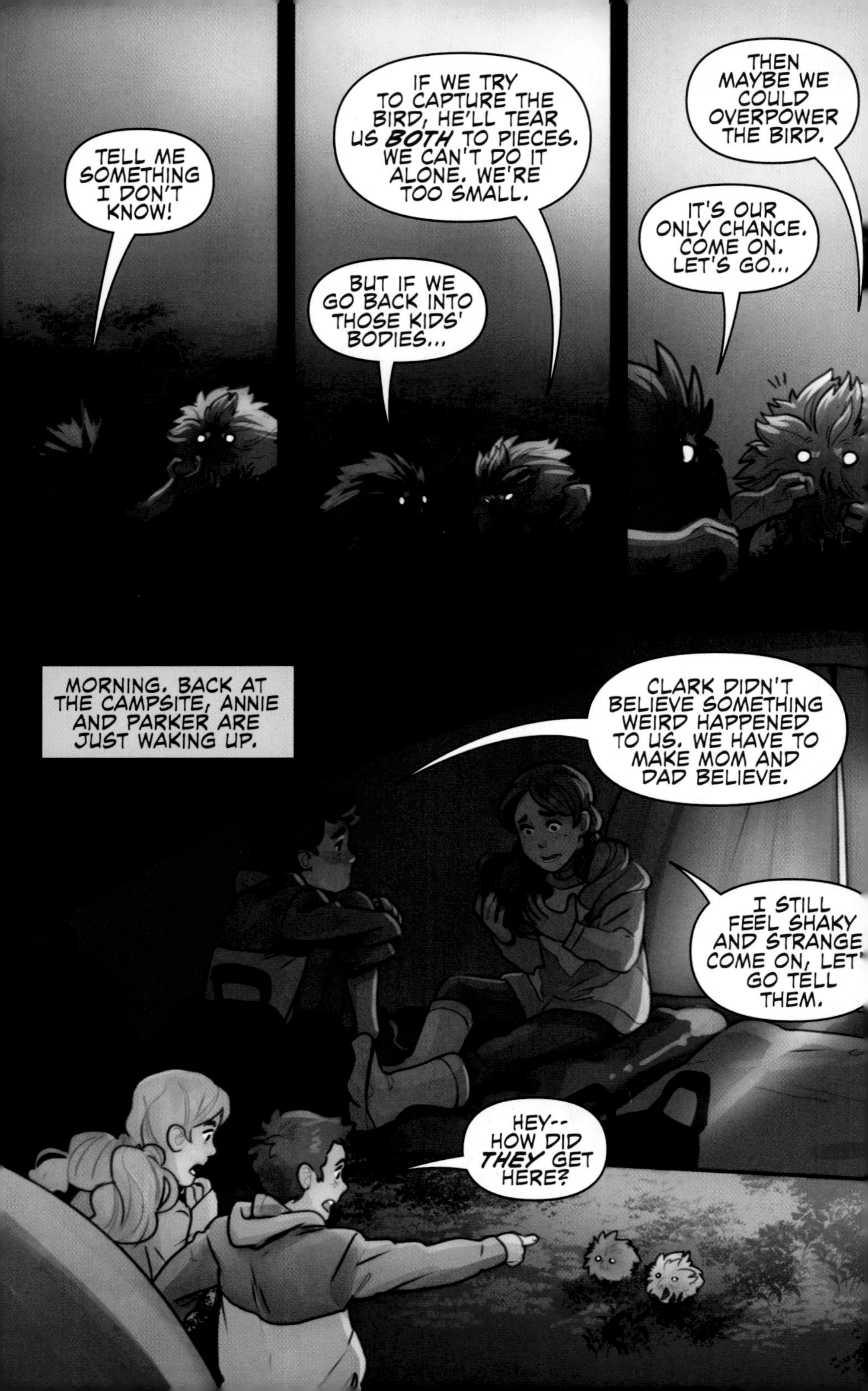
TELL ME SOMETHING I DON'T KNOW!
IF WE TRY TO CAPTURE THE BIRD, HE'LL TEAR US BOTH TO PIECES. WE CAN'T DO IT ALONE. WE'RE TOO SMALL.
BUT IF WE GO BACK INTO THOSE KIDS' BODIES...
THEN MAYBE WE COULD OVERPOWER THE BIRD.
IT'S OUR ONLY CHANCE. COME ON. LET'S GO...
MORNING. BACK AT THE CAMPSITE, ANNIE AND PARKER ARE JUST WAKING UP.
CLARK DIDN'T BELIEVE SOMETHING WEIRD HAPPENED TO US. WE HAVE TO MAKE MOM AND DAD BELIEVE.
I STILL FEEL SHAKY AND STRANGE COME ON, LET' GO TELL THEM.
HEY-- HOW DID THEY GET HERE?

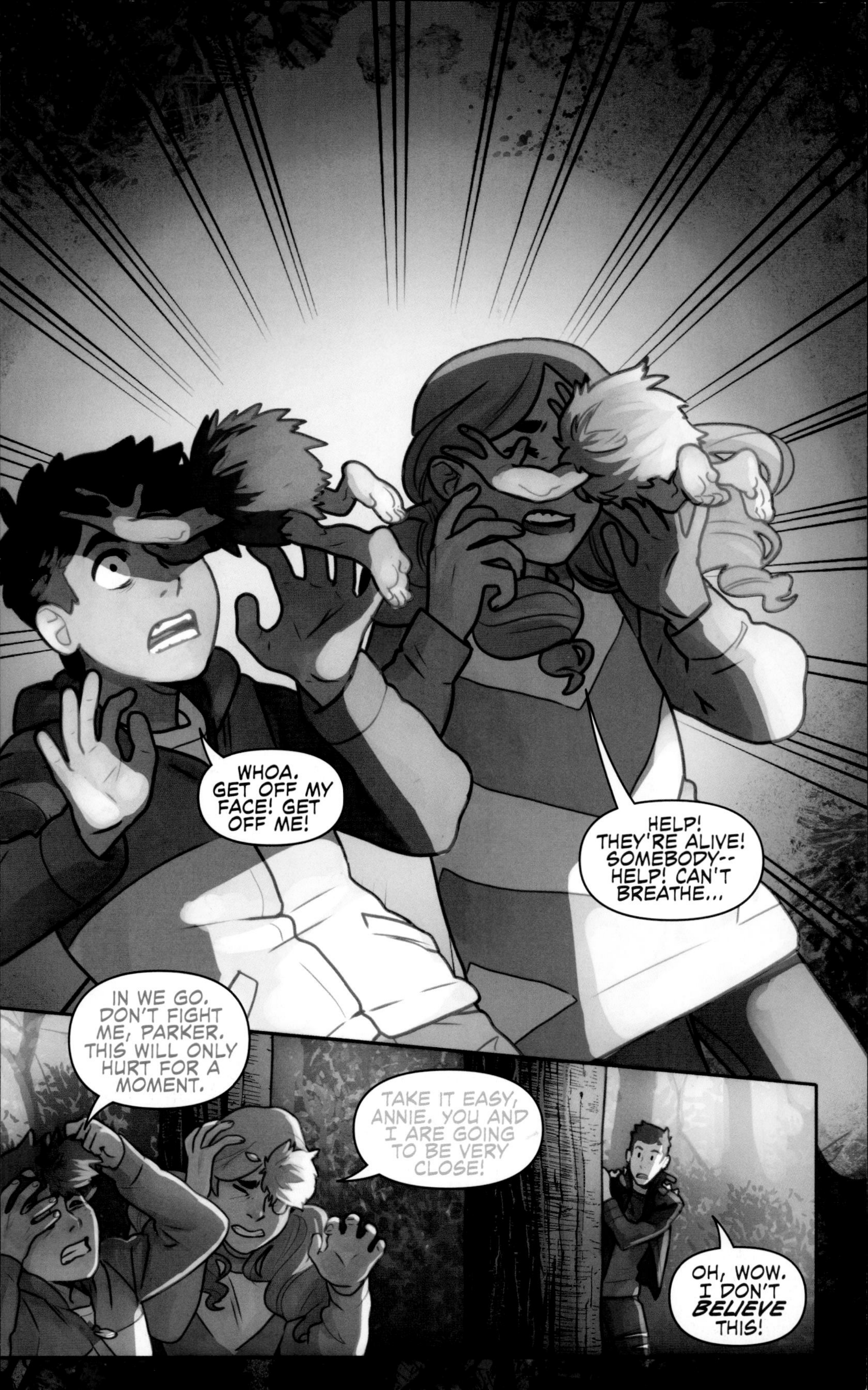
WHOA. GET OFF MY FACE! GET OFF ME!
HELP! THEY'RE ALIVE! SOMEBODY-- HELP! CAN'T BREATHE...
IN WE GO. DON'T FIGHT ME, PARKER. THIS WILL ONLY HURT FOR A MOMENT.
TAKE IT EASY, ANNIE. YOU AND I ARE GOING TO BE VERY CLOSE!
OH, WOW. I DON'T *BELIEVE* THIS!

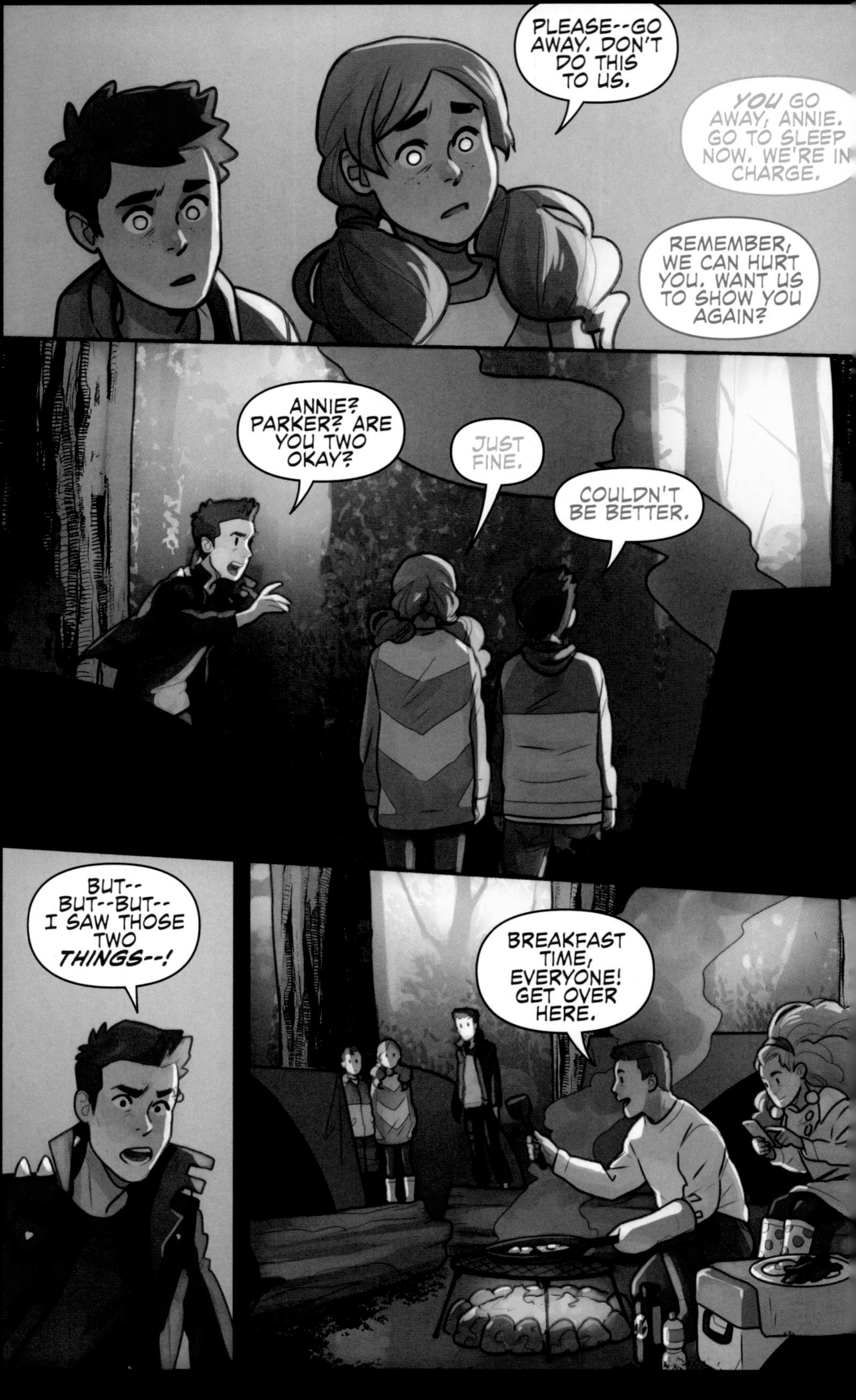
PLEASE--GO AWAY. DON'T DO THIS TO US.
YOU GO AWAY, ANNIE. GO TO SLEEP NOW. WE'RE IN CHARGE.
REMEMBER, WE CAN HURT YOU. WANT US TO SHOW YOU AGAIN?
ANNIE? PARKER? ARE YOU TWO OKAY?
JUST FINE.
COULDN'T BE BETTER.
BUT-- BUT--BUT-- I SAW THOSE TWO THINGS--!
BREAKFAST TIME, EVERYONE! GET OVER HERE.

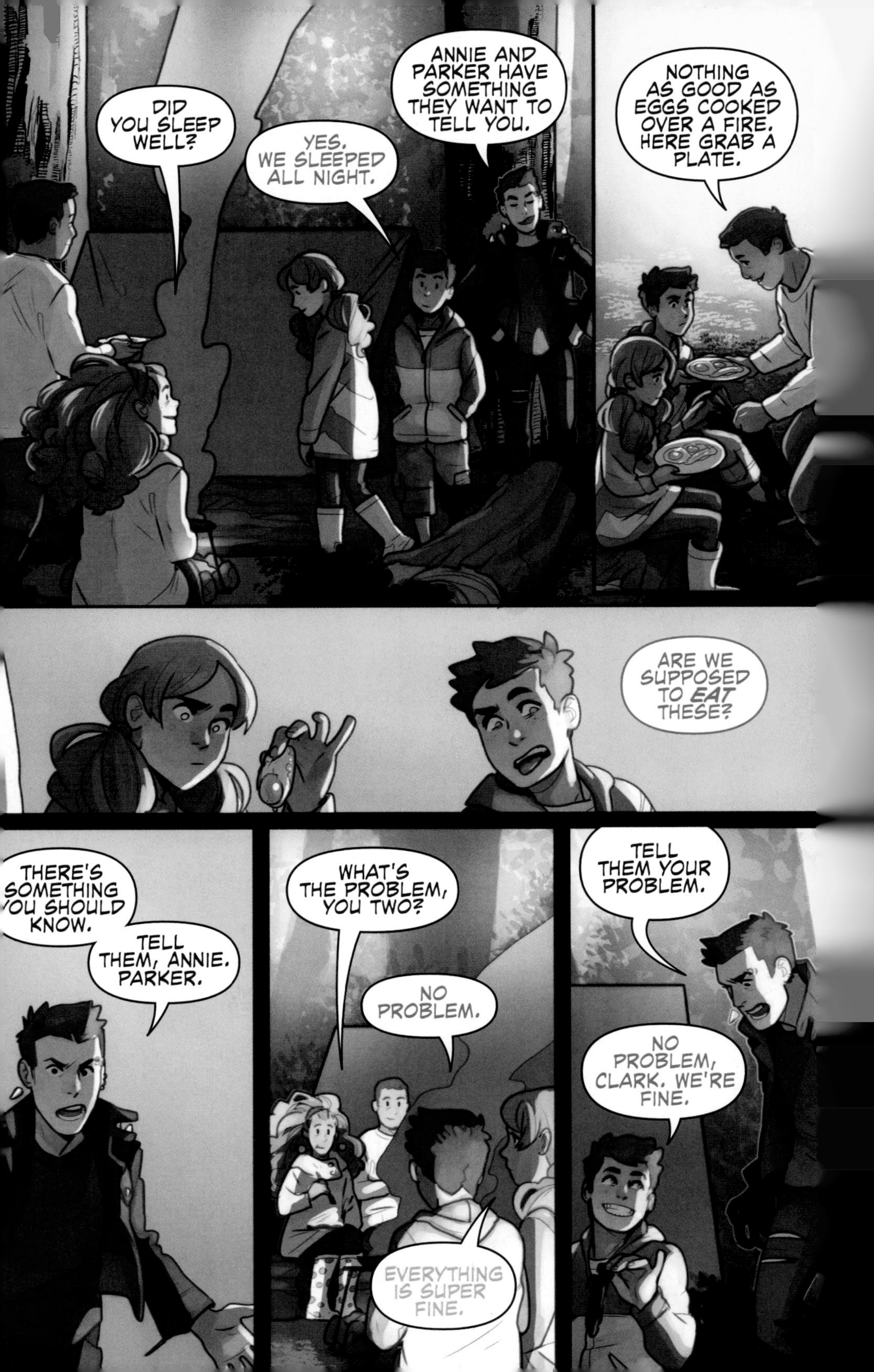
DID YOU SLEEP WELL?
YES. WE SLEEPED ALL NIGHT.
ANNIE AND PARKER HAVE SOMETHING THEY WANT TO TELL YOU.
NOTHING AS GOOD AS EGGS COOKED OVER A FIRE. HERE GRAB A PLATE.
ARE WE SUPPOSED TO EAT THESE?
THERE'S SOMETHING YOU SHOULD KNOW.
TELL THEM, ANNIE. PARKER.
WHAT'S THE PROBLEM, YOU TWO?
NO PROBLEM.
EVERYTHING IS SUPER FINE.
TELL THEM YOUR PROBLEM.
NO PROBLEM, CLARK. WE'RE FINE.

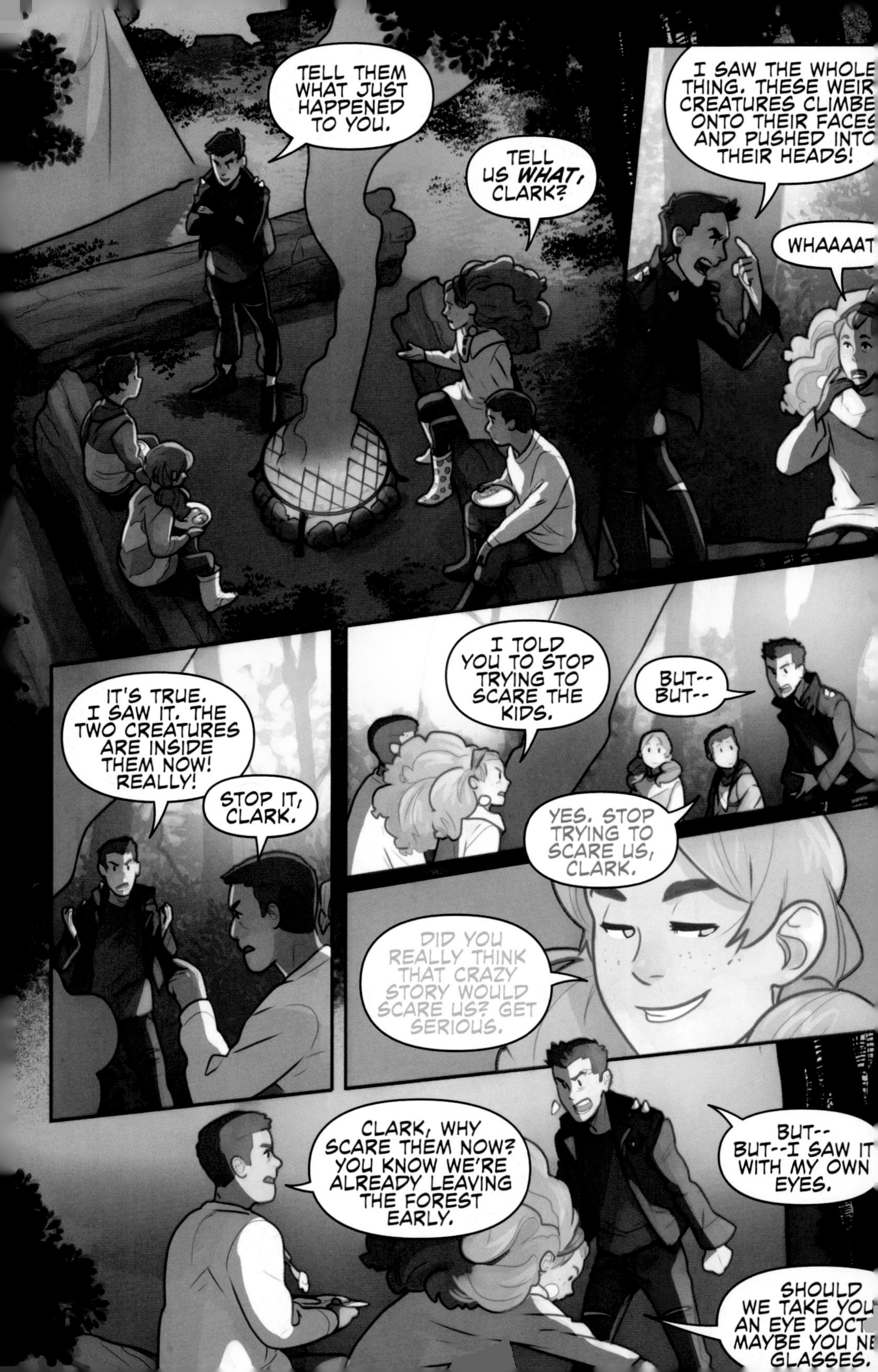
TELL THEM WHAT JUST HAPPENED TO YOU.
TELL US *WHAT*, CLARK?
I SAW THE WHOLE THING. THESE WEIR CREATURES CLIMBE ONTO THEIR FACES AND PUSHED INTO THEIR HEADS!
WHAAAAT
IT'S TRUE. I SAW IT. THE TWO CREATURES ARE INSIDE THEM NOW! REALLY!
STOP IT, CLARK.
I TOLD YOU TO STOP TRYING TO SCARE THE KIDS.
BUT-- BUT--
YES. STOP TRYING TO SCARE US, CLARK.
DID YOU REALLY THINK THAT CRAZY STORY WOULD SCARE US? GET SERIOUS.
CLARK, WHY SCARE THEM NOW? YOU KNOW WE'RE ALREADY LEAVING THE FOREST EARLY.
BUT-- BUT--I SAW IT WITH MY OWN EYES.
SHOULD WE TAKE YOU AN EYE DOCT MAYBE YOU NE GLASSES.

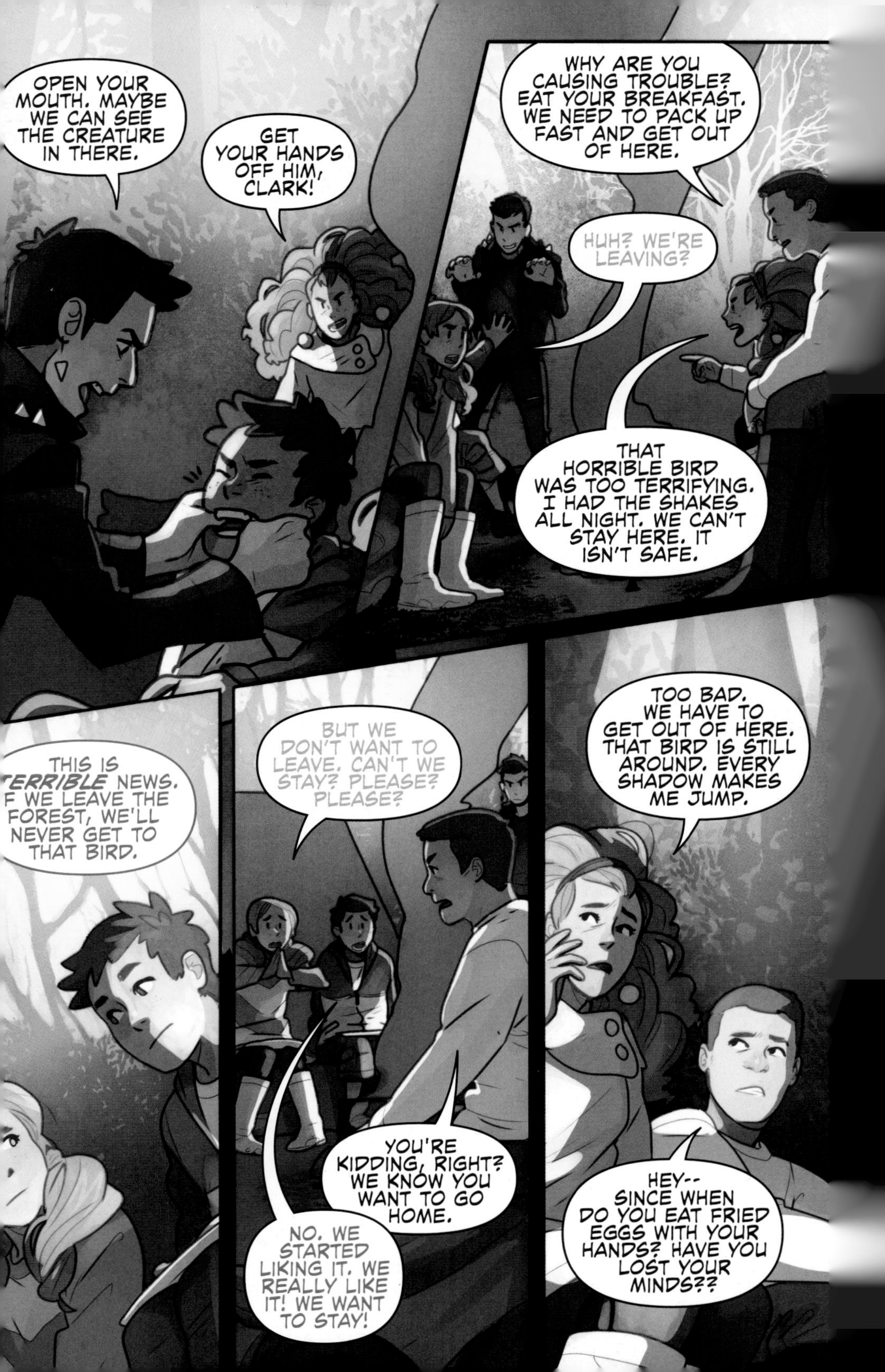
OPEN YOUR MOUTH. MAYBE WE CAN SEE THE CREATURE IN THERE.
GET YOUR HANDS OFF HIM, CLARK!
WHY ARE YOU CAUSING TROUBLE? EAT YOUR BREAKFAST. WE NEED TO PACK UP FAST AND GET OUT OF HERE.
HUH? WE'RE LEAVING?
THAT HORRIBLE BIRD WAS TOO TERRIFYING. I HAD THE SHAKES ALL NIGHT. WE CAN'T STAY HERE. IT ISN'T SAFE.
THIS IS TERRIBLE NEWS. F WE LEAVE THE FOREST, WE'LL NEVER GET TO THAT BIRD.
BUT WE DON'T WANT TO LEAVE. CAN'T WE STAY? PLEASE? PLEASE?
YOU'RE KIDDING, RIGHT? WE KNOW YOU WANT TO GO HOME.
NO. WE STARTED LIKING IT. WE REALLY LIKE IT! WE WANT TO STAY!
TOO BAD. WE HAVE TO GET OUT OF HERE. THAT BIRD IS STILL AROUND. EVERY SHADOW MAKES ME JUMP.
HEY-- SINCE WHEN DO YOU EAT FRIED EGGS WITH YOUR HANDS? HAVE YOU LOST YOUR MINDS??

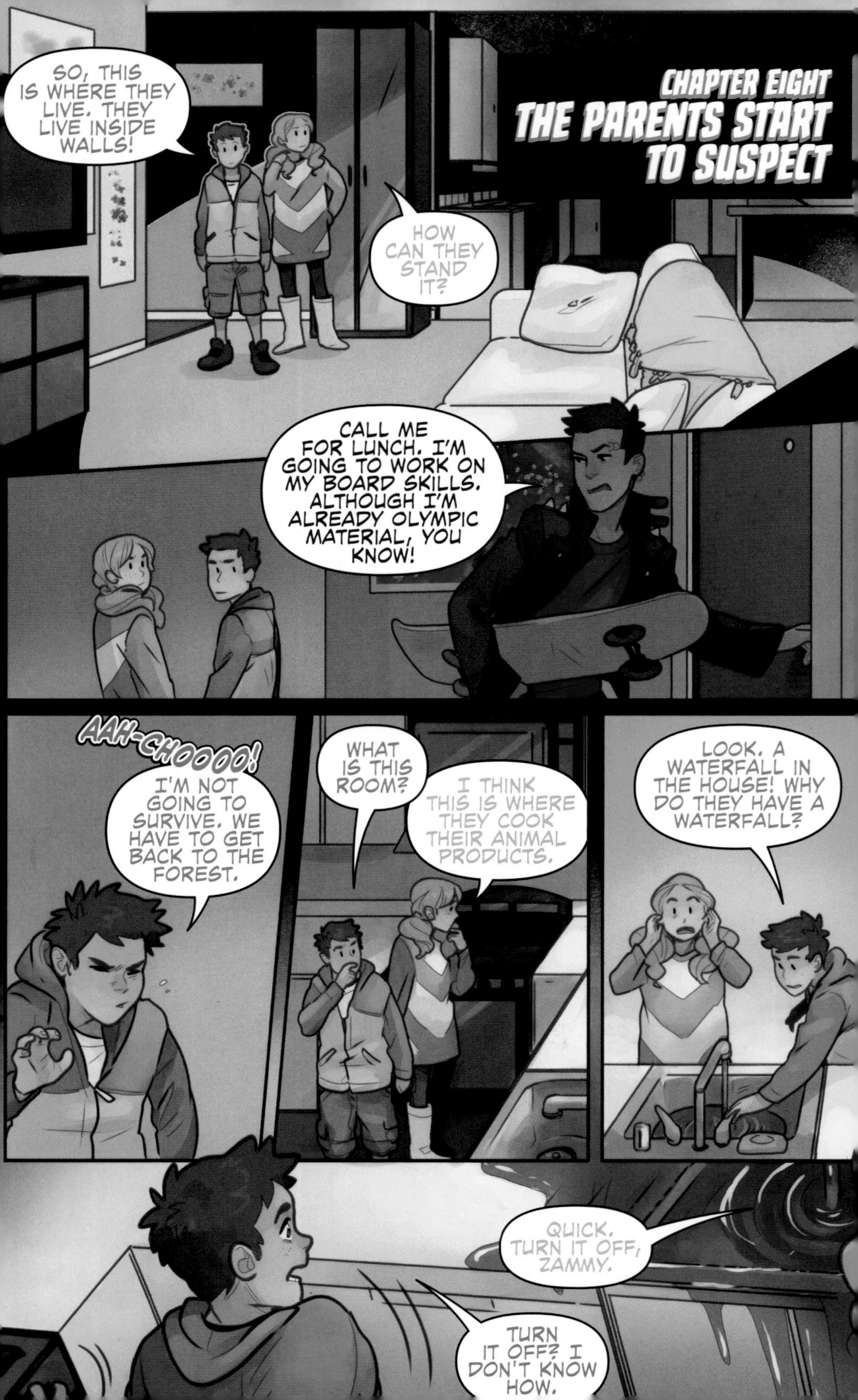

CHAPTER EIGHT
THE PARENTS START TO SUSPECT
SO, THIS IS WHERE THEY LIVE. THEY LIVE INSIDE WALLS!
HOW CAN THEY STAND IT?
CALL ME FOR LUNCH. I'M GOING TO WORK ON MY BOARD SKILLS. ALTHOUGH I'M ALREADY OLYMPIC MATERIAL, YOU KNOW!
AAH-CHOOOOO!
I'M NOT GOING TO SURVIVE. WE HAVE TO GET BACK TO THE FOREST.
WHAT IS THIS ROOM?
I THINK THIS IS WHERE THEY COOK THEIR ANIMAL PRODUCTS.
LOOK. A WATERFALL IN THE HOUSE! WHY DO THEY HAVE A WATERFALL?
QUICK. TURN IT OFF, ZAMMY.
TURN IT OFF? I DON'T KNOW HOW.

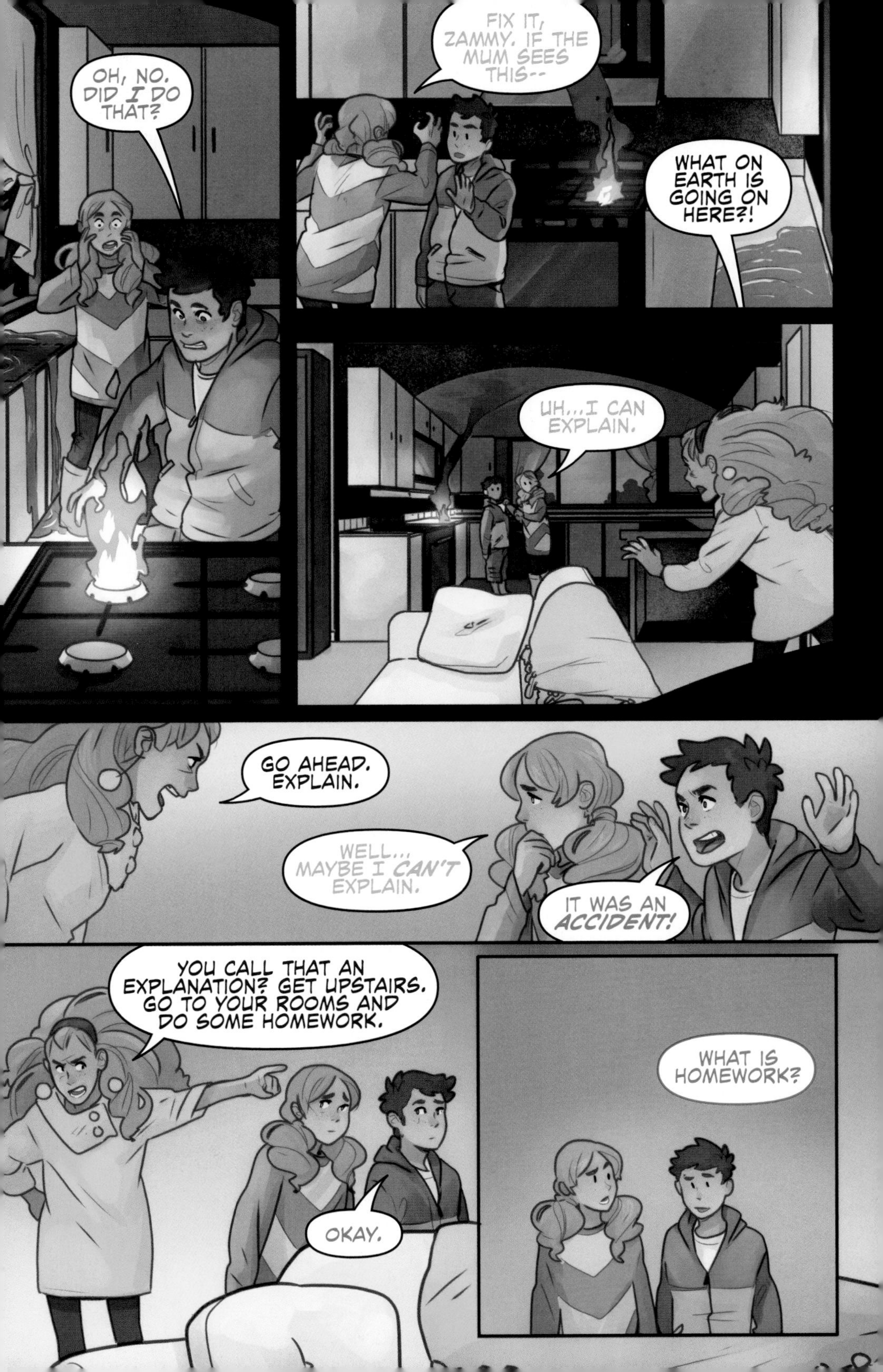
OH, NO. DID I DO THAT?
FIX IT, ZAMMY. IF THE MUM SEES THIS--
WHAT ON EARTH IS GOING ON HERE?!
UH...I CAN EXPLAIN.
GO AHEAD. EXPLAIN.
WELL... MAYBE I CAN'T EXPLAIN.
IT WAS AN ACCIDENT!
YOU CALL THAT AN EXPLANATION? GET UPSTAIRS. GO TO YOUR ROOMS AND DO SOME HOMEWORK.
OKAY.
WHAT IS HOMEWORK?

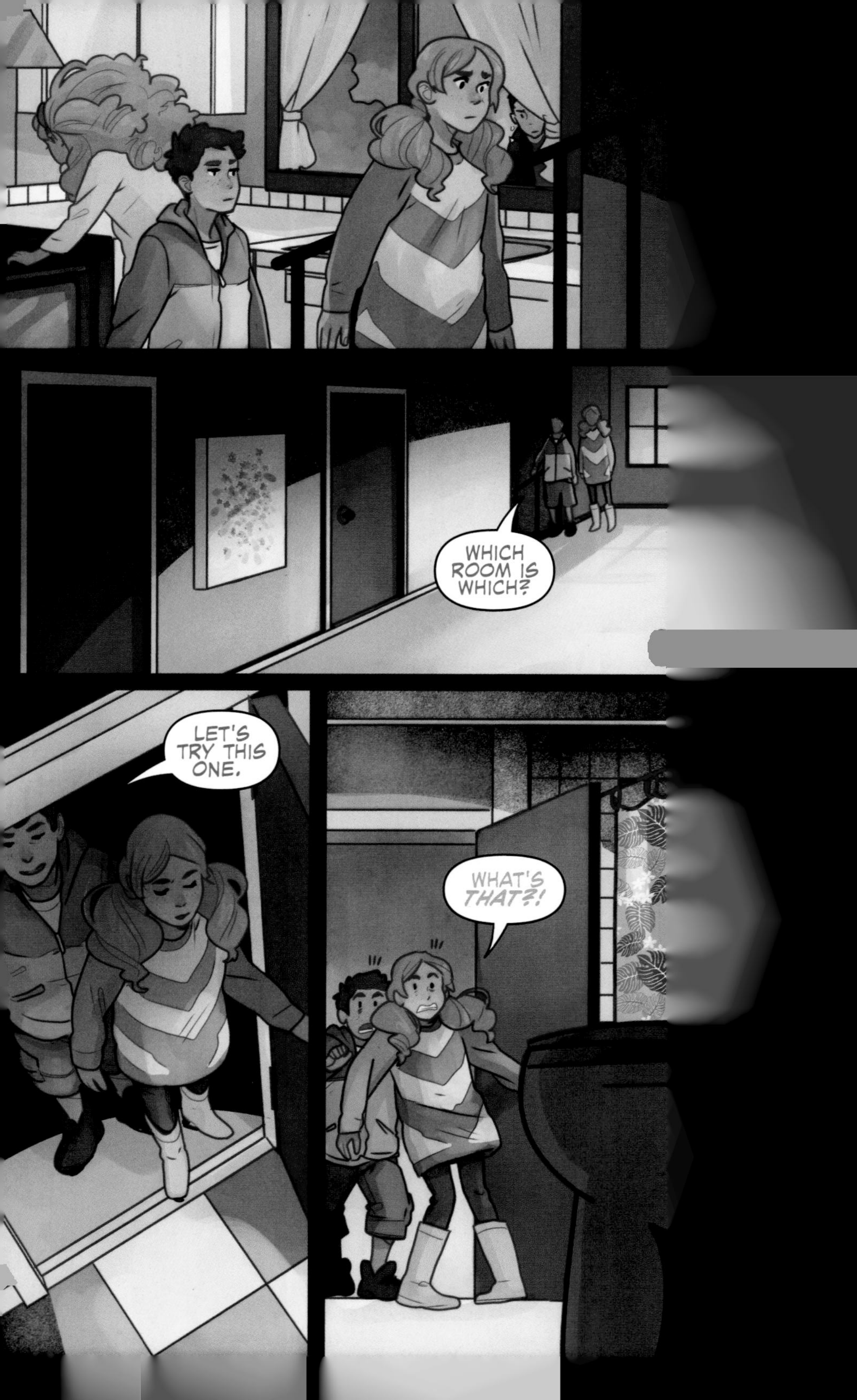
WHICH ROOM IS WHICH?
LET'S TRY THIS ONE.
WHAT'S THAT?!

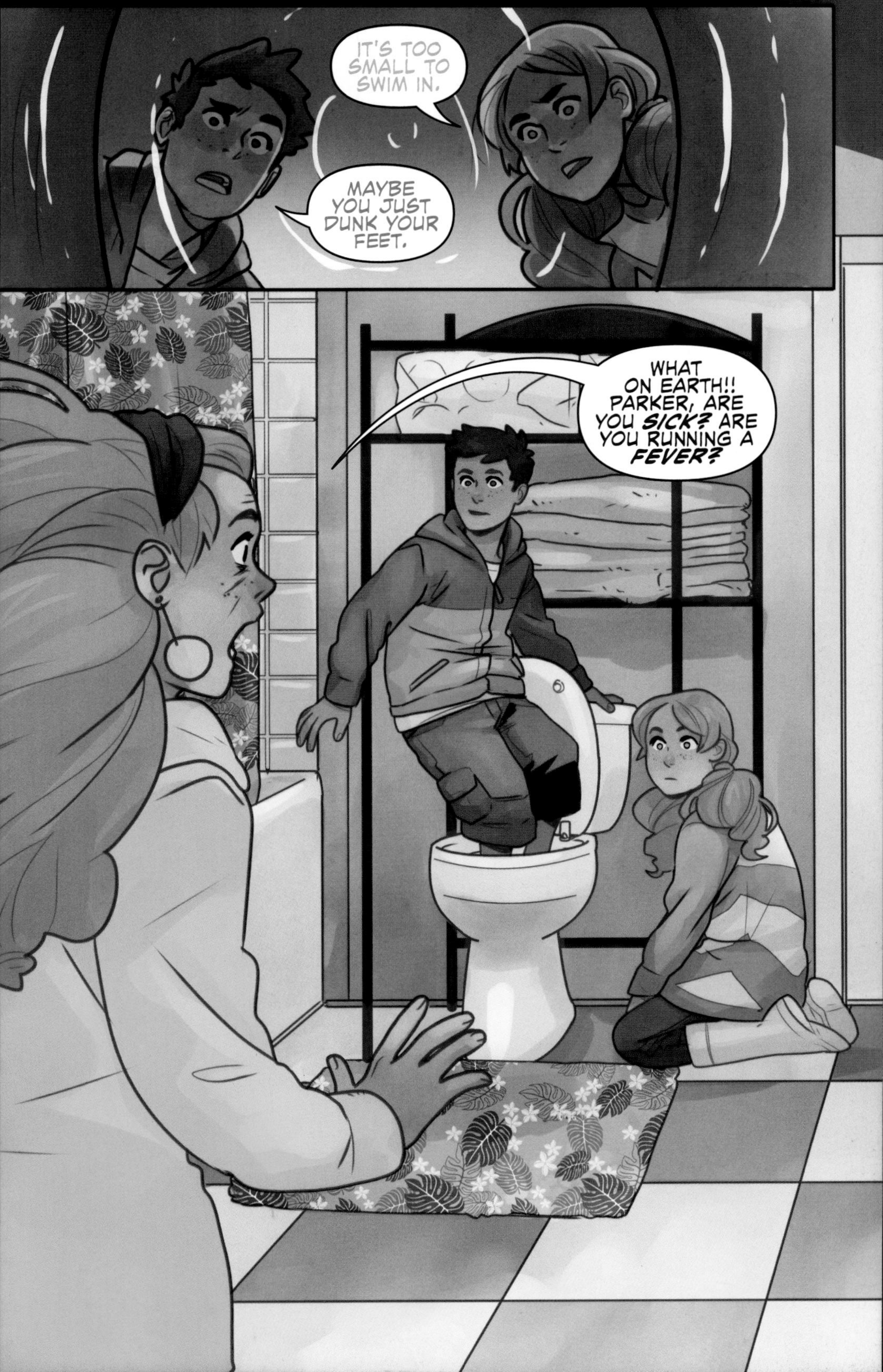
IT'S TOO SMALL TO SWIM IN.
MAYBE YOU JUST DUNK YOUR FEET.
WHAT ON EARTH!! PARKER, ARE YOU SICK? ARE YOU RUNNING A FEVER?

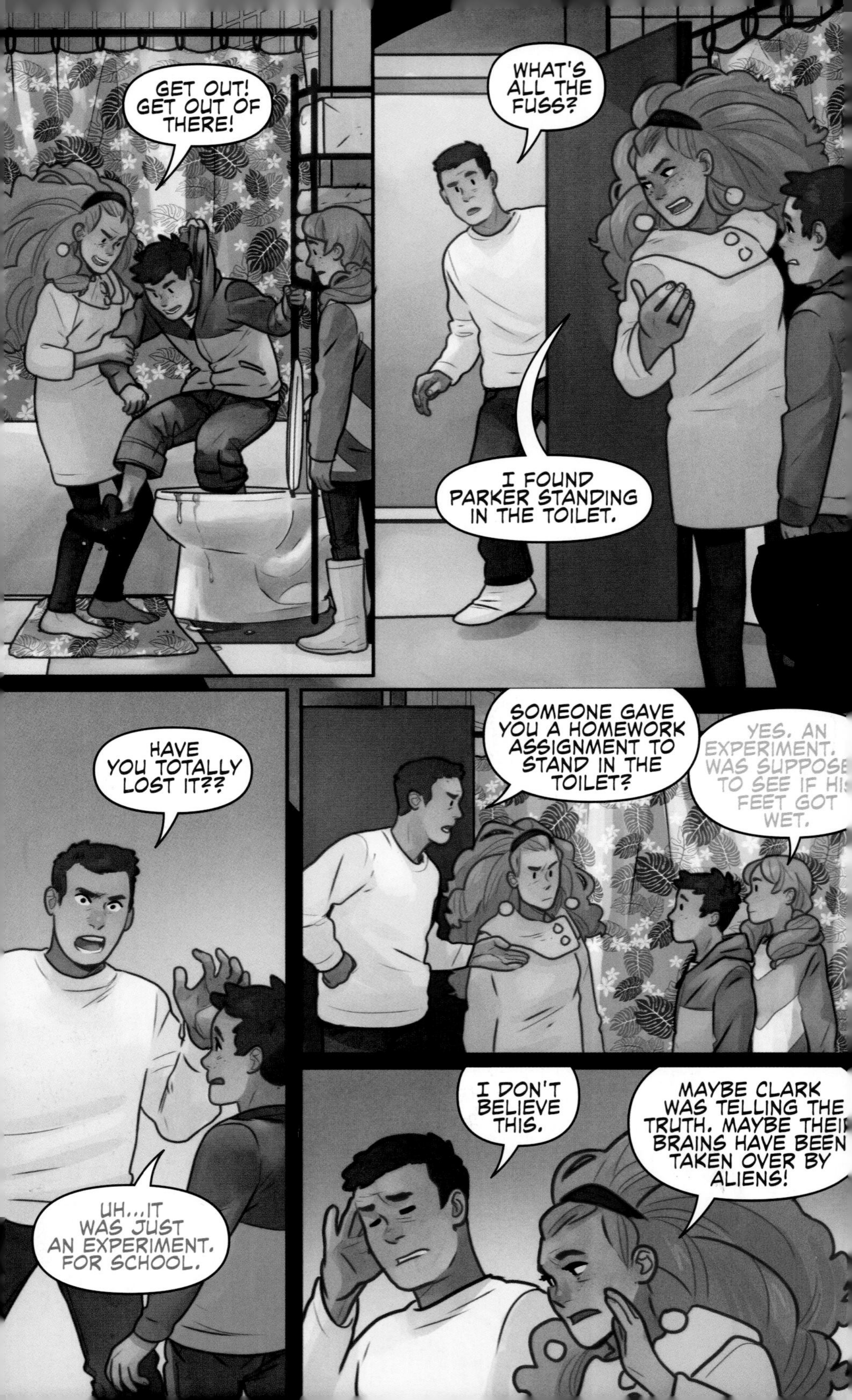
GET OUT! GET OUT OF THERE!
WHAT'S ALL THE FUSS?
I FOUND PARKER STANDING IN THE TOILET.
HAVE YOU TOTALLY LOST IT??
UH...IT WAS JUST AN EXPERIMENT. FOR SCHOOL.
SOMEONE GAVE YOU A HOMEWORK ASSIGNMENT TO STAND IN THE TOILET?
YES. AN EXPERIMENT. WAS SUPPOSE TO SEE IF HI FEET GOT WET.
I DON'T BELIEVE THIS.
MAYBE CLARK WAS TELLING THE TRUTH. MAYBE THEI BRAINS HAVE BEEN TAKEN OVER BY ALIENS!

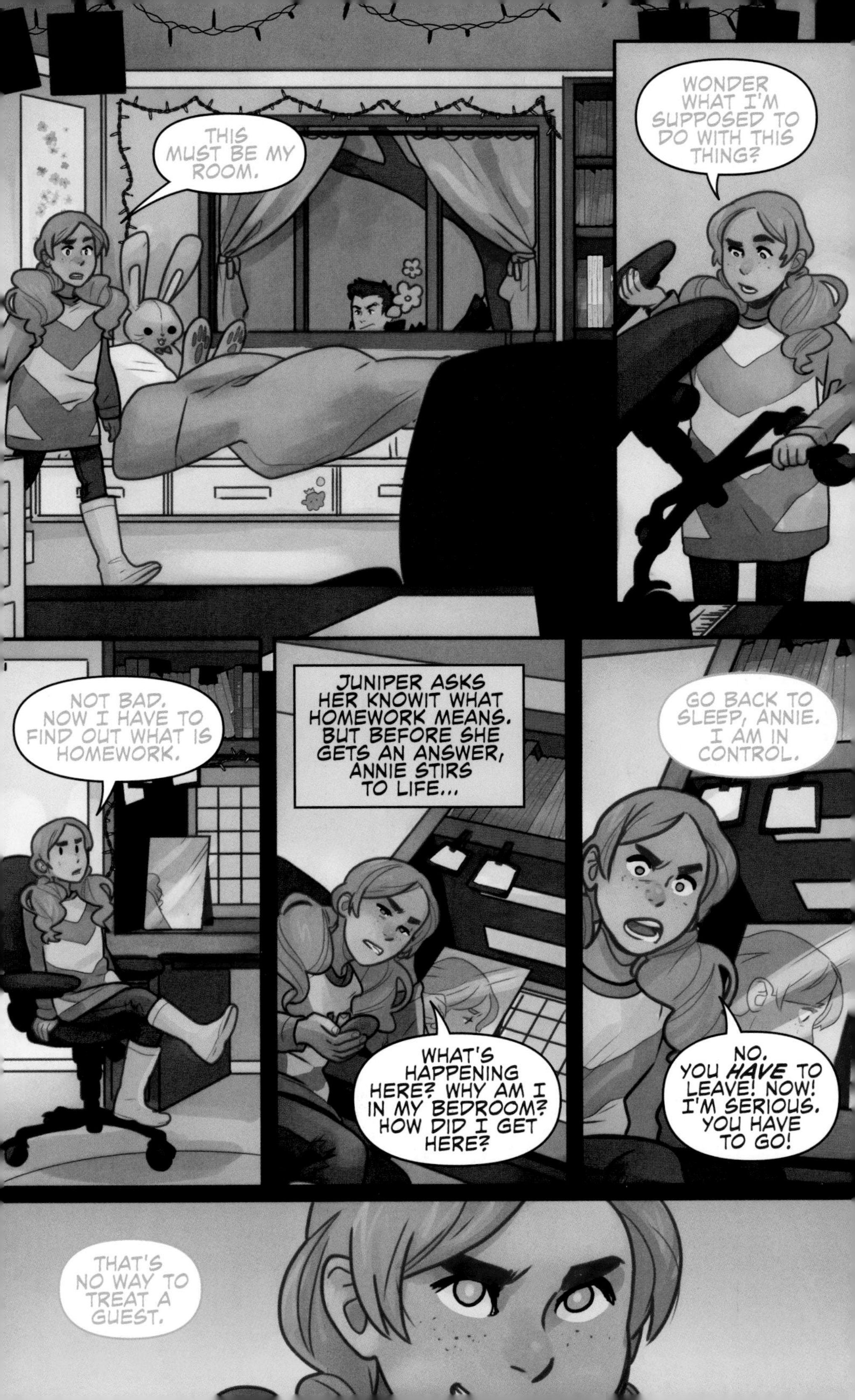
THIS MUST BE MY ROOM.
WONDER WHAT I'M SUPPOSED TO DO WITH THIS THING?
NOT BAD. NOW I HAVE TO FIND OUT WHAT IS HOMEWORK.
JUNIPER ASKS HER KNOWIT WHAT HOMEWORK MEANS. BUT BEFORE SHE GETS AN ANSWER, ANNIE STIRS TO LIFE...
WHAT'S HAPPENING HERE? WHY AM I IN MY BEDROOM? HOW DID I GET HERE?
GO BACK TO SLEEP, ANNIE. I AM IN CONTROL.
NO. YOU *HAVE* TO LEAVE! NOW! I'M SERIOUS. YOU HAVE TO GO!
THAT'S NO WAY TO TREAT A GUEST.

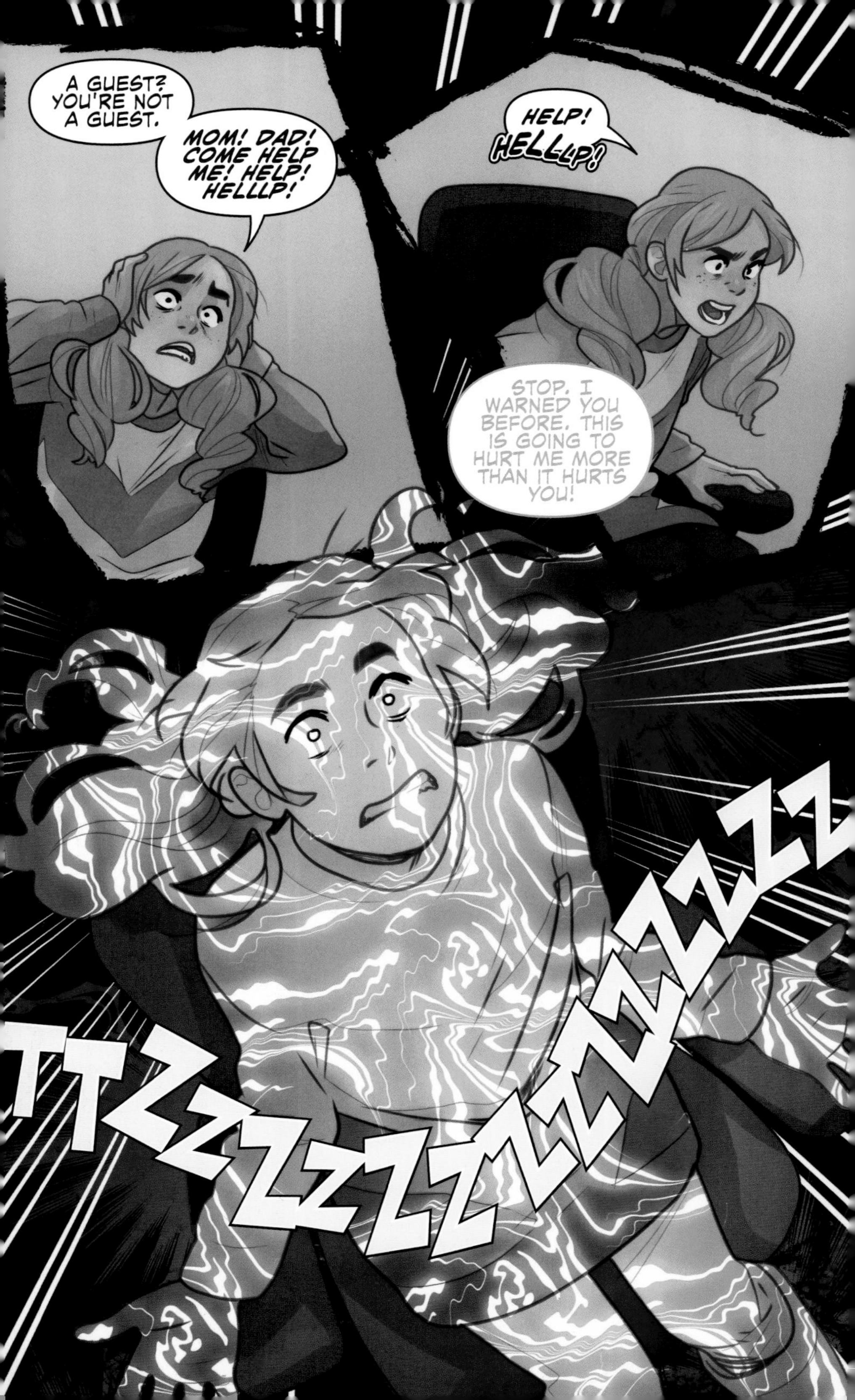
A GUEST? YOU'RE NOT A GUEST.
MOM! DAD! COME HELP ME! HELP! HELLLP!
HELP! HELLLLP!
STOP. I WARNED YOU BEFORE. THIS IS GOING TO HURT ME MORE THAN IT HURTS YOU!
TTZZZZZZZZZZZZZZ

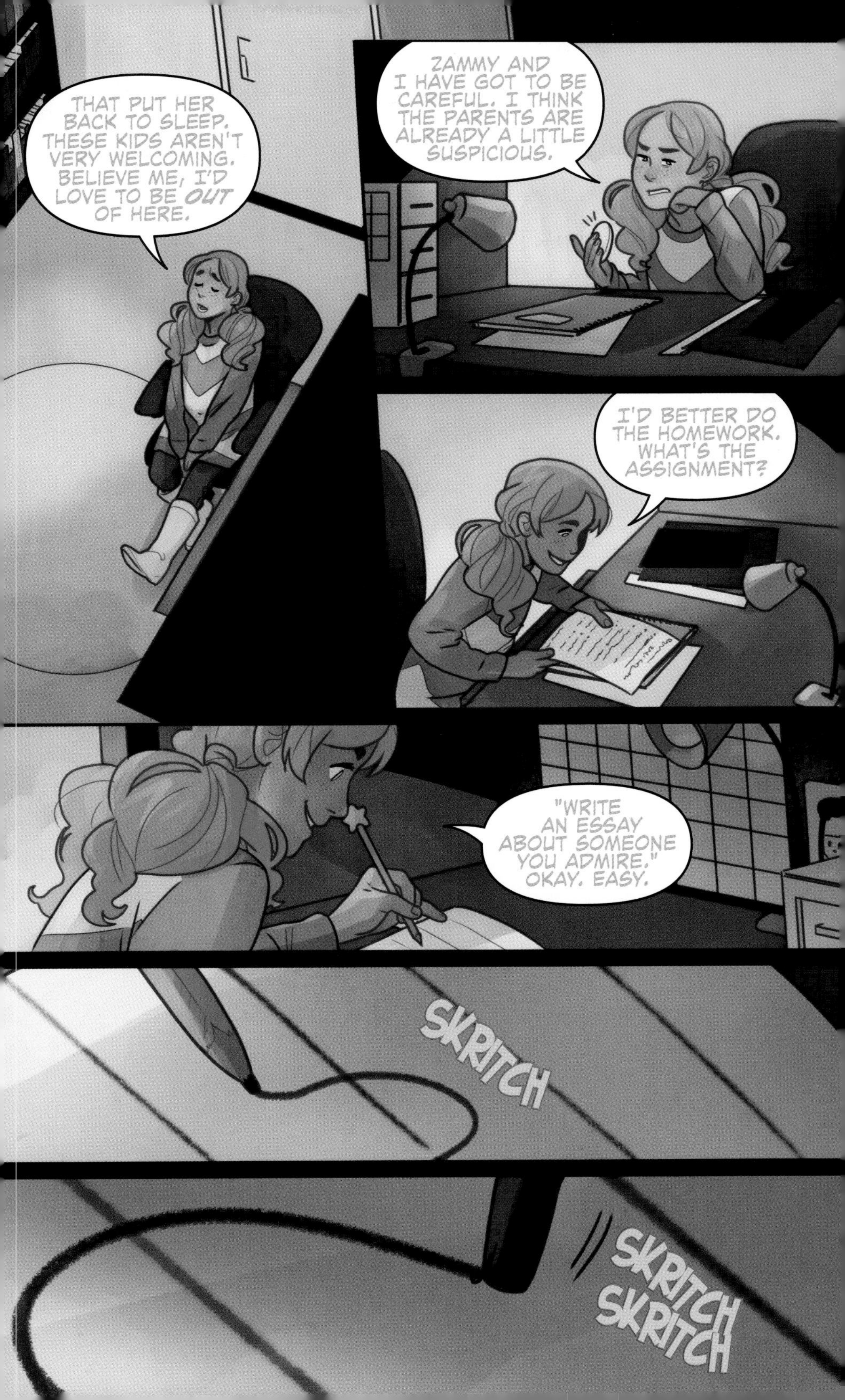
THAT PUT HER BACK TO SLEEP. THESE KIDS AREN'T VERY WELCOMING. BELIEVE ME, I'D LOVE TO BE *OUT* OF HERE.
ZAMMY AND I HAVE GOT TO BE CAREFUL. I THINK THE PARENTS ARE ALREADY A LITTLE SUSPICIOUS.
I'D BETTER DO THE HOMEWORK. WHAT'S THE ASSIGNMENT?
"WRITE AN ESSAY ABOUT SOMEONE YOU ADMIRE." OKAY. EASY.
SKRITCH
SKRITCH SKRITCH

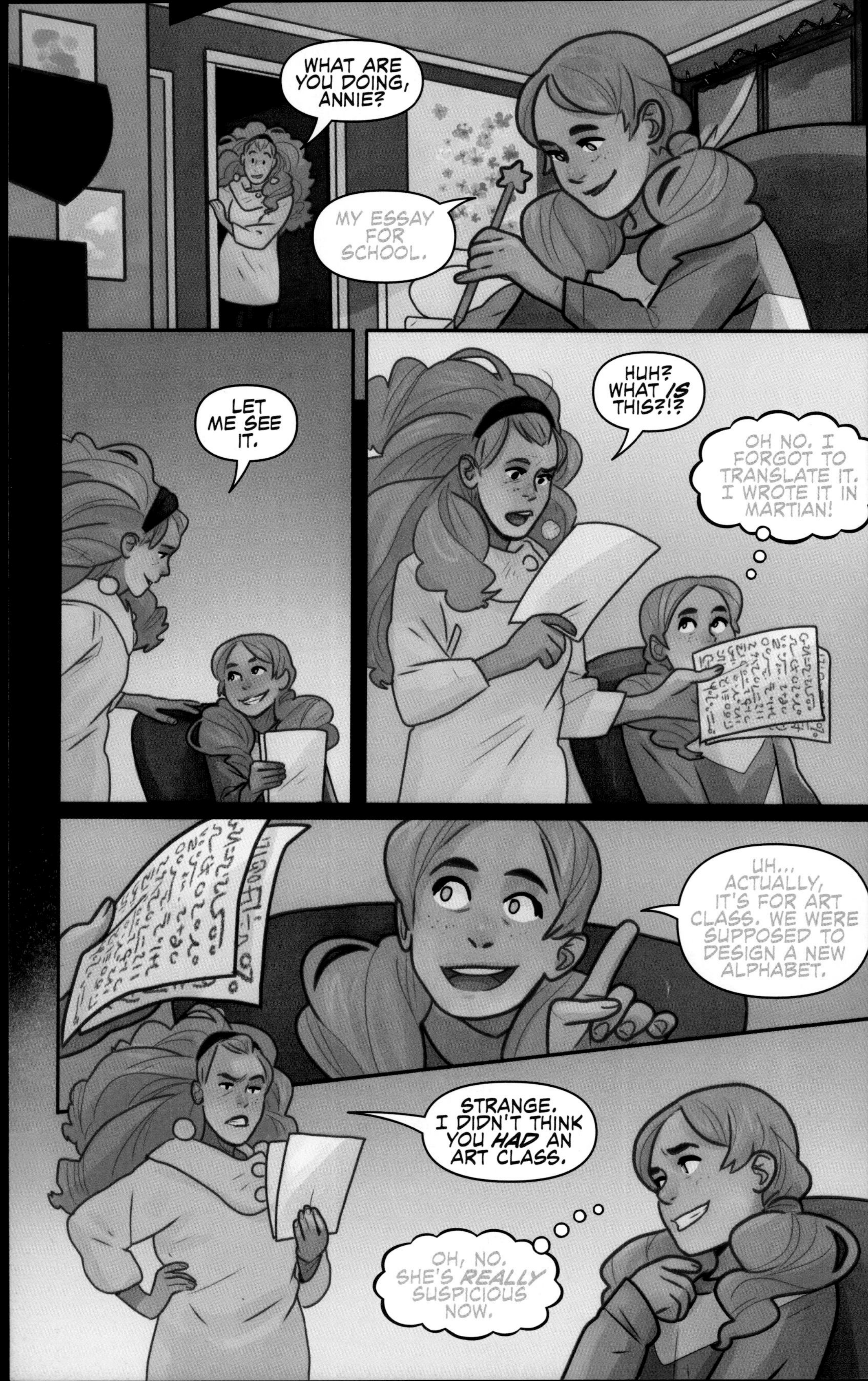
WHAT ARE YOU DOING, ANNIE?
MY ESSAY FOR SCHOOL.
LET ME SEE IT.
HUH? WHAT *IS* THIS?!?
OH NO. I FORGOT TO TRANSLATE IT. I WROTE IT IN MARTIAN!
UH... ACTUALLY, IT'S FOR ART CLASS. WE WERE SUPPOSED TO DESIGN A NEW ALPHABET.
STRANGE. I DIDN'T THINK YOU *HAD* AN ART CLASS.
OH, NO. SHE'S *REALLY* SUSPICIOUS NOW.

CHAPTER NINE
LET'S TEAR DAVID IN HALF

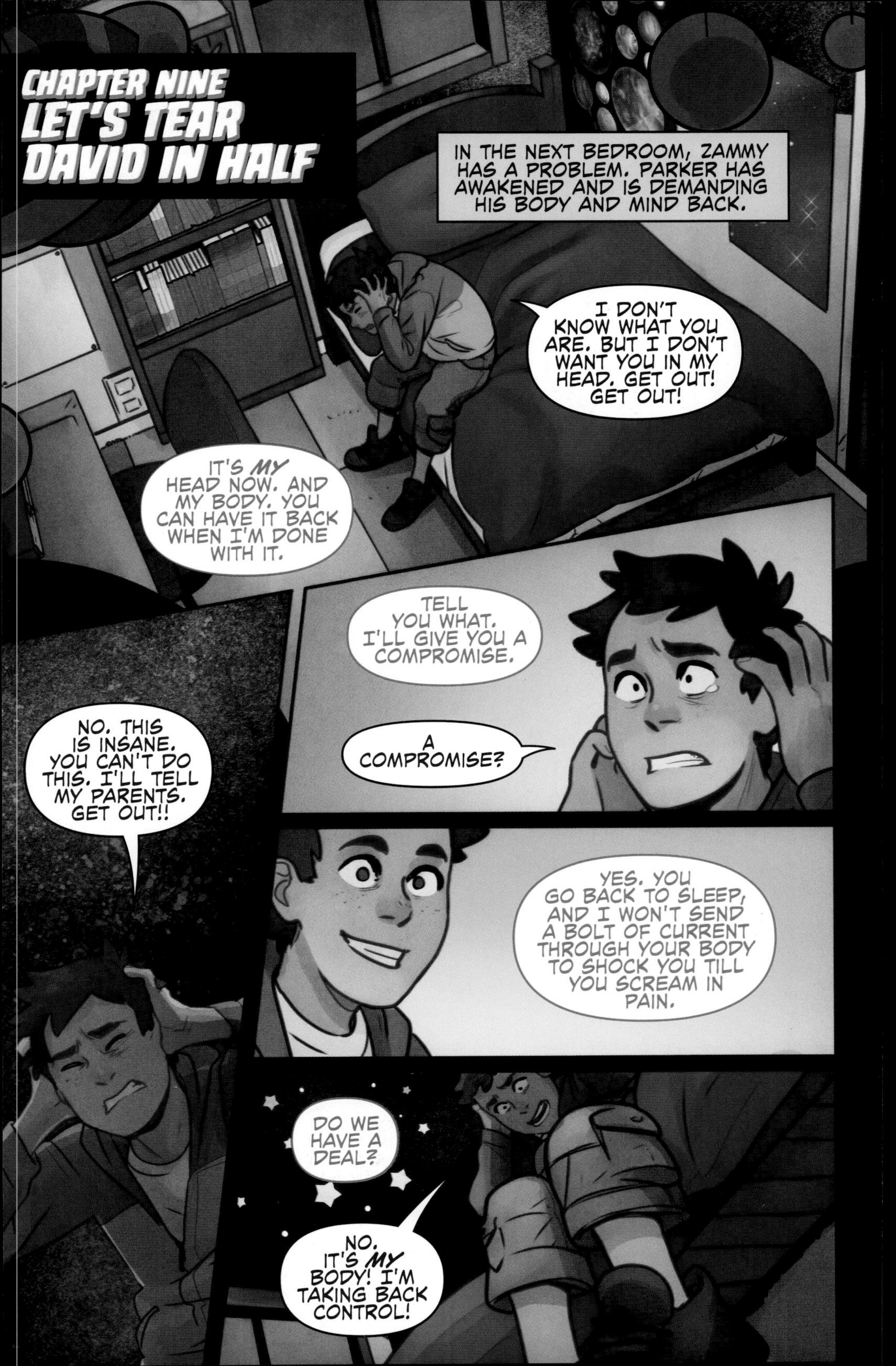
IN THE NEXT BEDROOM, ZAMMY HAS A PROBLEM. PARKER HAS AWAKENED AND IS DEMANDING HIS BODY AND MIND BACK.
I DON'T KNOW WHAT YOU ARE. BUT I DON'T WANT YOU IN MY HEAD. GET OUT! GET OUT!
IT'S *MY* HEAD NOW. AND MY BODY. YOU CAN HAVE IT BACK WHEN I'M DONE WITH IT.
TELL YOU WHAT. I'LL GIVE YOU A COMPROMISE.
A COMPROMISE?
NO. THIS IS INSANE. YOU CAN'T DO THIS. I'LL TELL MY PARENTS. GET OUT!!
YES. YOU GO BACK TO SLEEP, AND I WON'T SEND A BOLT OF CURRENT THROUGH YOUR BODY TO SHOCK YOU TILL YOU SCREAM IN PAIN.
DO WE HAVE A DEAL?
NO. IT'S *MY* BODY! I'M TAKING BACK CONTROL!

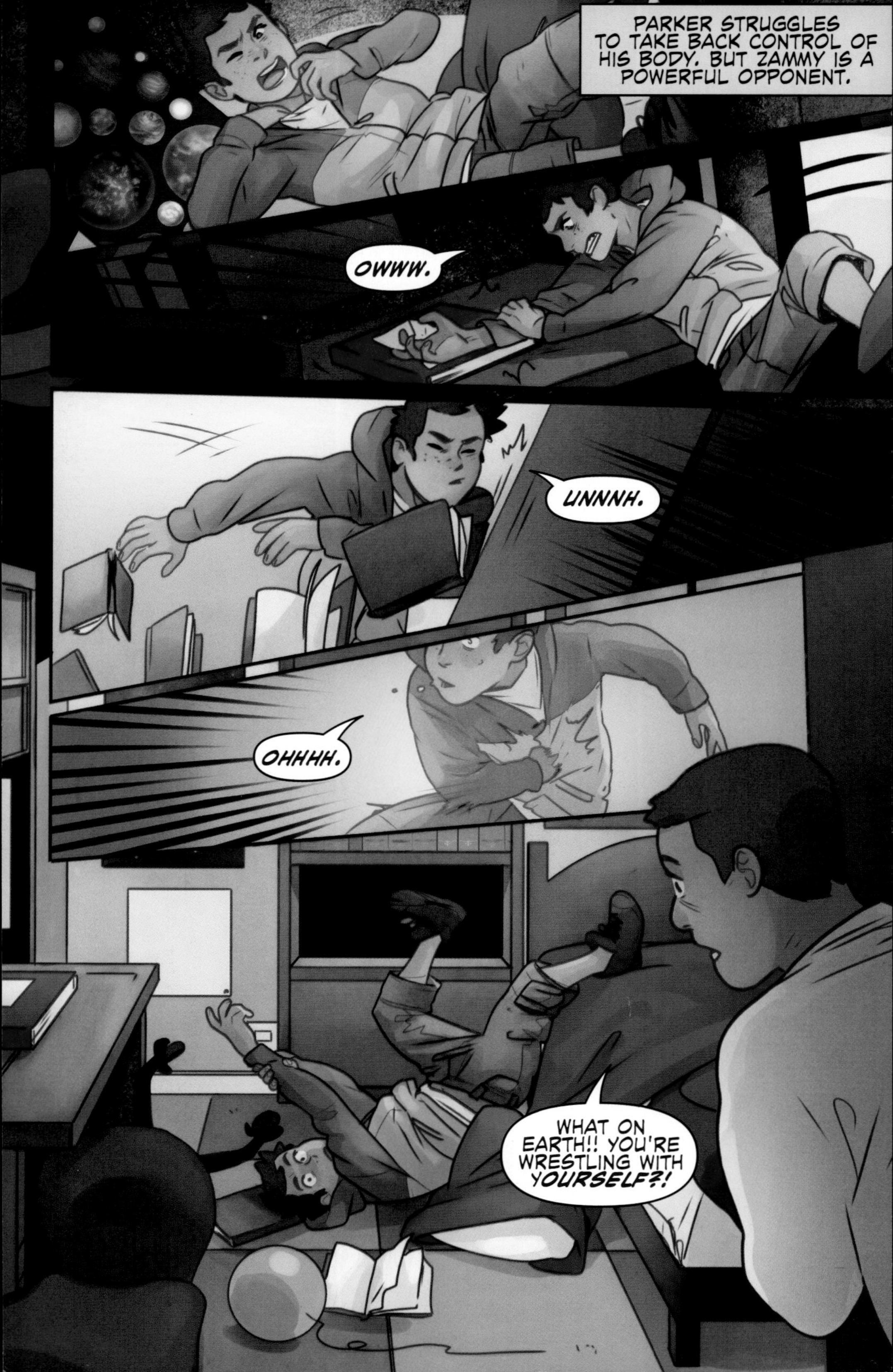
PARKER STRUGGLES TO TAKE BACK CONTROL OF HIS BODY. BUT ZAMMY IS A POWERFUL OPPONENT.
OWWW.
UNNNH.
OHHHH.
WHAT ON EARTH!! YOU'RE WRESTLING WITH *YOURSELF*?!

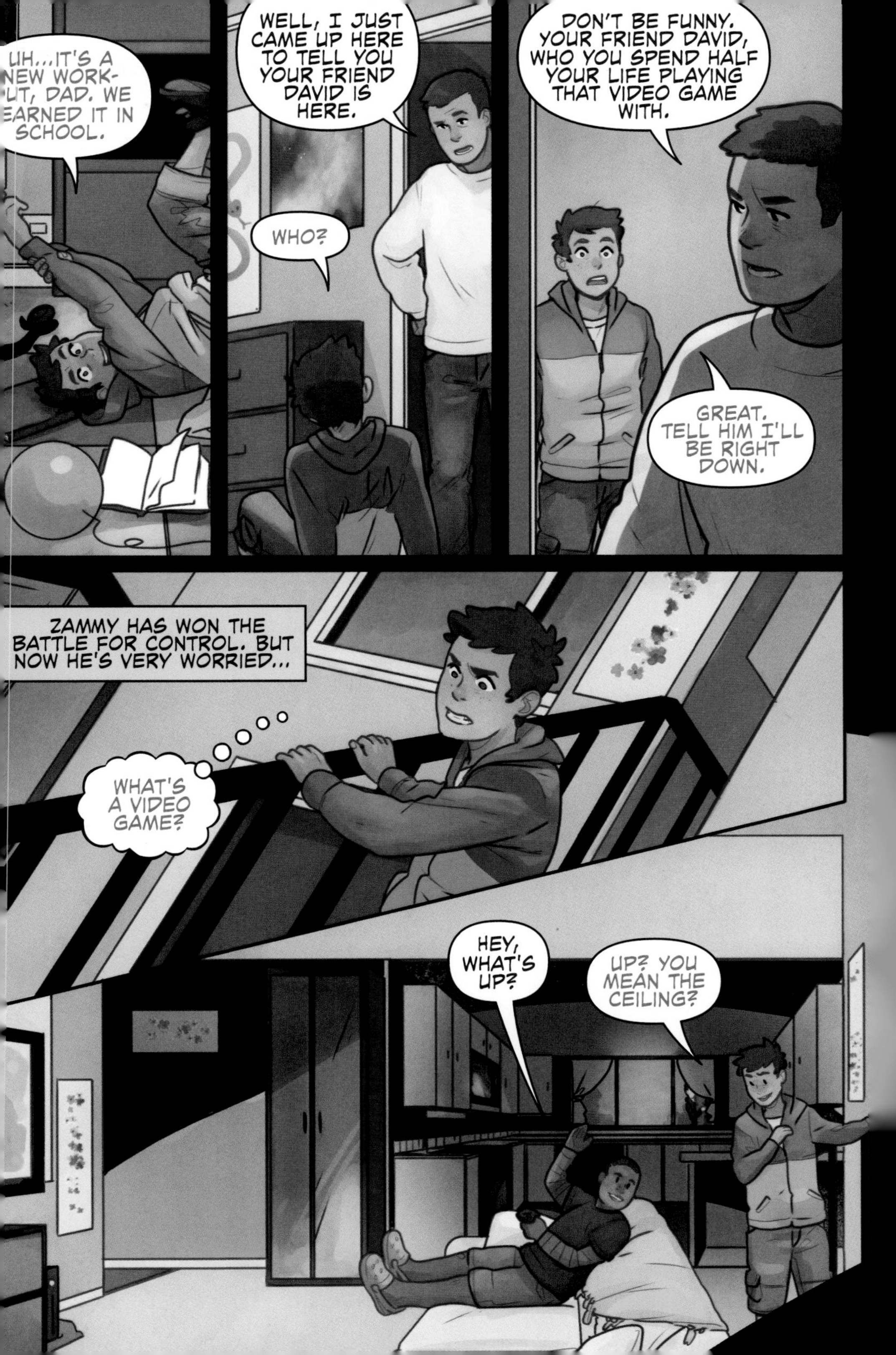
UH...IT'S A NEW WORK-UT, DAD. WE EARNED IT IN SCHOOL.
WELL, I JUST CAME UP HERE TO TELL YOU YOUR FRIEND DAVID IS HERE.
WHO?
DON'T BE FUNNY. YOUR FRIEND DAVID, WHO YOU SPEND HALF YOUR LIFE PLAYING THAT VIDEO GAME WITH.
GREAT. TELL HIM I'LL BE RIGHT DOWN.
ZAMMY HAS WON THE BATTLE FOR CONTROL. BUT NOW HE'S VERY WORRIED...
WHAT'S A VIDEO GAME?
HEY, WHAT'S UP?
UP? YOU MEAN THE CEILING?

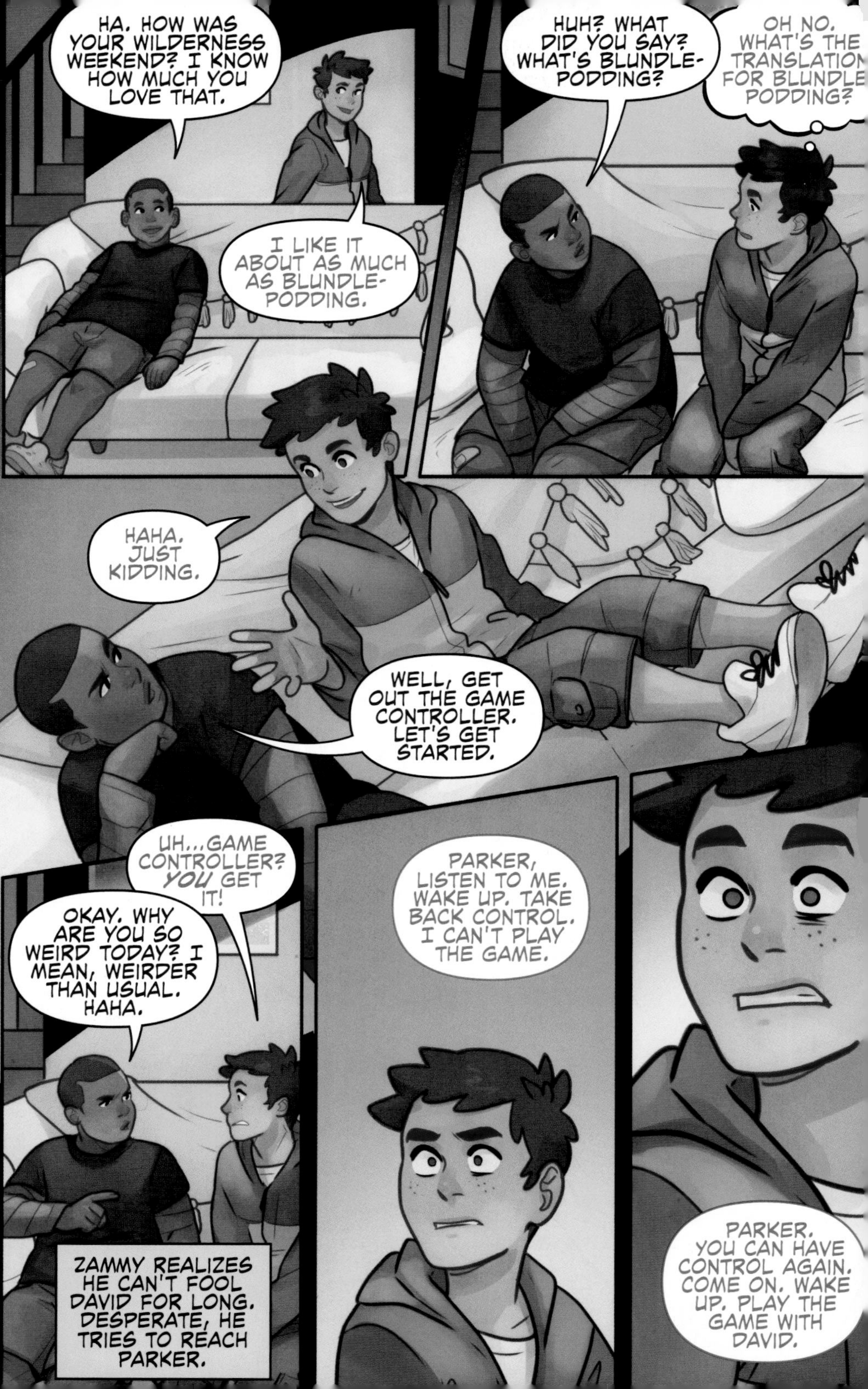
HA. HOW WAS YOUR WILDERNESS WEEKEND? I KNOW HOW MUCH YOU LOVE THAT.
I LIKE IT ABOUT AS MUCH AS BLUNDLE-PODDING.
HUH? WHAT DID YOU SAY? WHAT'S BLUNDLE-PODDING?
OH NO. WHAT'S THE TRANSLATION FOR BLUNDLE PODDING?
HAHA. JUST KIDDING.
WELL, GET OUT THE GAME CONTROLLER. LET'S GET STARTED.
UH...GAME CONTROLLER? YOU GET IT!
OKAY. WHY ARE YOU SO WEIRD TODAY? I MEAN, WEIRDER THAN USUAL. HAHA.
ZAMMY REALIZES HE CAN'T FOOL DAVID FOR LONG. DESPERATE, HE TRIES TO REACH PARKER.
PARKER, LISTEN TO ME. WAKE UP. TAKE BACK CONTROL. I CAN'T PLAY THE GAME.
PARKER. YOU CAN HAVE CONTROL AGAIN. COME ON. WAKE UP. PLAY THE GAME WITH DAVID.

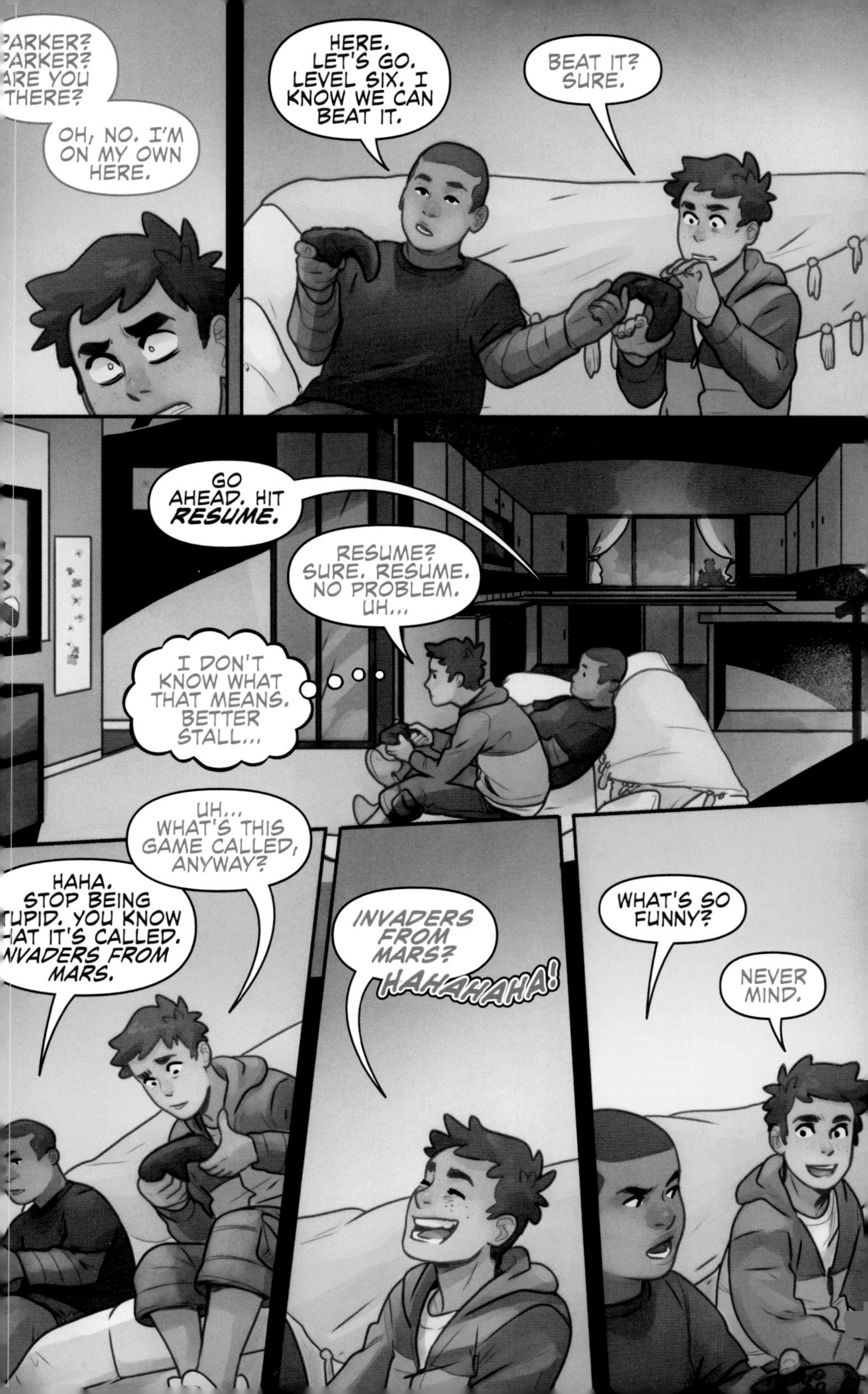

PARKER? PARKER? ARE YOU THERE?
OH, NO. I'M ON MY OWN HERE.
HERE. LET'S GO. LEVEL SIX. I KNOW WE CAN BEAT IT.
BEAT IT? SURE.
GO AHEAD. HIT *RESUME.*
RESUME? SURE. RESUME. NO PROBLEM. UH...
I DON'T KNOW WHAT THAT MEANS. BETTER STALL...
UH... WHAT'S THIS GAME CALLED, ANYWAY?
HAHA. STOP BEING STUPID. YOU KNOW WHAT IT'S CALLED. INVADERS FROM MARS.
INVADERS FROM MARS?
HAHAHAHAHA!
WHAT'S SO FUNNY?
NEVER MIND.

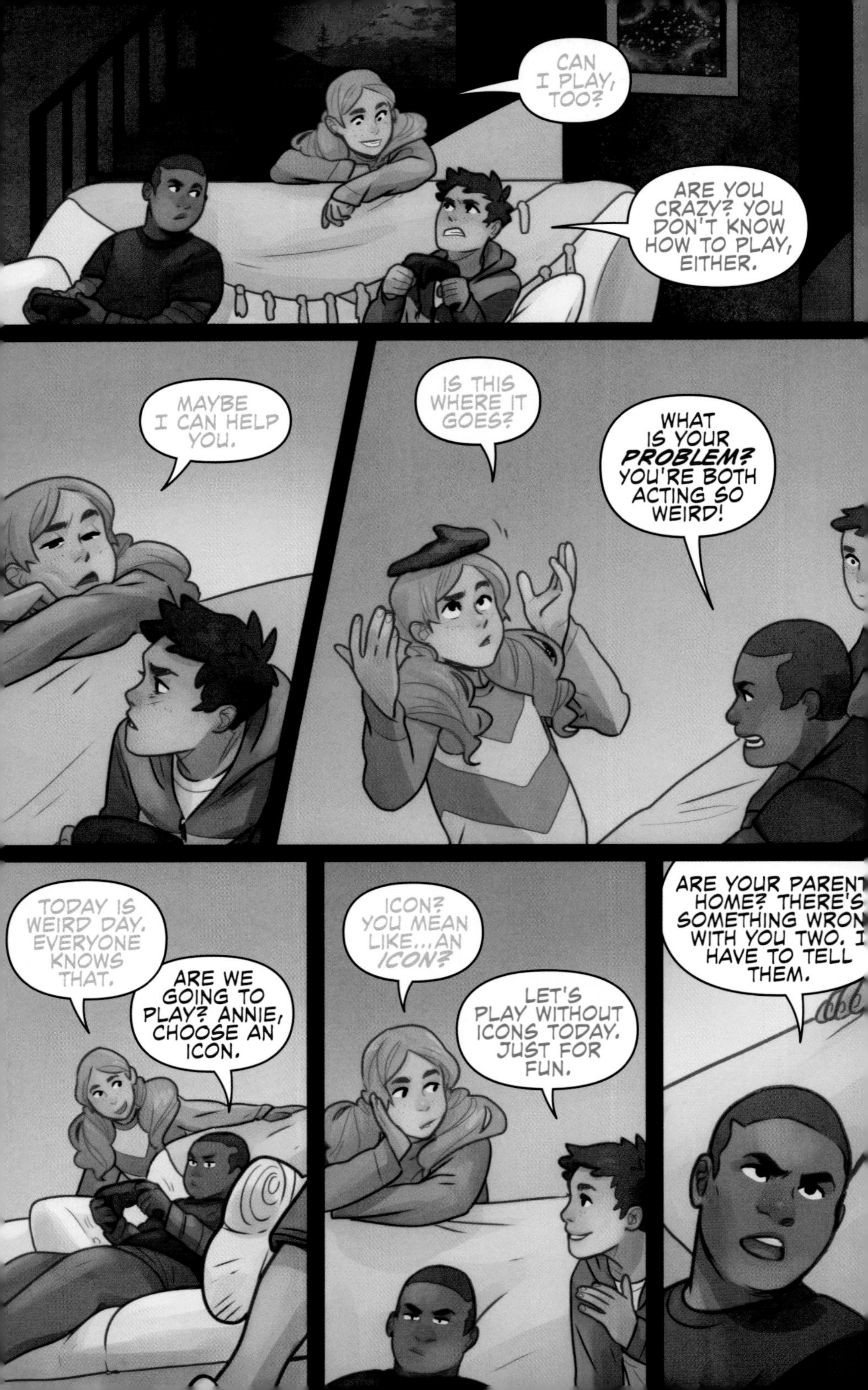

CAN I PLAY, TOO?
ARE YOU CRAZY? YOU DON'T KNOW HOW TO PLAY, EITHER.
MAYBE I CAN HELP YOU.
IS THIS WHERE IT GOES?
WHAT IS YOUR PROBLEM? YOU'RE BOTH ACTING SO WEIRD!
TODAY IS WEIRD DAY. EVERYONE KNOWS THAT.
ARE WE GOING TO PLAY? ANNIE, CHOOSE AN ICON.
ICON? YOU MEAN LIKE...AN ICON?
LET'S PLAY WITHOUT ICONS TODAY. JUST FOR FUN.
ARE YOUR PARENT HOME? THERE'S SOMETHING WRON WITH YOU TWO. I HAVE TO TELL THEM.

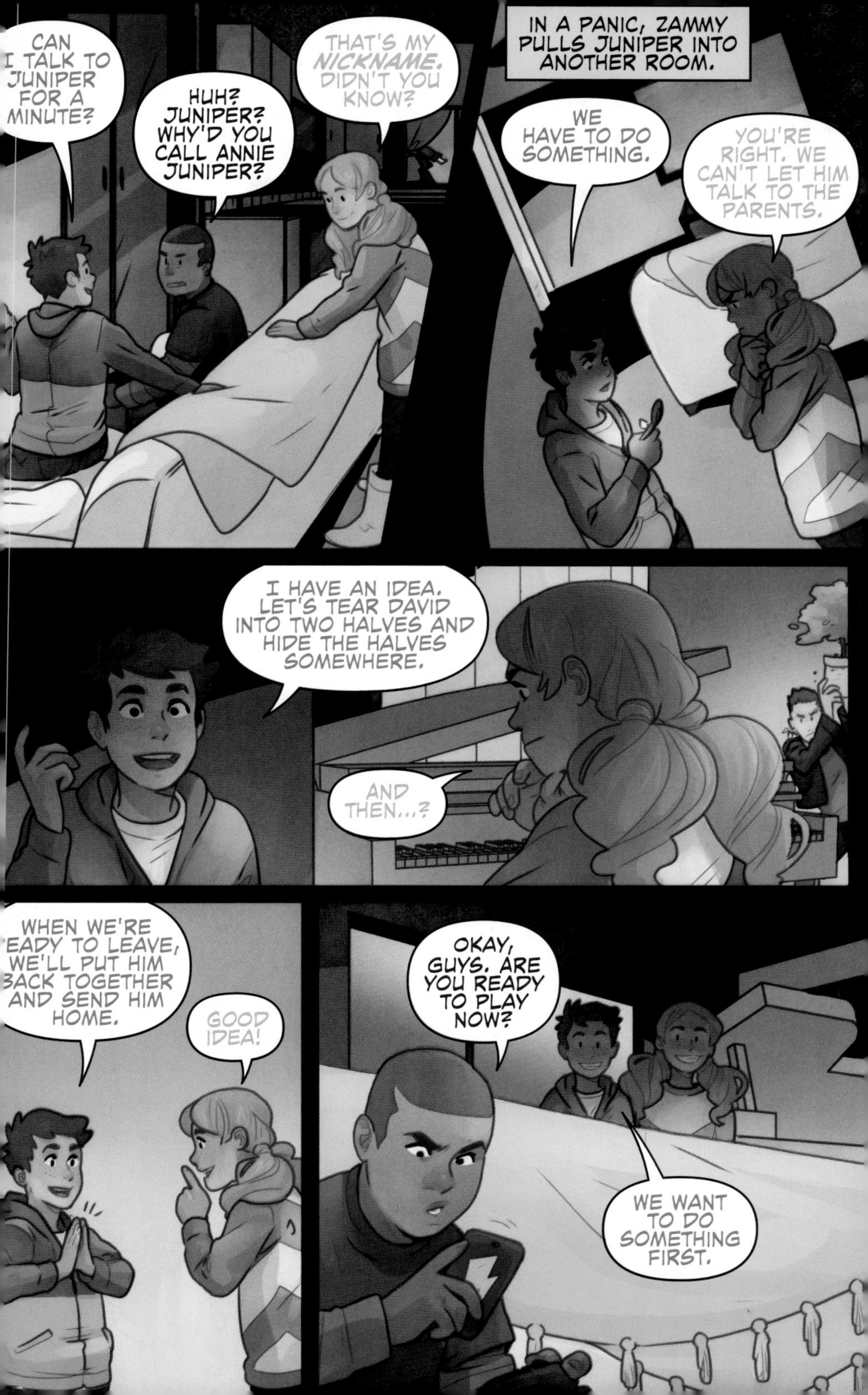
CAN I TALK TO JUNIPER FOR A MINUTE?
HUH? JUNIPER? WHY'D YOU CALL ANNIE JUNIPER?
THAT'S MY *NICKNAME*. DIDN'T YOU KNOW?
IN A PANIC, ZAMMY PULLS JUNIPER INTO ANOTHER ROOM.
WE HAVE TO DO SOMETHING.
YOU'RE RIGHT. WE CAN'T LET HIM TALK TO THE PARENTS.
I HAVE AN IDEA. LET'S TEAR DAVID INTO TWO HALVES AND HIDE THE HALVES SOMEWHERE.
AND THEN...?
WHEN WE'RE READY TO LEAVE, WE'LL PUT HIM BACK TOGETHER AND SEND HIM HOME.
GOOD IDEA!
OKAY, GUYS. ARE YOU READY TO PLAY NOW?
WE WANT TO DO SOMETHING FIRST.

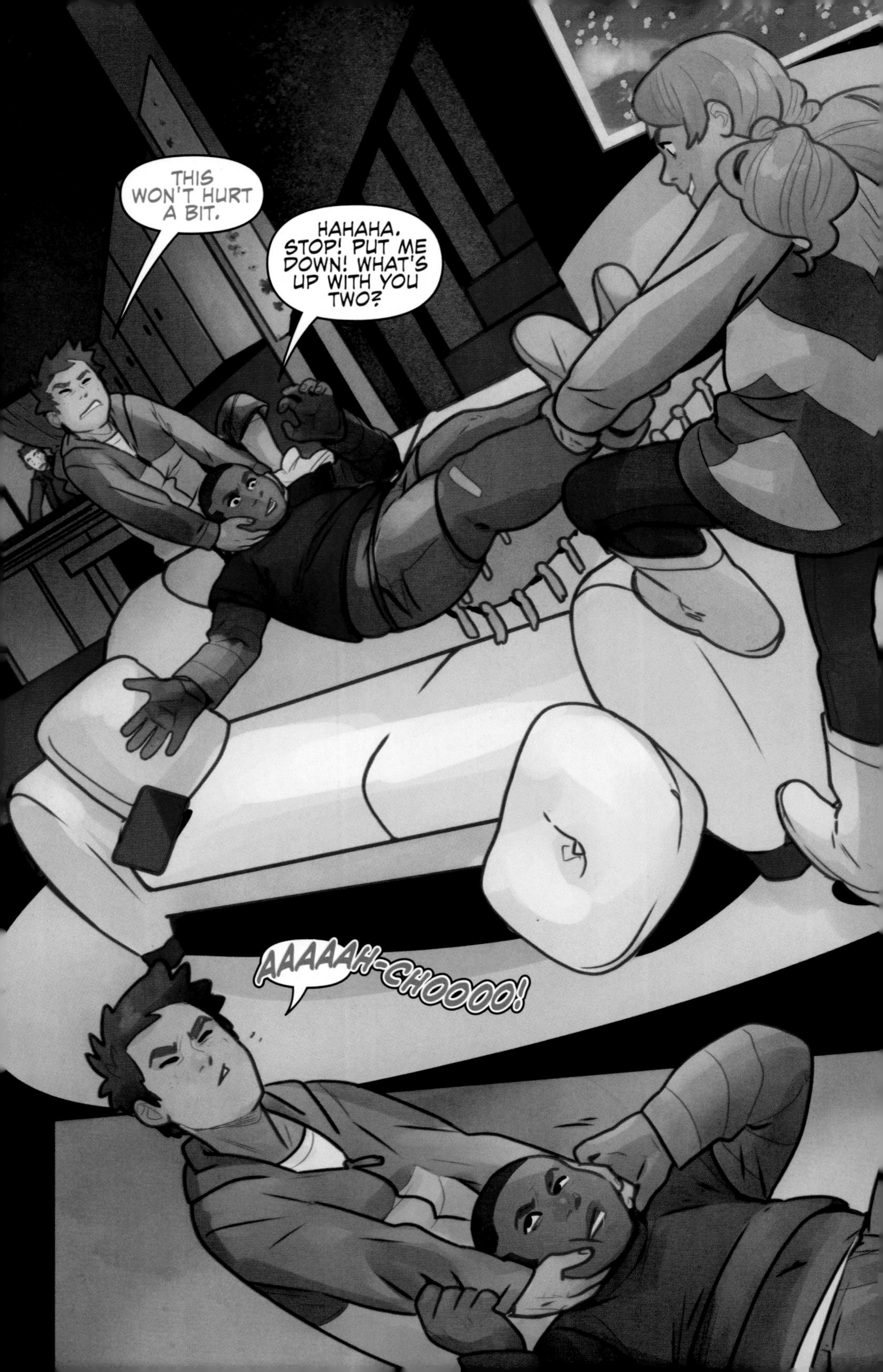
THIS WON'T HURT A BIT.
HAHAHA. STOP! PUT ME DOWN! WHAT'S UP WITH YOU TWO?
AAAAAH-CHOOOOO!

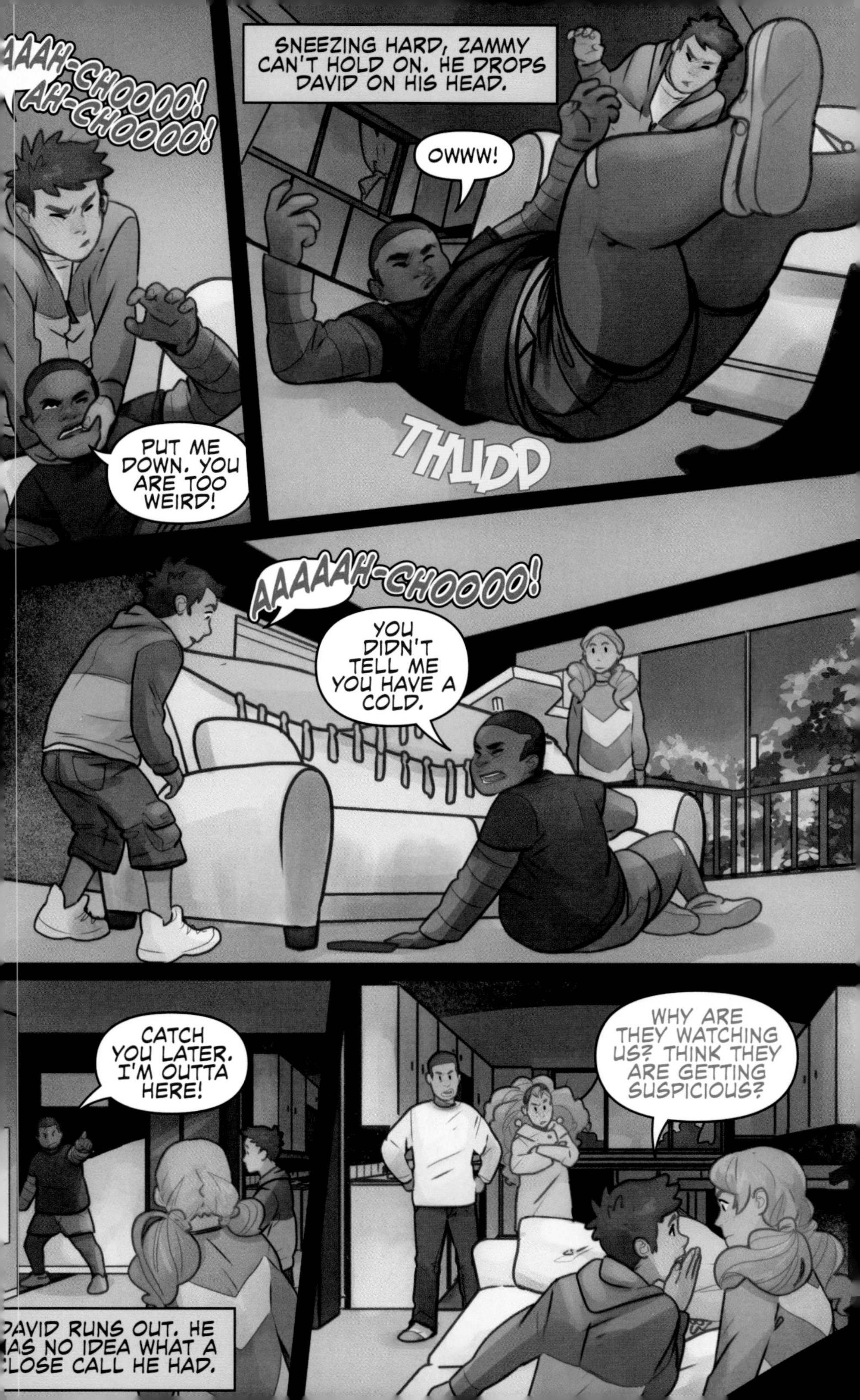
AAAAH-CHOOOOO!
AH-CHOOOOO!
PUT ME DOWN. YOU ARE TOO WEIRD!
SNEEZING HARD, ZAMMY CAN'T HOLD ON. HE DROPS DAVID ON HIS HEAD.
OWWW!
THUDD
AAAAAH-CHOOOOO!
YOU DIDN'T TELL ME YOU HAVE A COLD.
CATCH YOU LATER. I'M OUTTA HERE!
DAVID RUNS OUT. HE HAS NO IDEA WHAT A CLOSE CALL HE HAD.
WHY ARE THEY WATCHING US? THINK THEY ARE GETTING SUSPICIOUS?

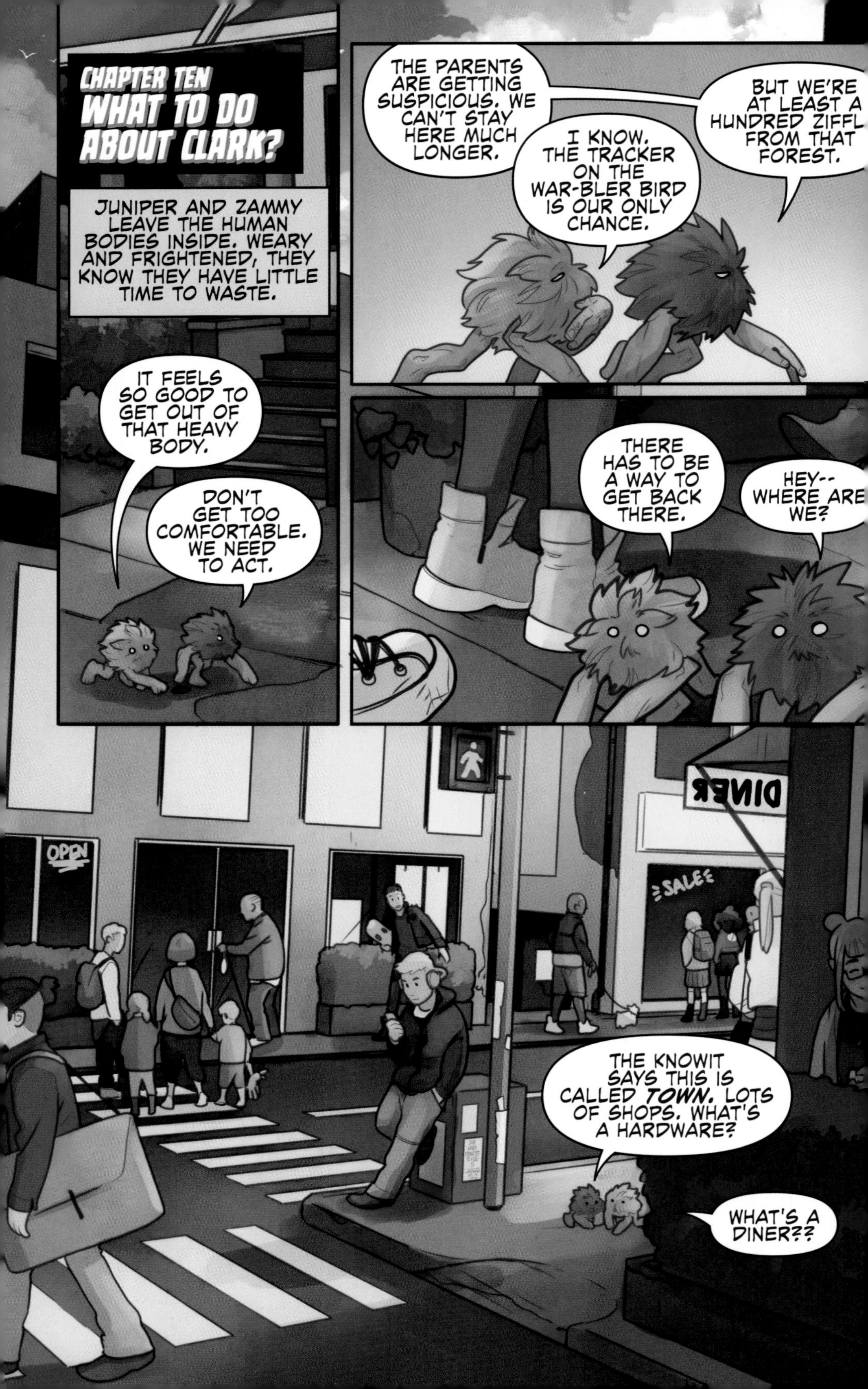
CHAPTER TEN
WHAT TO DO ABOUT CLARK?
JUNIPER AND ZAMMY LEAVE THE HUMAN BODIES INSIDE. WEARY AND FRIGHTENED, THEY KNOW THEY HAVE LITTLE TIME TO WASTE.
IT FEELS SO GOOD TO GET OUT OF THAT HEAVY BODY.
DON'T GET TOO COMFORTABLE. WE NEED TO ACT.
THE PARENTS ARE GETTING SUSPICIOUS. WE CAN'T STAY HERE MUCH LONGER.
I KNOW. THE TRACKER ON THE WAR-BLER BIRD IS OUR ONLY CHANCE.
BUT WE'RE AT LEAST A HUNDRED ZIFFL FROM THAT FOREST.
THERE HAS TO BE A WAY TO GET BACK THERE.
HEY-- WHERE ARE WE?
OPEN
DINER
SALE
THE KNOWIT SAYS THIS IS CALLED TOWN. LOTS OF SHOPS. WHAT'S A HARDWARE?
WHAT'S A DINER??

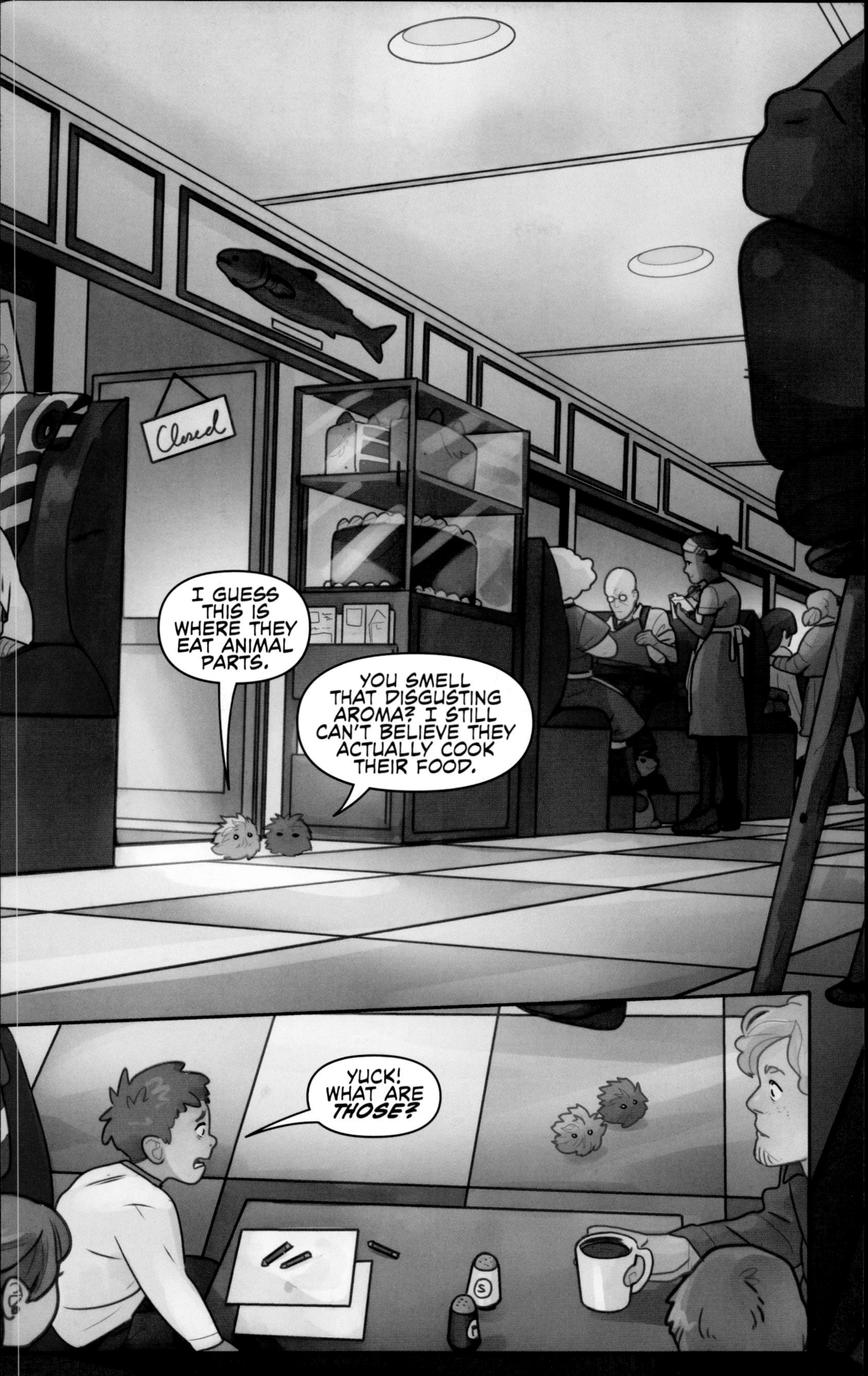
Closed
I GUESS THIS IS WHERE THEY EAT ANIMAL PARTS.
YOU SMELL THAT DISGUSTING AROMA? I STILL CAN'T BELIEVE THEY ACTUALLY COOK THEIR FOOD.
YUCK! WHAT ARE *THOSE?*

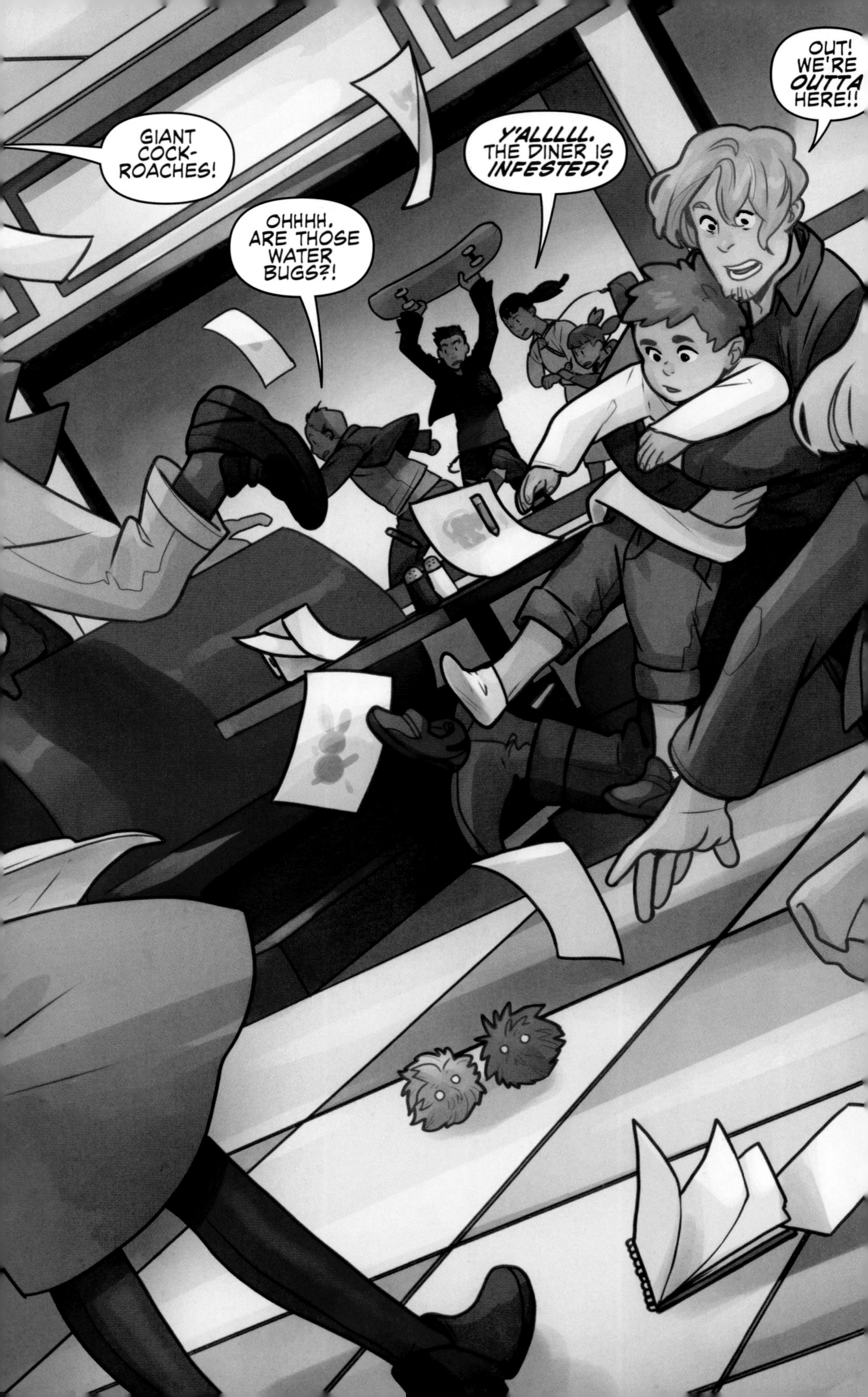
GIANT COCK-ROACHES!
OHHHH. ARE THOSE WATER BUGS?!
Y'ALLLLL. THE DINER IS *INFESTED!*
OUT! WE'RE *OUTTA* HERE!!

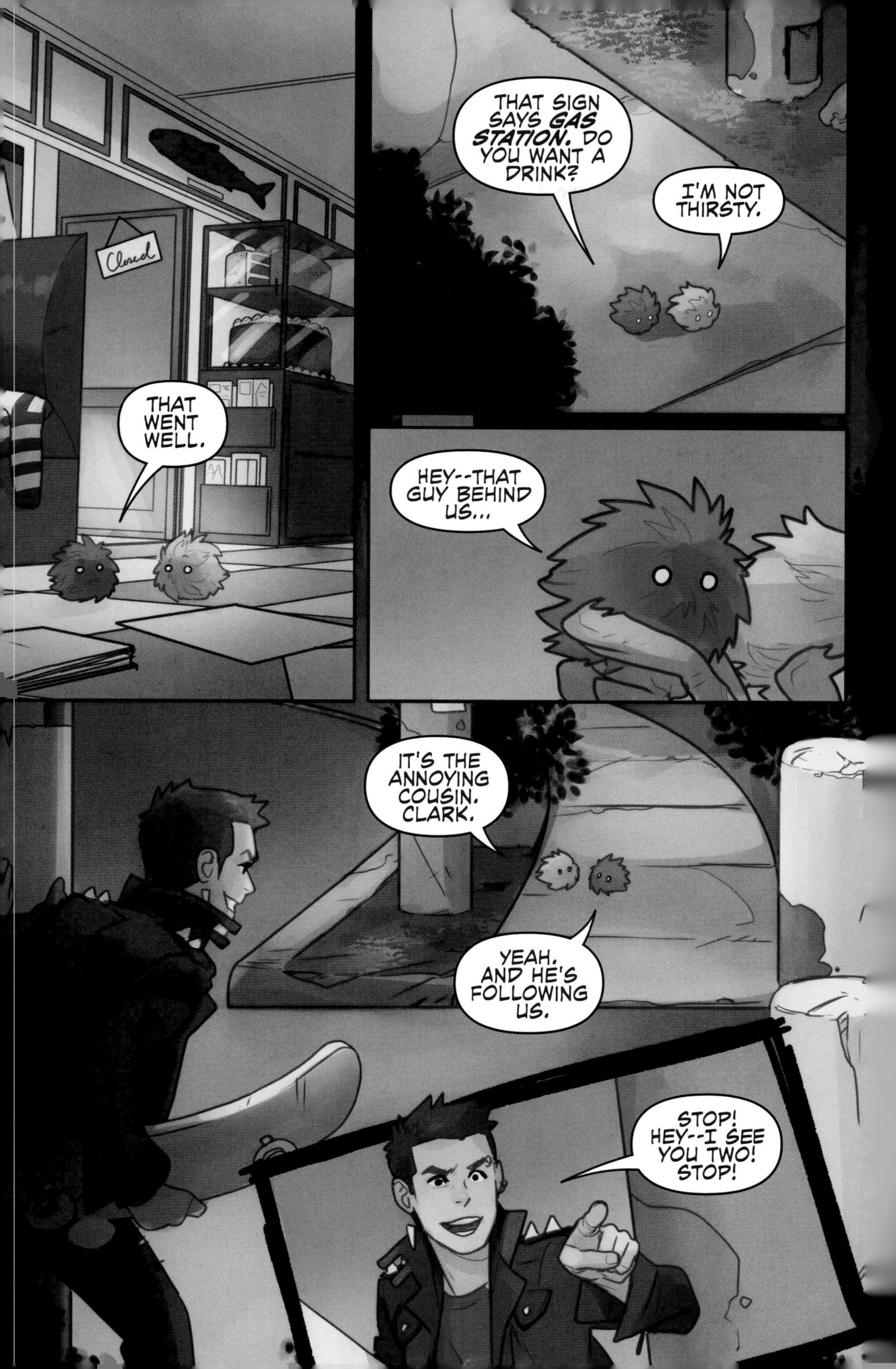
Closed
THAT WENT WELL.
THAT SIGN SAYS GAS STATION. DO YOU WANT A DRINK?
I'M NOT THIRSTY.
HEY--THAT GUY BEHIND US...
IT'S THE ANNOYING COUSIN. CLARK.
YEAH. AND HE'S FOLLOWING US.
STOP! HEY--I SEE YOU TWO! STOP!

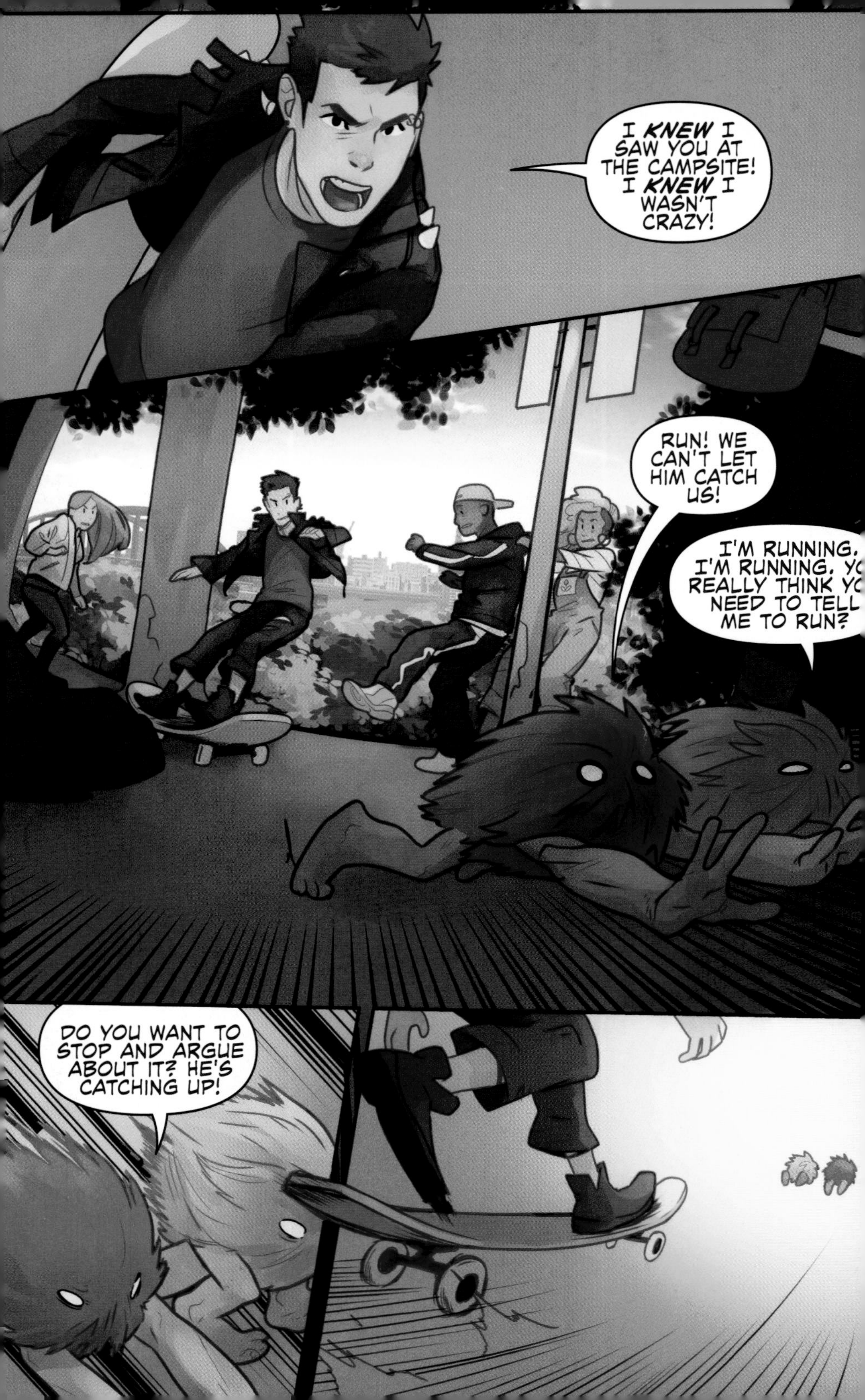
I KNEW I SAW YOU AT THE CAMPSITE! I KNEW I WASN'T CRAZY!
RUN! WE CAN'T LET HIM CATCH US!
I'M RUNNING. I'M RUNNING. YO REALLY THINK YO NEED TO TELL ME TO RUN?
DO YOU WANT TO STOP AND ARGUE ABOUT IT? HE'S CATCHING UP!

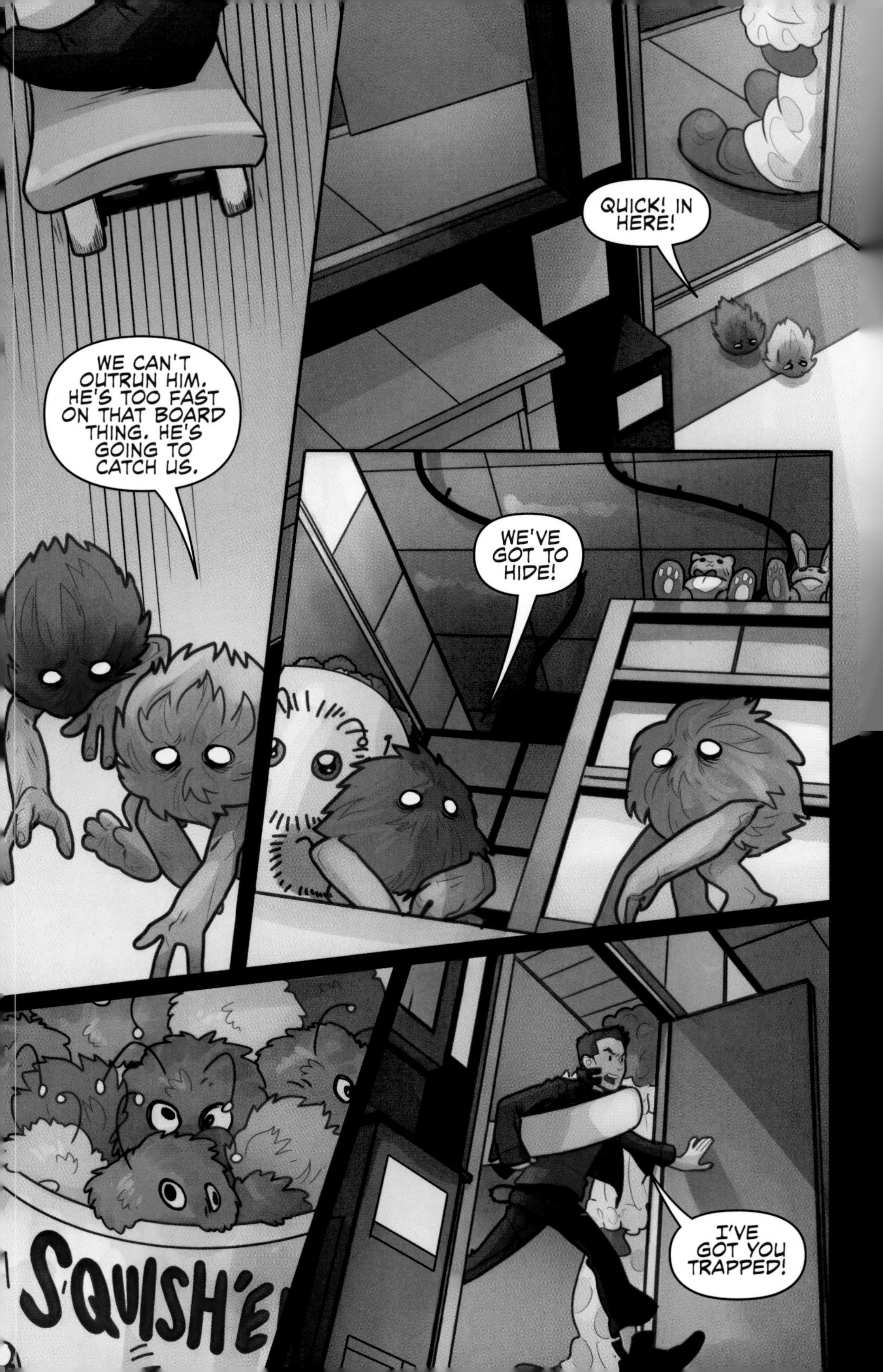
QUICK! IN HERE!
WE CAN'T OUTRUN HIM. HE'S TOO FAST ON THAT BOARD THING. HE'S GOING TO CATCH US.
WE'VE GOT TO HIDE!
SQUISH'E
I'VE GOT YOU TRAPPED!

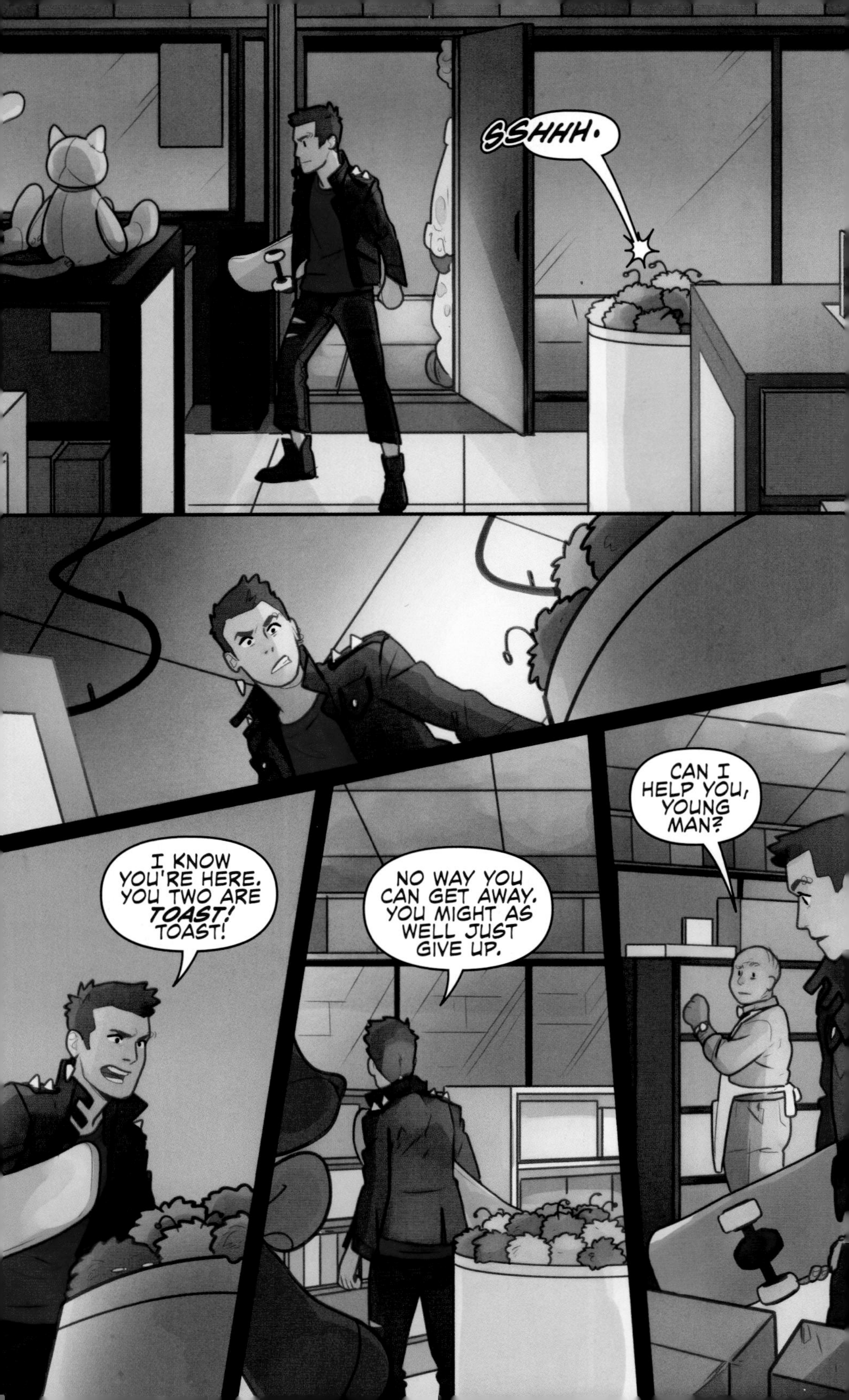
SSHHH.
I KNOW YOU'RE HERE. YOU TWO ARE TOAST! TOAST!
NO WAY YOU CAN GET AWAY. YOU MIGHT AS WELL JUST GIVE UP.
CAN I HELP YOU, YOUNG MAN?

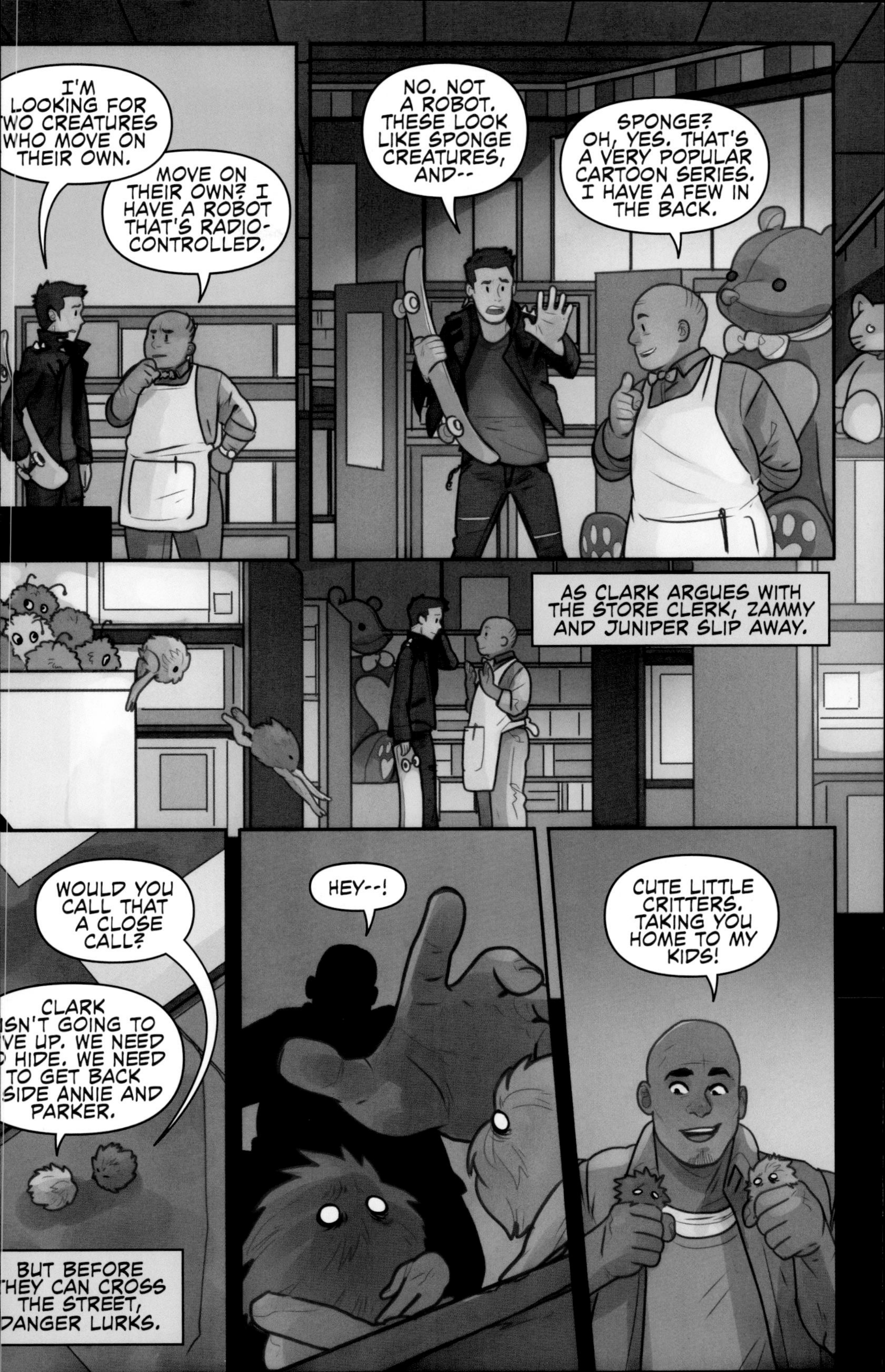
I'M LOOKING FOR TWO CREATURES WHO MOVE ON THEIR OWN.
MOVE ON THEIR OWN? I HAVE A ROBOT THAT'S RADIO-CONTROLLED.
NO, NOT A ROBOT. THESE LOOK LIKE SPONGE CREATURES, AND--
SPONGE? OH, YES. THAT'S A VERY POPULAR CARTOON SERIES. I HAVE A FEW IN THE BACK.
AS CLARK ARGUES WITH THE STORE CLERK, ZAMMY AND JUNIPER SLIP AWAY.
WOULD YOU CALL THAT A CLOSE CALL?
CLARK ISN'T GOING TO GIVE UP. WE NEED TO HIDE. WE NEED TO GET BACK INSIDE ANNIE AND PARKER.
BUT BEFORE THEY CAN CROSS THE STREET, DANGER LURKS.
HEY--!
CUTE LITTLE CRITTERS. TAKING YOU HOME TO MY KIDS!

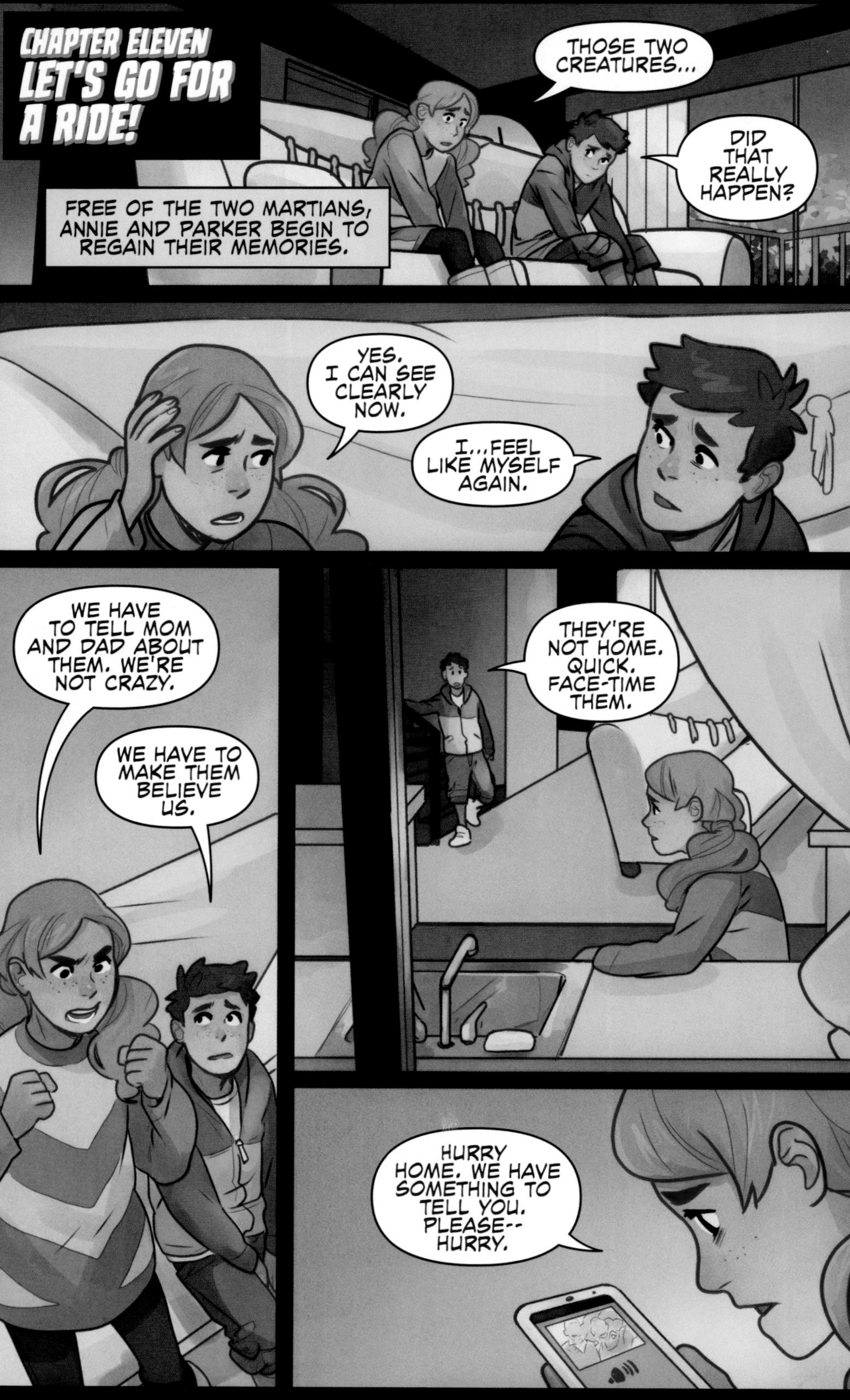
CHAPTER ELEVEN
LET'S GO FOR A RIDE!
THOSE TWO CREATURES...
DID THAT REALLY HAPPEN?
FREE OF THE TWO MARTIANS, ANNIE AND PARKER BEGIN TO REGAIN THEIR MEMORIES.
YES, I CAN SEE CLEARLY NOW.
I...FEEL LIKE MYSELF AGAIN.
WE HAVE TO TELL MOM AND DAD ABOUT THEM. WE'RE NOT CRAZY.
WE HAVE TO MAKE THEM BELIEVE US.
THEY'RE NOT HOME. QUICK. FACE-TIME THEM.
HURRY HOME. WE HAVE SOMETHING TO TELL YOU. PLEASE-- HURRY.

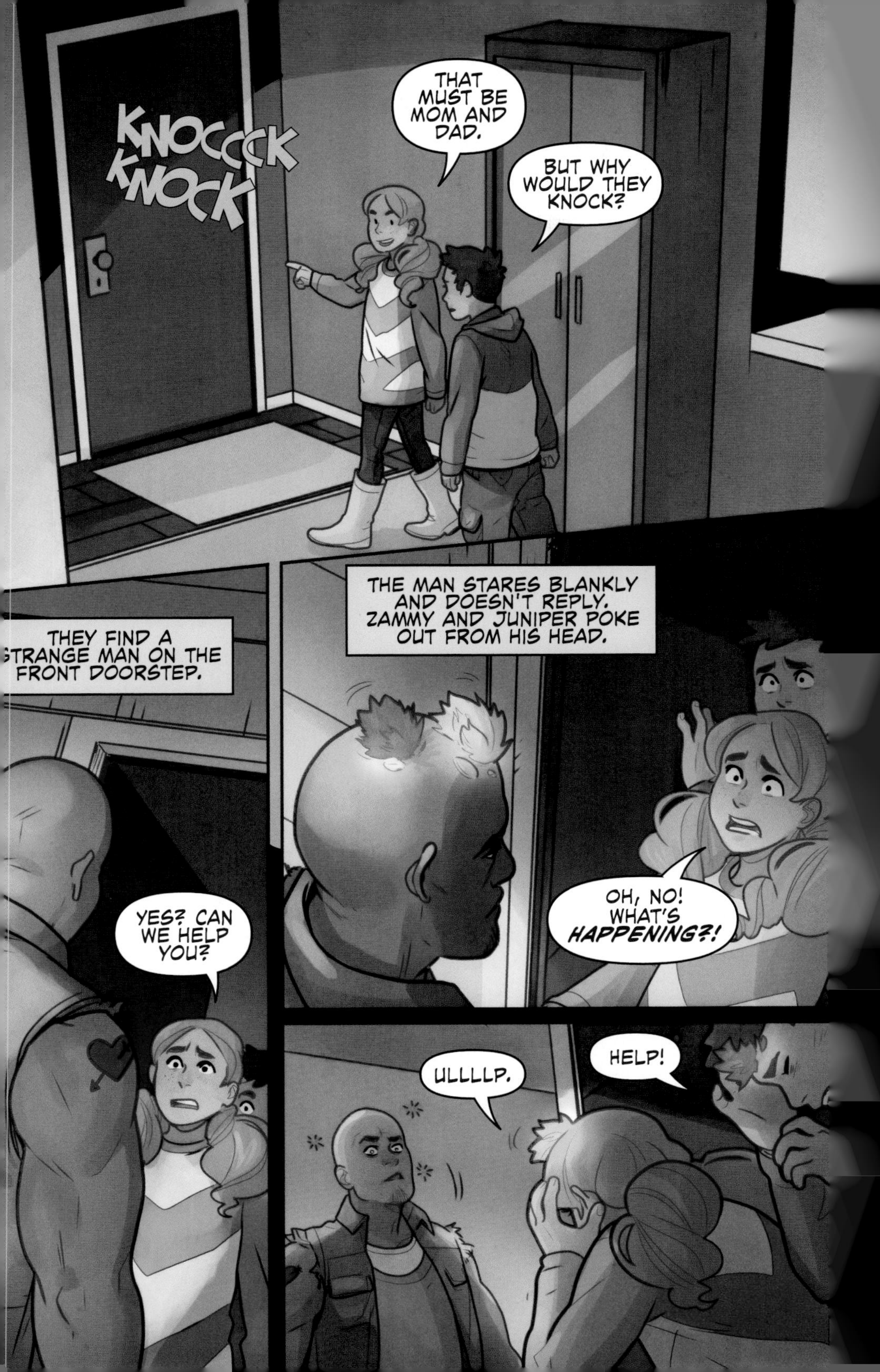
KNOCCCK KNOCK
THAT MUST BE MOM AND DAD.
BUT WHY WOULD THEY KNOCK?
THEY FIND A STRANGE MAN ON THE FRONT DOORSTEP.
YES? CAN WE HELP YOU?
THE MAN STARES BLANKLY AND DOESN'T REPLY. ZAMMY AND JUNIPER POKE OUT FROM HIS HEAD.
OH, NO! WHAT'S *HAPPENING?!*
ULLLLP.
HELP!

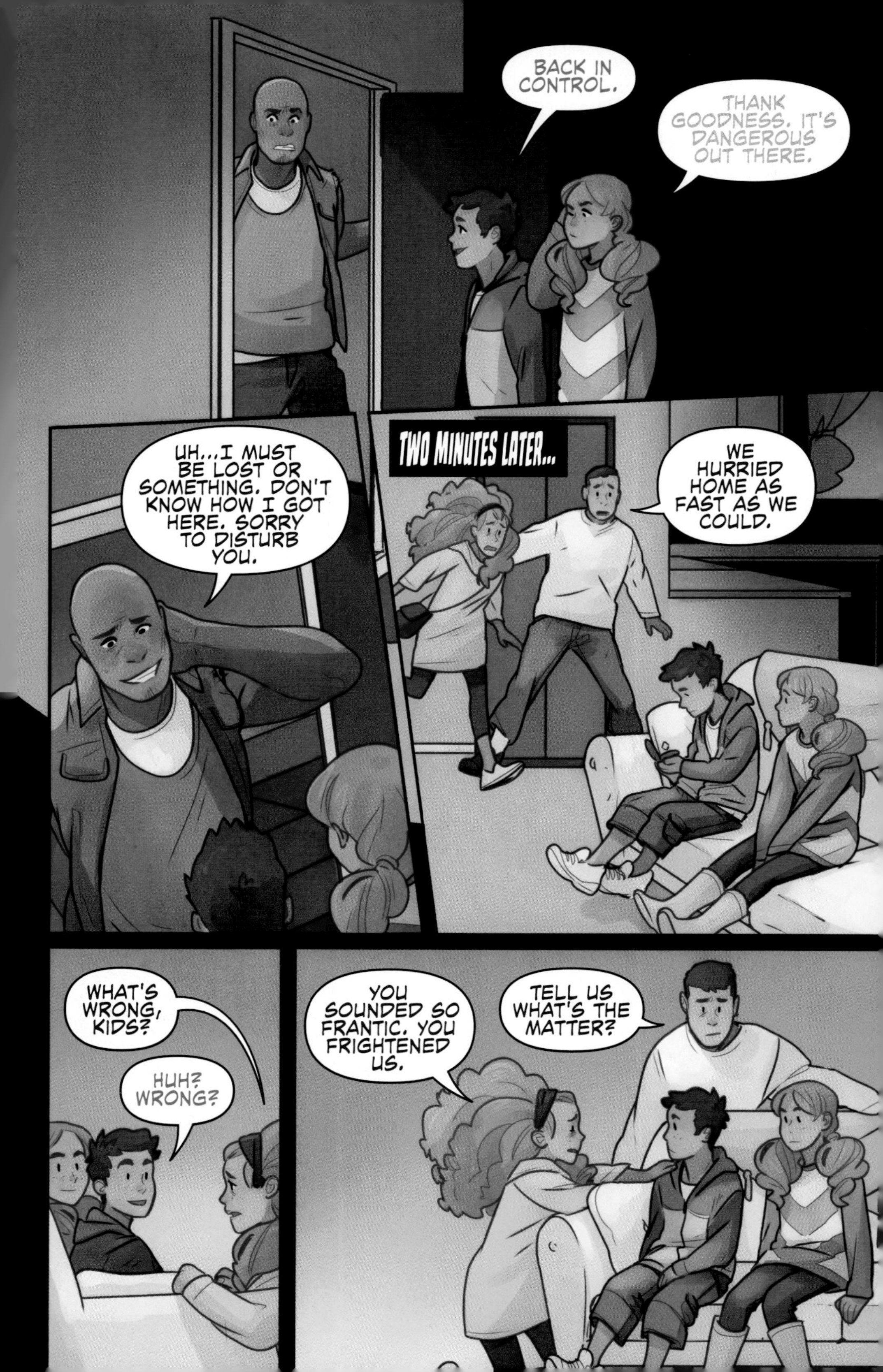
BACK IN CONTROL.
THANK GOODNESS. IT'S DANGEROUS OUT THERE.
UH...I MUST BE LOST OR SOMETHING. DON'T KNOW HOW I GOT HERE. SORRY TO DISTURB YOU.
TWO MINUTES LATER...
WE HURRIED HOME AS FAST AS WE COULD.
WHAT'S WRONG, KIDS?
HUH? WRONG?
YOU SOUNDED SO FRANTIC. YOU FRIGHTENED US.
TELL US WHAT'S THE MATTER?

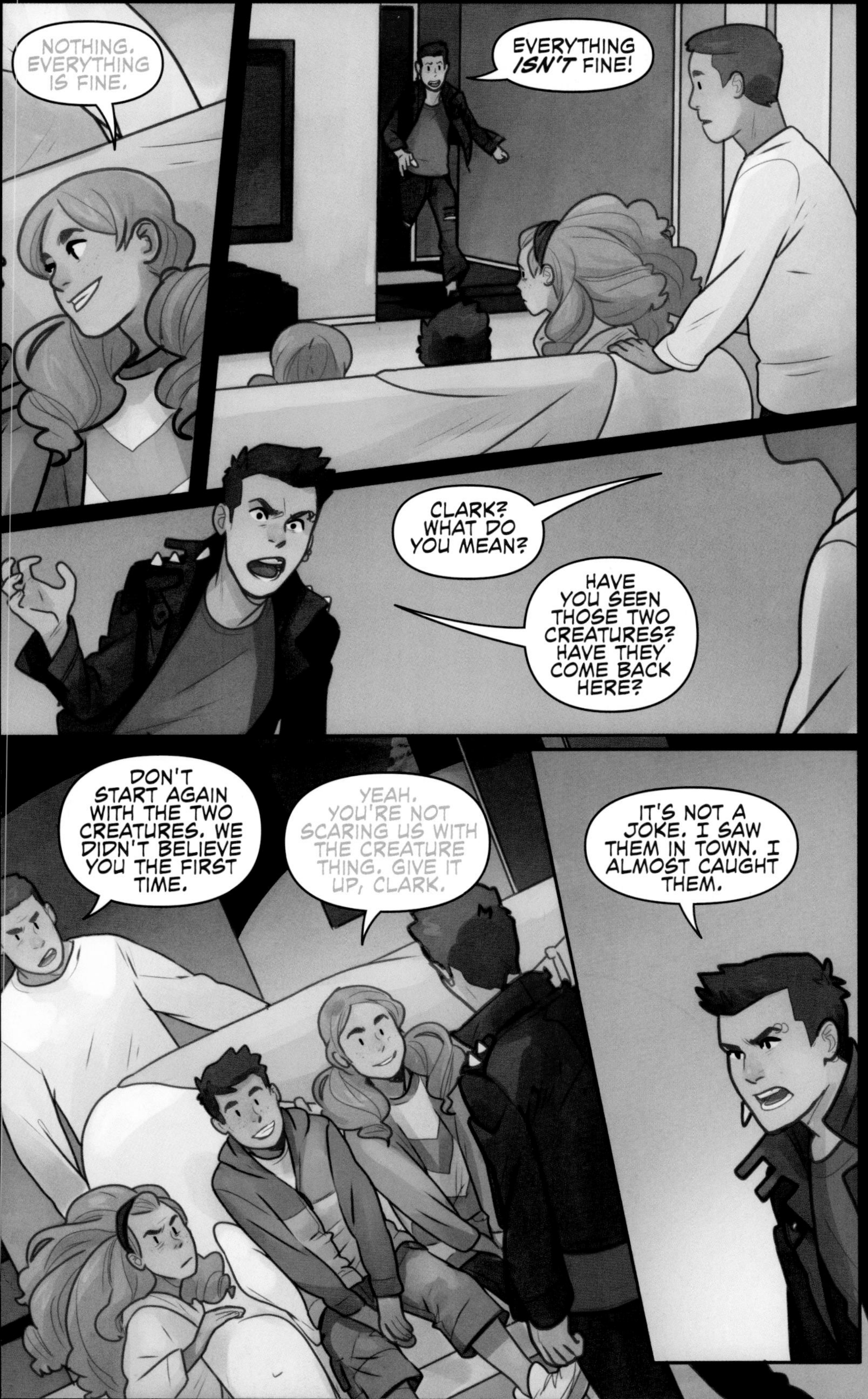
NOTHING. EVERYTHING IS FINE.
EVERYTHING *ISN'T* FINE!
CLARK? WHAT DO YOU MEAN?
HAVE YOU SEEN THOSE TWO CREATURES? HAVE THEY COME BACK HERE?
DON'T START AGAIN WITH THE TWO CREATURES. WE DIDN'T BELIEVE YOU THE FIRST TIME.
YEAH. YOU'RE NOT SCARING US WITH THE CREATURE THING. GIVE IT UP, CLARK.
IT'S NOT A JOKE. I SAW THEM IN TOWN. I ALMOST CAUGHT THEM.

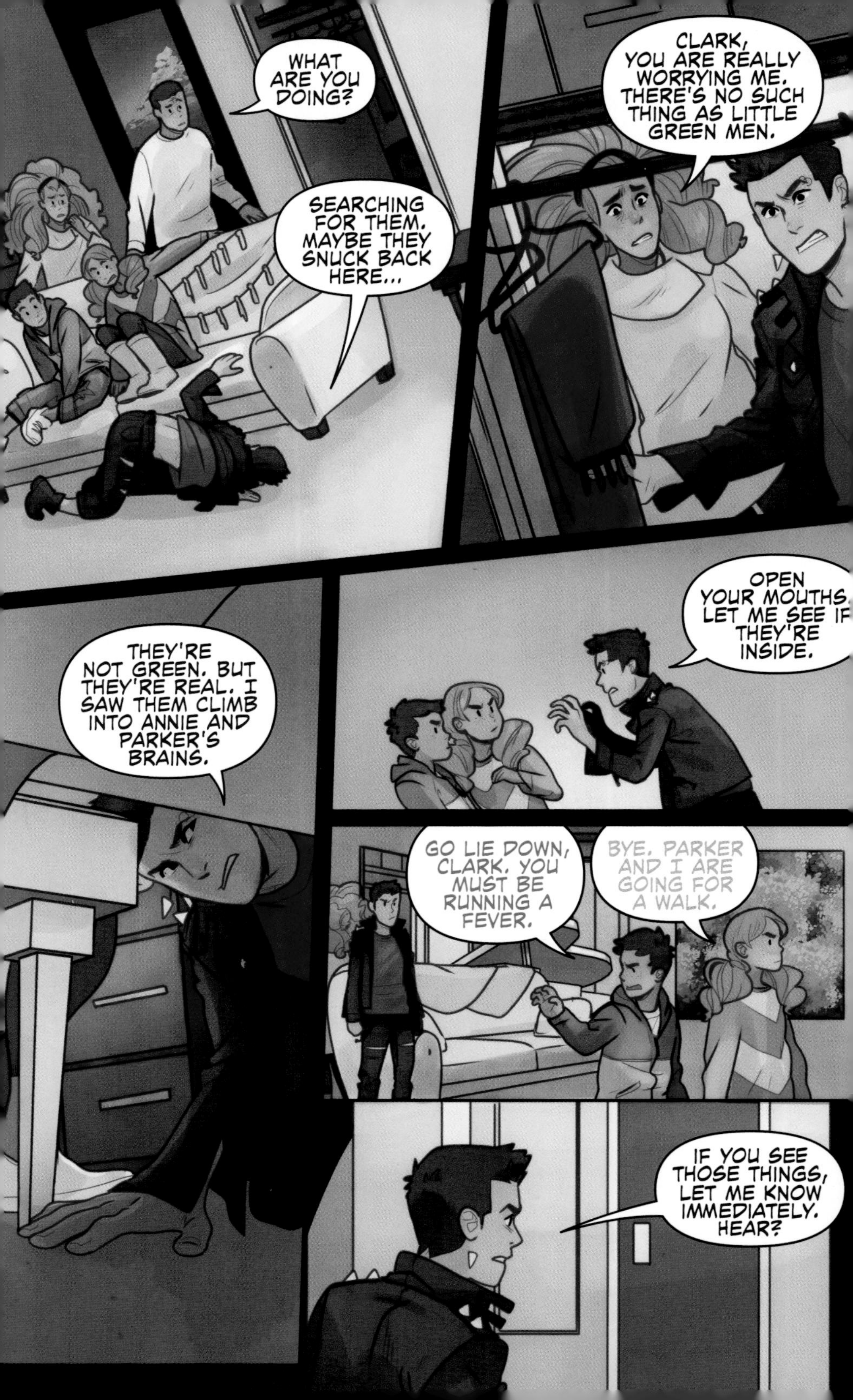
WHAT ARE YOU DOING?
SEARCHING FOR THEM. MAYBE THEY SNUCK BACK HERE...
CLARK, YOU ARE REALLY WORRYING ME. THERE'S NO SUCH THING AS LITTLE GREEN MEN.
THEY'RE NOT GREEN. BUT THEY'RE REAL. I SAW THEM CLIMB INTO ANNIE AND PARKER'S BRAINS.
OPEN YOUR MOUTHS. LET ME SEE IF THEY'RE INSIDE.
GO LIE DOWN, CLARK. YOU MUST BE RUNNING A FEVER.
BYE. PARKER AND I ARE GOING FOR A WALK.
IF YOU SEE THOSE THINGS, LET ME KNOW IMMEDIATELY. HEAR?

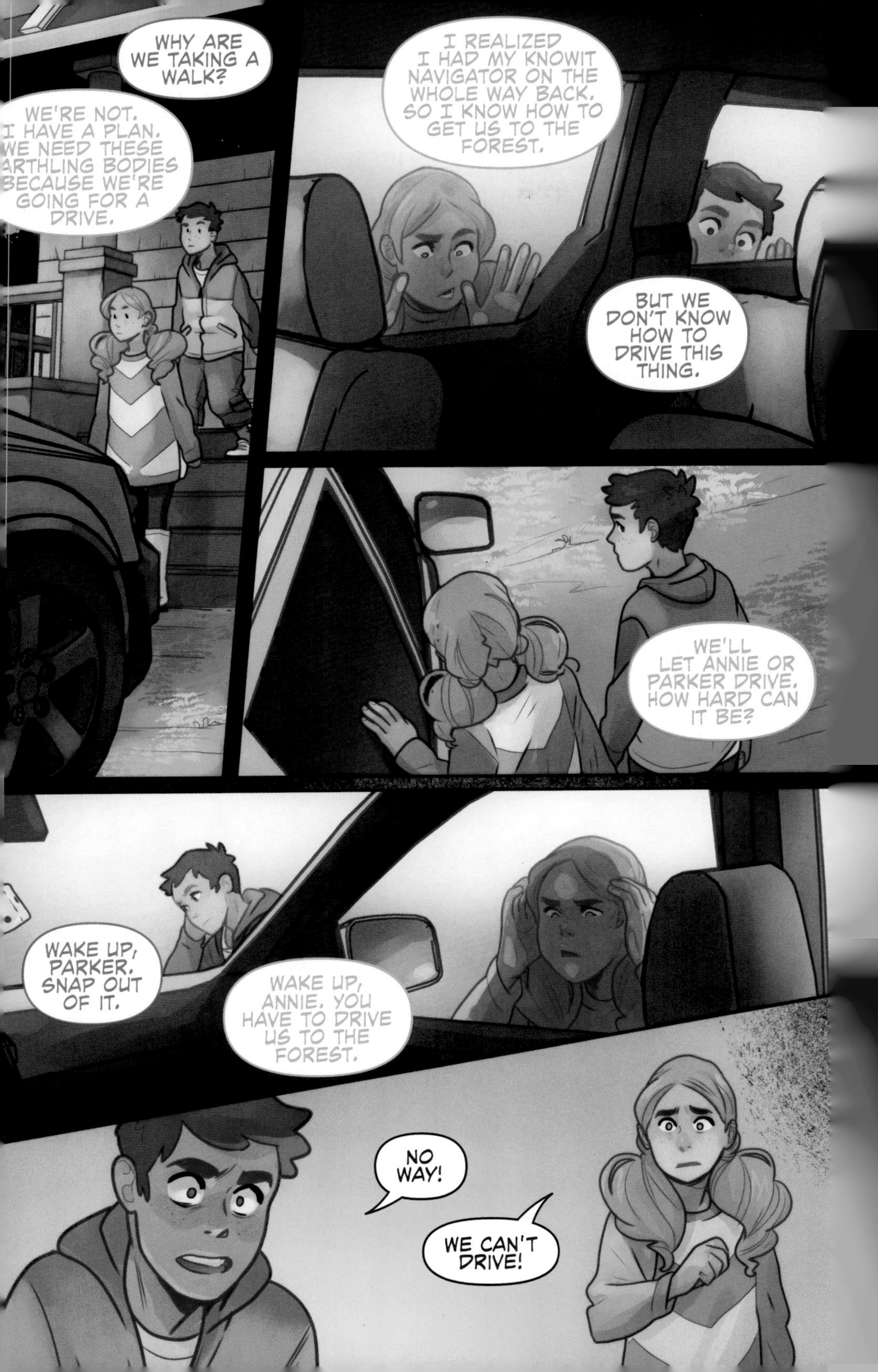
WHY ARE WE TAKING A WALK?
WE'RE NOT. I HAVE A PLAN. WE NEED THESE ARTHLING BODIES BECAUSE WE'RE GOING FOR A DRIVE.
I REALIZED I HAD MY KNOWIT NAVIGATOR ON THE WHOLE WAY BACK, SO I KNOW HOW TO GET US TO THE FOREST.
BUT WE DON'T KNOW HOW TO DRIVE THIS THING.
WE'LL LET ANNIE OR PARKER DRIVE. HOW HARD CAN IT BE?
WAKE UP, PARKER. SNAP OUT OF IT.
WAKE UP, ANNIE. YOU HAVE TO DRIVE US TO THE FOREST.
NO WAY!
WE CAN'T DRIVE!

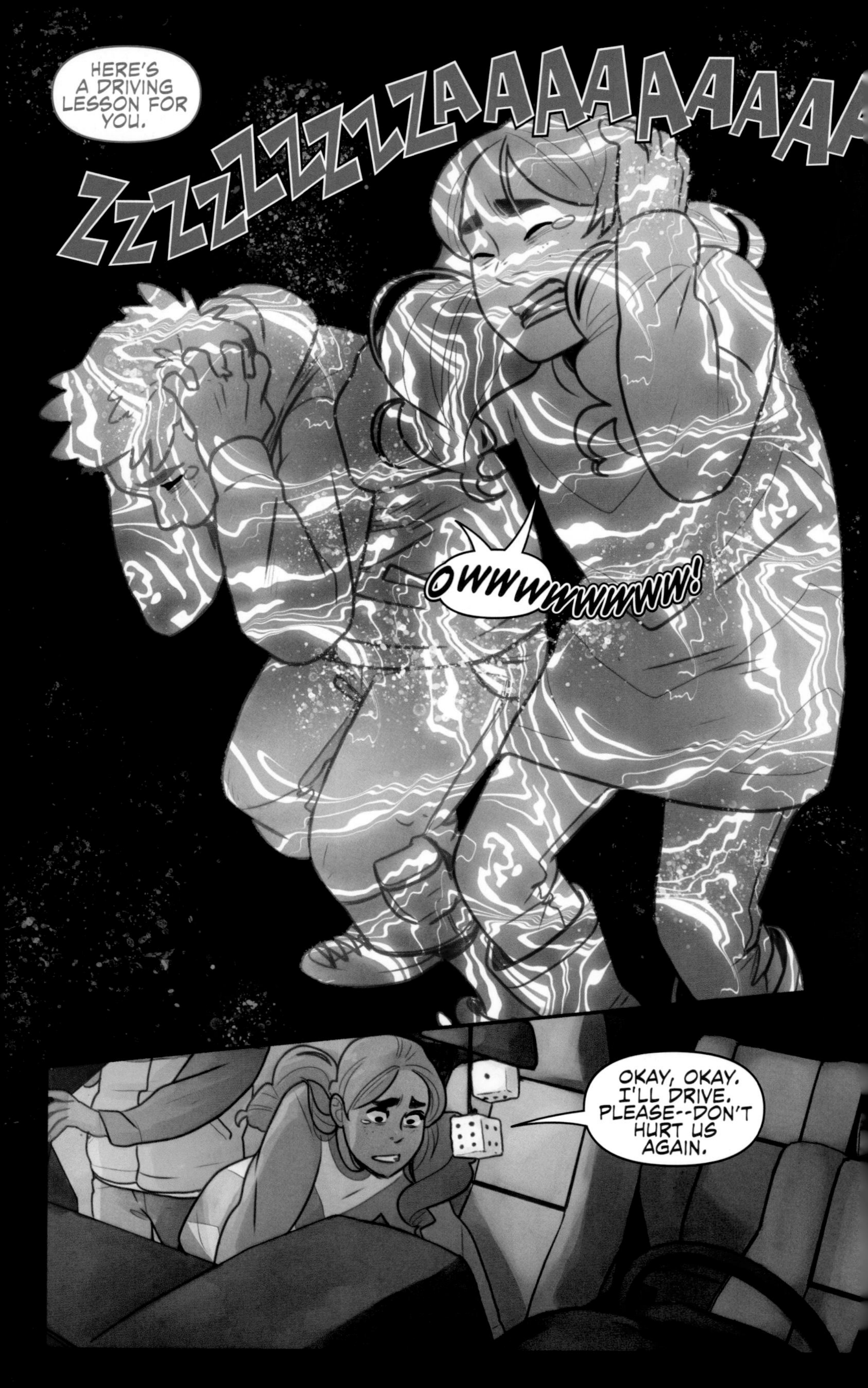
HERE'S A DRIVING LESSON FOR YOU.
ZZZZZZZZZZAAAAAAAAAA
OWWWWWWWW!
OKAY, OKAY. I'LL DRIVE. PLEASE--DON'T HURT US AGAIN.

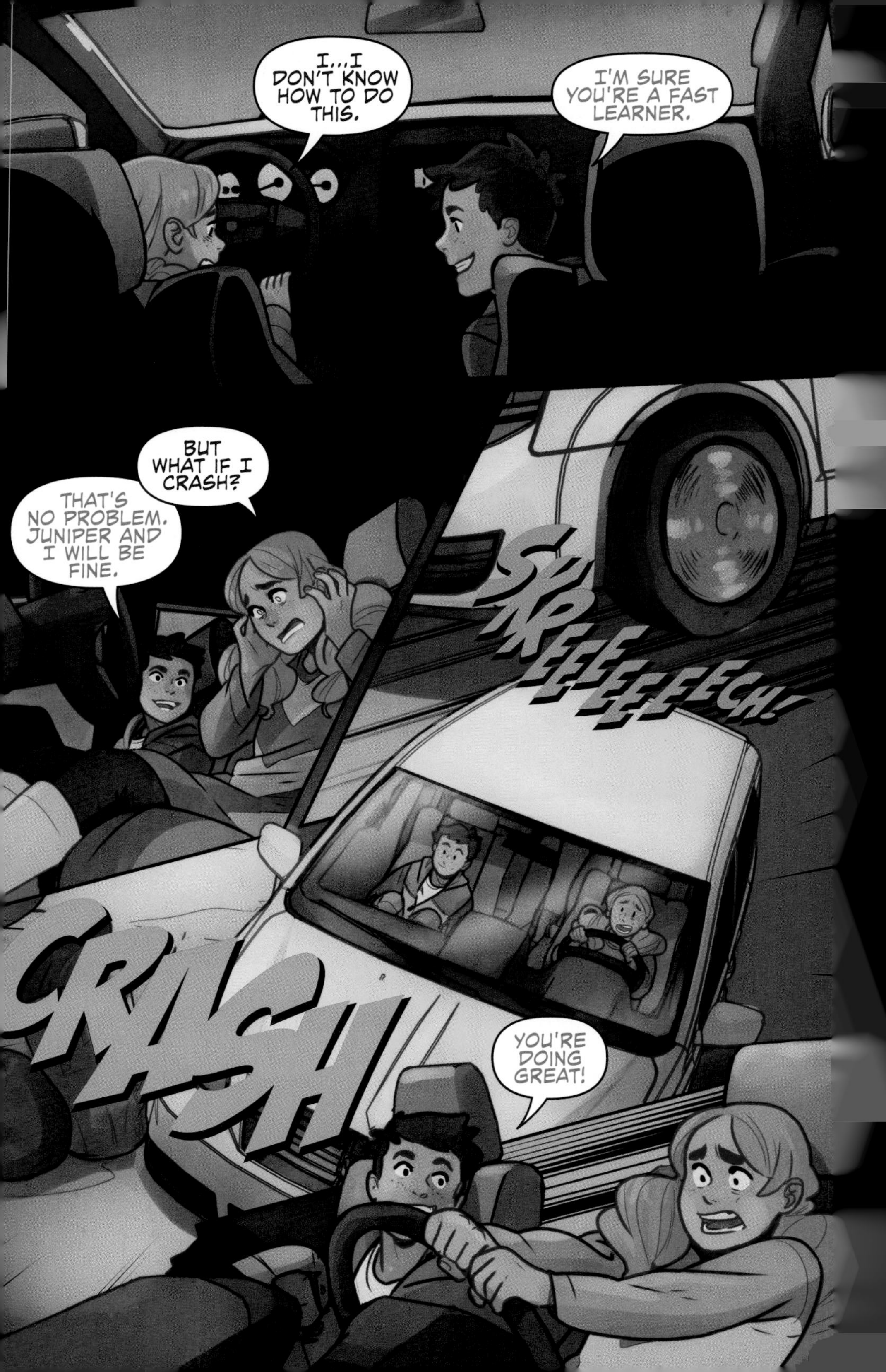
I...I DON'T KNOW HOW TO DO THIS.
I'M SURE YOU'RE A FAST LEARNER.
BUT WHAT IF I CRASH?
THAT'S NO PROBLEM. JUNIPER AND I WILL BE FINE.
SKREEEEEEEECH!
CRASH
YOU'RE DOING GREAT!

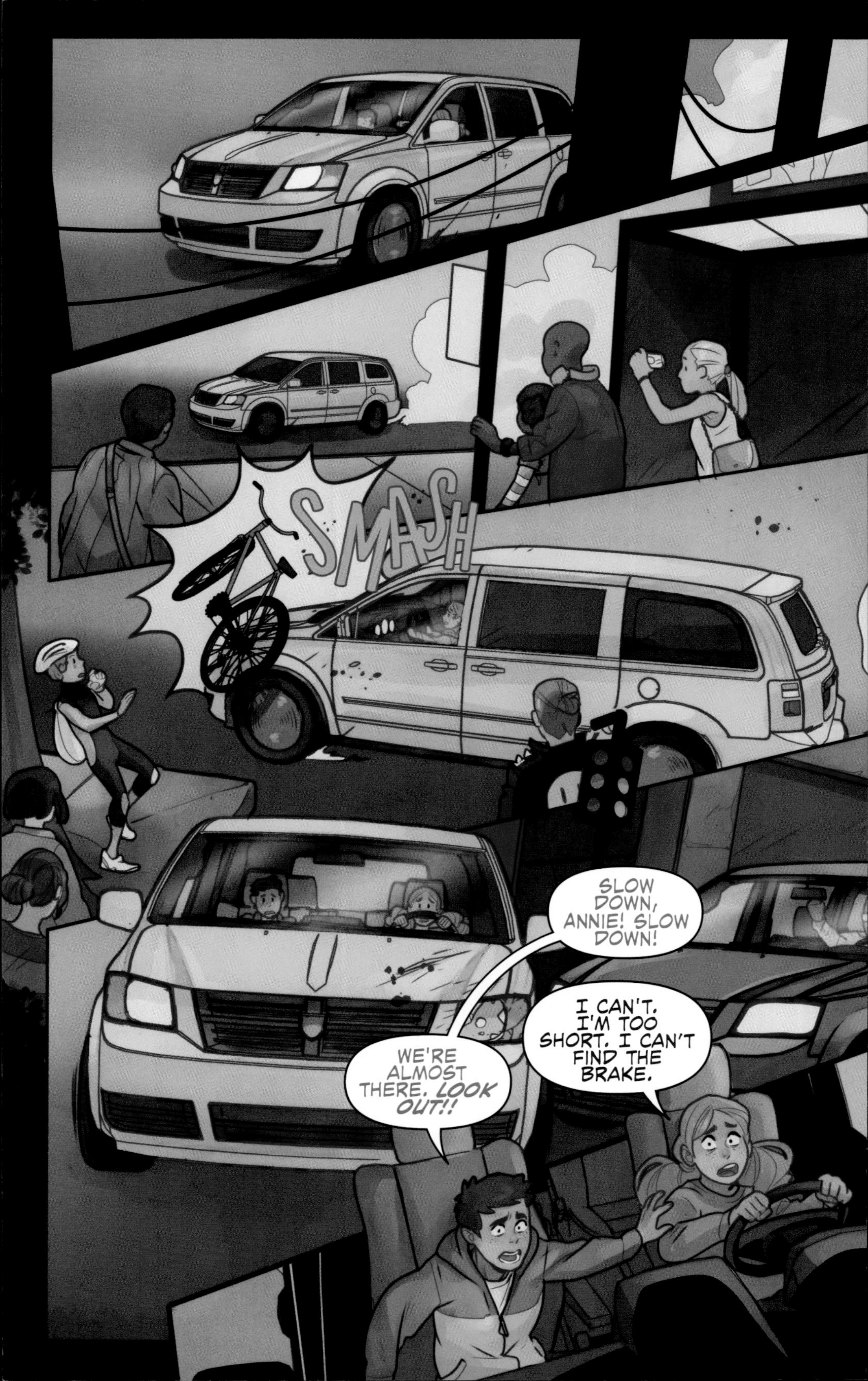
SMASH
SLOW DOWN, ANNIE! SLOW DOWN!
I CAN'T. I'M TOO SHORT. I CAN'T FIND THE BRAKE.
WE'RE ALMOST THERE. LOOK OUT!!

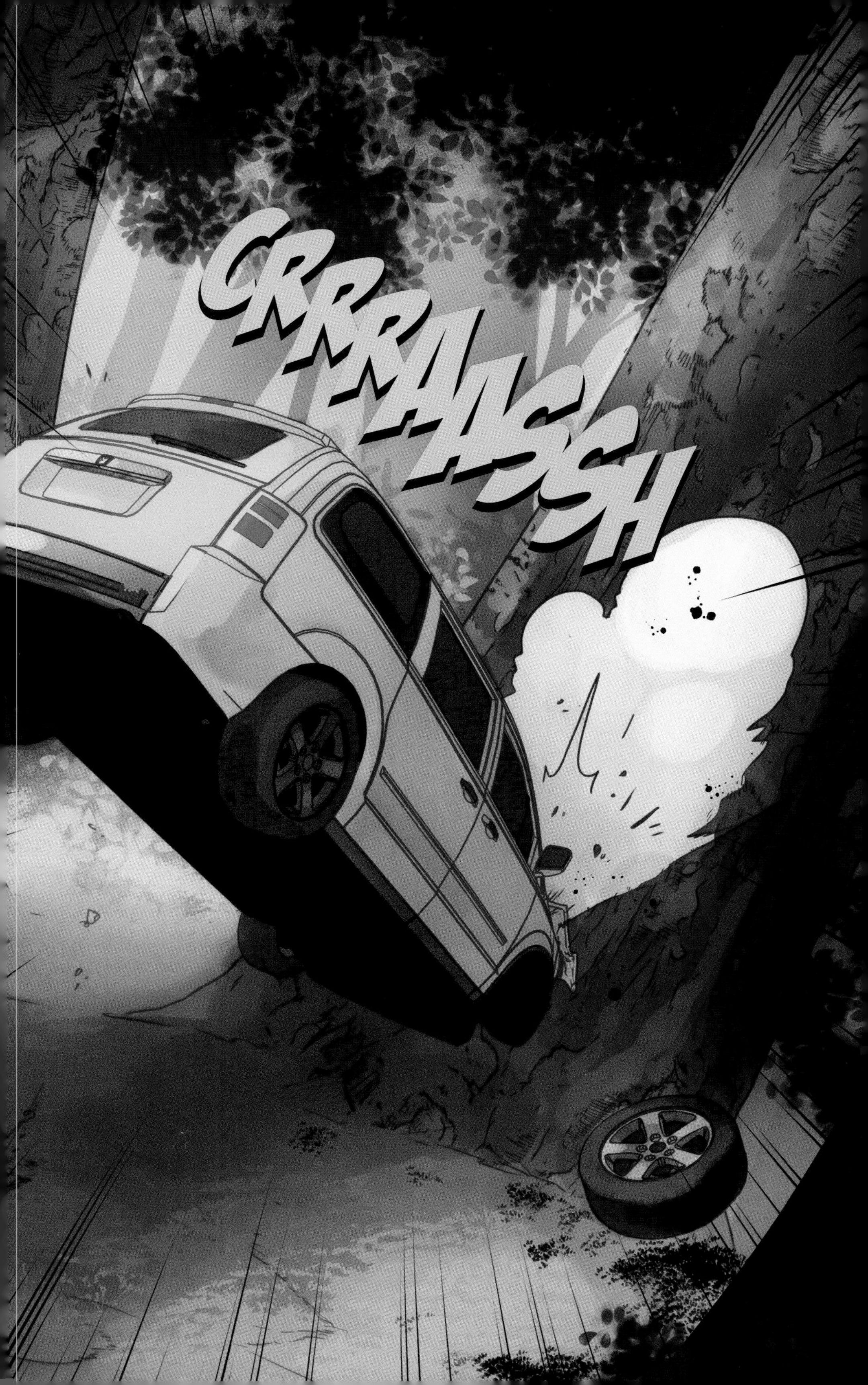
CRRRAASSH

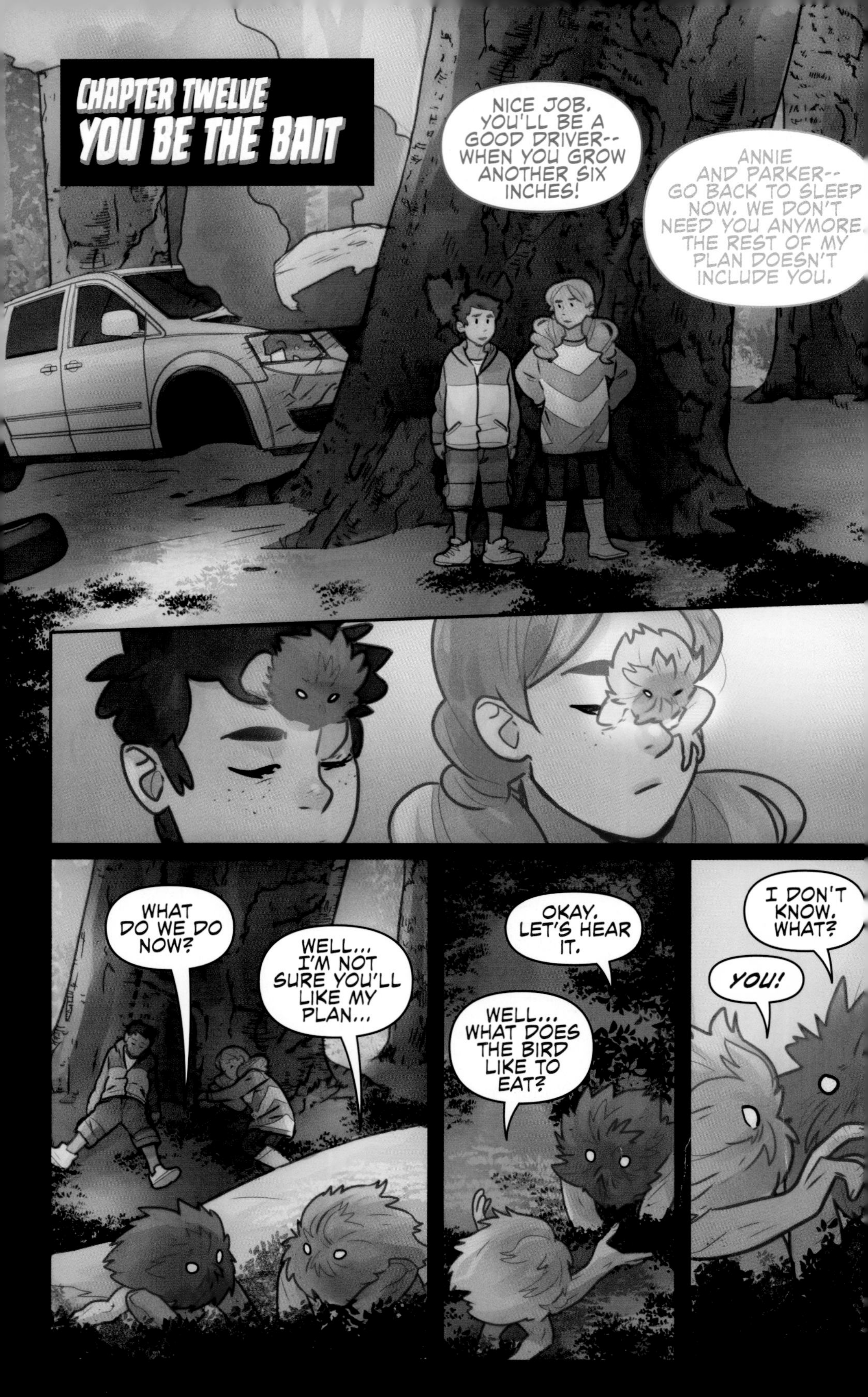
CHAPTER TWELVE
YOU BE THE BAIT
NICE JOB. YOU'LL BE A GOOD DRIVER-- WHEN YOU GROW ANOTHER SIX INCHES!
ANNIE AND PARKER-- GO BACK TO SLEEP NOW. WE DON'T NEED YOU ANYMORE. THE REST OF MY PLAN DOESN'T INCLUDE YOU.
WHAT DO WE DO NOW?
WELL... I'M NOT SURE YOU'LL LIKE MY PLAN...
OKAY. LET'S HEAR IT.
WELL... WHAT DOES THE BIRD LIKE TO EAT?
I DON'T KNOW. WHAT?
YOU!

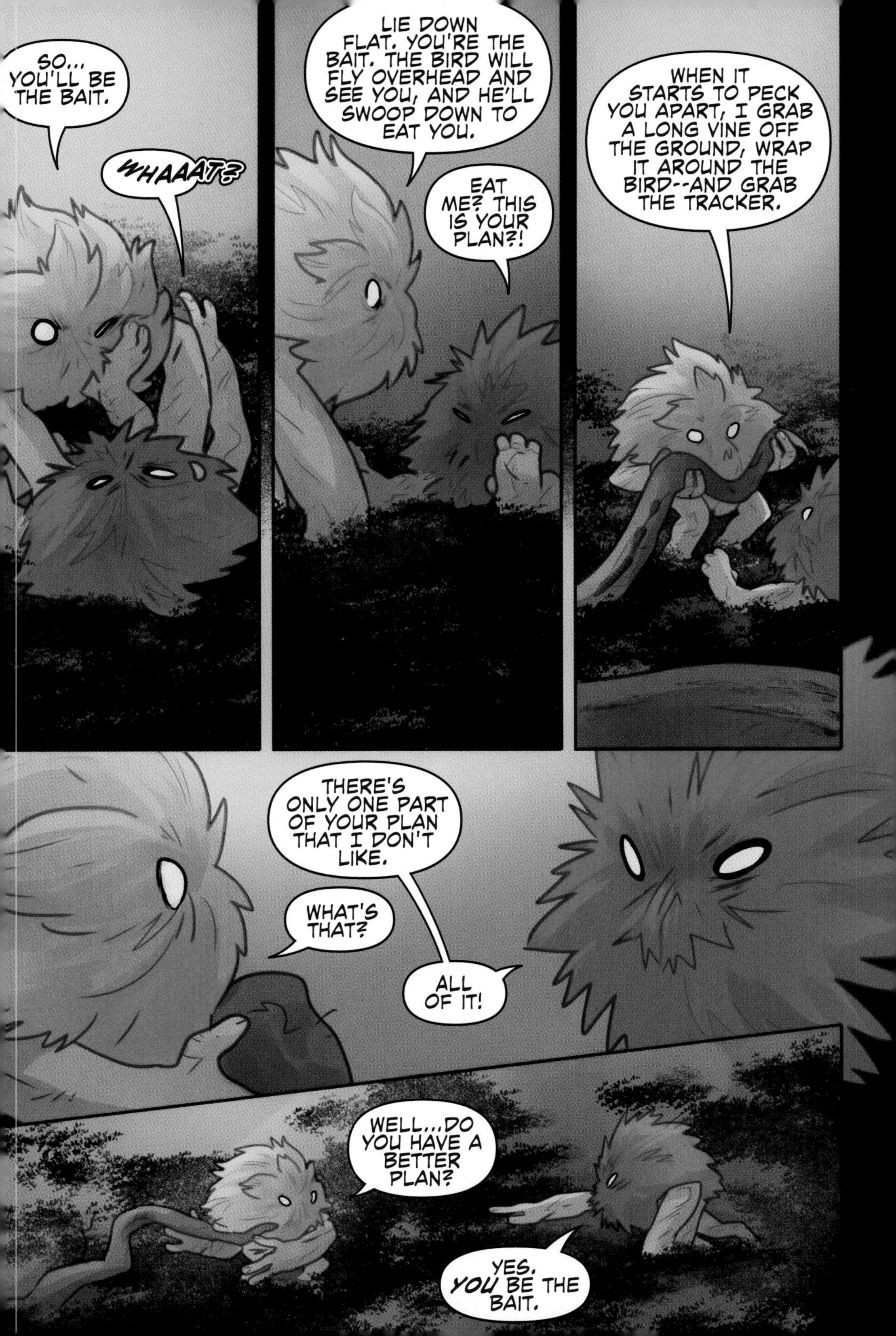
SO... YOU'LL BE THE BAIT.
WHAAAT?
LIE DOWN FLAT. YOU'RE THE BAIT. THE BIRD WILL FLY OVERHEAD AND SEE YOU, AND HE'LL SWOOP DOWN TO EAT YOU.
EAT ME? THIS IS YOUR PLAN?!
WHEN IT STARTS TO PECK YOU APART, I GRAB A LONG VINE OFF THE GROUND, WRAP IT AROUND THE BIRD--AND GRAB THE TRACKER.
THERE'S ONLY ONE PART OF YOUR PLAN THAT I DON'T LIKE.
WHAT'S THAT?
ALL OF IT!
WELL...DO YOU HAVE A BETTER PLAN?
YES. YOU BE THE BAIT.

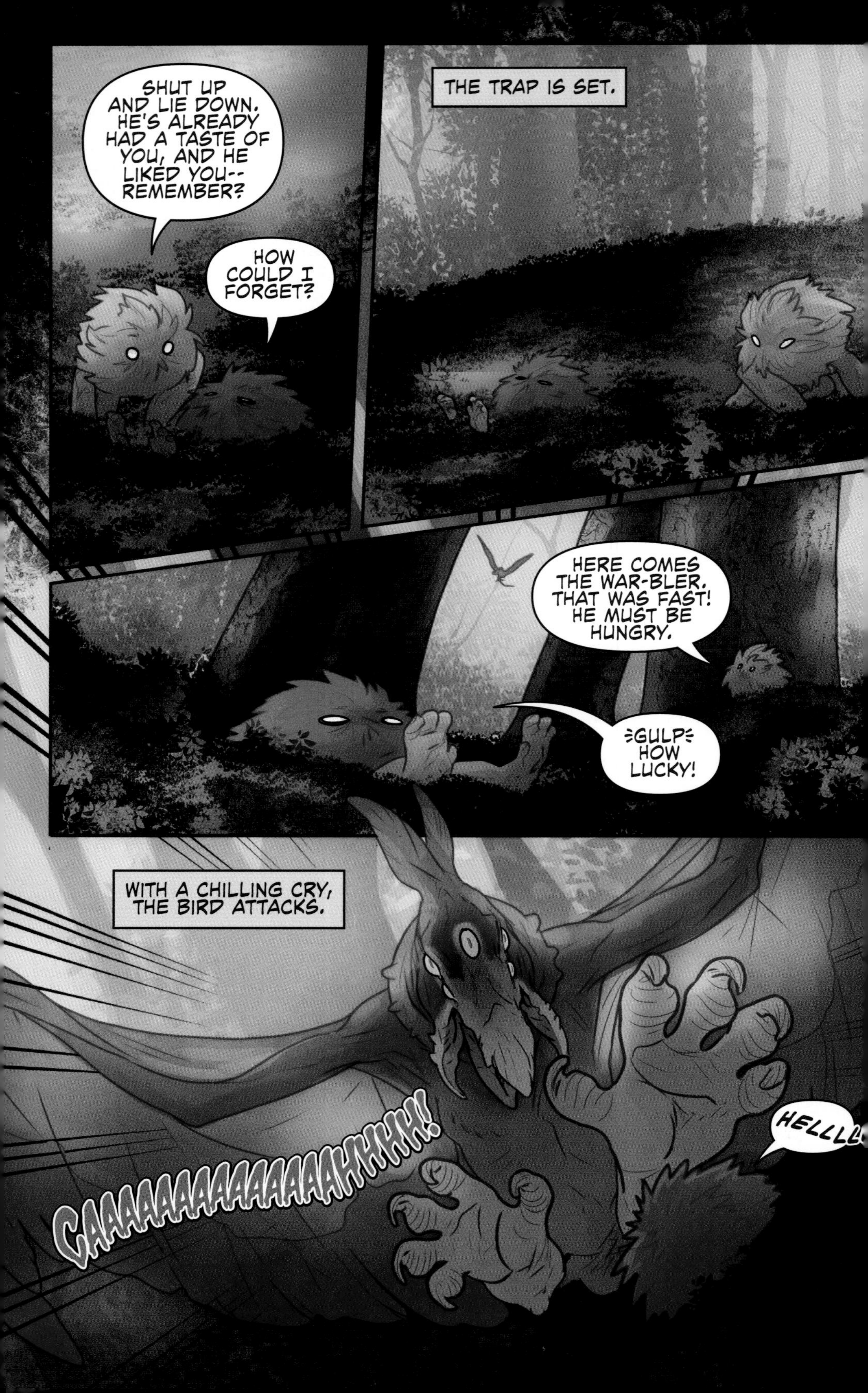

SHUT UP AND LIE DOWN. HE'S ALREADY HAD A TASTE OF YOU, AND HE LIKED YOU--REMEMBER?
HOW COULD I FORGET?
THE TRAP IS SET.
HERE COMES THE WAR-BLER. THAT WAS FAST! HE MUST BE HUNGRY.
GULP HOW LUCKY!
WITH A CHILLING CRY, THE BIRD ATTACKS.
CAAAAAAAAAAAAAAHHHH!
HELLLL

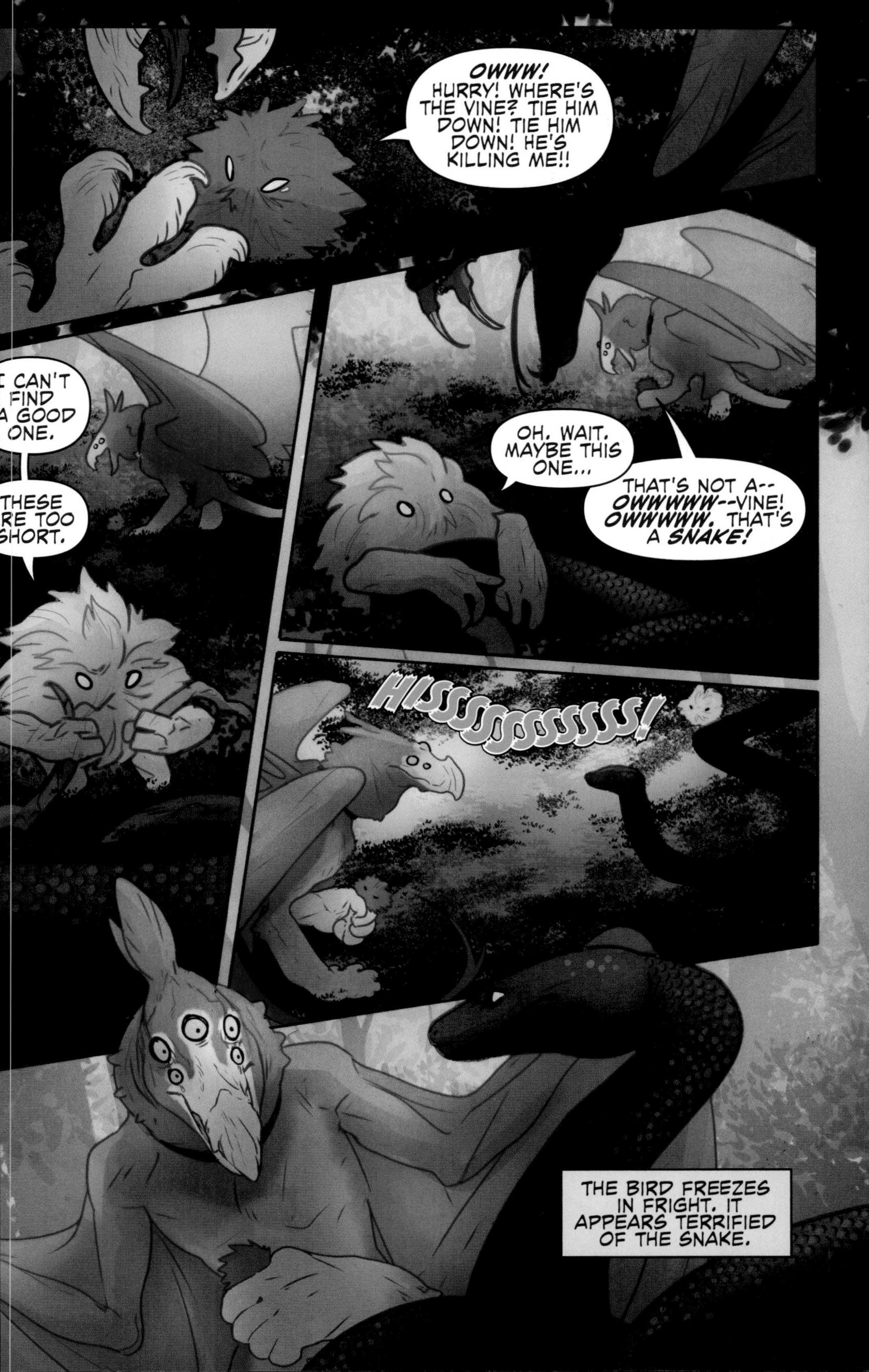

OWWW! HURRY! WHERE'S THE VINE? TIE HIM DOWN! TIE HIM DOWN! HE'S KILLING ME!!
I CAN'T FIND A GOOD ONE.
THESE ARE TOO SHORT.
OH. WAIT. MAYBE THIS ONE...
THAT'S NOT A--OWWWWW--VINE! OWWWWW. THAT'S A SNAKE!
HISSSSSSSSSSSS!
THE BIRD FREEZES IN FRIGHT. IT APPEARS TERRIFIED OF THE SNAKE.

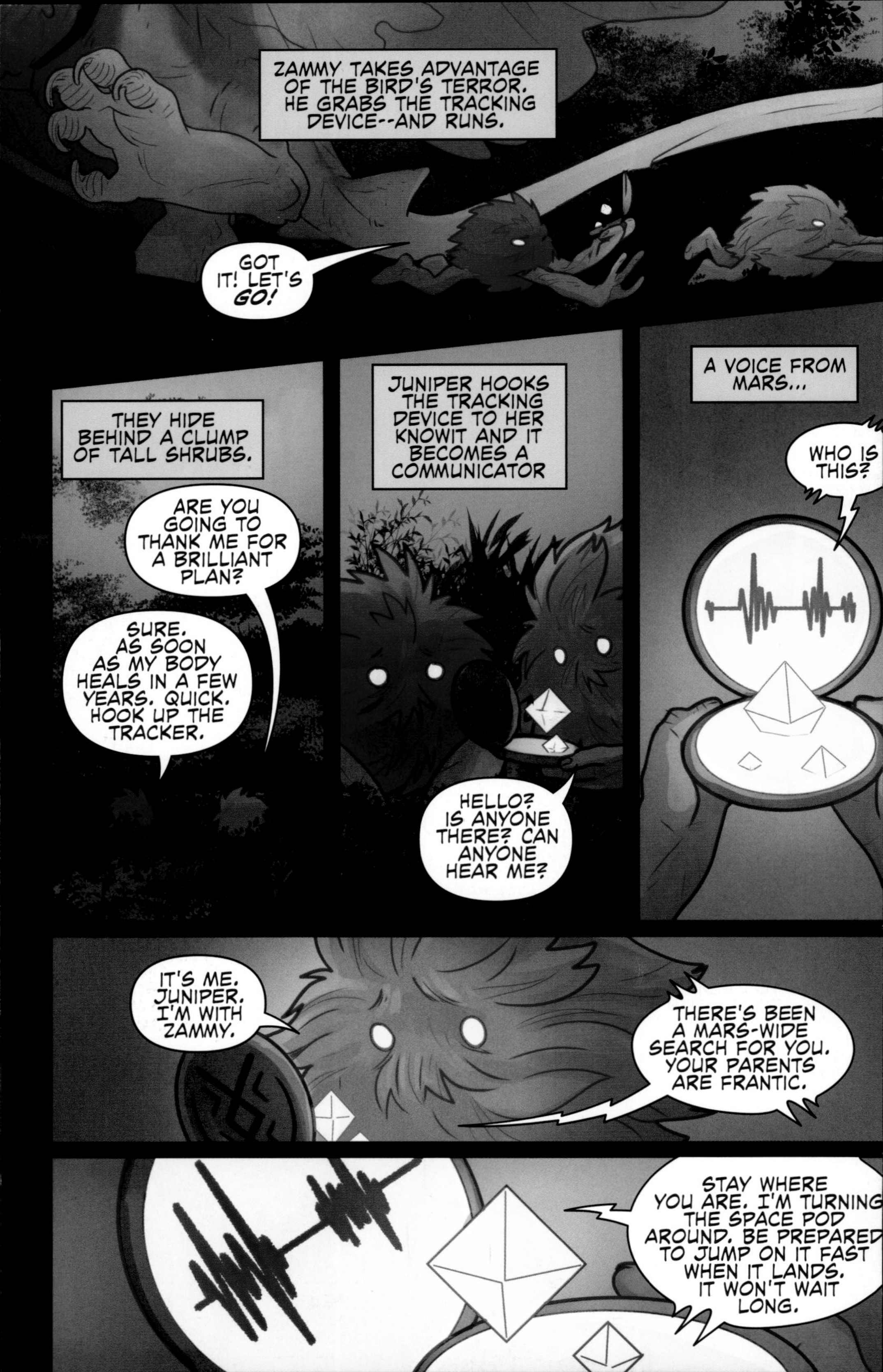
ZAMMY TAKES ADVANTAGE OF THE BIRD'S TERROR. HE GRABS THE TRACKING DEVICE--AND RUNS.
GOT IT! LET'S *GO!*
THEY HIDE BEHIND A CLUMP OF TALL SHRUBS.
ARE YOU GOING TO THANK ME FOR A BRILLIANT PLAN?
SURE. AS SOON AS MY BODY HEALS IN A FEW YEARS. QUICK. HOOK UP THE TRACKER.
JUNIPER HOOKS THE TRACKING DEVICE TO HER KNOWIT AND IT BECOMES A COMMUNICATOR
HELLO? IS ANYONE THERE? CAN ANYONE HEAR ME?
A VOICE FROM MARS...
WHO IS THIS?
IT'S ME. JUNIPER. I'M WITH ZAMMY.
THERE'S BEEN A MARS-WIDE SEARCH FOR YOU. YOUR PARENTS ARE FRANTIC.
STAY WHERE YOU ARE. I'M TURNING THE SPACE POD AROUND. BE PREPARED TO JUMP ON IT FAST WHEN IT LANDS. IT WON'T WAIT LONG.

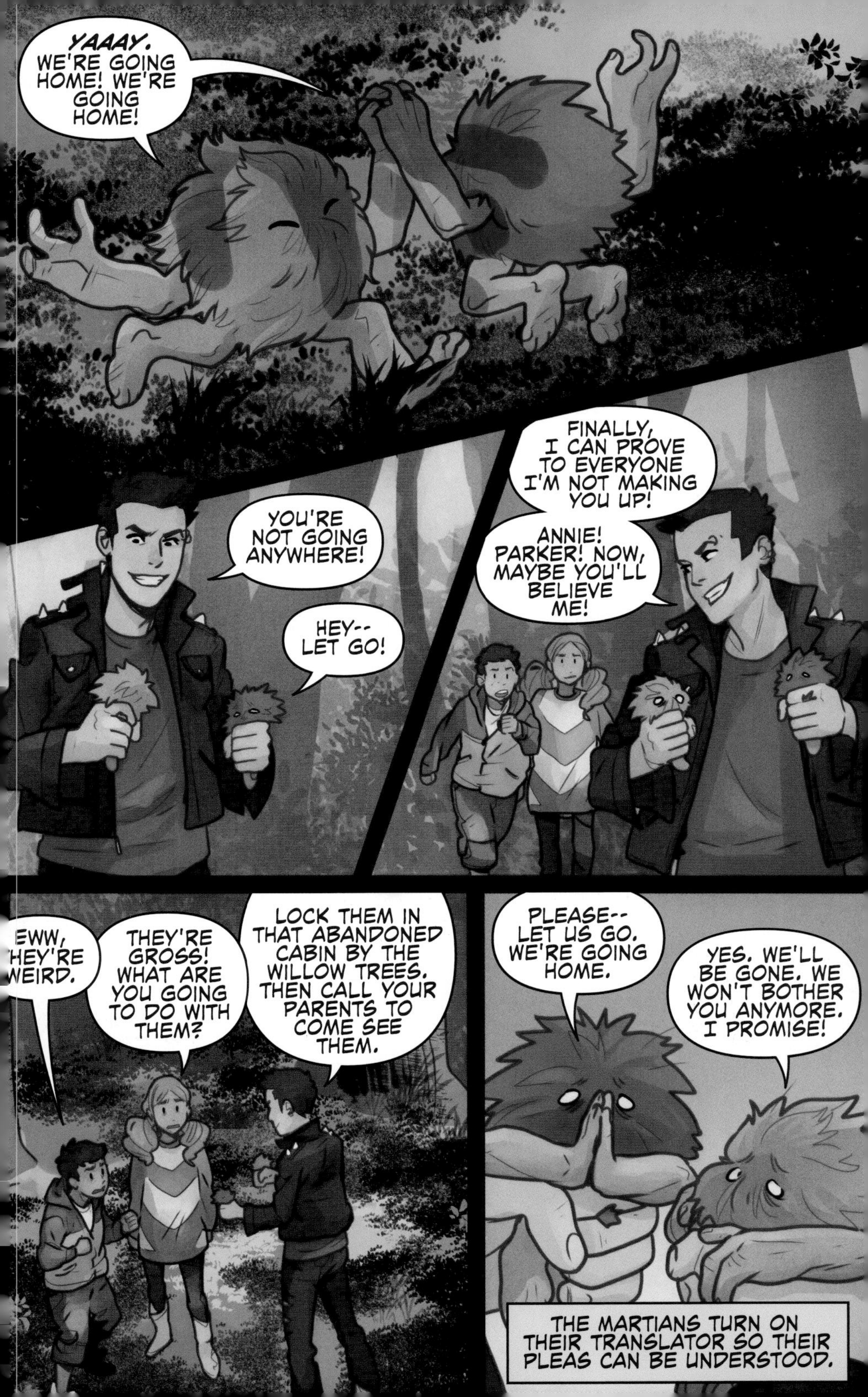
YAAAY. WE'RE GOING HOME! WE'RE GOING HOME!
YOU'RE NOT GOING ANYWHERE!
HEY-- LET GO!
FINALLY, I CAN PROVE TO EVERYONE I'M NOT MAKING YOU UP!
ANNIE! PARKER! NOW, MAYBE YOU'LL BELIEVE ME!
EWW, THEY'RE WEIRD.
THEY'RE GROSS! WHAT ARE YOU GOING TO DO WITH THEM?
LOCK THEM IN THAT ABANDONED CABIN BY THE WILLOW TREES. THEN CALL YOUR PARENTS TO COME SEE THEM.
PLEASE-- LET US GO. WE'RE GOING HOME.
YES. WE'LL BE GONE. WE WON'T BOTHER YOU ANYMORE. I PROMISE!
THE MARTIANS TURN ON THEIR TRANSLATOR SO THEIR PLEAS CAN BE UNDERSTOOD.

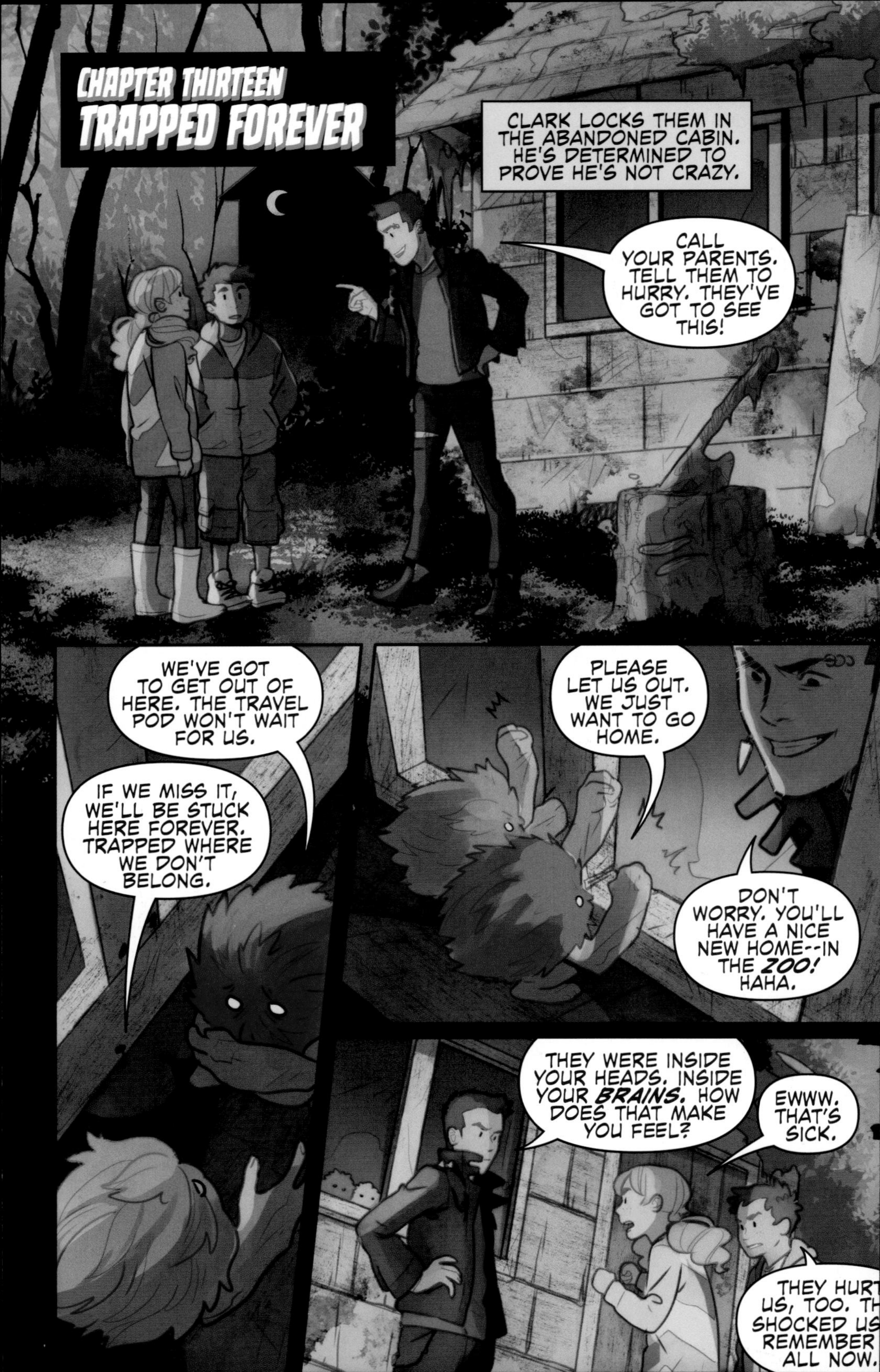
CHAPTER THIRTEEN
TRAPPED FOREVER
CLARK LOCKS THEM IN THE ABANDONED CABIN. HE'S DETERMINED TO PROVE HE'S NOT CRAZY.
CALL YOUR PARENTS. TELL THEM TO HURRY. THEY'VE GOT TO SEE THIS!
WE'VE GOT TO GET OUT OF HERE. THE TRAVEL POD WON'T WAIT FOR US.
IF WE MISS IT, WE'LL BE STUCK HERE FOREVER. TRAPPED WHERE WE DON'T BELONG.
PLEASE LET US OUT. WE JUST WANT TO GO HOME.
DON'T WORRY. YOU'LL HAVE A NICE NEW HOME--IN THE ZOO! HAHA.
THEY WERE INSIDE YOUR HEADS. INSIDE YOUR BRAINS. HOW DOES THAT MAKE YOU FEEL?
EWWW. THAT'S SICK.
THEY HURT US, TOO. TH SHOCKED US REMEMBER ALL NOW.

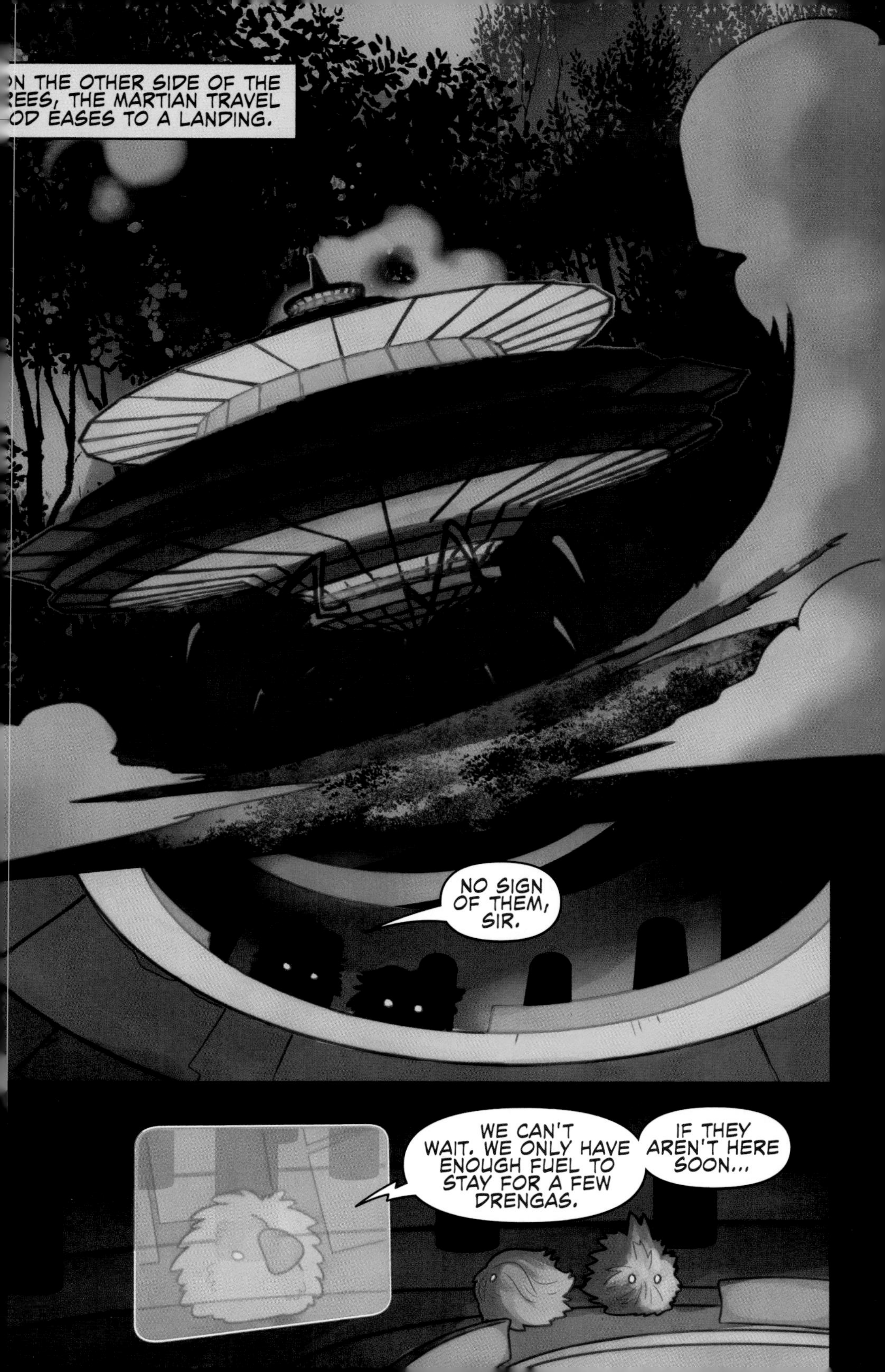
ON THE OTHER SIDE OF THE TREES, THE MARTIAN TRAVEL POD EASES TO A LANDING.
NO SIGN OF THEM, SIR.
WE CAN'T WAIT. WE ONLY HAVE ENOUGH FUEL TO STAY FOR A FEW DRENGAS.
IF THEY AREN'T HERE SOON...

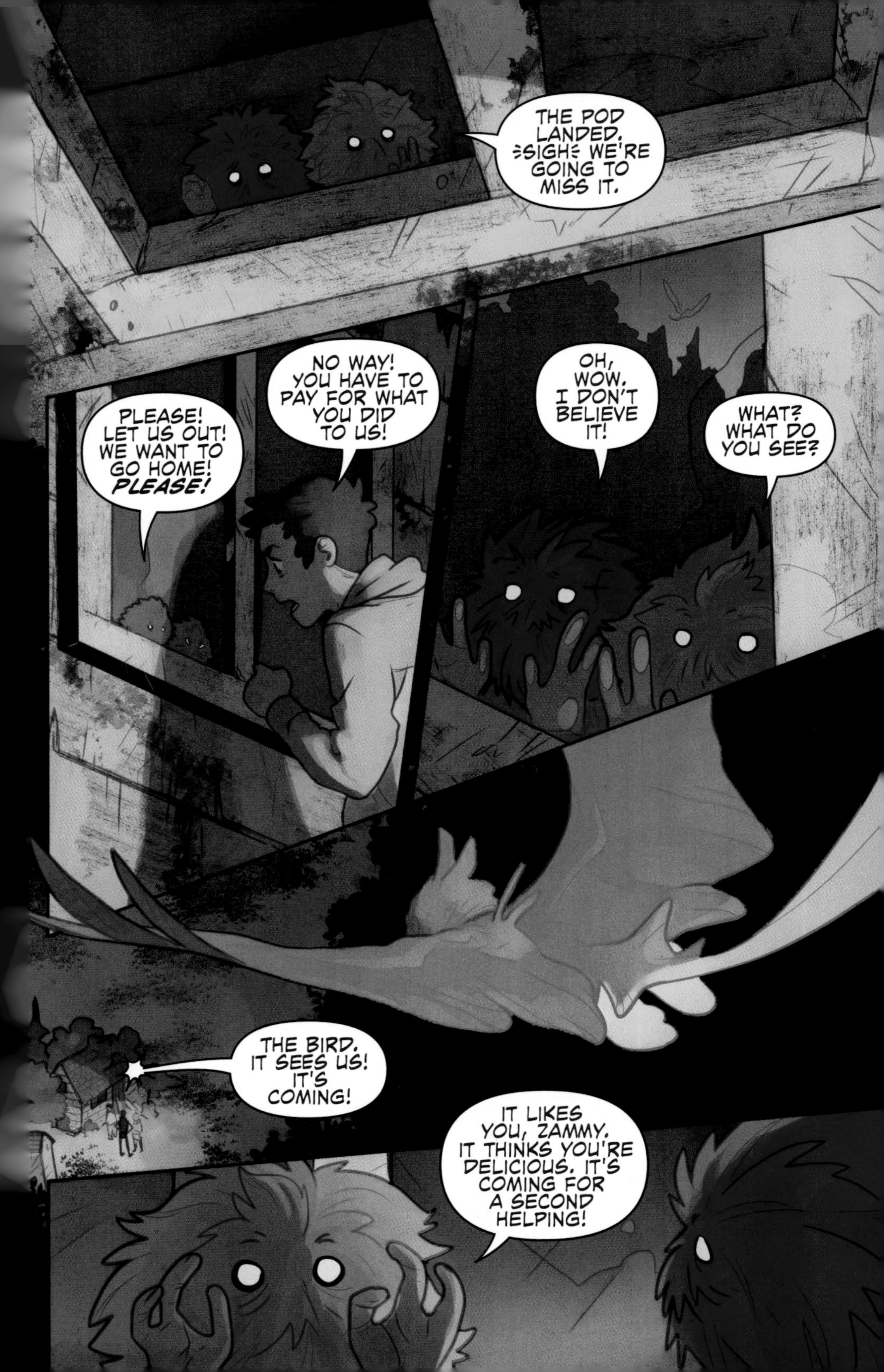
THE POD LANDED. ≋SIGH≋ WE'RE GOING TO MISS IT.
PLEASE! LET US OUT! WE WANT TO GO HOME! *PLEASE!*
NO WAY! YOU HAVE TO PAY FOR WHAT YOU DID TO US!
OH, WOW. I DON'T BELIEVE IT!
WHAT? WHAT DO YOU SEE?
THE BIRD. IT SEES US! IT'S COMING!
IT LIKES YOU, ZAMMY. IT THINKS YOU'RE DELICIOUS. IT'S COMING FOR A SECOND HELPING!

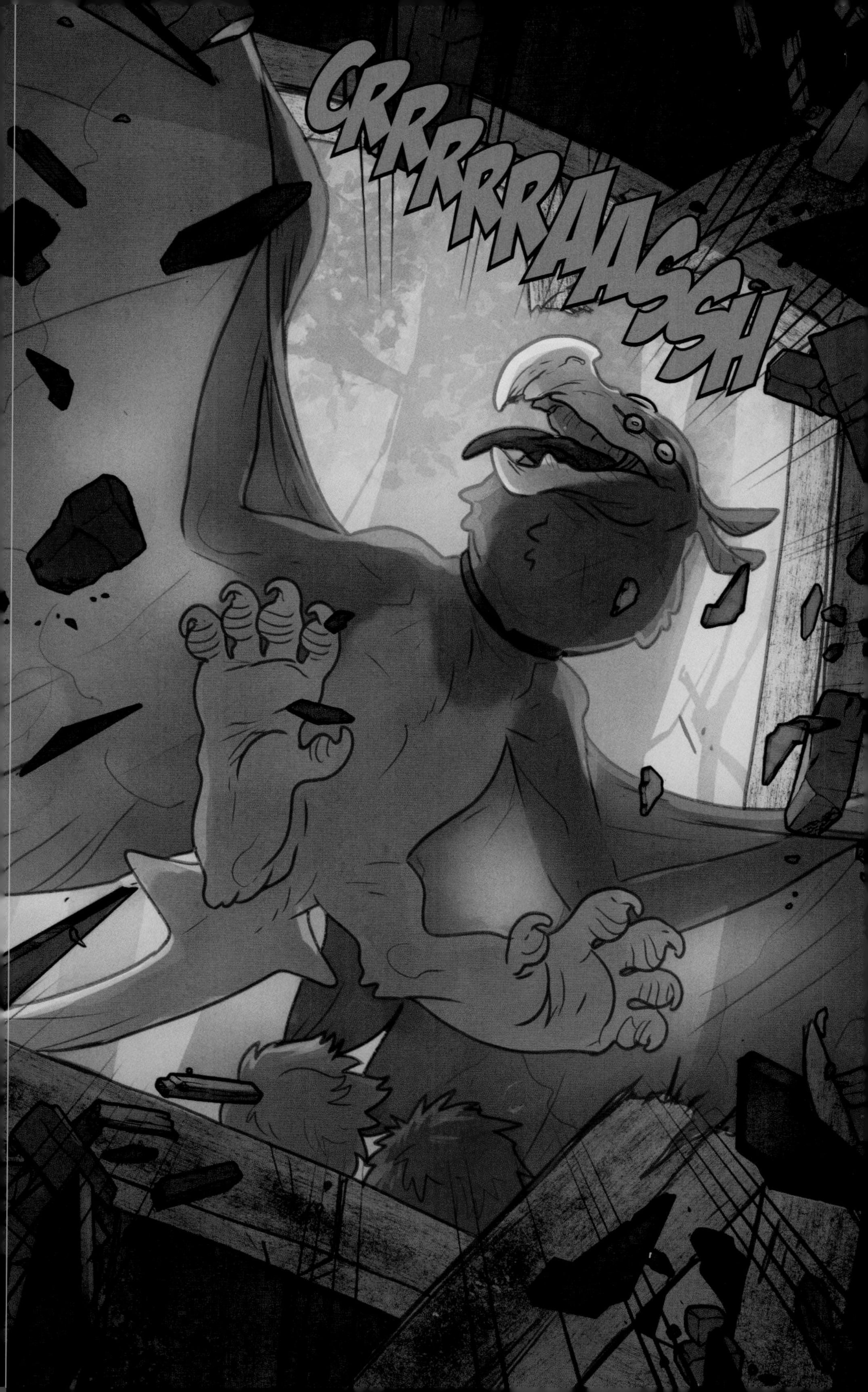
CRRRRRAAGGH

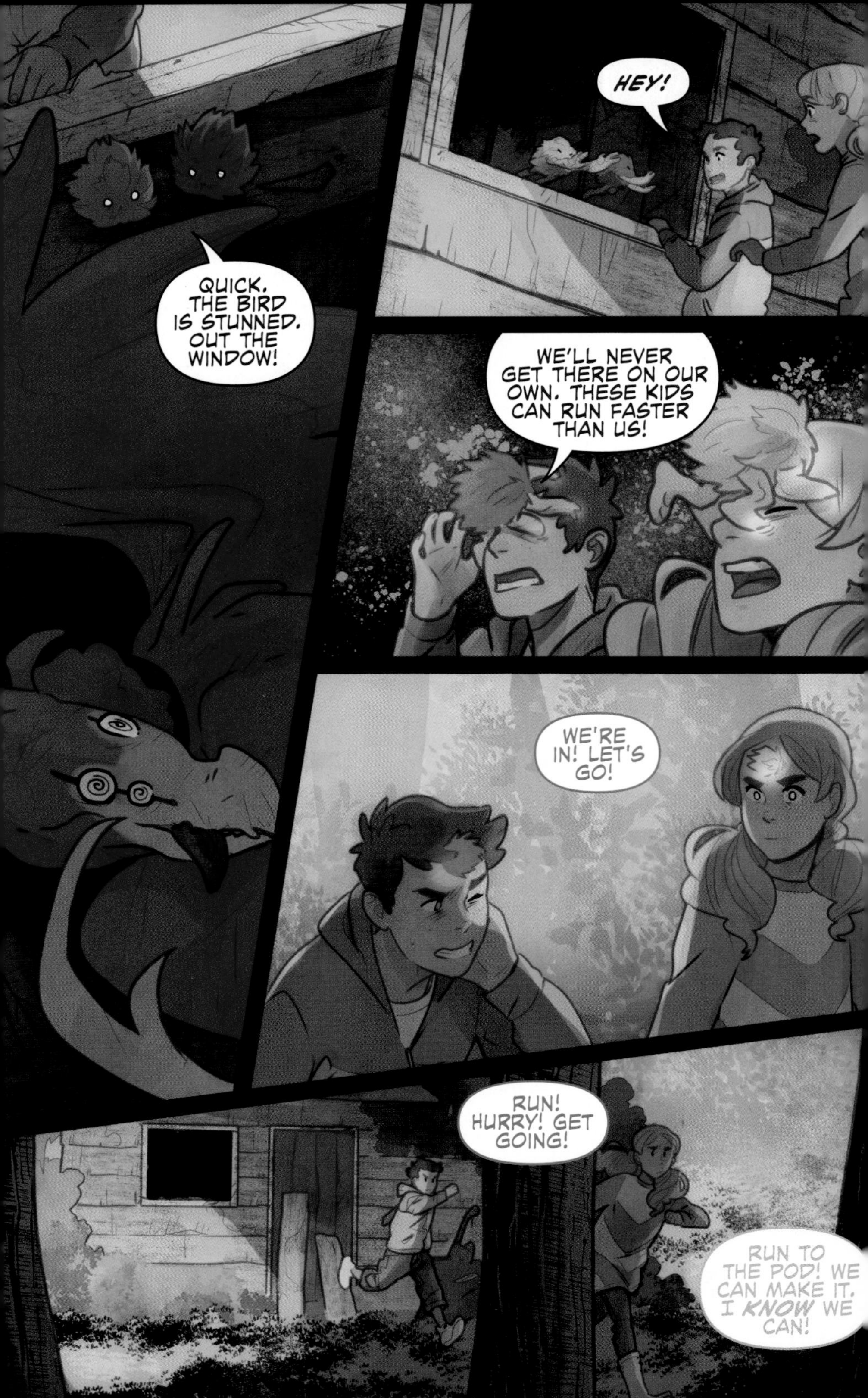
QUICK, THE BIRD IS STUNNED. OUT THE WINDOW!
HEY!
WE'LL NEVER GET THERE ON OUR OWN. THESE KIDS CAN RUN FASTER THAN US!
WE'RE IN! LET'S GO!
RUN! HURRY! GET GOING!
RUN TO THE POD! WE CAN MAKE IT. I *KNOW* WE CAN!

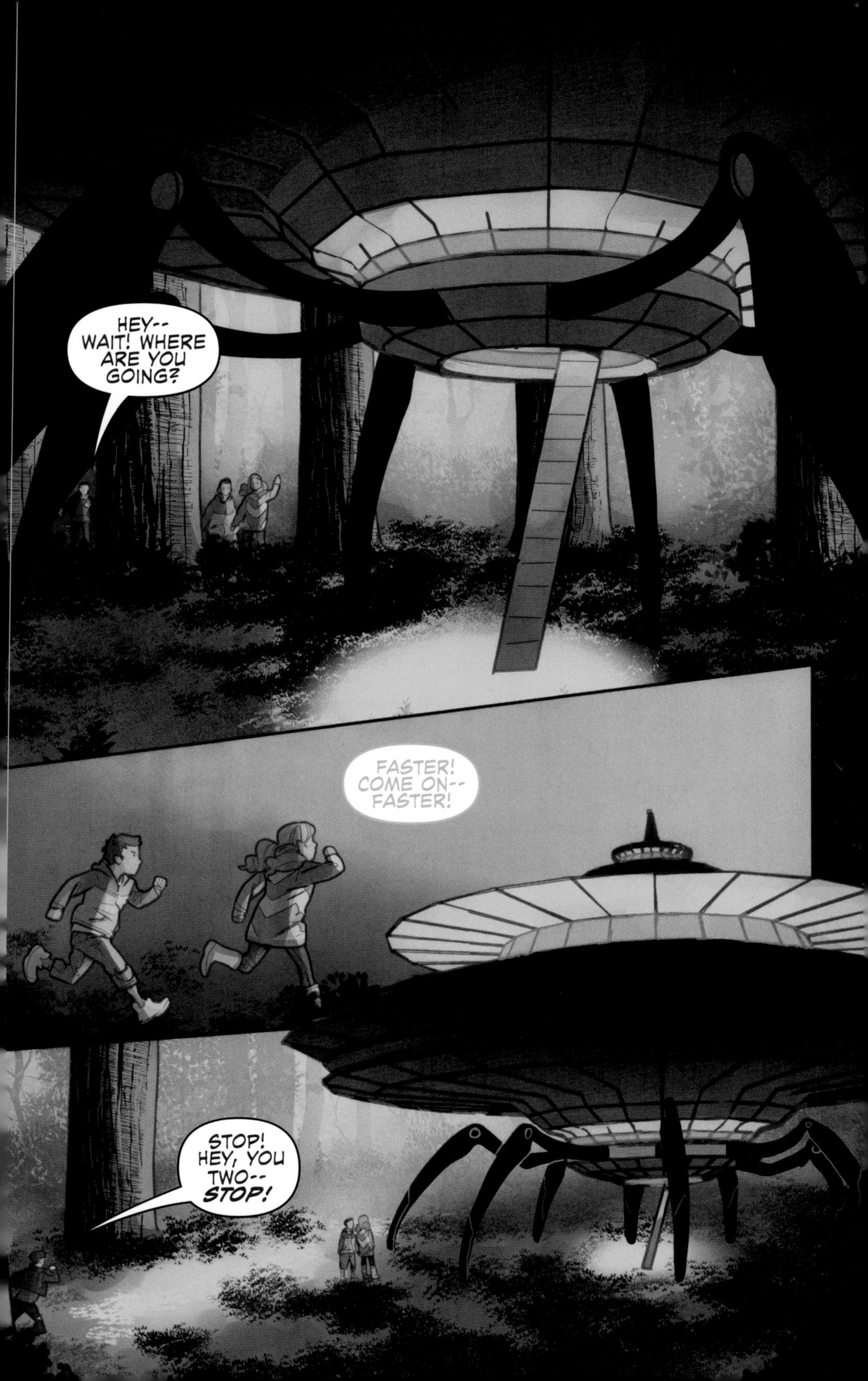
HEY-- WAIT! WHERE ARE YOU GOING?
FASTER! COME ON-- FASTER!
STOP! HEY, YOU TWO-- STOP!

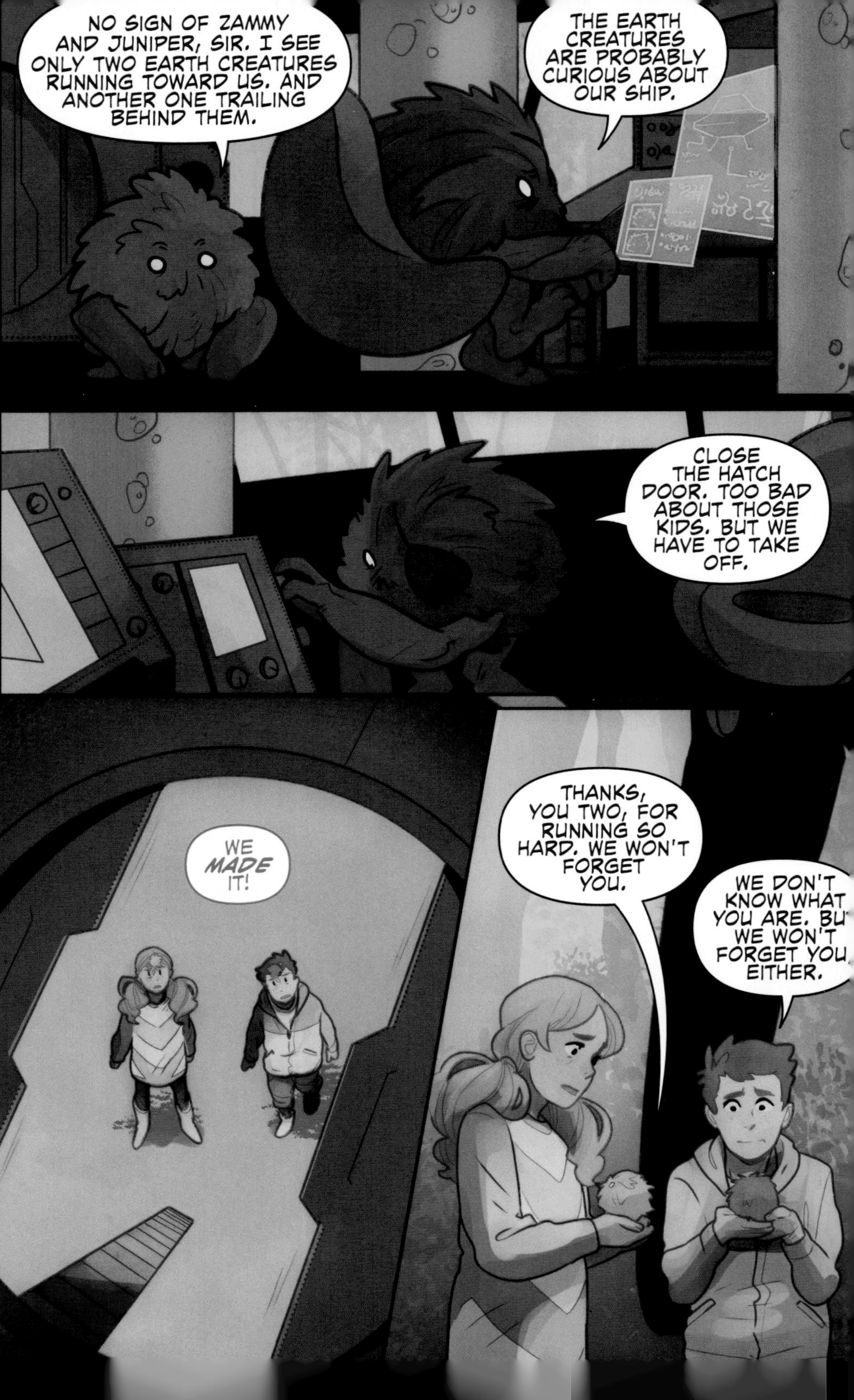
NO SIGN OF ZAMMY AND JUNIPER, SIR. I SEE ONLY TWO EARTH CREATURES RUNNING TOWARD US. AND ANOTHER ONE TRAILING BEHIND THEM.
THE EARTH CREATURES ARE PROBABLY CURIOUS ABOUT OUR SHIP.
CLOSE THE HATCH DOOR. TOO BAD ABOUT THOSE KIDS. BUT WE HAVE TO TAKE OFF.
WE MADE IT!
THANKS, YOU TWO, FOR RUNNING SO HARD. WE WON'T FORGET YOU.
WE DON'T KNOW WHAT YOU ARE. BU WE WON'T FORGET YOU EITHER.

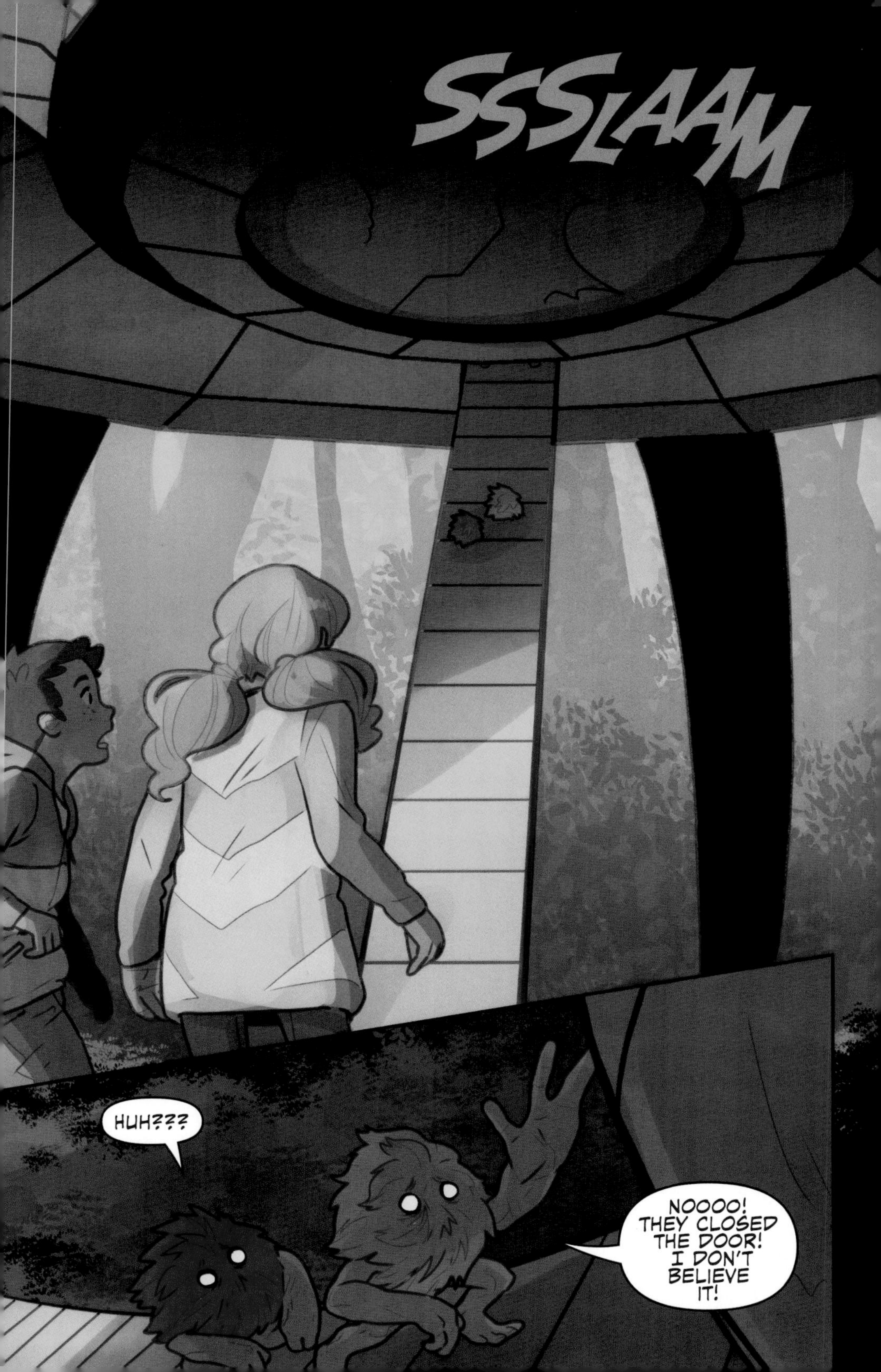
SSSLAAM
HUH???
NOOOO! THEY CLOSED THE DOOR! I DON'T BELIEVE IT!

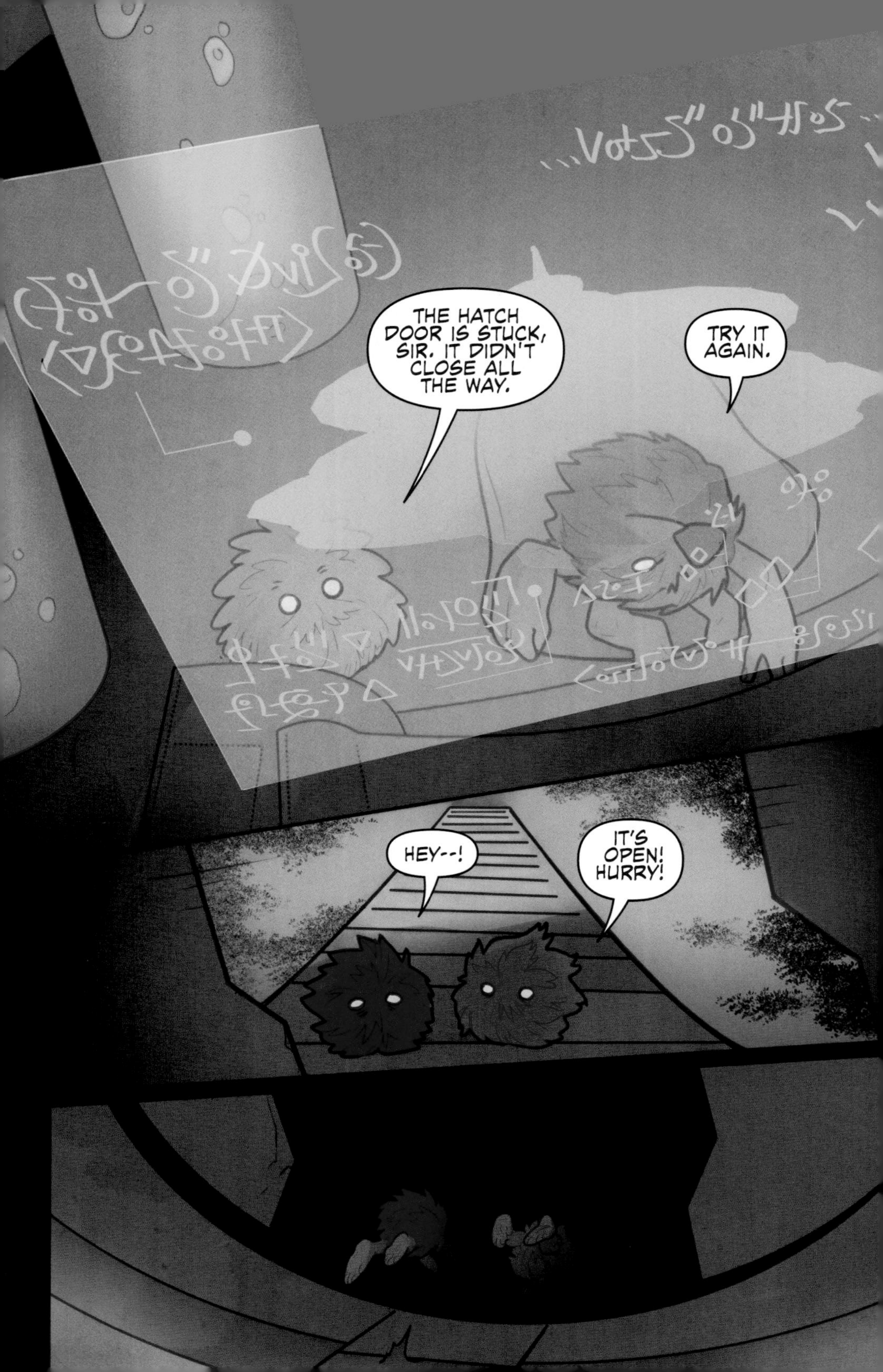
THE HATCH DOOR IS STUCK, SIR. IT DIDN'T CLOSE ALL THE WAY.
TRY IT AGAIN.
HEY--!
IT'S OPEN! HURRY!

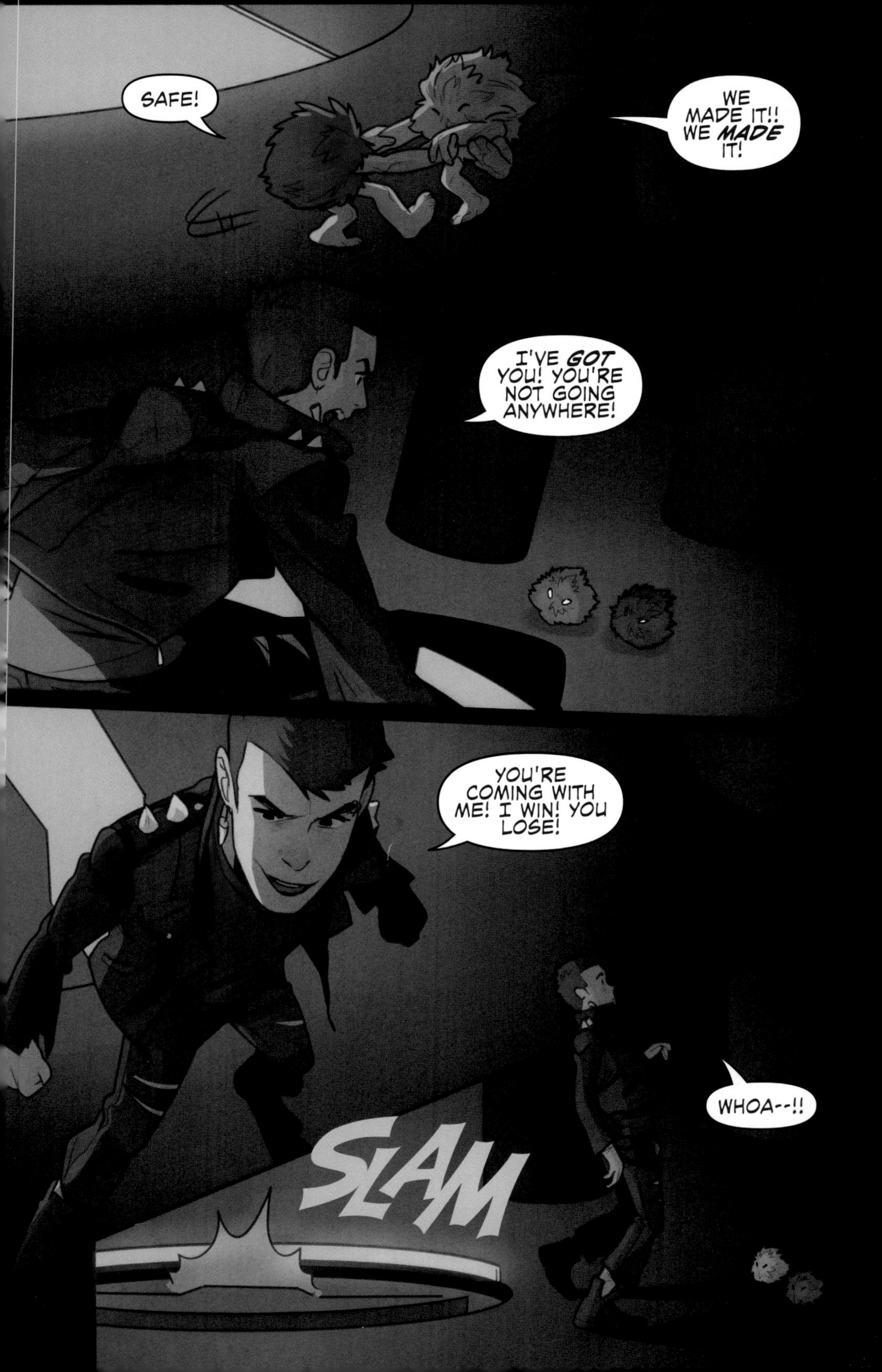
SAFE!
WE MADE IT!! WE MADE IT!
I'VE GOT YOU! YOU'RE NOT GOING ANYWHERE!
YOU'RE COMING WITH ME! I WIN! YOU LOSE!
SLAM
WHOA--!!

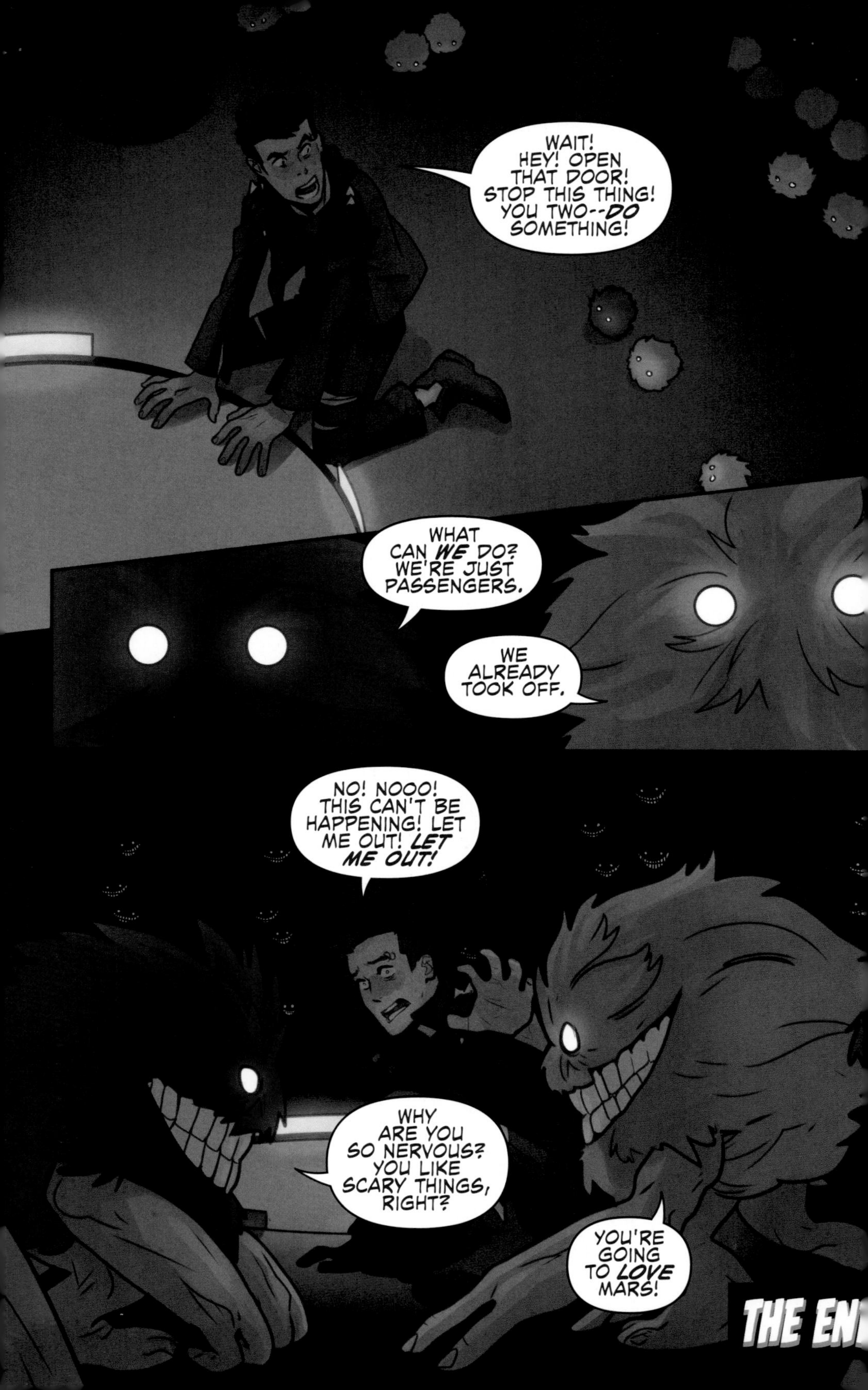
WAIT! HEY! OPEN THAT DOOR! STOP THIS THING! YOU TWO--*DO* SOMETHING!
WHAT CAN *WE* DO? WE'RE JUST PASSENGERS.
WE ALREADY TOOK OFF.
NO! NOOO! THIS CAN'T BE HAPPENING! LET ME OUT! *LET ME OUT!*
WHY ARE YOU SO NERVOUS? YOU LIKE SCARY THINGS, RIGHT?
YOU'RE GOING TO *LOVE* MARS!
THE EN

JUST

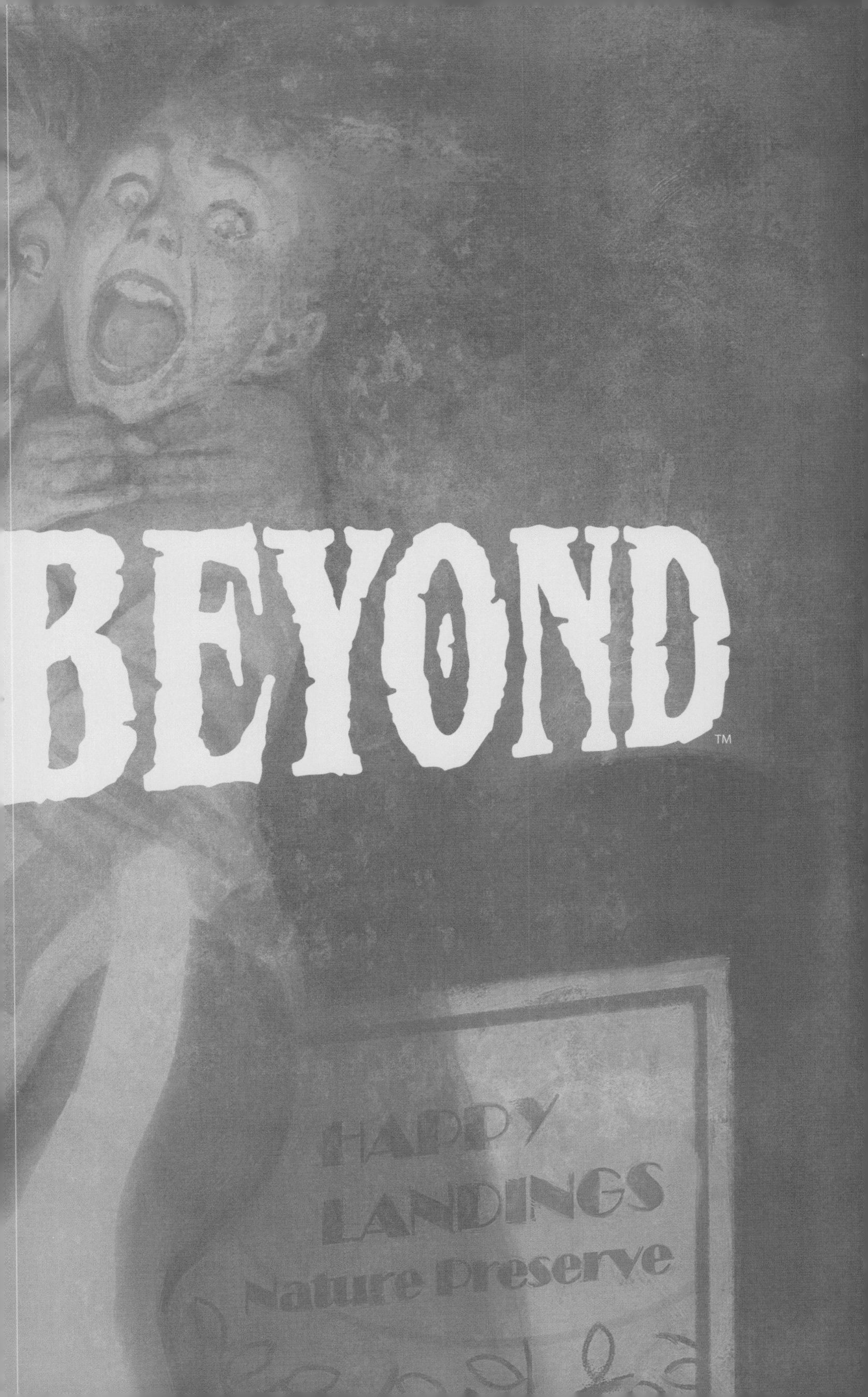
BEYOND™
HAPPY
LANDINGS
Nature Preserve

ABOUT THE
AUTHORS

R.L. Stine

R.L. Stine is one of the best-selling children's authors in history. His *Goosebumps* and *Fear Street* series have sold more than 400 million copies around the world and have been translated into 32 languages. He has had several TV series based on his work, and two feature films, *Goosebumps* (2015) and *Goosebumps 2: Haunted Halloween* (2018) starring Jack Black as R.L. Stine. *Just Beyond* is Stine's first-ever series of original graphic novels. He lives in New York City with his wife Jane, an editor and publisher.

Kelly & Nicole Matthews

Kelly and Nichole Matthews are twin sisters (and totally not four cats in a trench coat) who work as freelance comic book artists and illustrators just north of the Emerald City. They've worked on a number of titles that you may have heard of (and maybe even read!) including *Jim Henson's The Power of the Dark Crystal*, *Pandora's Legacy*, and *Toil & Trouble*. They have an original webcomic, *Maskless*, that you can read for free on Hiveworks.

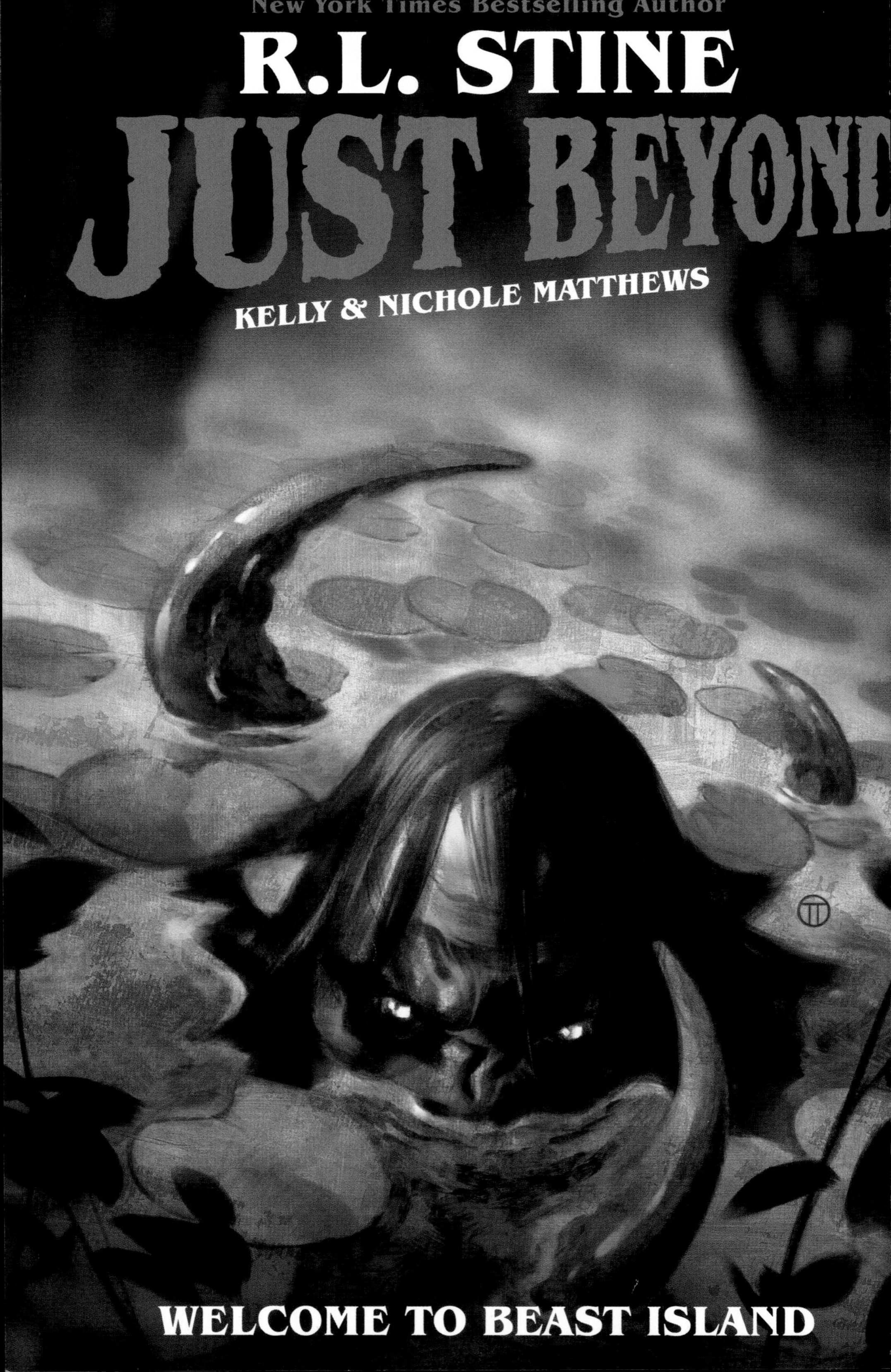
New York Times Bestselling Author
R.L. STINE
JUST BEYOND
KELLY & NICHOLE MATTHEWS
WELCOME TO BEAST ISLAND

YOUR SCARY SNEAK PEEK!

Written by
R.L. Stine

Illustrated by
Kelly & Nichole Matthews

Lettered by
Mike Fiorentino

Cover by
Julian Totino Tedesco

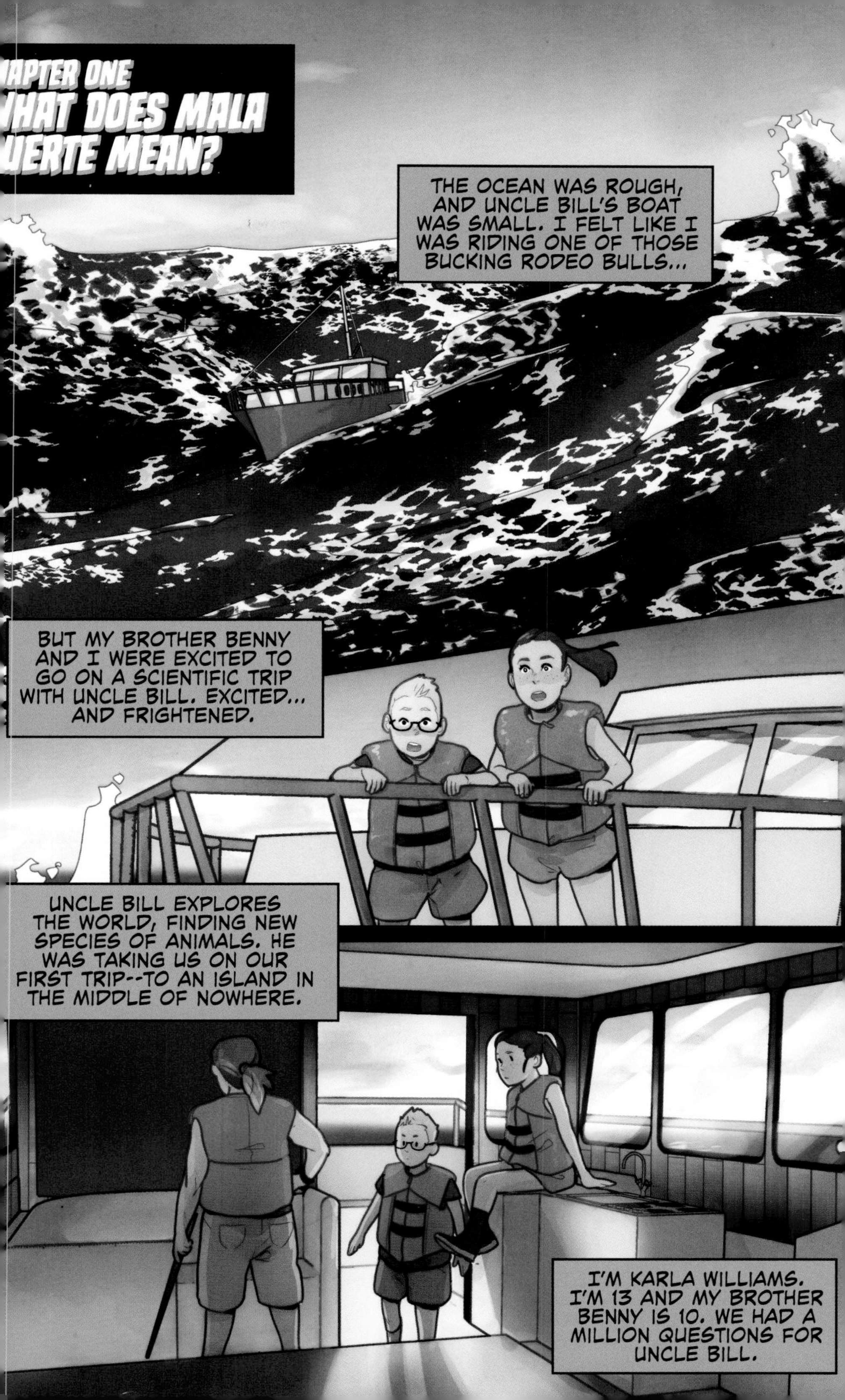

APTER ONE
HAT DOES MALA
UERTE MEAN?
THE OCEAN WAS ROUGH, AND UNCLE BILL'S BOAT WAS SMALL. I FELT LIKE I WAS RIDING ONE OF THOSE BUCKING RODEO BULLS...
BUT MY BROTHER BENNY AND I WERE EXCITED TO GO ON A SCIENTIFIC TRIP WITH UNCLE BILL. EXCITED... AND FRIGHTENED.
UNCLE BILL EXPLORES THE WORLD, FINDING NEW SPECIES OF ANIMALS. HE WAS TAKING US ON OUR FIRST TRIP--TO AN ISLAND IN THE MIDDLE OF NOWHERE.
I'M KARLA WILLIAMS. I'M 13 AND MY BROTHER BENNY IS 10. WE HAD A MILLION QUESTIONS FOR UNCLE BILL.

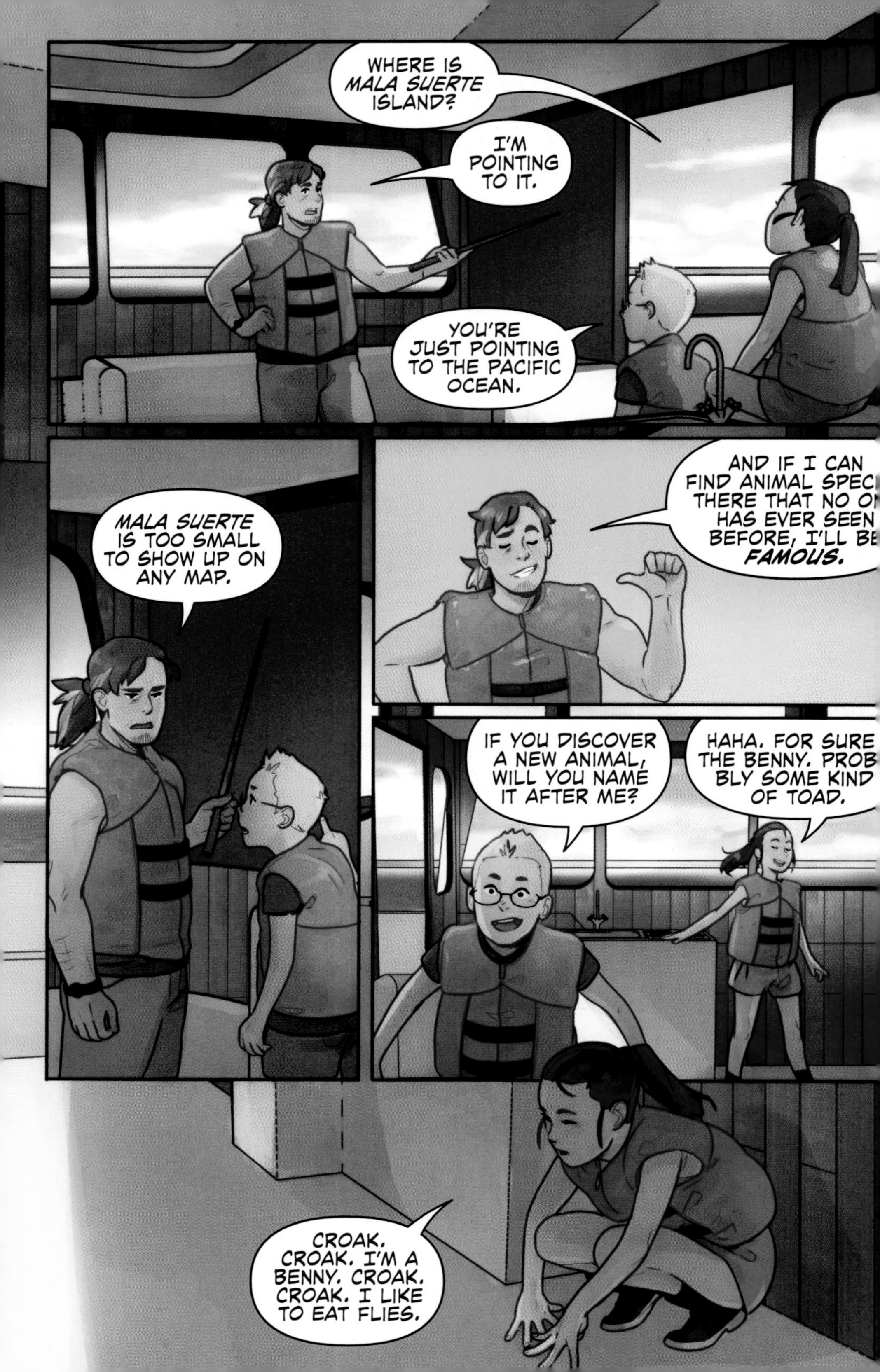
WHERE IS MALA SUERTE ISLAND?
I'M POINTING TO IT.
YOU'RE JUST POINTING TO THE PACIFIC OCEAN.
MALA SUERTE IS TOO SMALL TO SHOW UP ON ANY MAP.
AND IF I CAN FIND ANIMAL SPEC THERE THAT NO O HAS EVER SEEN BEFORE, I'LL BE FAMOUS.
IF YOU DISCOVER A NEW ANIMAL, WILL YOU NAME IT AFTER ME?
HAHA. FOR SURE THE BENNY. PROB BLY SOME KIND OF TOAD.
CROAK. CROAK. I'M A BENNY. CROAK. CROAK. I LIKE TO EAT FLIES.

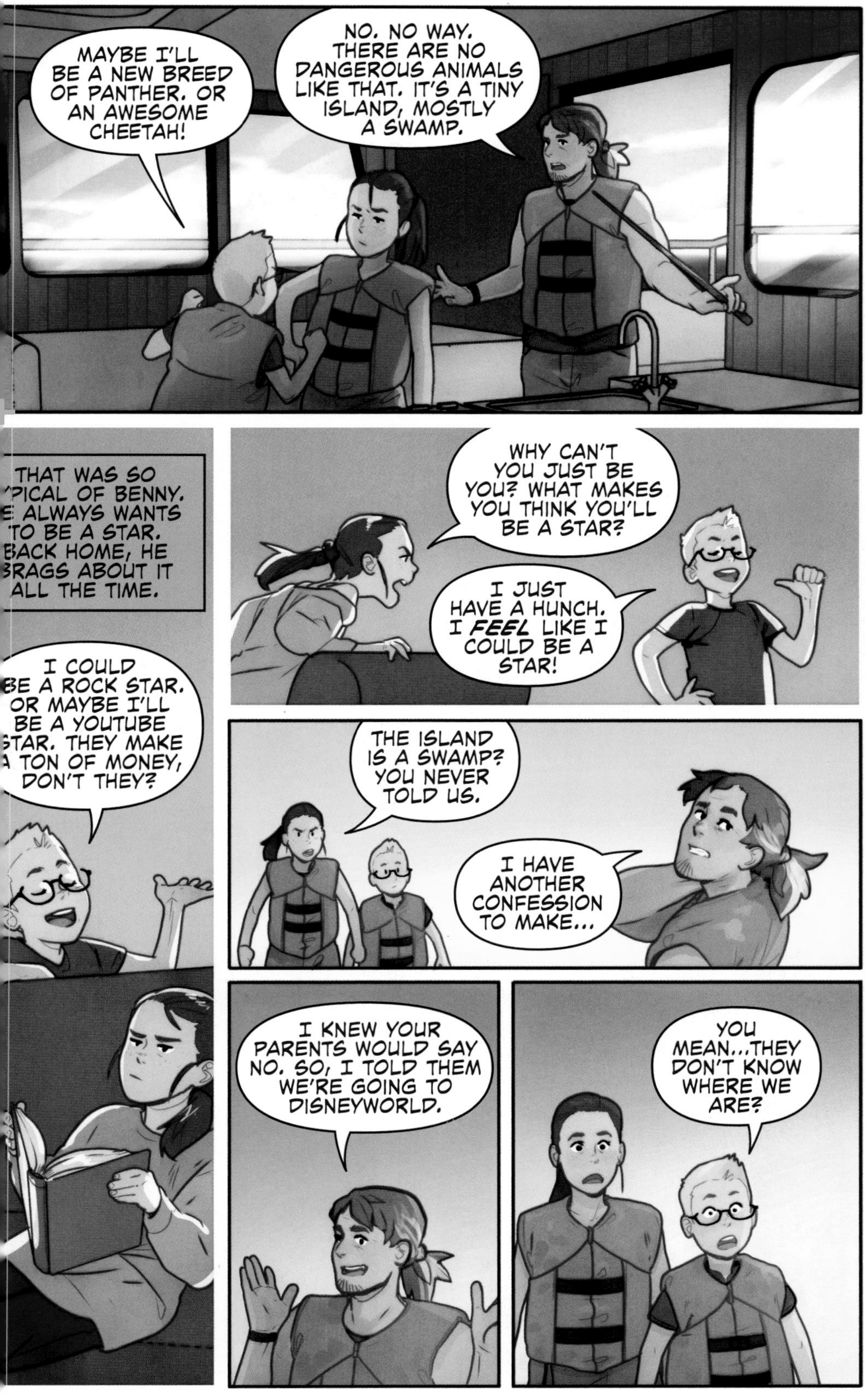
MAYBE I'LL BE A NEW BREED OF PANTHER. OR AN AWESOME CHEETAH!
NO. NO WAY. THERE ARE NO DANGEROUS ANIMALS LIKE THAT. IT'S A TINY ISLAND, MOSTLY A SWAMP.
THAT WAS SO PICAL OF BENNY. E ALWAYS WANTS TO BE A STAR. BACK HOME, HE RAGS ABOUT IT ALL THE TIME.
I COULD BE A ROCK STAR. OR MAYBE I'LL BE A YOUTUBE TAR. THEY MAKE TON OF MONEY, DON'T THEY?
WHY CAN'T YOU JUST BE YOU? WHAT MAKES YOU THINK YOU'LL BE A STAR?
I JUST HAVE A HUNCH. I *FEEL* LIKE I COULD BE A STAR!
THE ISLAND IS A SWAMP? YOU NEVER TOLD US.
I HAVE ANOTHER CONFESSION TO MAKE...
I KNEW YOUR PARENTS WOULD SAY NO. SO, I TOLD THEM WE'RE GOING TO DISNEYWORLD.
YOU MEAN...THEY DON'T KNOW WHERE WE ARE?

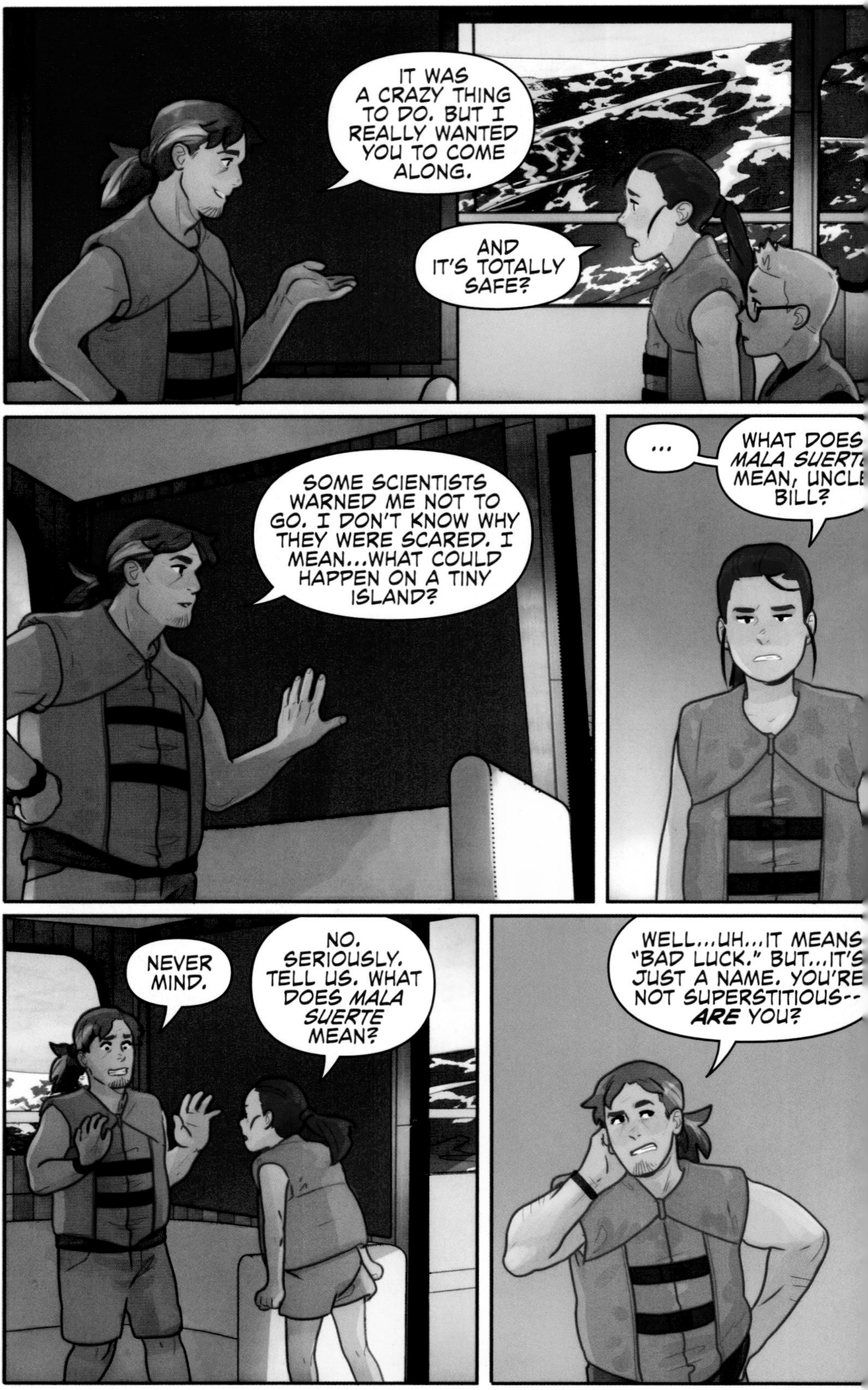
IT WAS A CRAZY THING TO DO. BUT I REALLY WANTED YOU TO COME ALONG.
AND IT'S TOTALLY SAFE?
SOME SCIENTISTS WARNED ME NOT TO GO. I DON'T KNOW WHY THEY WERE SCARED. I MEAN...WHAT COULD HAPPEN ON A TINY ISLAND?
...
WHAT DOES *MALA SUERT* MEAN, UNCL BILL?
NEVER MIND.
NO. SERIOUSLY. TELL US. WHAT DOES *MALA SUERTE* MEAN?
WELL...UH...IT MEANS "BAD LUCK." BUT...IT'S JUST A NAME. YOU'RE NOT SUPERSTITIOUS-- ***ARE*** YOU?

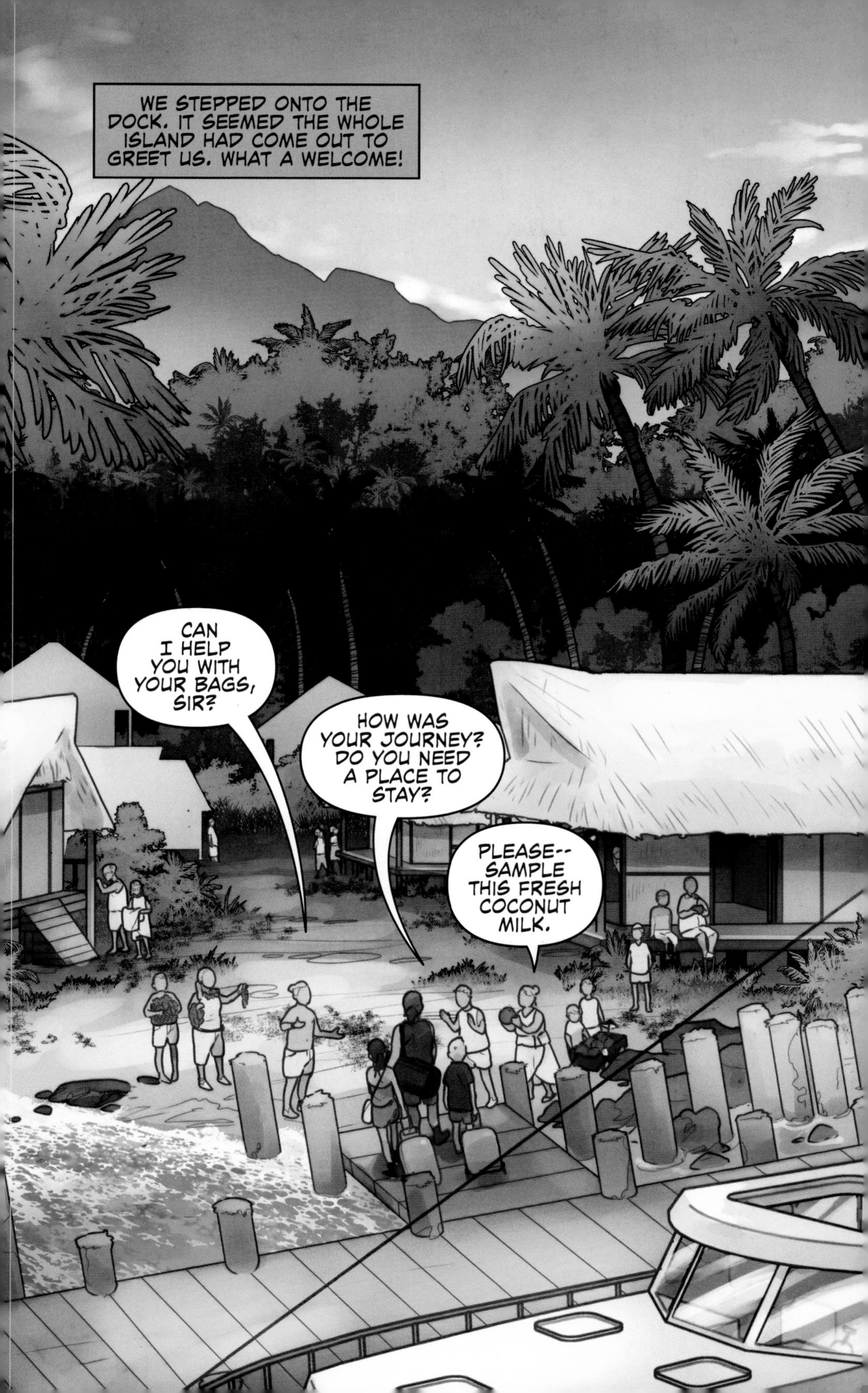
WE STEPPED ONTO THE DOCK. IT SEEMED THE WHOLE ISLAND HAD COME OUT TO GREET US. WHAT A WELCOME!
CAN I HELP YOU WITH YOUR BAGS, SIR?
HOW WAS YOUR JOURNEY? DO YOU NEED A PLACE TO STAY?
PLEASE-- SAMPLE THIS FRESH COCONUT MILK.

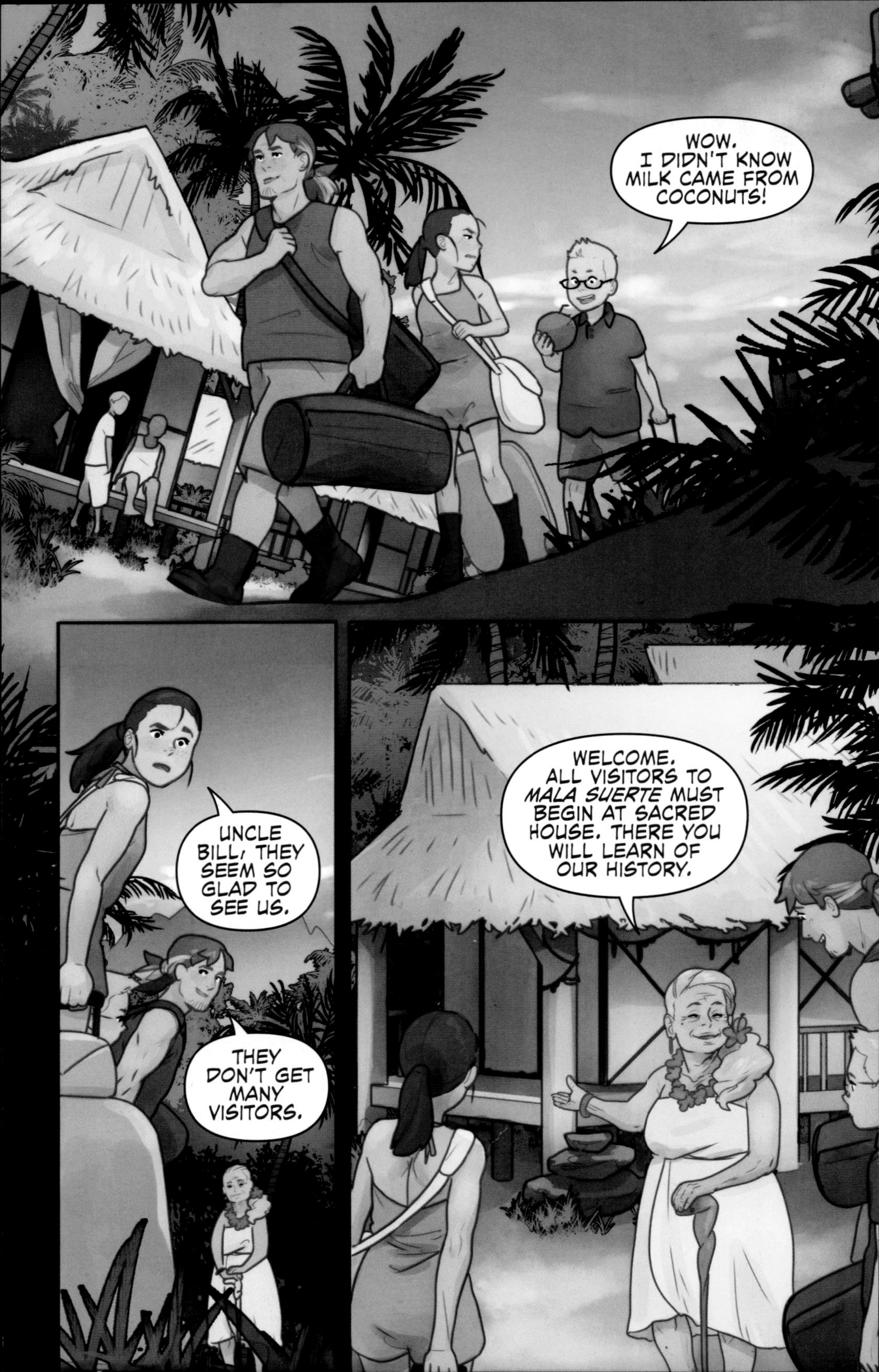
WOW. I DIDN'T KNOW MILK CAME FROM COCONUTS!
UNCLE BILL, THEY SEEM SO GLAD TO SEE US.
THEY DON'T GET MANY VISITORS.
WELCOME. ALL VISITORS TO *MALA SUERTE* MUST BEGIN AT SACRED HOUSE. THERE YOU WILL LEARN OF OUR HISTORY.

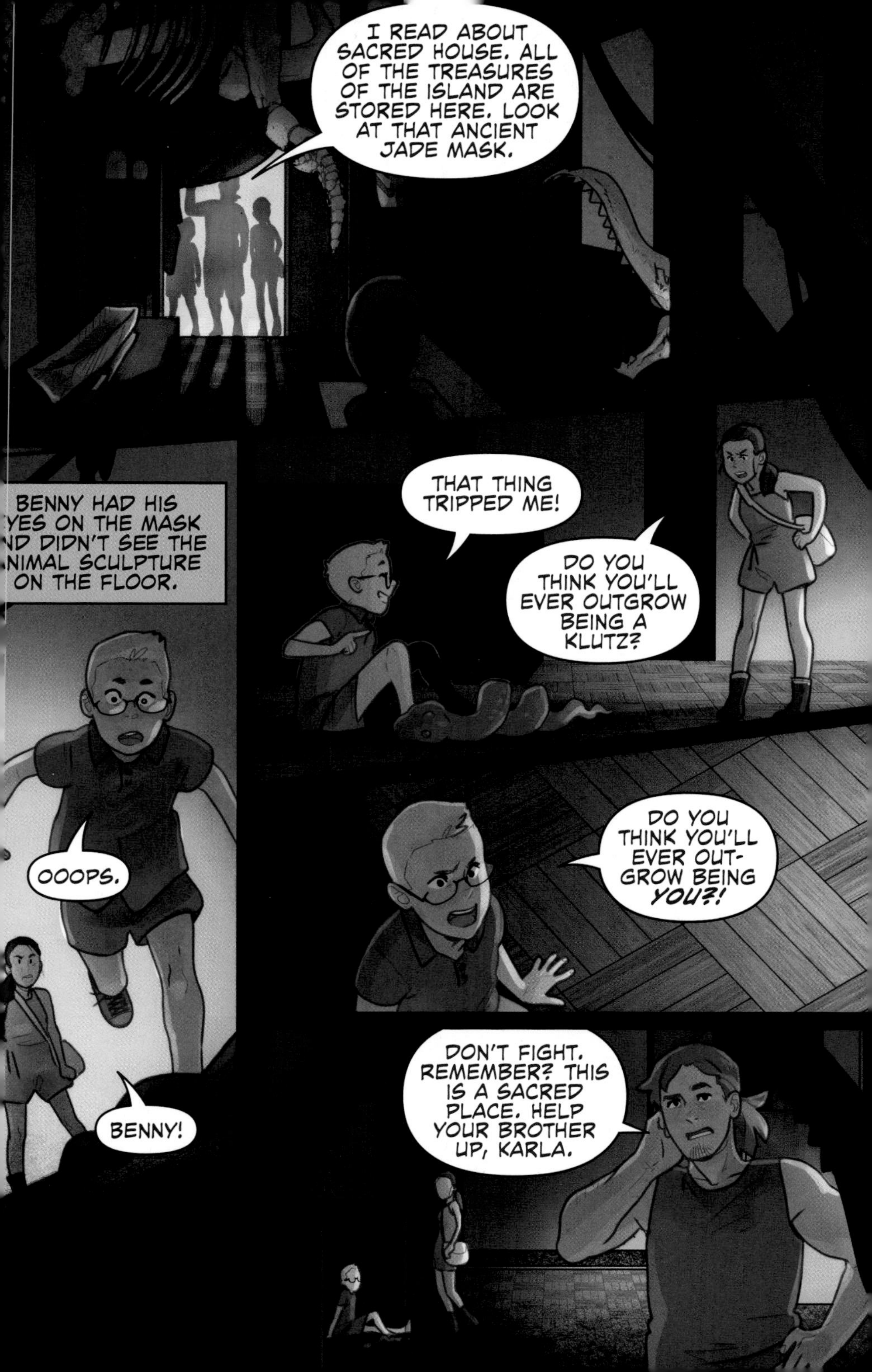

I READ ABOUT SACRED HOUSE. ALL OF THE TREASURES OF THE ISLAND ARE STORED HERE. LOOK AT THAT ANCIENT JADE MASK.
BENNY HAD HIS
ON THE MASK
DIDN'T SEE THE
SCULPTURE
ON THE FLOOR.
OOOPS.
BENNY!
THAT THING TRIPPED ME!
DO YOU THINK YOU'LL EVER OUTGROW BEING A KLUTZ?
DO YOU THINK YOU'LL EVER OUT-GROW BEING *YOU?!*
DON'T FIGHT. REMEMBER? THIS IS A SACRED PLACE. HELP YOUR BROTHER UP, KARLA.

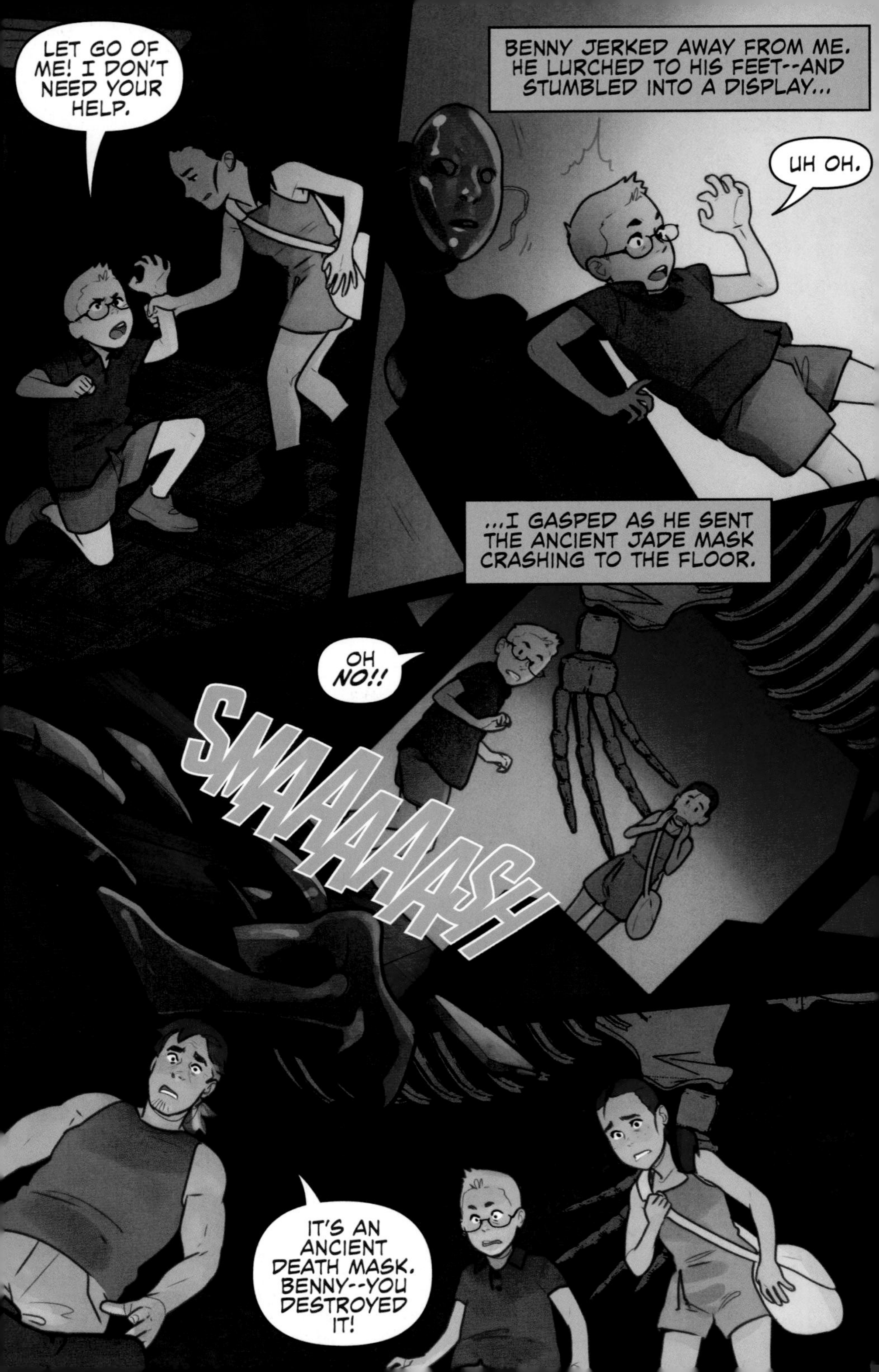
LET GO OF ME! I DON'T NEED YOUR HELP.
BENNY JERKED AWAY FROM ME. HE LURCHED TO HIS FEET--AND STUMBLED INTO A DISPLAY...
UH OH.
...I GASPED AS HE SENT THE ANCIENT JADE MASK CRASHING TO THE FLOOR.
OH NO!!
SMAAAAASH
IT'S AN ANCIENT DEATH MASK. BENNY--YOU DESTROYED IT!

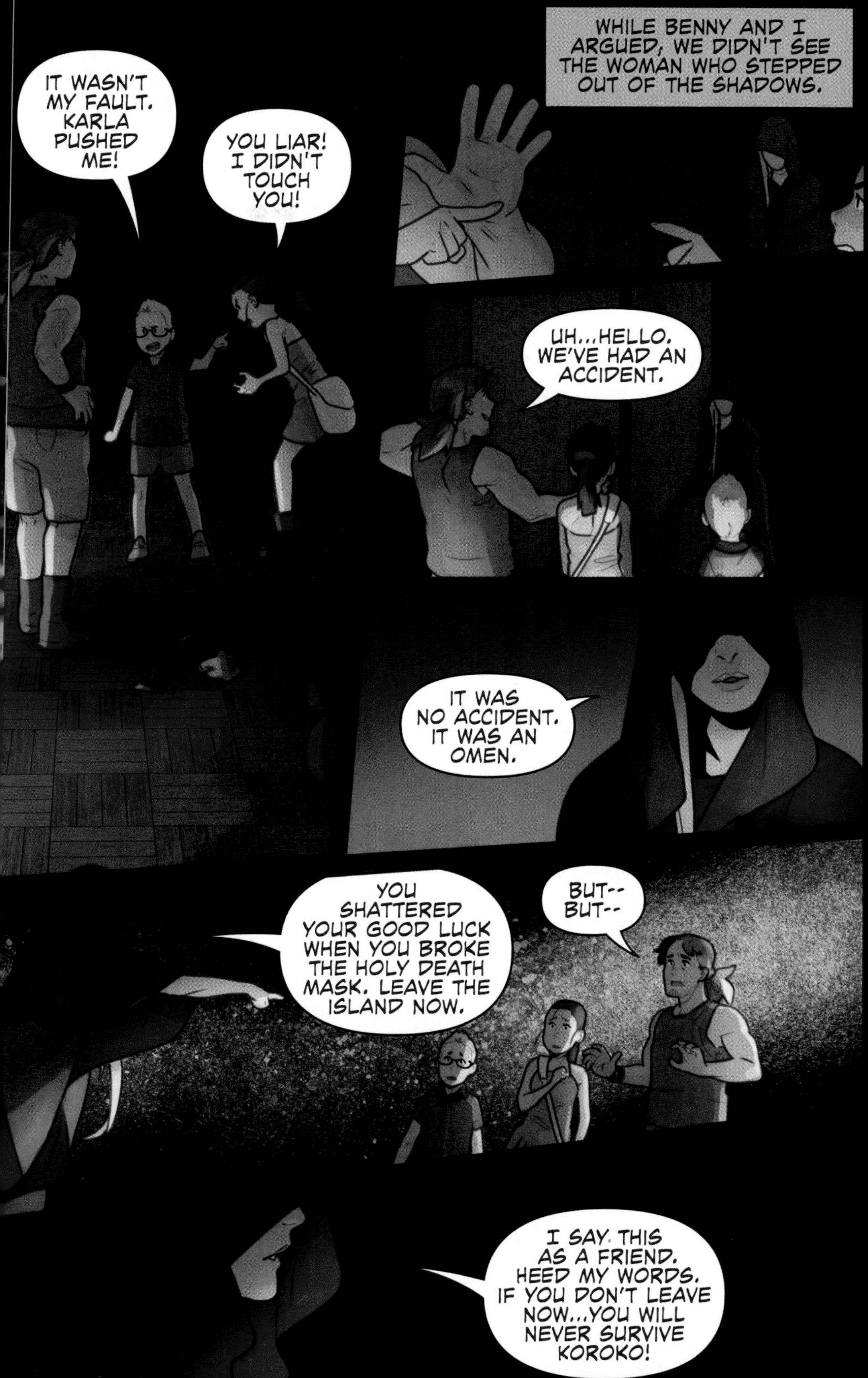
IT WASN'T MY FAULT. KARLA PUSHED ME!
YOU LIAR! I DIDN'T TOUCH YOU!
WHILE BENNY AND I ARGUED, WE DIDN'T SEE THE WOMAN WHO STEPPED OUT OF THE SHADOWS.
UH...HELLO. WE'VE HAD AN ACCIDENT.
IT WAS NO ACCIDENT. IT WAS AN OMEN.
YOU SHATTERED YOUR GOOD LUCK WHEN YOU BROKE THE HOLY DEATH MASK. LEAVE THE ISLAND NOW.
BUT-- BUT--
I SAY THIS AS A FRIEND. HEED MY WORDS. IF YOU DON'T LEAVE NOW...YOU WILL NEVER SURVIVE KOROKO!

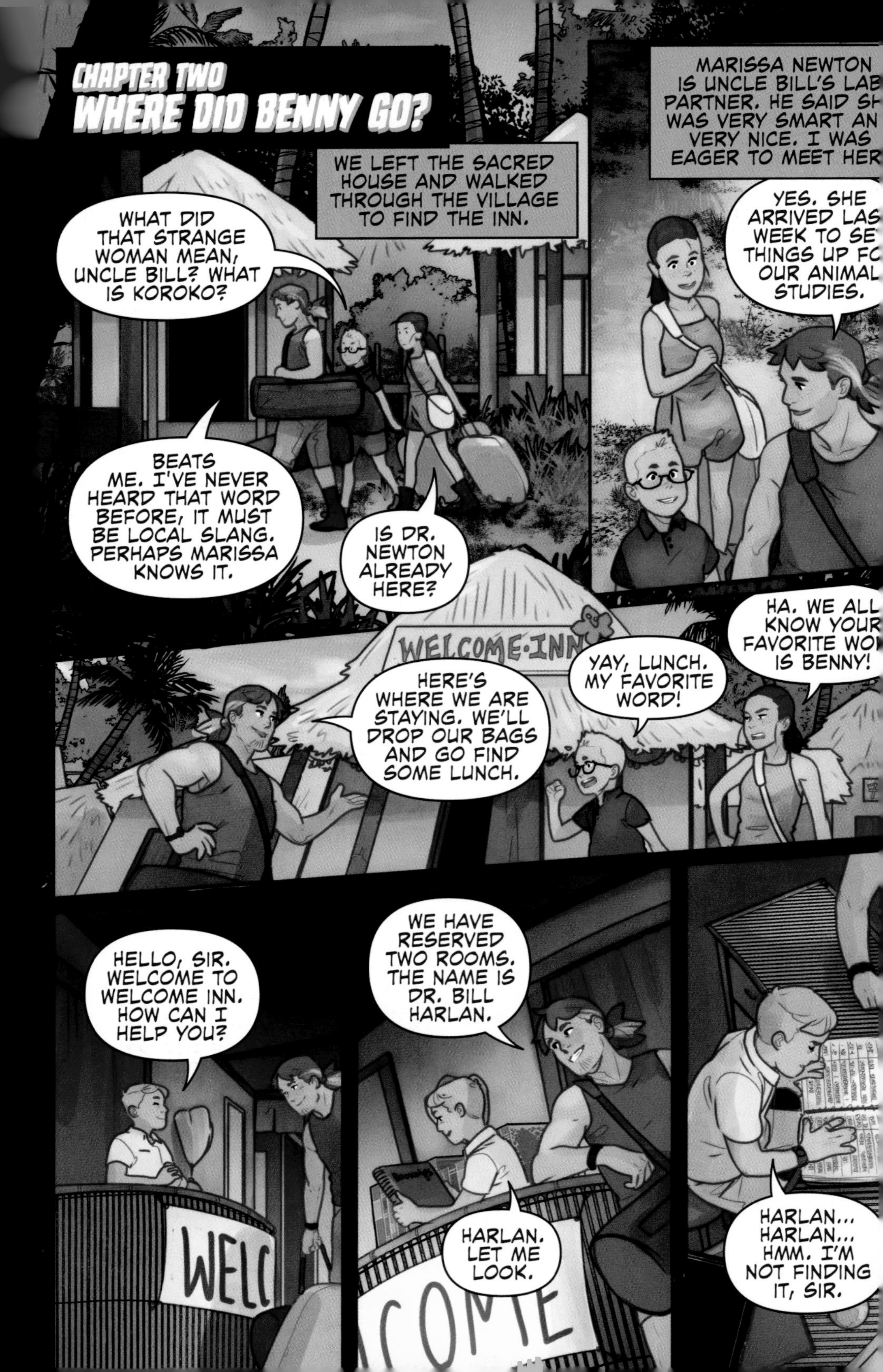

CHAPTER TWO
WHERE DID BENNY GO?
WE LEFT THE SACRED HOUSE AND WALKED THROUGH THE VILLAGE TO FIND THE INN.
WHAT DID THAT STRANGE WOMAN MEAN, UNCLE BILL? WHAT IS KOROKO?
BEATS ME. I'VE NEVER HEARD THAT WORD BEFORE, IT MUST BE LOCAL SLANG. PERHAPS MARISSA KNOWS IT.
IS DR. NEWTON ALREADY HERE?
MARISSA NEWTON IS UNCLE BILL'S LAB PARTNER. HE SAID SH WAS VERY SMART AN VERY NICE. I WAS EAGER TO MEET HER
YES. SHE ARRIVED LAS WEEK TO SE THINGS UP FO OUR ANIMAL STUDIES.
WELCOME·INN
HERE'S WHERE WE ARE STAYING. WE'LL DROP OUR BAGS AND GO FIND SOME LUNCH.
YAY, LUNCH. MY FAVORITE WORD!
HA. WE ALL KNOW YOUR FAVORITE WO IS BENNY!
HELLO, SIR. WELCOME TO WELCOME INN. HOW CAN I HELP YOU?
WELC
WE HAVE RESERVED TWO ROOMS. THE NAME IS DR. BILL HARLAN.
HARLAN. LET ME LOOK.
COME
HARLAN... HARLAN... HMM. I'M NOT FINDING IT, SIR.

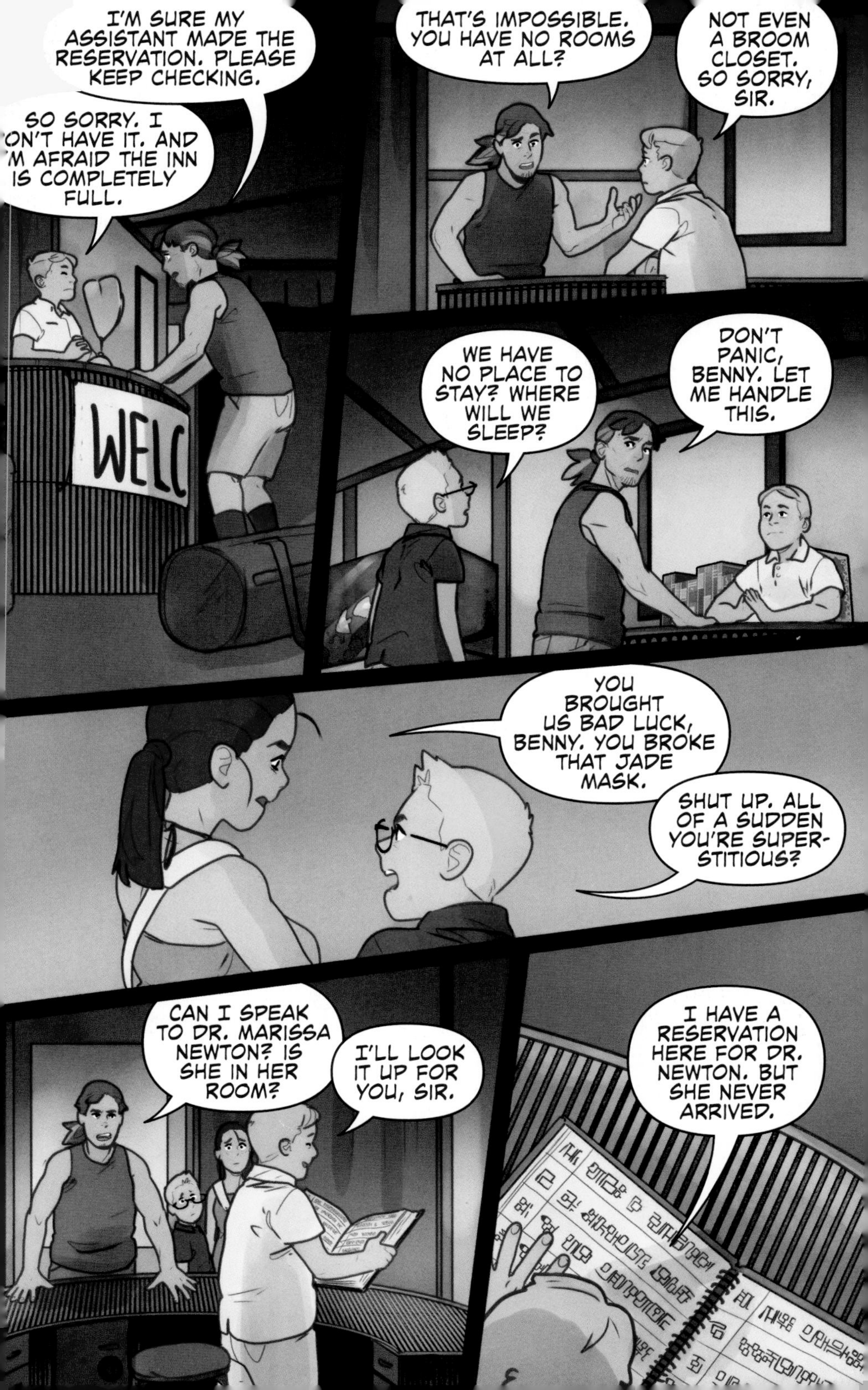
I'M SURE MY ASSISTANT MADE THE RESERVATION. PLEASE KEEP CHECKING.
SO SORRY. I ON'T HAVE IT. AND 'M AFRAID THE INN IS COMPLETELY FULL.
WELC
THAT'S IMPOSSIBLE. YOU HAVE NO ROOMS AT ALL?
NOT EVEN A BROOM CLOSET. SO SORRY, SIR.
WE HAVE NO PLACE TO STAY? WHERE WILL WE SLEEP?
DON'T PANIC, BENNY. LET ME HANDLE THIS.
YOU BROUGHT US BAD LUCK, BENNY. YOU BROKE THAT JADE MASK.
SHUT UP. ALL OF A SUDDEN YOU'RE SUPER-STITIOUS?
CAN I SPEAK TO DR. MARISSA NEWTON? IS SHE IN HER ROOM?
I'LL LOOK IT UP FOR YOU, SIR.
I HAVE A RESERVATION HERE FOR DR. NEWTON. BUT SHE NEVER ARRIVED.

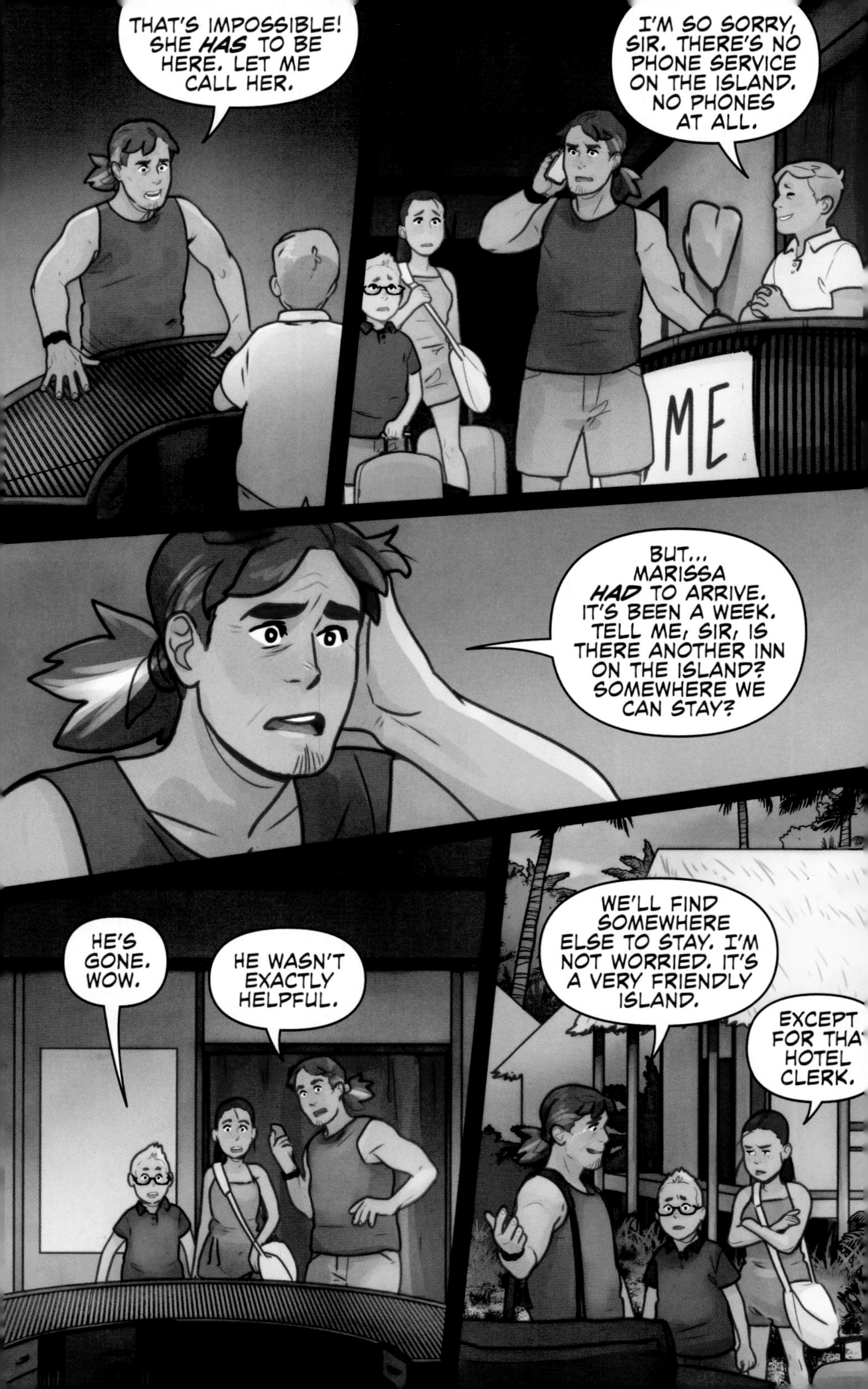
THAT'S IMPOSSIBLE! SHE HAS TO BE HERE. LET ME CALL HER.
I'M SO SORRY, SIR. THERE'S NO PHONE SERVICE ON THE ISLAND. NO PHONES AT ALL.
ME
BUT... MARISSA HAD TO ARRIVE. IT'S BEEN A WEEK. TELL ME, SIR, IS THERE ANOTHER INN ON THE ISLAND? SOMEWHERE WE CAN STAY?
HE'S GONE. WOW.
HE WASN'T EXACTLY HELPFUL.
WE'LL FIND SOMEWHERE ELSE TO STAY. I'M NOT WORRIED. IT'S A VERY FRIENDLY ISLAND.
EXCEPT FOR THA HOTEL CLERK.

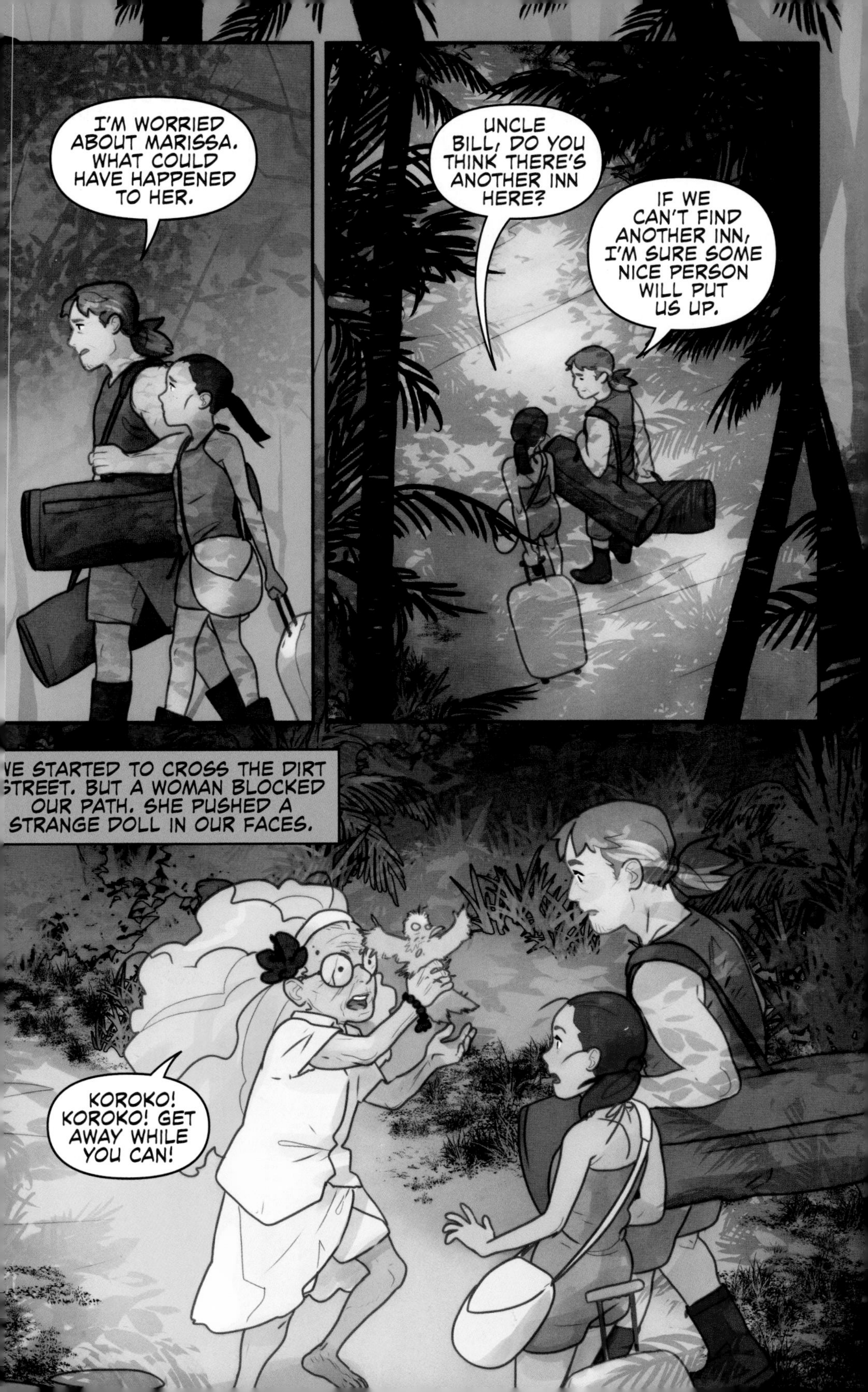
I'M WORRIED ABOUT MARISSA. WHAT COULD HAVE HAPPENED TO HER.
UNCLE BILL, DO YOU THINK THERE'S ANOTHER INN HERE?
IF WE CAN'T FIND ANOTHER INN, I'M SURE SOME NICE PERSON WILL PUT US UP.
WE STARTED TO CROSS THE DIRT STREET. BUT A WOMAN BLOCKED OUR PATH. SHE PUSHED A STRANGE DOLL IN OUR FACES.
KOROKO! KOROKO! GET AWAY WHILE YOU CAN!

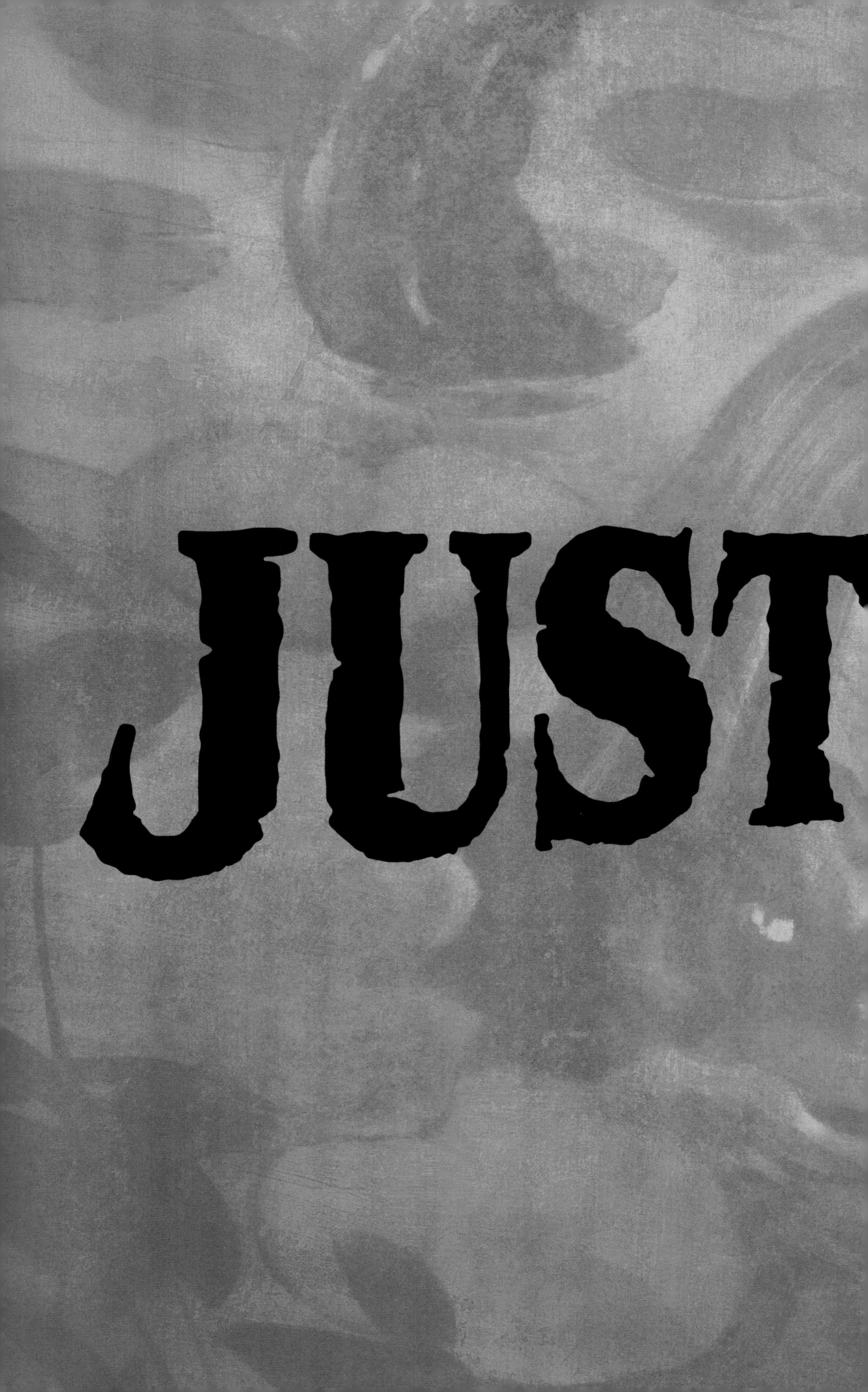
JUST

BEYOND

™

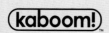

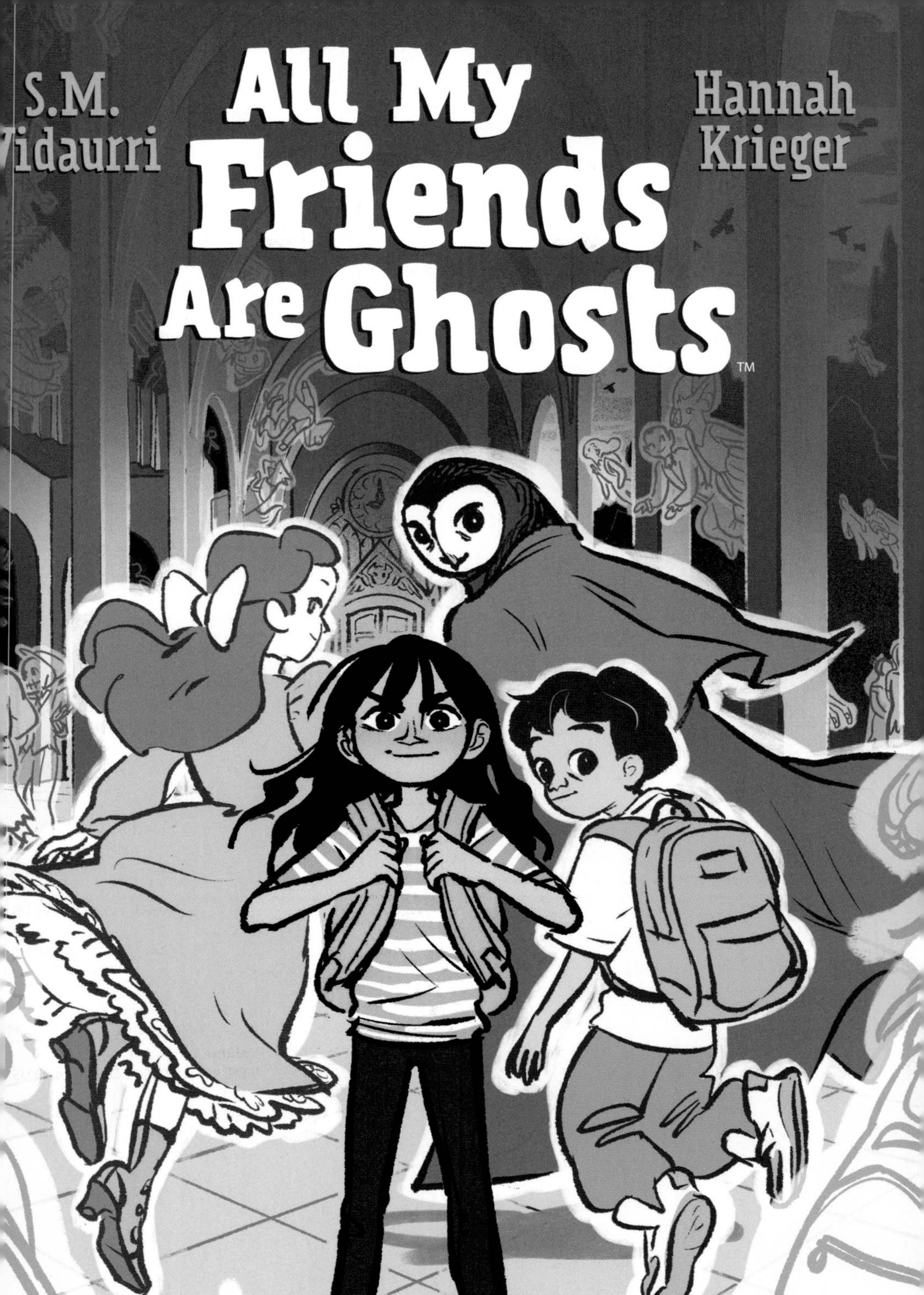
S.M. Vidaurri
All My Friends Are Ghosts™
Hannah Krieger

Written by
S.M. Vidaurri

Illustrated by
Hannah Krieger

Colored by
Hannah Krieger
with **S.M. Vidaurri**

Lettered by
Mike Fiorentino

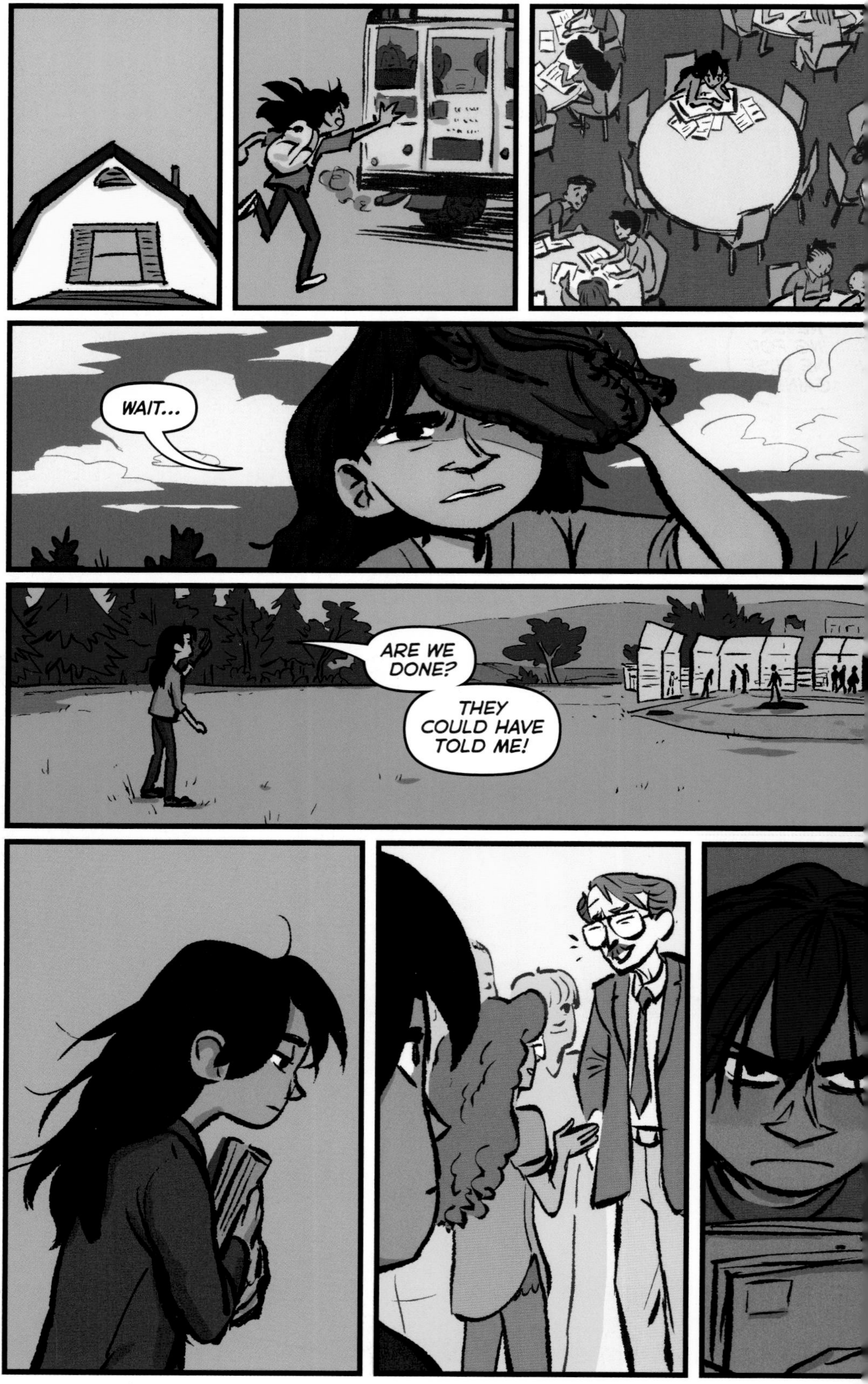
WAIT...
ARE WE DONE?
THEY COULD HAVE TOLD ME!

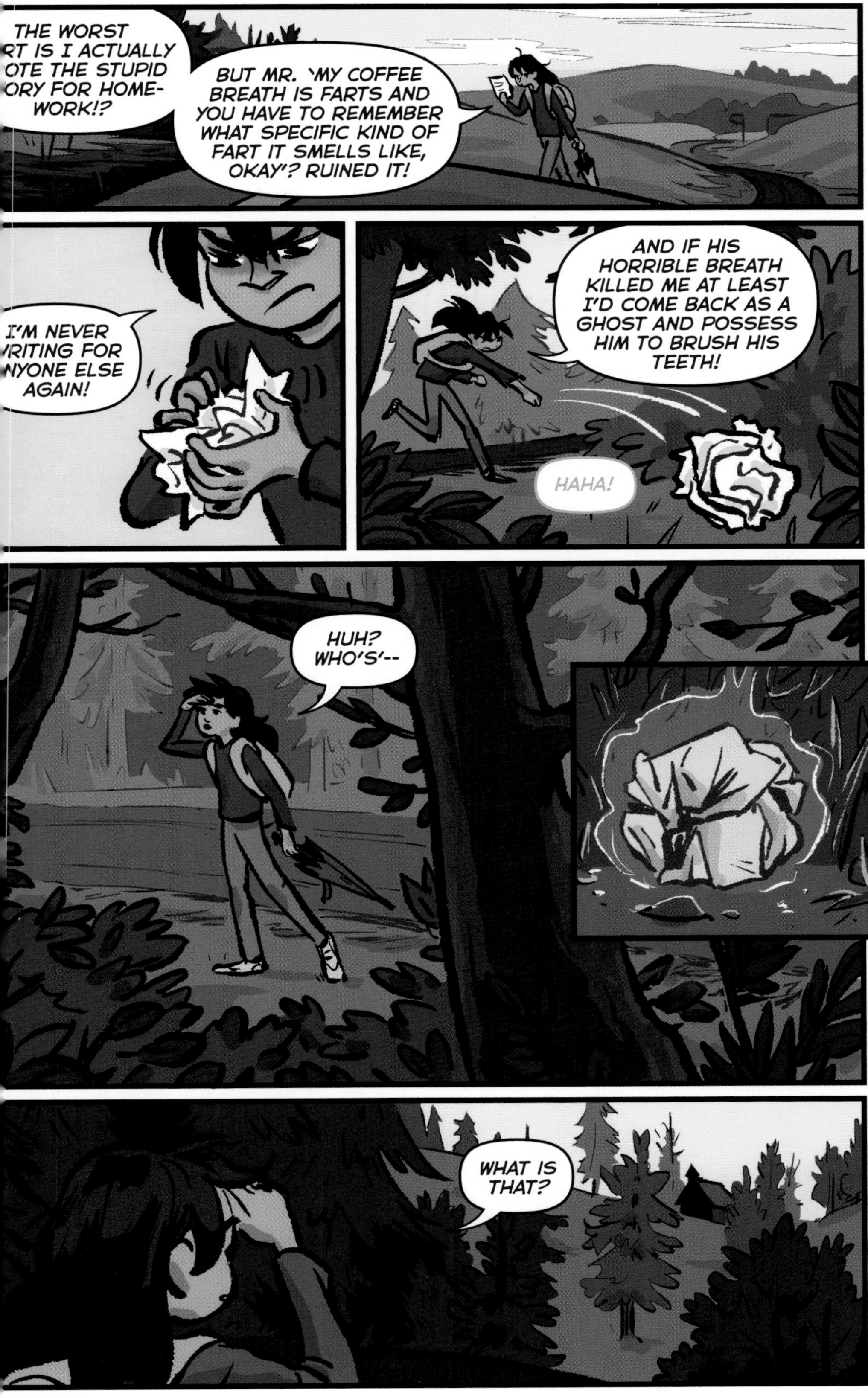
THE WORST
RT IS I ACTUALLY
OTE THE STUPID
ORY FOR HOME-
WORK!?
BUT MR. 'MY COFFEE BREATH IS FARTS AND YOU HAVE TO REMEMBER WHAT SPECIFIC KIND OF FART IT SMELLS LIKE, OKAY'? RUINED IT!
I'M NEVER
RITING FOR
NYONE ELSE
AGAIN!
AND IF HIS HORRIBLE BREATH KILLED ME AT LEAST I'D COME BACK AS A GHOST AND POSSESS HIM TO BRUSH HIS TEETH!
HAHA!
HUH? WHO'S'--
WHAT IS THAT?

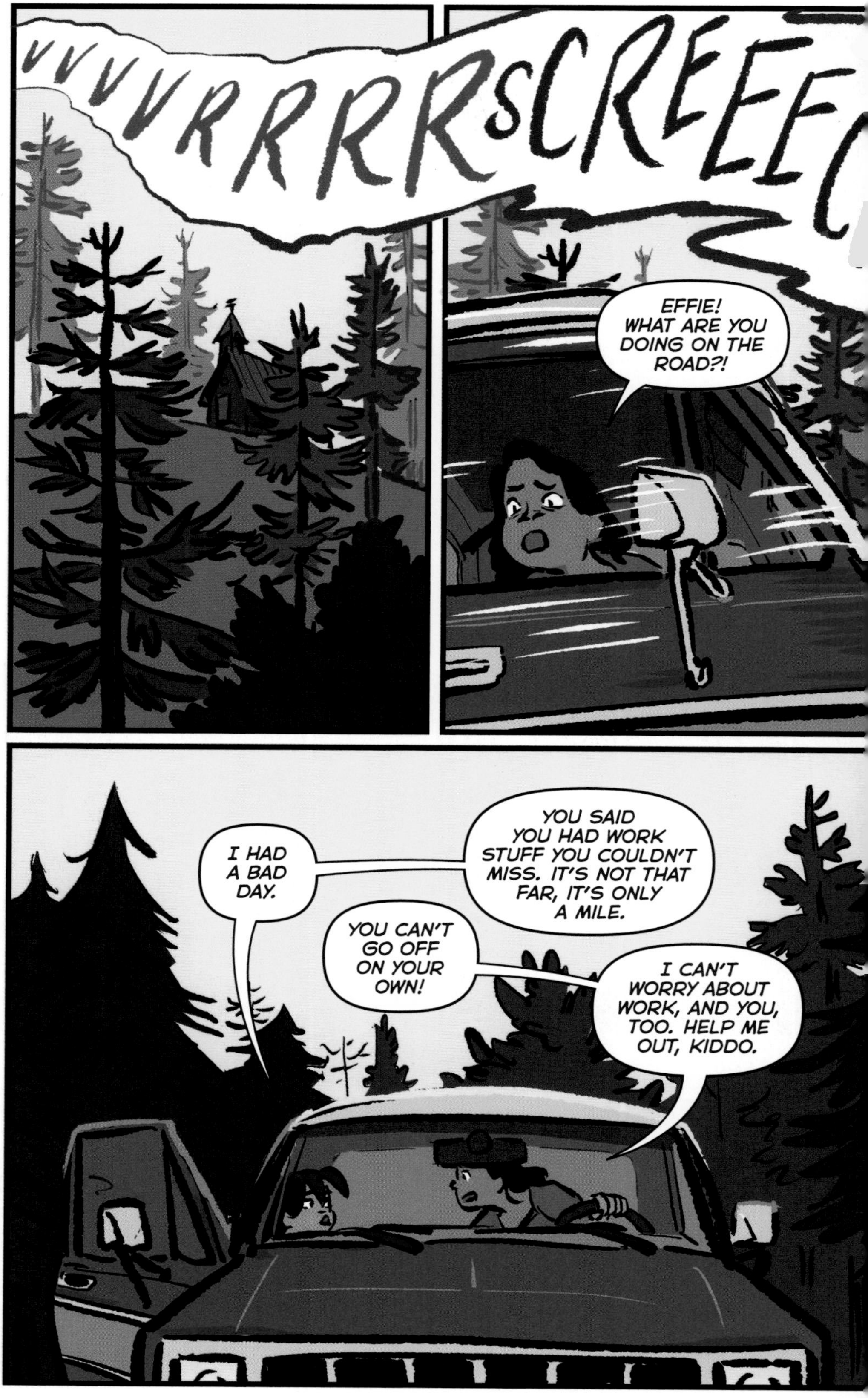
VVVVRRRRSCREEEC
EFFIE! WHAT ARE YOU DOING ON THE ROAD?!
I HAD A BAD DAY.
YOU SAID YOU HAD WORK STUFF YOU COULDN'T MISS. IT'S NOT THAT FAR, IT'S ONLY A MILE.
YOU CAN'T GO OFF ON YOUR OWN!
I CAN'T WORRY ABOUT WORK, AND YOU, TOO. HELP ME OUT, KIDDO.

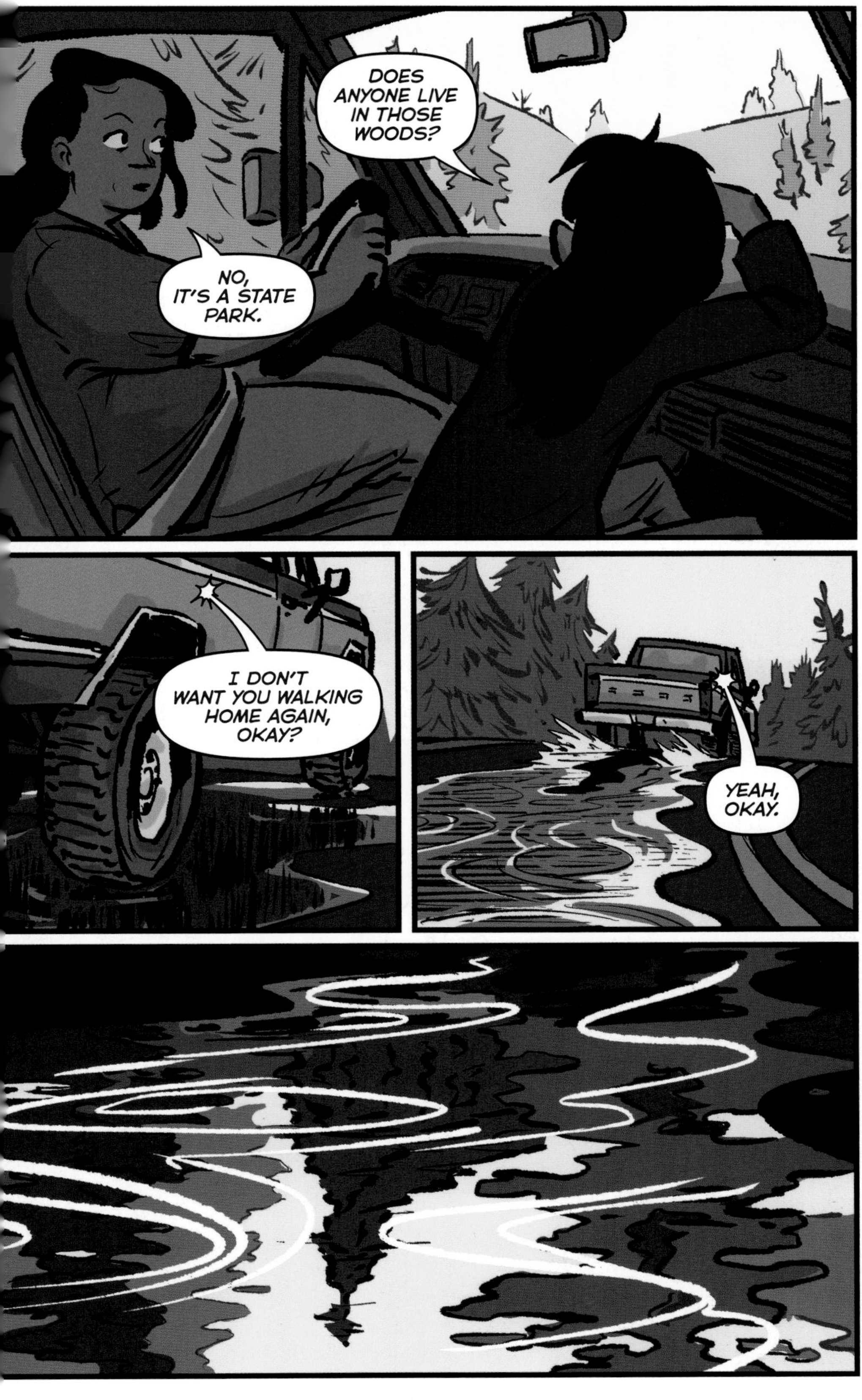
DOES ANYONE LIVE IN THOSE WOODS?
NO, IT'S A STATE PARK.
I DON'T WANT YOU WALKING HOME AGAIN, OKAY?
YEAH, OKAY.

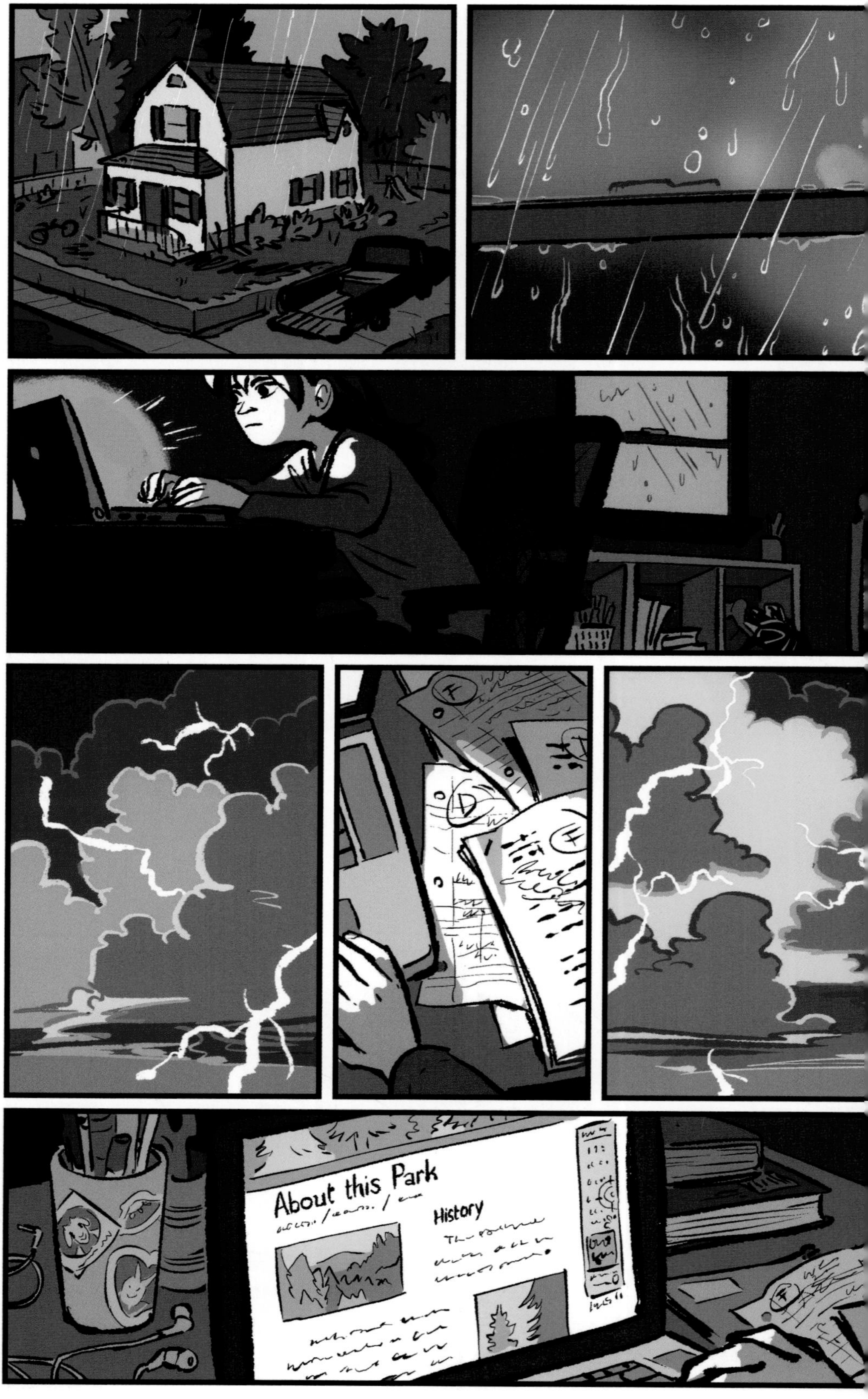
About this Park
History

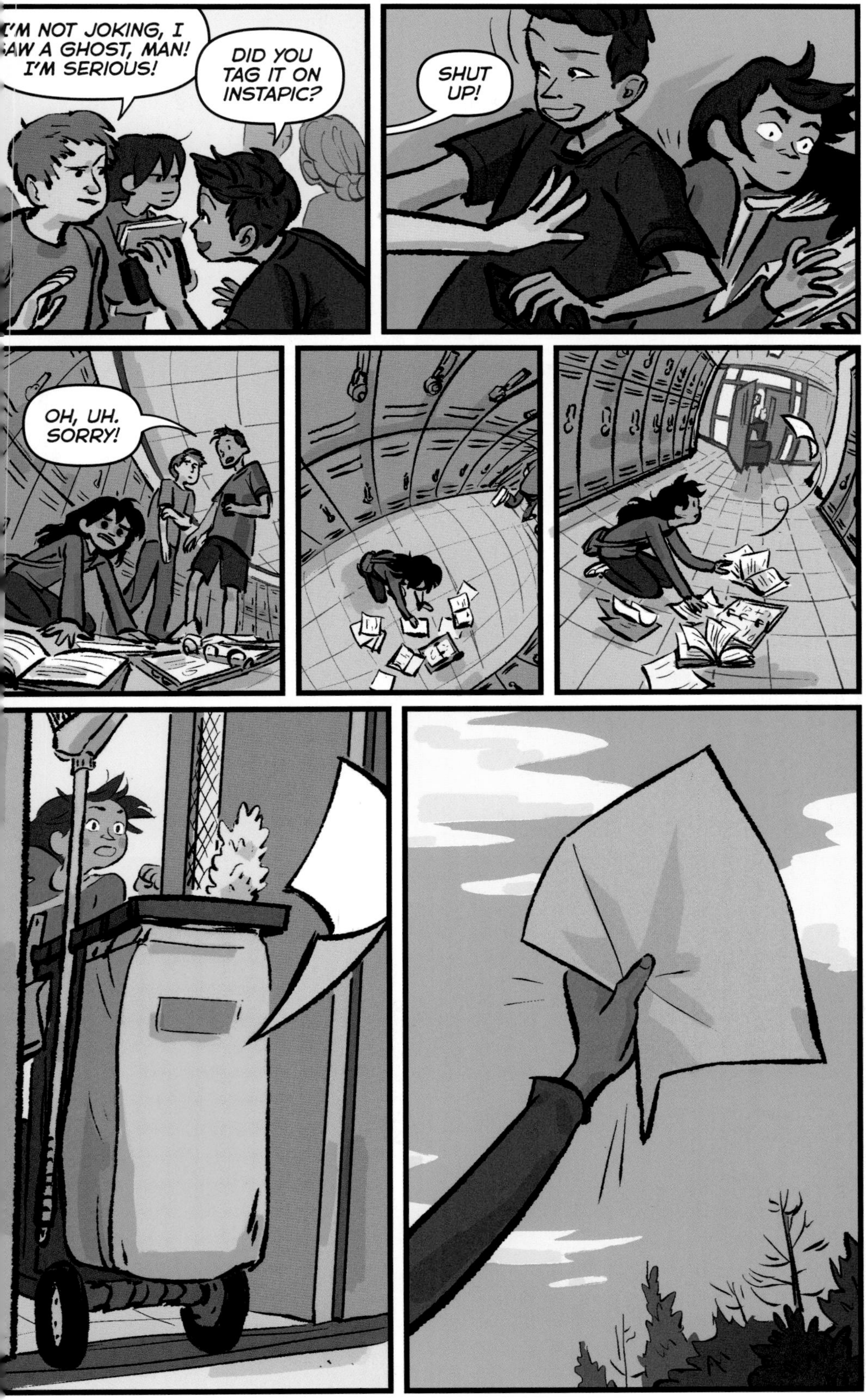
I'M NOT JOKING, I SAW A GHOST, MAN! I'M SERIOUS!
DID YOU TAG IT ON INSTAPIC?
SHUT UP!
OH, UH. SORRY!

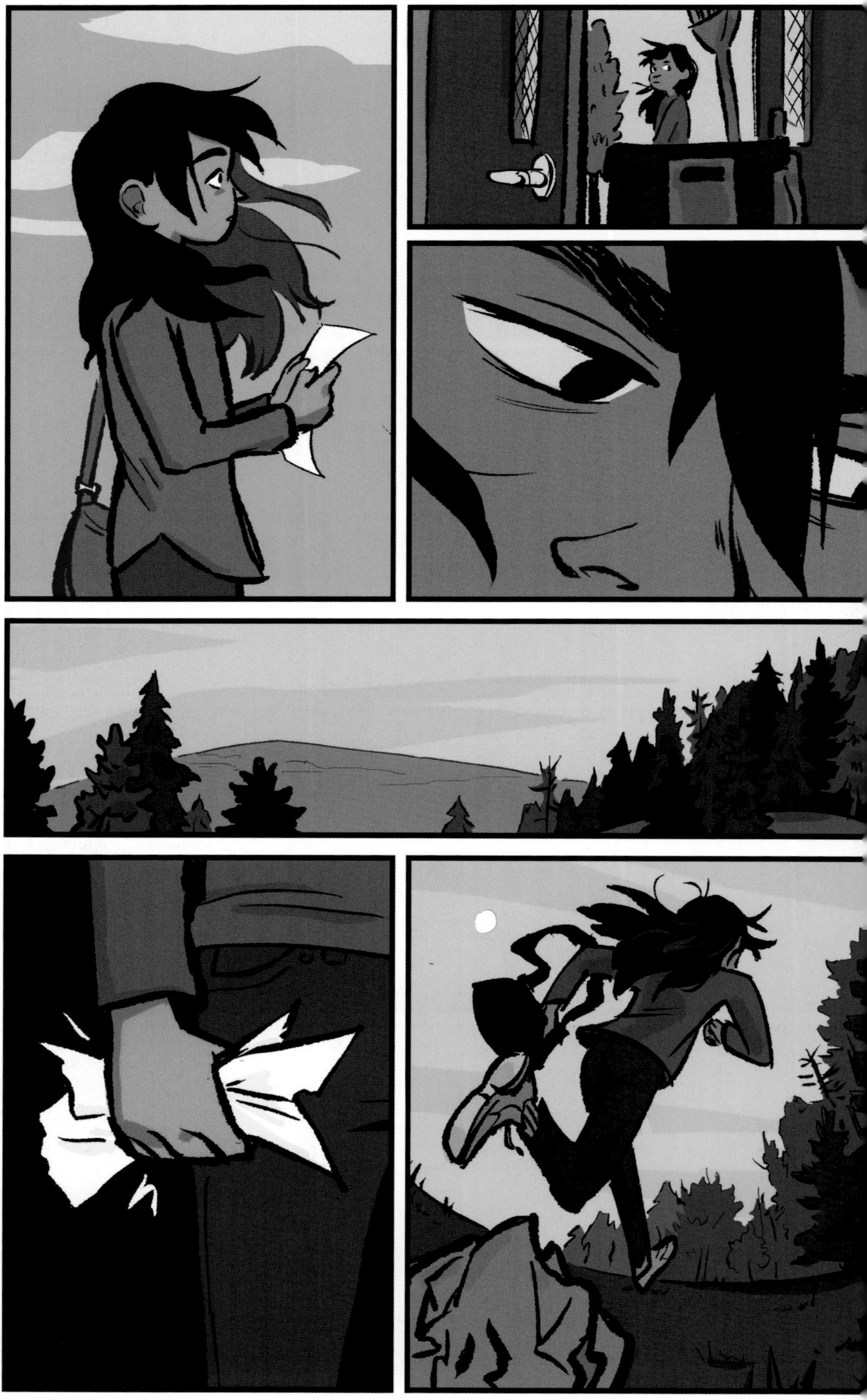

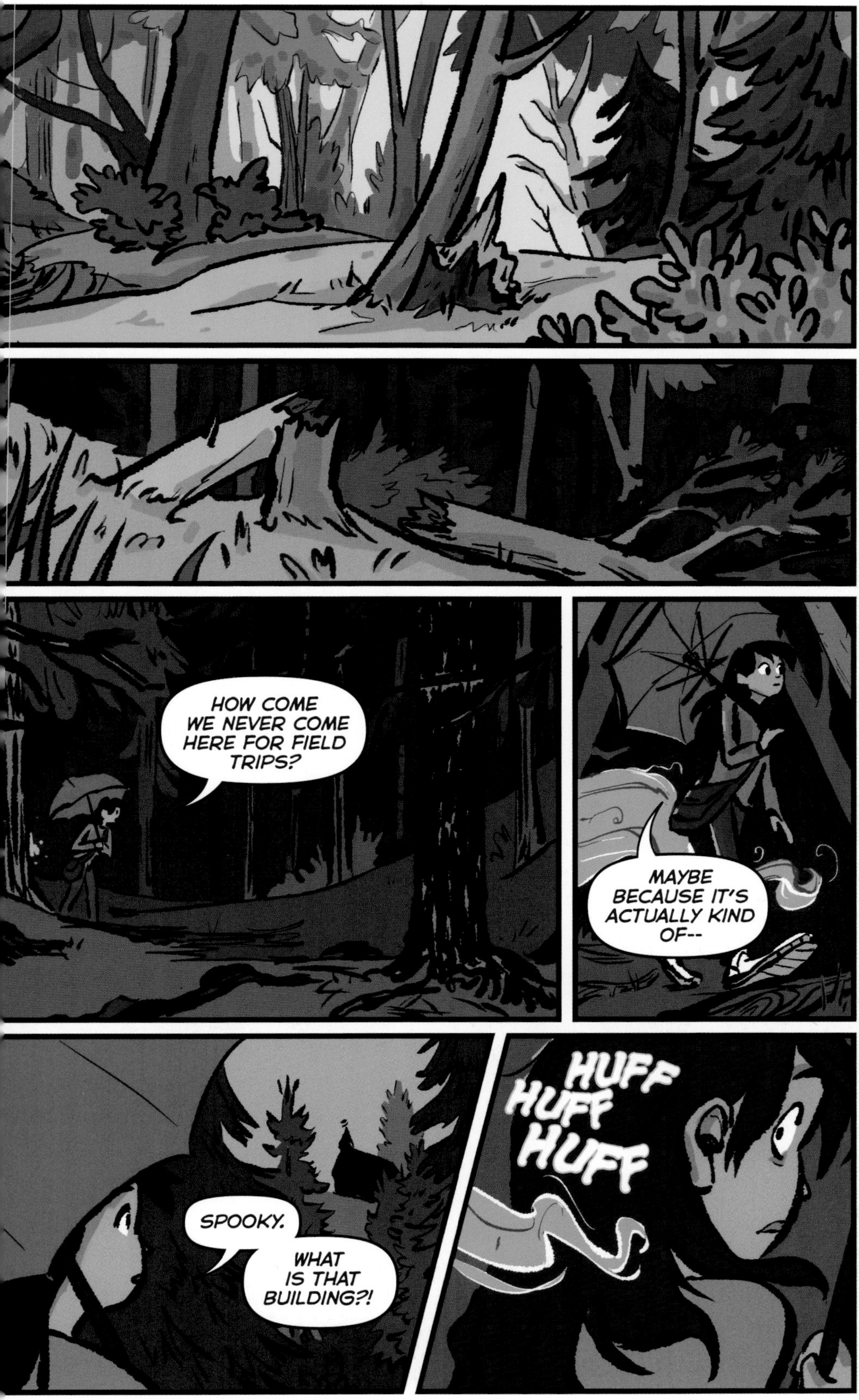
HOW COME WE NEVER COME HERE FOR FIELD TRIPS?
MAYBE BECAUSE IT'S ACTUALLY KIND OF--
SPOOKY.
WHAT IS THAT BUILDING?!
HUFF HUFF HUFF

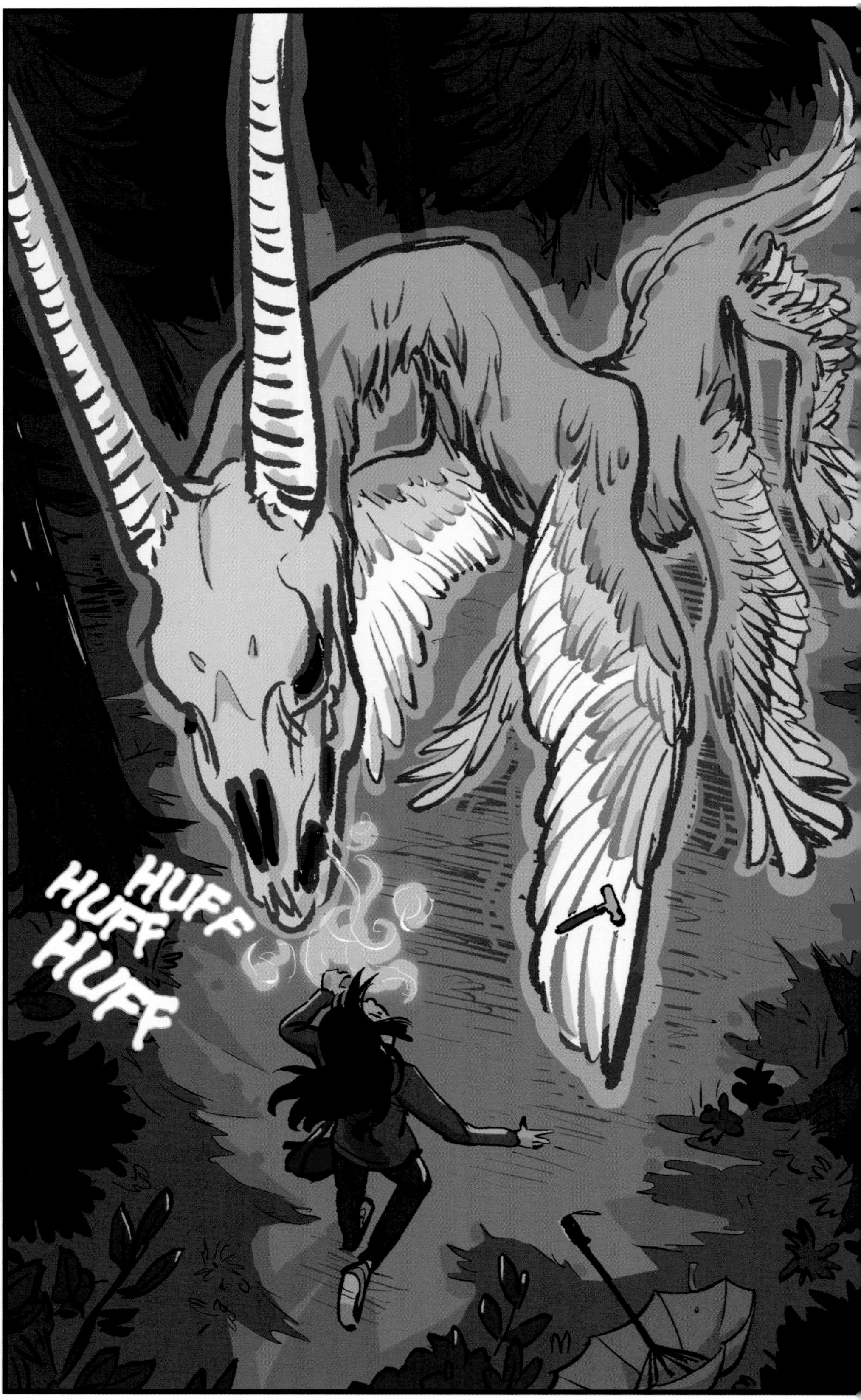
HUFF
HUFF
HUFF

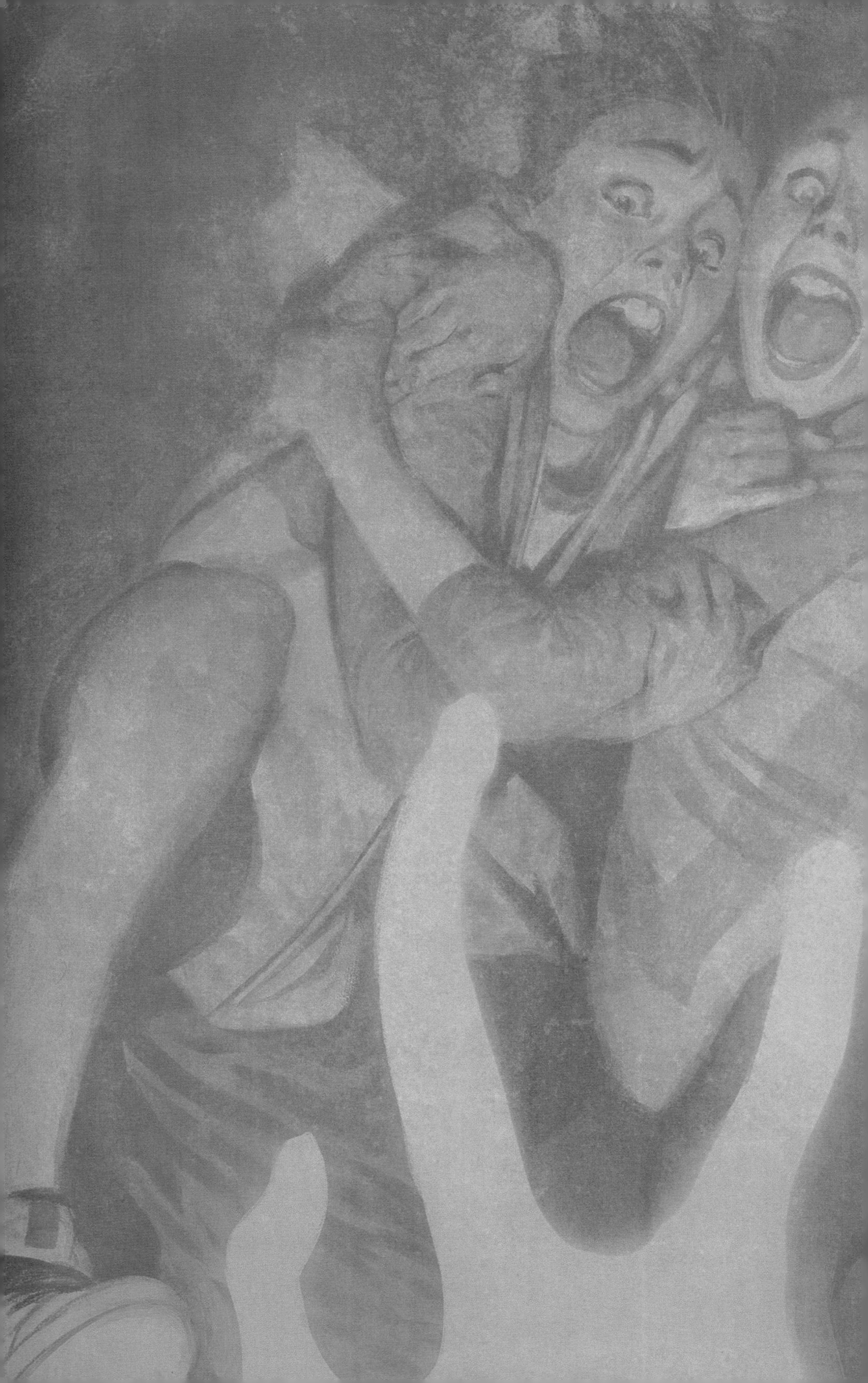

To find a teaching guide for

JUST BEYOND™

THE HORROR AT HAPPY LANDINGS

please go to **boom-studios.com/JustBeyondHaHL**